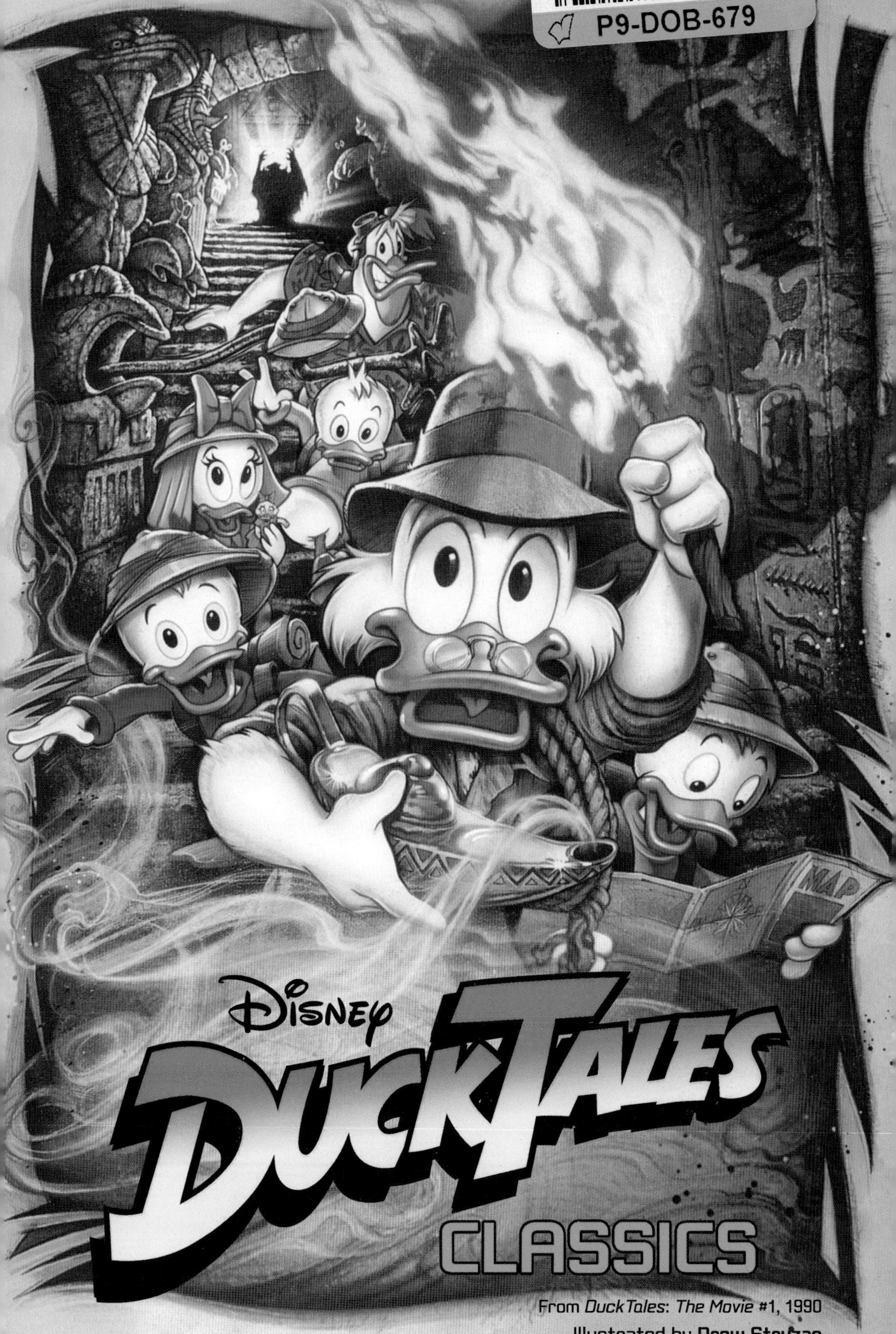
MAP
Disney
DuckTales
CLASSICS

From *DuckTales: The Movie* #1, 1990
Illustrated by Drew Struzan

Cover Artist: **Tello-Team**

Cover Colorist: **Marco Colletti**

Title Page Restoration: **Erik Rosengarten**

Archival Editor: **David Gerstein**

Collection Editors: **Justin Eisinger and Alonzo Simon**

Collection Designer: **Clyde Grapa**

Publisher: **Greg Goldstein**

For international rights, contact licensing@idwpublishing.com

Special thanks to Stefano Ambrosio, Stefano Attardi, Julie Dorris, Julia Gabrick, Marco Ghiglione, Jodi Hammerwold, Manny Mederos, Eugene Paraszczuk, Carlotta Quattrocolo, Roberto Santillo, Christopher Troise, and Camilla Vedove. for their invaluable assistance.

ISBN: 978-1-68405-296-7   21 20 19 18   1 2 3 4

Greg Goldstein, President & Publisher • **John Barber**, Editor-in-Chief • **Robbie Robbins**, EVP/Sr. Graphic Artist • **Cara Morrison**, Chief Financial Officer
Matthew Ruzicka, Chief Financial Officer • **Anita Frazier**, SVP of Sales and Marketing • **David Hedgecock**, Associate Publisher • **Jerry Bennington**,
VP of New Product Development • **Lorelei Bunjes**, VP of Digital Services • **Justin Eisinger**, Editorial Director, Graphic Novels & Collections • **Eric Moss**,
Senior Director, Licensing and Business Development

Ted Adams, Founder and CEO of IDW Media Holdings

Facebook: facebook.com/idwpublishing • Twitter: @idwpublishing • YouTube: youtube.com/idwpublishing
Tumblr: tumblr.idwpublishing.com • Instagram: instagram.com/idwpublishing

www.IDWPUBLISHING.com

The Bedeviled Dime
From *DuckTales* (series I) #8, 1989
Writer, Artist and Letterer: **William Van Horn**
Colorist: **Susan Daigle-Leach**

Flights of Fancy
From *DuckTales* (series I) #4, 1988
Writer: **Gary Leach**
Artist and Letterer: **William Van Horn**
Colorist: **Susan Daigle-Leach**

The Whistling Ghost
From *DuckTales* (series I) #10, 1989
Writer, Artist and Letterer: **William Van Horn**
Colorist: **Susan Daigle-Leach**

A Dolt From the Blue
From Danish *Anders And & Co.* #19/1996
First USA Publication in
Walt Disney's Comics and Stories #618, 1997
Writer, Artist and Letterer: **William Van Horn**
Colorist: **Susan Daigle-Leach**

The Billion Bean Stampede
From *DuckTales* (series I) #13, 1990
Writer: **John Lustig**
Artist and Letterer: **William Van Horn**
Colorists: **William Van Horn and Susan Daigle-Leach**

Seeing the Blight
From *DuckTales* (series I) #5, 1989
Writer, Artist and Letterer: **William Van Horn**
Colorists: **Susan Daigle-Leach** and **Digikore Studios**

Coin of the Realm
From *DuckTales* (series I) #6, 1989
Writer, Artist and Letterer: **William Van Horn**
Colorists: **Susan Daigle-Leach** and **Digikore Studios**

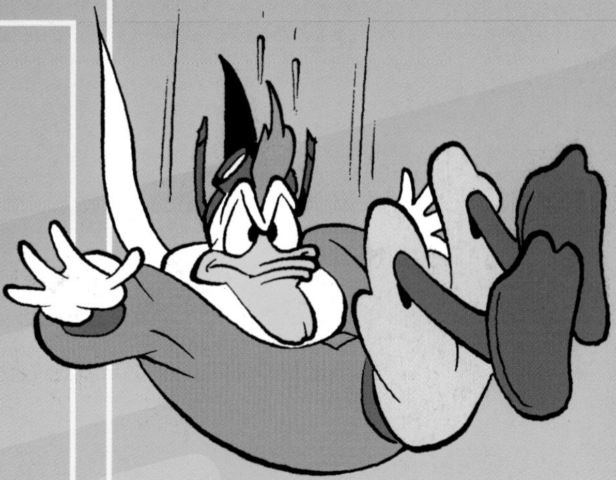

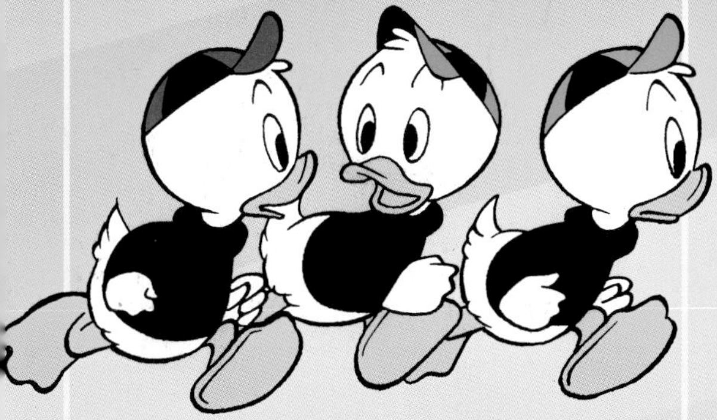

Just Another Hang-Up
From Danish *Anders And & Co.* #32/1996
First USA Publication in
Walt Disney's Comics and Stories #622, 1998
Writer, Artist and Letterer: **William Van Horn**
Colorist: **Susan Daigle-Leach**

Windfall on Mt. G'zoontight
From *DuckTales* (series I) #7, 1989
Writer: **John Lustig**
Artist and Letterer: **William Van Horn**
Colorist: **Scott Rockwell**

All Quacked Up
From Danish *Anders And & Co.* #46/1996
First USA Publication in
Walt Disney's Comics and Stories #623, 1998
Writer, Artist and Letterer: **William Van Horn**
Colorists: **Susan Daigle-Leach** and **Digikore Studios**

Sky-High Hi-Jinks
From *DuckTales* (series I) #11, 1990
Writer: **John Lustig**
Artist and Letterer: **William Van Horn**
Colorists: **William Van Horn** and **Susan Daigle-Leach**

Treasure of the Lost Lamp
From *DuckTales: The Movie* #1, 1990
Screenplay: **Alan Burnett**
Adaptation: **John Lustig**
Artists: **Carlos Valenti, Cosme Quartieri,**
Robert Bat, and **Rubén Torreiro**
Letterer: **John Clark**
Colorists: **Jo Meugniot** with **David Gerstein**

From *DuckTales* (series I) #8, 1989
Artist: **William Van Horn**
Colorist: **David Gerstein**

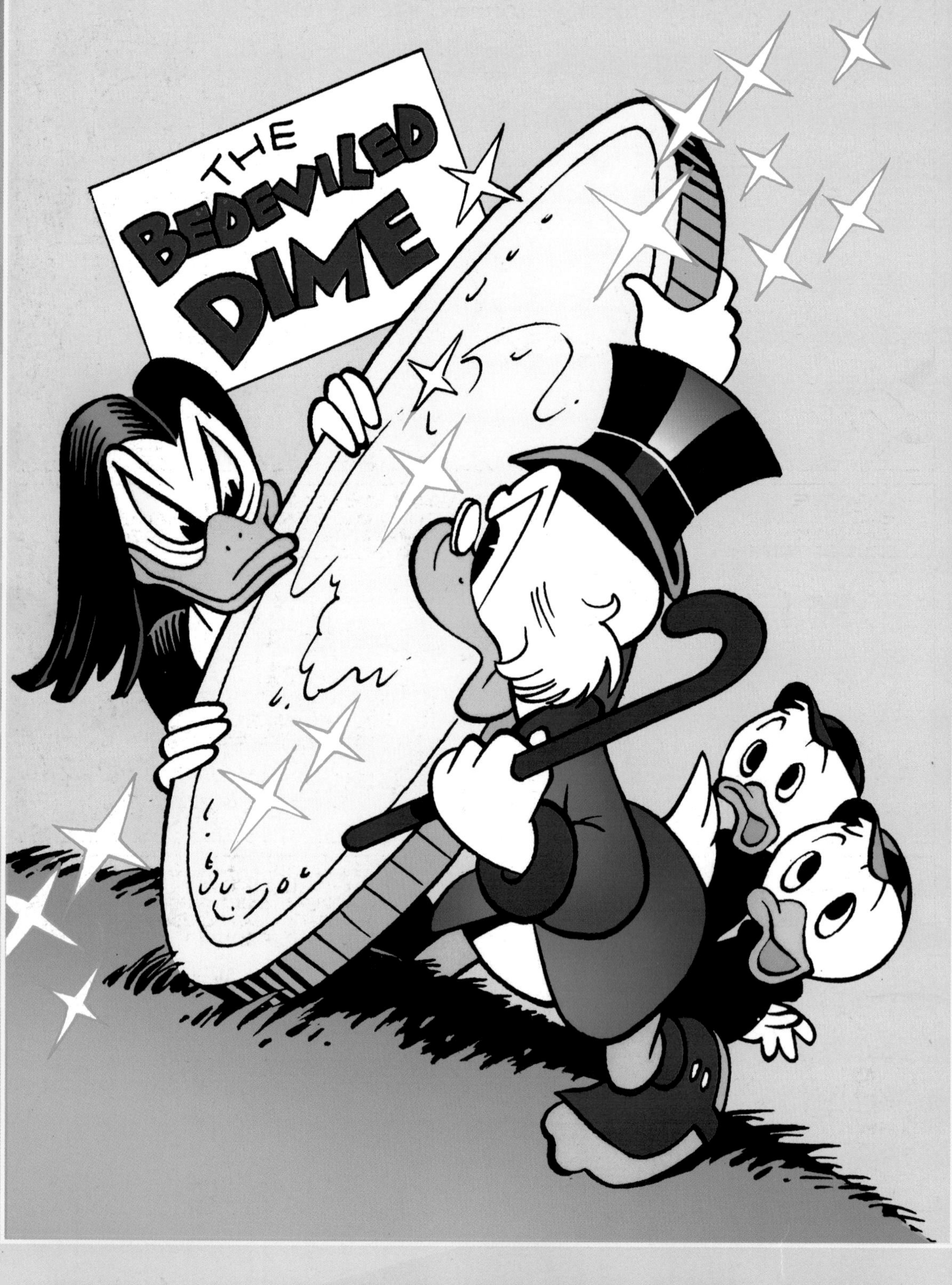
THE
BEDEVILED
DIME

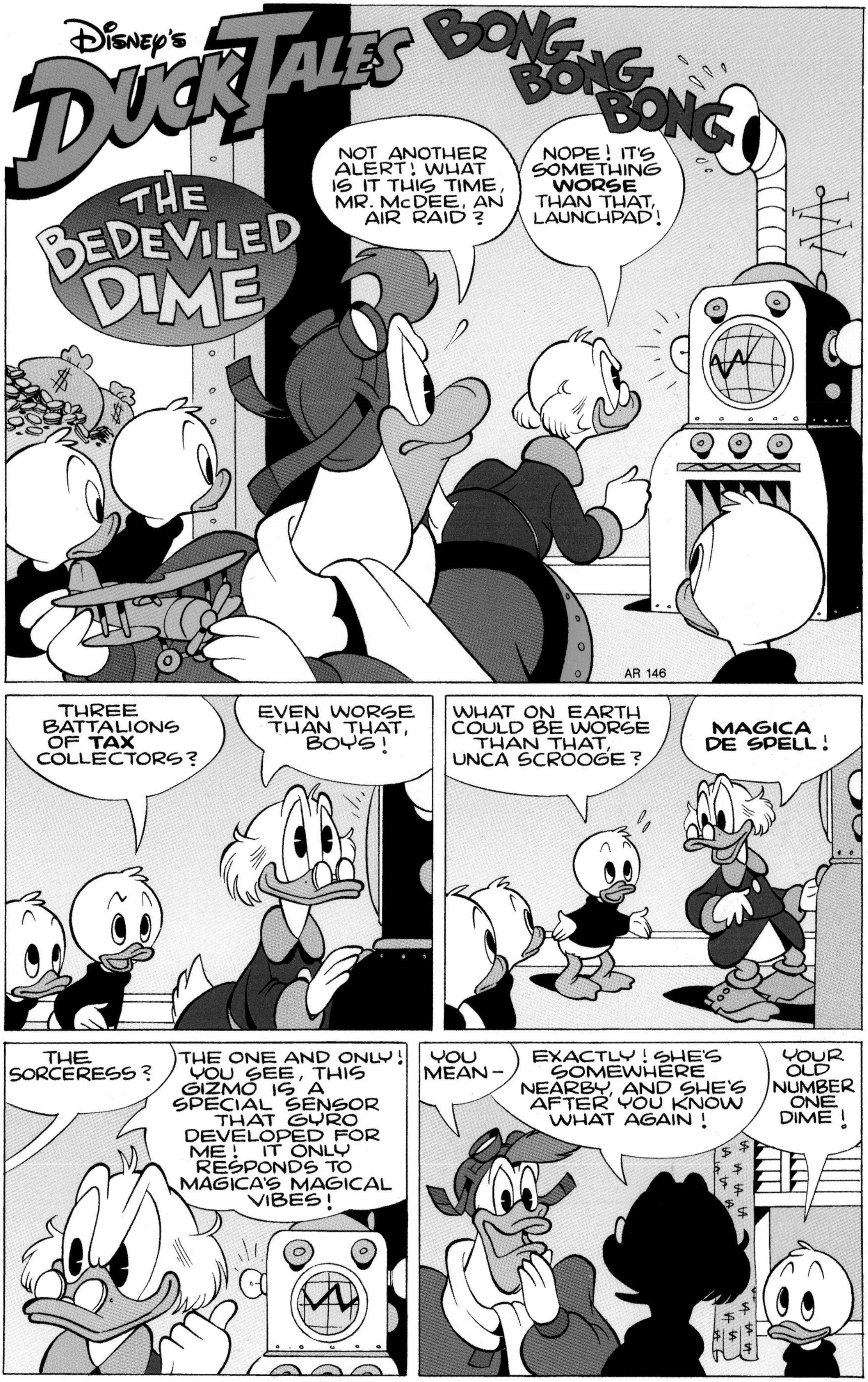
DISNEY'S DUCKTALES
THE BEDEVILED DIME
BONG BONG BONG
NOT ANOTHER ALERT! WHAT IS IT THIS TIME, MR. McDEE, AN AIR RAID?
NOPE! IT'S SOMETHING WORSE THAN THAT, LAUNCHPAD!
AR 146
THREE BATTALIONS OF TAX COLLECTORS?
EVEN WORSE THAN THAT, BOYS!
WHAT ON EARTH COULD BE WORSE THAN THAT, UNCA SCROOGE?
MAGICA DE SPELL!
THE SORCERESS?
THE ONE AND ONLY! YOU SEE, THIS GIZMO IS A SPECIAL SENSOR THAT GYRO DEVELOPED FOR ME! IT ONLY RESPONDS TO MAGICA'S MAGICAL VIBES!
YOU MEAN-
EXACTLY! SHE'S SOMEWHERE NEARBY, AND SHE'S AFTER YOU KNOW WHAT AGAIN!
YOUR OLD NUMBER ONE DIME!

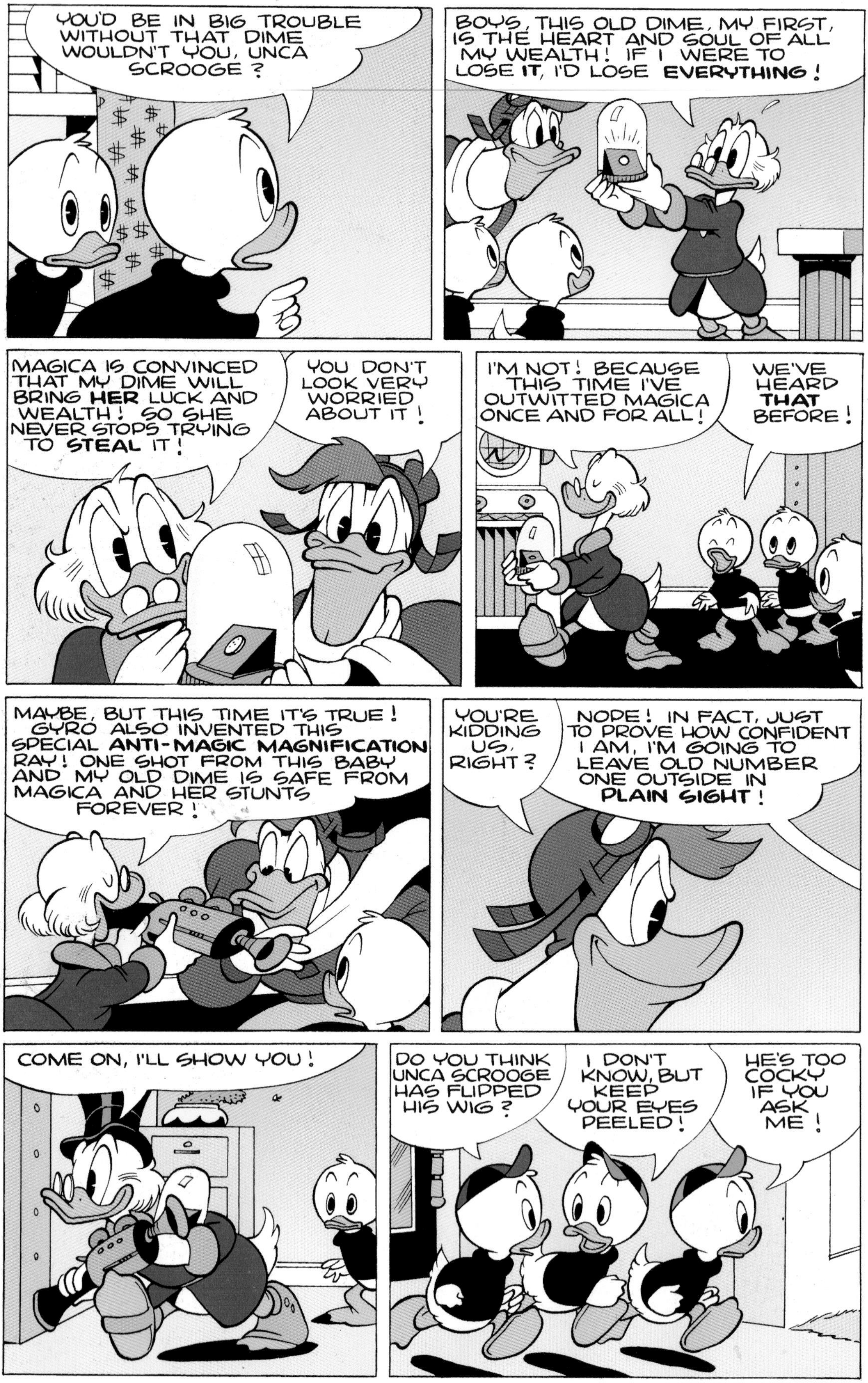

YOU'D BE IN BIG TROUBLE WITHOUT THAT DIME WOULDN'T YOU, UNCA SCROOGE ?
BOYS, THIS OLD DIME, MY FIRST, IS THE HEART AND SOUL OF ALL MY WEALTH ! IF I WERE TO LOSE IT, I'D LOSE EVERYTHING !
MAGICA IS CONVINCED THAT MY DIME WILL BRING HER LUCK AND WEALTH ! SO SHE NEVER STOPS TRYING TO STEAL IT !
YOU DON'T LOOK VERY WORRIED ABOUT IT !
I'M NOT ! BECAUSE THIS TIME I'VE OUTWITTED MAGICA ONCE AND FOR ALL !
WE'VE HEARD THAT BEFORE !
MAYBE, BUT THIS TIME IT'S TRUE ! GYRO ALSO INVENTED THIS SPECIAL ANTI-MAGIC MAGNIFICATION RAY ! ONE SHOT FROM THIS BABY AND MY OLD DIME IS SAFE FROM MAGICA AND HER STUNTS FOREVER !
YOU'RE KIDDING US, RIGHT ?
NOPE ! IN FACT, JUST TO PROVE HOW CONFIDENT I AM, I'M GOING TO LEAVE OLD NUMBER ONE OUTSIDE IN PLAIN SIGHT !
COME ON, I'LL SHOW YOU !
DO YOU THINK UNCA SCROOGE HAS FLIPPED HIS WIG ?
I DON'T KNOW, BUT KEEP YOUR EYES PEELED !
HE'S TOO COCKY IF YOU ASK ME !

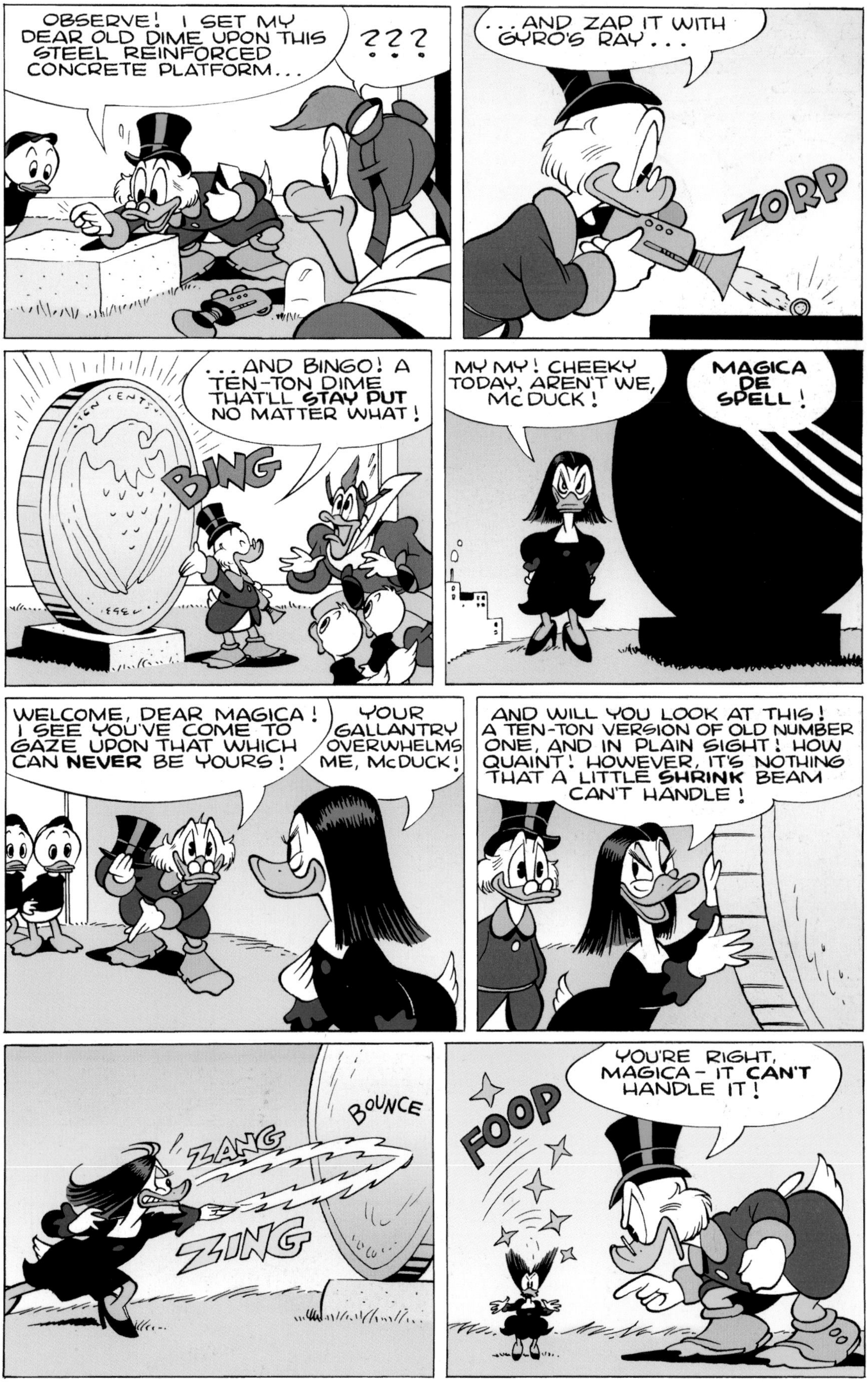
OBSERVE! I SET MY DEAR OLD DIME UPON THIS STEEL REINFORCED CONCRETE PLATFORM...
???
...AND ZAP IT WITH GYRO'S RAY...
ZORP
...AND BINGO! A TEN-TON DIME THAT'LL STAY PUT NO MATTER WHAT!
BING
MY MY! CHEEKY TODAY, AREN'T WE, McDUCK!
MAGICA DE SPELL!
WELCOME, DEAR MAGICA! I SEE YOU'VE COME TO GAZE UPON THAT WHICH CAN NEVER BE YOURS!
YOUR GALLANTRY OVERWHELMS ME, McDUCK!
AND WILL YOU LOOK AT THIS! A TEN-TON VERSION OF OLD NUMBER ONE, AND IN PLAIN SIGHT! HOW QUAINT! HOWEVER, IT'S NOTHING THAT A LITTLE SHRINK BEAM CAN'T HANDLE!
BOUNCE
ZANG
ZING
FOOP
YOU'RE RIGHT, MAGICA- IT CAN'T HANDLE IT!

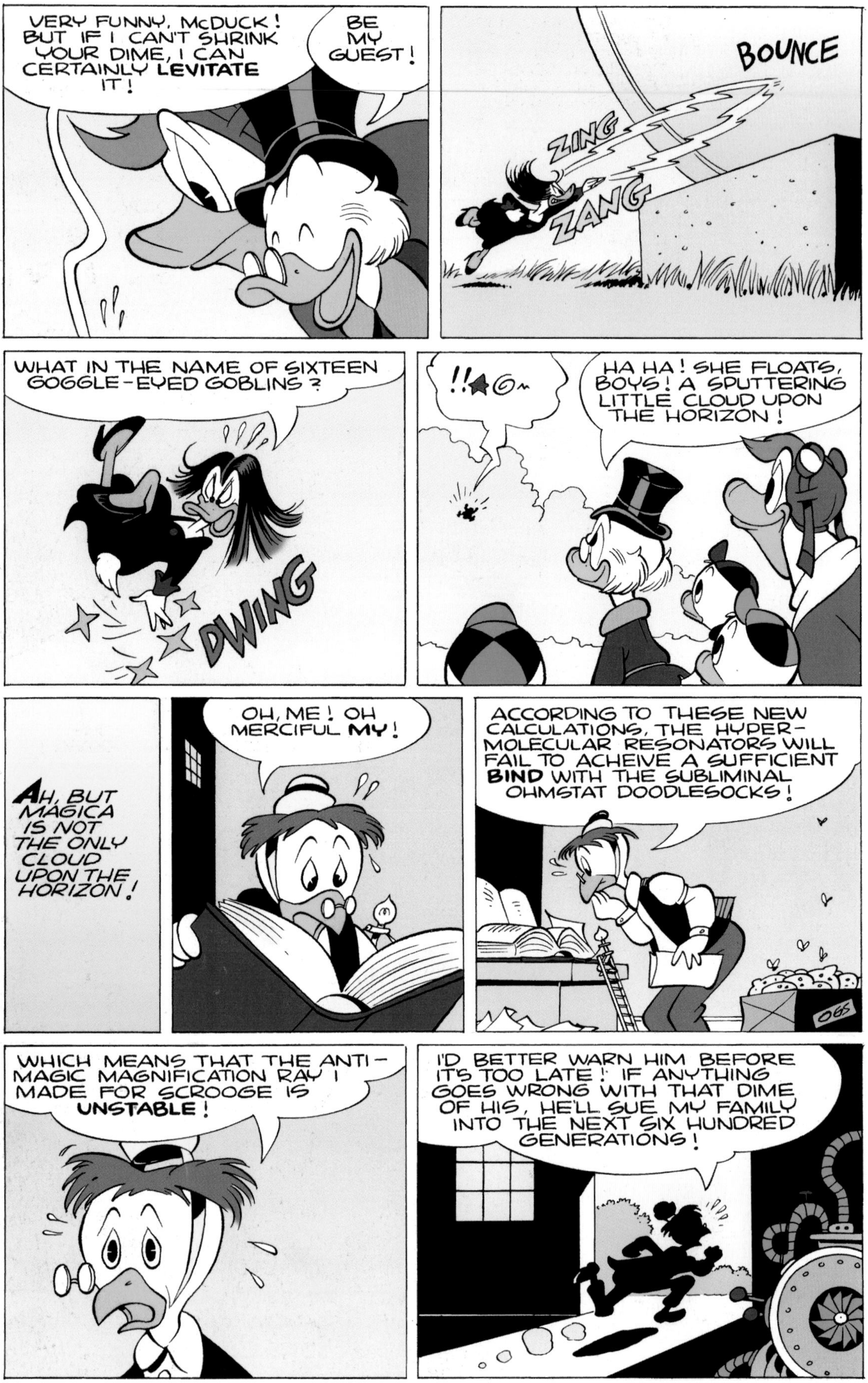
VERY FUNNY, McDUCK! BUT IF I CAN'T SHRINK YOUR DIME, I CAN CERTAINLY LEVITATE IT!
BE MY GUEST!
BOUNCE
ZING
ZANG
WHAT IN THE NAME OF SIXTEEN GOGGLE-EYED GOBLINS?
DWING
HA HA! SHE FLOATS, BOYS! A SPUTTERING LITTLE CLOUD UPON THE HORIZON!
AH, BUT MAGICA IS NOT THE ONLY CLOUD UPON THE HORIZON!
OH, ME! OH MERCIFUL MY!
ACCORDING TO THESE NEW CALCULATIONS, THE HYPER-MOLECULAR RESONATORS WILL FAIL TO ACHEIVE A SUFFICIENT BIND WITH THE SUBLIMINAL OHMSTAT DOODLESOCKS!
WHICH MEANS THAT THE ANTI-MAGIC MAGNIFICATION RAY I MADE FOR SCROOGE IS UNSTABLE!
I'D BETTER WARN HIM BEFORE IT'S TOO LATE! IF ANYTHING GOES WRONG WITH THAT DIME OF HIS, HE'LL SUE MY FAMILY INTO THE NEXT SIX HUNDRED GENERATIONS!

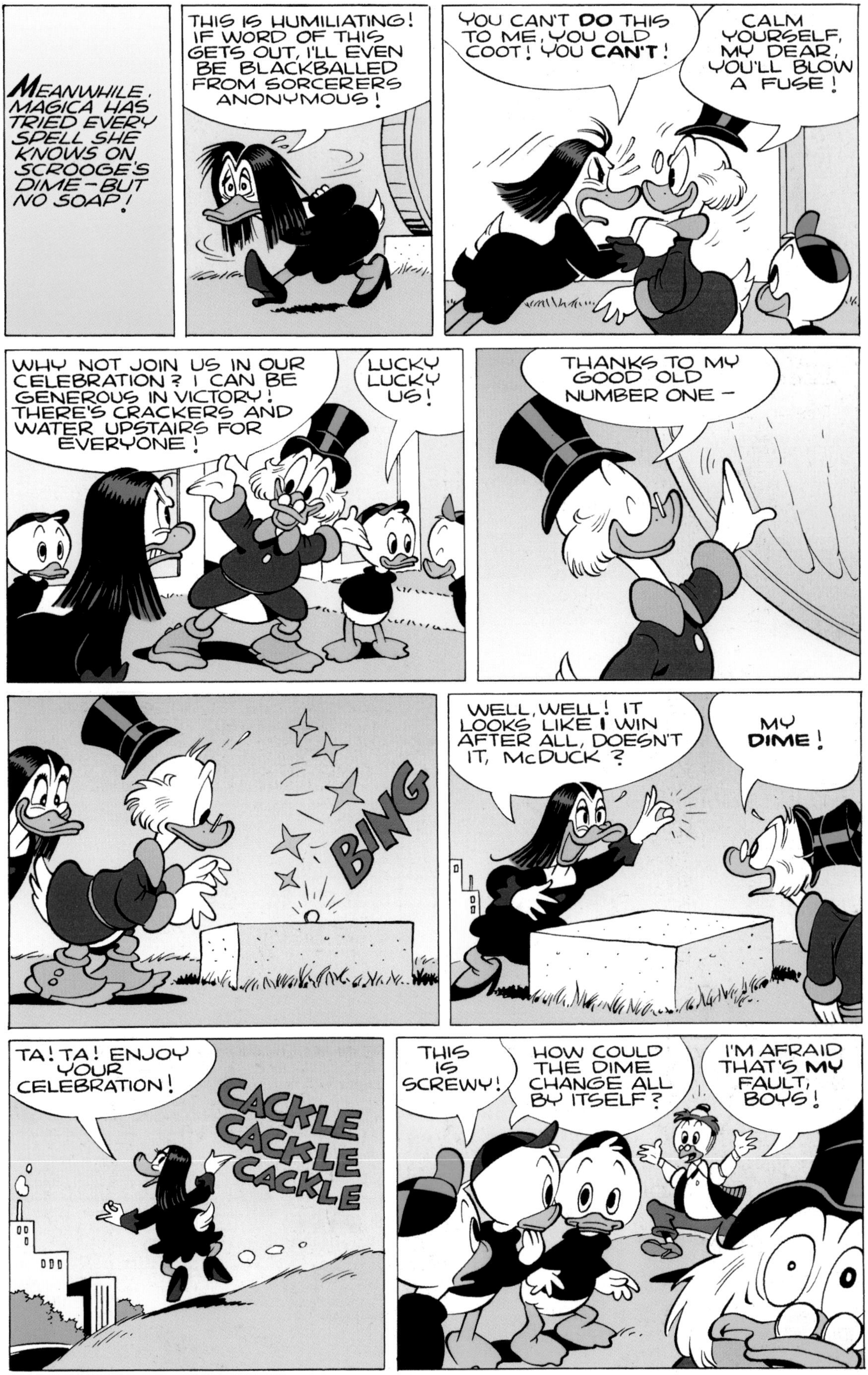
MEANWHILE, MAGICA HAS TRIED EVERY SPELL SHE KNOWS ON SCROOGE'S DIME—BUT NO SOAP!
THIS IS HUMILIATING! IF WORD OF THIS GETS OUT, I'LL EVEN BE BLACKBALLED FROM SORCERERS ANONYMOUS!
YOU CAN'T DO THIS TO ME, YOU OLD COOT! YOU CAN'T!
CALM YOURSELF, MY DEAR, YOU'LL BLOW A FUSE!
WHY NOT JOIN US IN OUR CELEBRATION? I CAN BE GENEROUS IN VICTORY! THERE'S CRACKERS AND WATER UPSTAIRS FOR EVERYONE!
LUCKY LUCKY US!
THANKS TO MY GOOD OLD NUMBER ONE—
BING
WELL, WELL! IT LOOKS LIKE I WIN AFTER ALL, DOESN'T IT, McDUCK?
MY DIME!
TA! TA! ENJOY YOUR CELEBRATION!
CACKLE CACKLE CACKLE
THIS IS SCREWY!
HOW COULD THE DIME CHANGE ALL BY ITSELF?
I'M AFRAID THAT'S MY FAULT, BOYS!

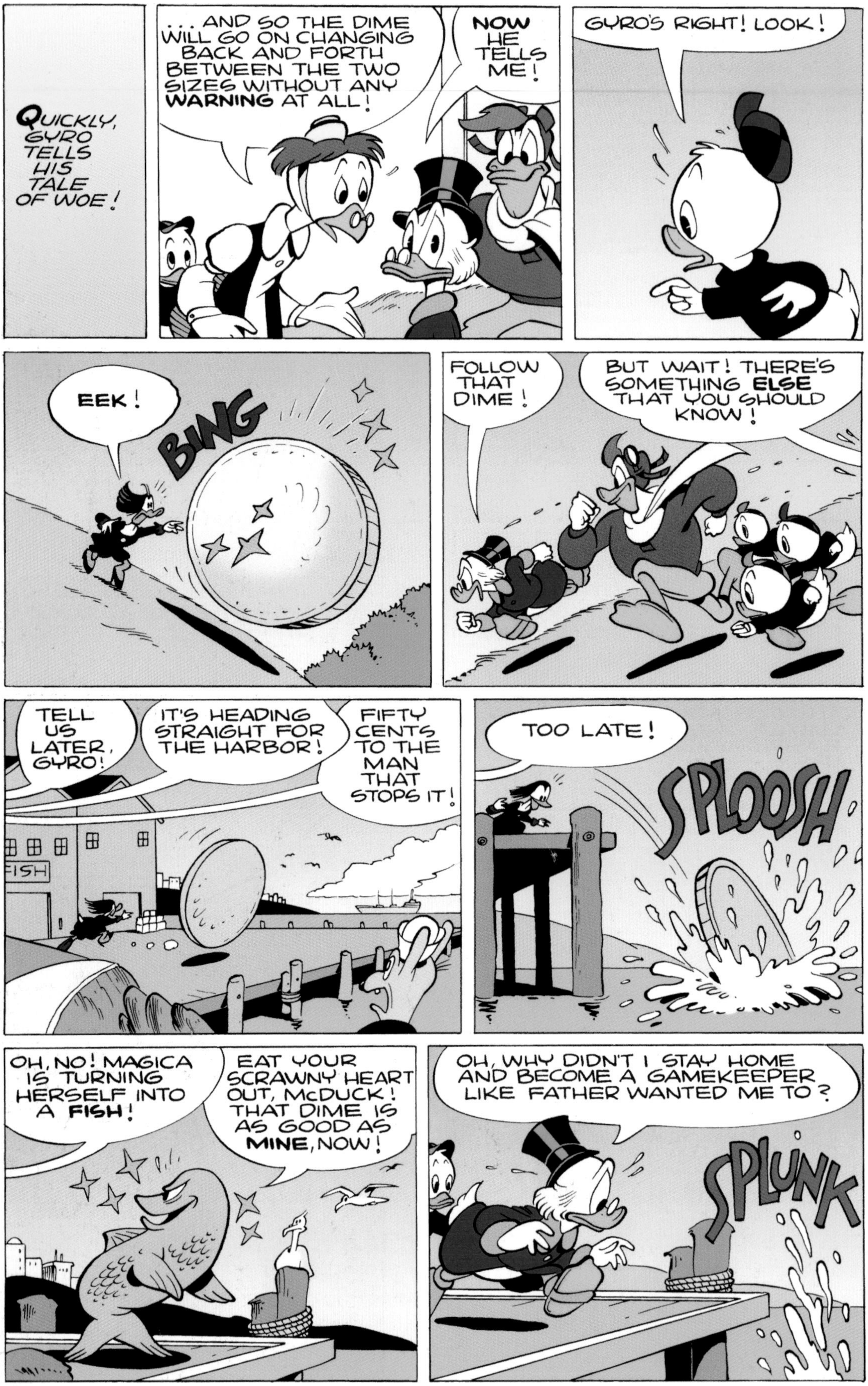
QUICKLY, GYRO TELLS HIS TALE OF WOE!
...AND SO THE DIME WILL GO ON CHANGING BACK AND FORTH BETWEEN THE TWO SIZES WITHOUT ANY WARNING AT ALL!
NOW HE TELLS ME!
GYRO'S RIGHT! LOOK!
EEK!
BING
FOLLOW THAT DIME!
BUT WAIT! THERE'S SOMETHING ELSE THAT YOU SHOULD KNOW!
TELL US LATER, GYRO!
IT'S HEADING STRAIGHT FOR THE HARBOR!
FIFTY CENTS TO THE MAN THAT STOPS IT!
FISH
TOO LATE!
SPLOOSH
OH, NO! MAGICA IS TURNING HERSELF INTO A FISH!
EAT YOUR SCRAWNY HEART OUT, McDUCK! THAT DIME IS AS GOOD AS MINE, NOW!
OH, WHY DIDN'T I STAY HOME AND BECOME A GAMEKEEPER LIKE FATHER WANTED ME TO?
SPLUNK

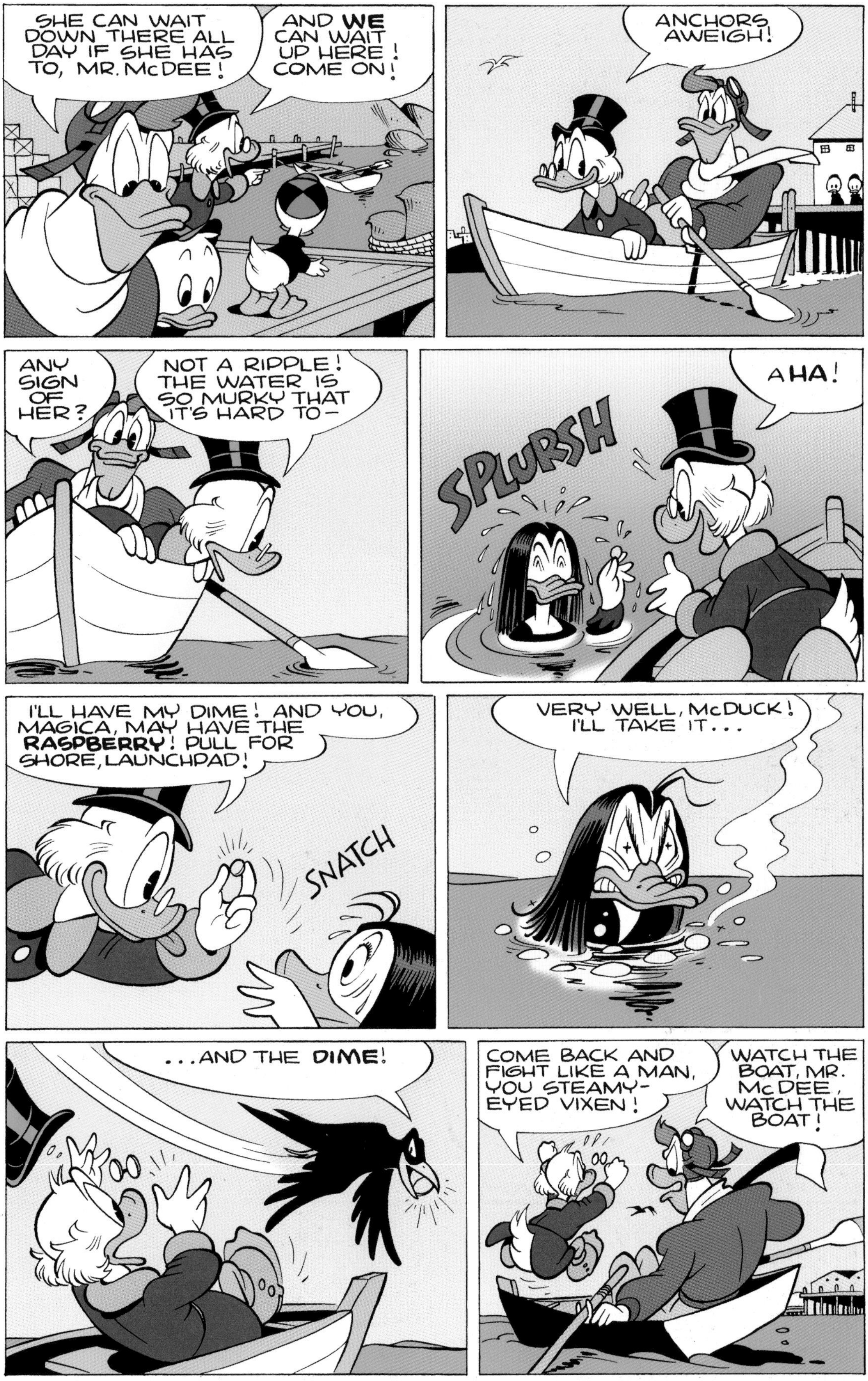
SHE CAN WAIT DOWN THERE ALL DAY IF SHE HAS TO, MR. McDEE!
AND **WE** CAN WAIT UP HERE! COME ON!
ANCHORS AWEIGH!
ANY SIGN OF HER?
NOT A RIPPLE! THE WATER IS SO MURKY THAT IT'S HARD TO–
SPLURSH
A **HA**!
I'LL HAVE MY DIME! AND YOU, MAGICA, MAY HAVE THE **RASPBERRY**! PULL FOR SHORE, LAUNCHPAD!
SNATCH
VERY WELL, McDUCK! I'LL TAKE IT...
...AND THE **DIME**!
COME BACK AND FIGHT LIKE A MAN, YOU STEAMY-EYED VIXEN!
WATCH THE BOAT, MR. McDEE, WATCH THE BOAT!

I'M IN THE CLEAR! NOW IF I CAN JUST GET BACK TO MY CHALET BEFORE THIS IDIOT DIME . . .

BING

. . . CHANGES!

THUD

WELL, WELL, WELL! ENCOUNTER A LITTLE DOWNDRAFT, DID YOU?

RANT! RAVE! **POX**! PESTILENCE AND CARNAGE!

I THINK MAGICA IS HAVING A BIT OF A FIT, UNCA SCROOGE!

MUSIC TO MY EARS, BOYS!

ROWF AUGH

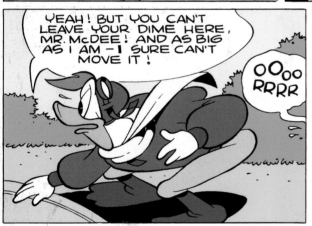

YEAH! BUT YOU CAN'T LEAVE YOUR DIME HERE, MR. McDEE! AND AS BIG AS I AM — I SURE CAN'T MOVE IT!

OOOOO RRRR

BIG? OF COURSE! WHY DIDN'T I THINK OF IT BEFORE?

I GUESS WE'LL JUST HAVE TO WAIT FOR THE DIME TO CHANGE AGAIN, THEN MAKE A RUN FOR IT!

FUMF

THAT WON'T BE NECESSARY, BOYS!

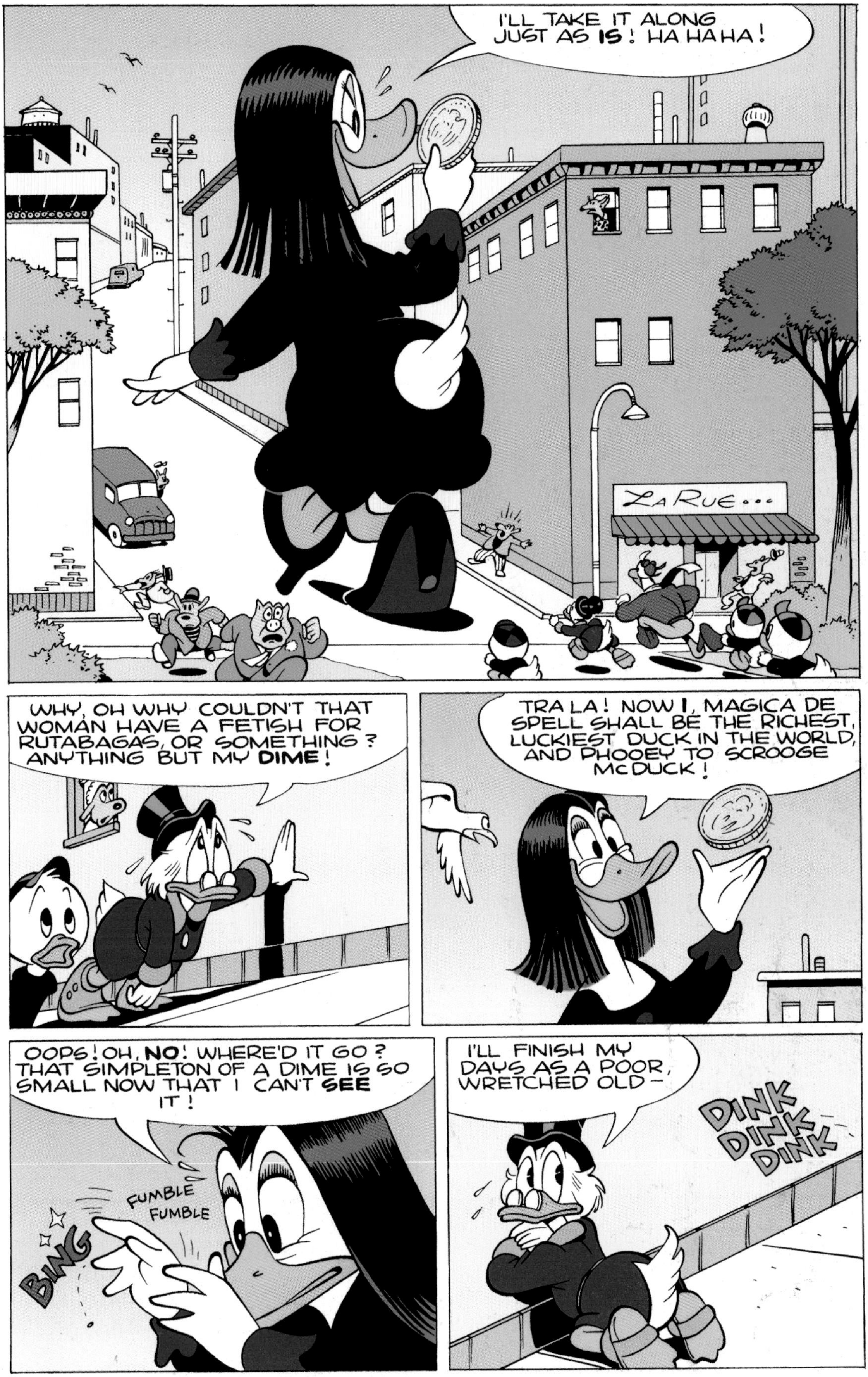
I'LL TAKE IT ALONG JUST AS IS! HA HA HA!
LA RUE...
WHY, OH WHY COULDN'T THAT WOMAN HAVE A FETISH FOR RUTABAGAS, OR SOMETHING? ANYTHING BUT MY DIME!
TRA LA! NOW I, MAGICA DE SPELL SHALL BE THE RICHEST, LUCKIEST DUCK IN THE WORLD, AND PHOOEY TO SCROOGE McDUCK!
OOPS! OH, NO! WHERE'D IT GO? THAT SIMPLETON OF A DIME IS SO SMALL NOW THAT I CAN'T SEE IT!
FUMBLE FUMBLE
BING
I'LL FINISH MY DAYS AS A POOR, WRETCHED OLD—
DINK DINK DINK

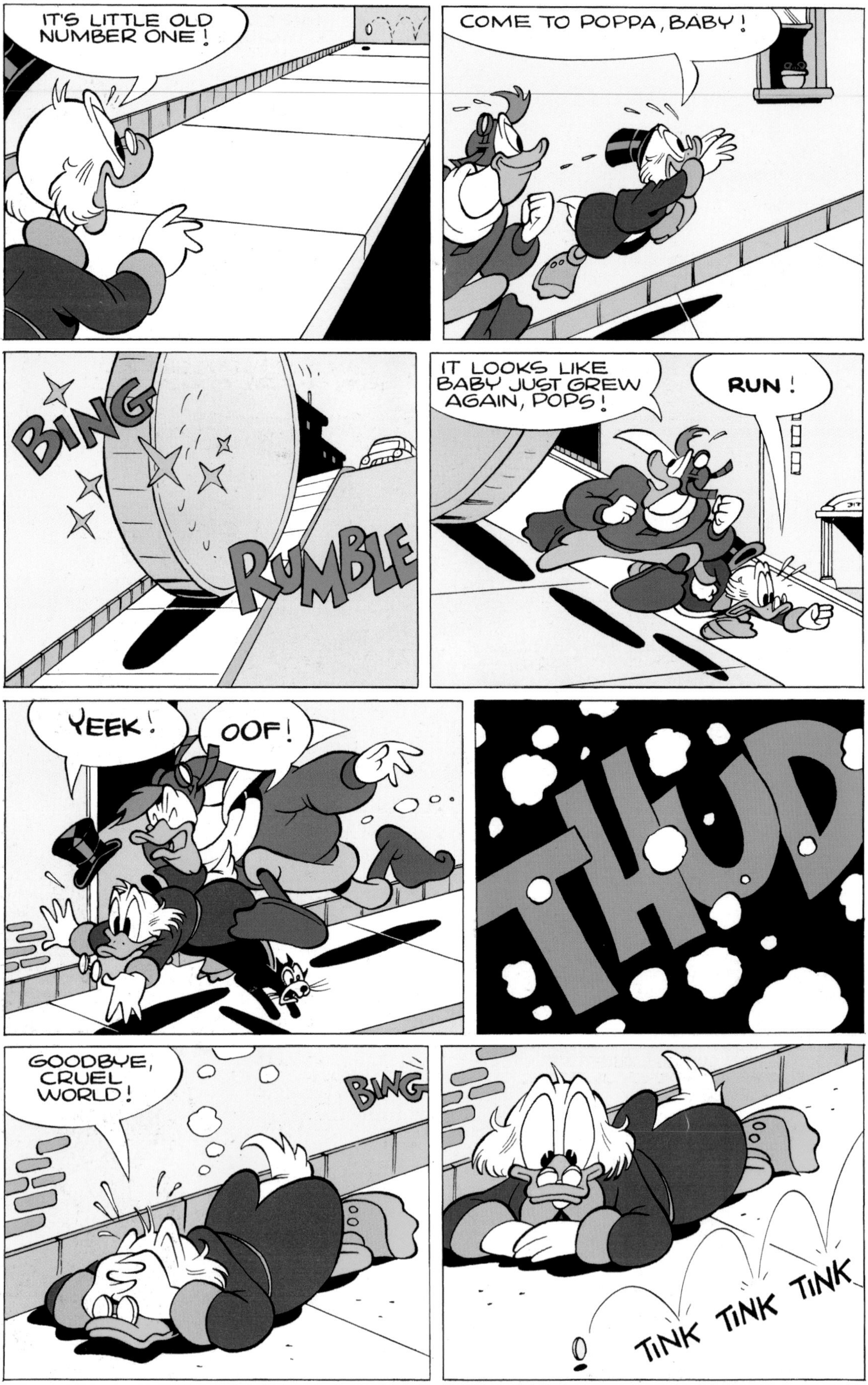
IT'S LITTLE OLD NUMBER ONE!
COME TO POPPA, BABY!
BING
RUMBLE
IT LOOKS LIKE BABY JUST GREW AGAIN, POPS!
RUN!
YEEK!
OOF!
THUD
GOODBYE, CRUEL WORLD!
BING
TINK TINK TINK

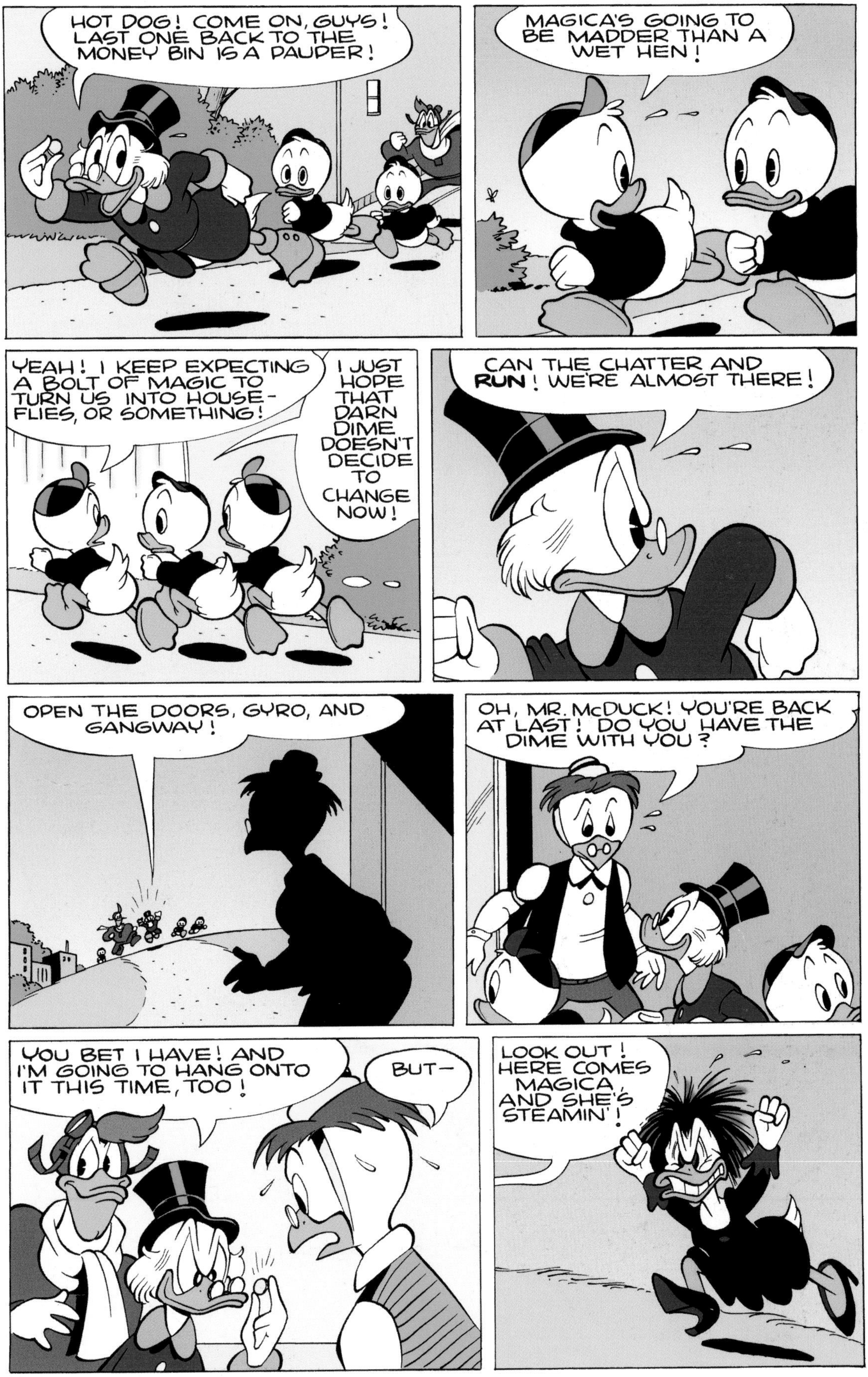
HOT DOG! COME ON, GUYS! LAST ONE BACK TO THE MONEY BIN IS A PAUPER!
MAGICA'S GOING TO BE MADDER THAN A WET HEN!
YEAH! I KEEP EXPECTING A BOLT OF MAGIC TO TURN US INTO HOUSE-FLIES, OR SOMETHING!
I JUST HOPE THAT DARN DIME DOESN'T DECIDE TO CHANGE NOW!
CAN THE CHATTER AND RUN! WE'RE ALMOST THERE!
OPEN THE DOORS, GYRO, AND GANGWAY!
OH, MR. McDUCK! YOU'RE BACK AT LAST! DO YOU HAVE THE DIME WITH YOU?
YOU BET I HAVE! AND I'M GOING TO HANG ONTO IT THIS TIME, TOO!
BUT—
LOOK OUT! HERE COMES MAGICA, AND SHE'S STEAMIN'!

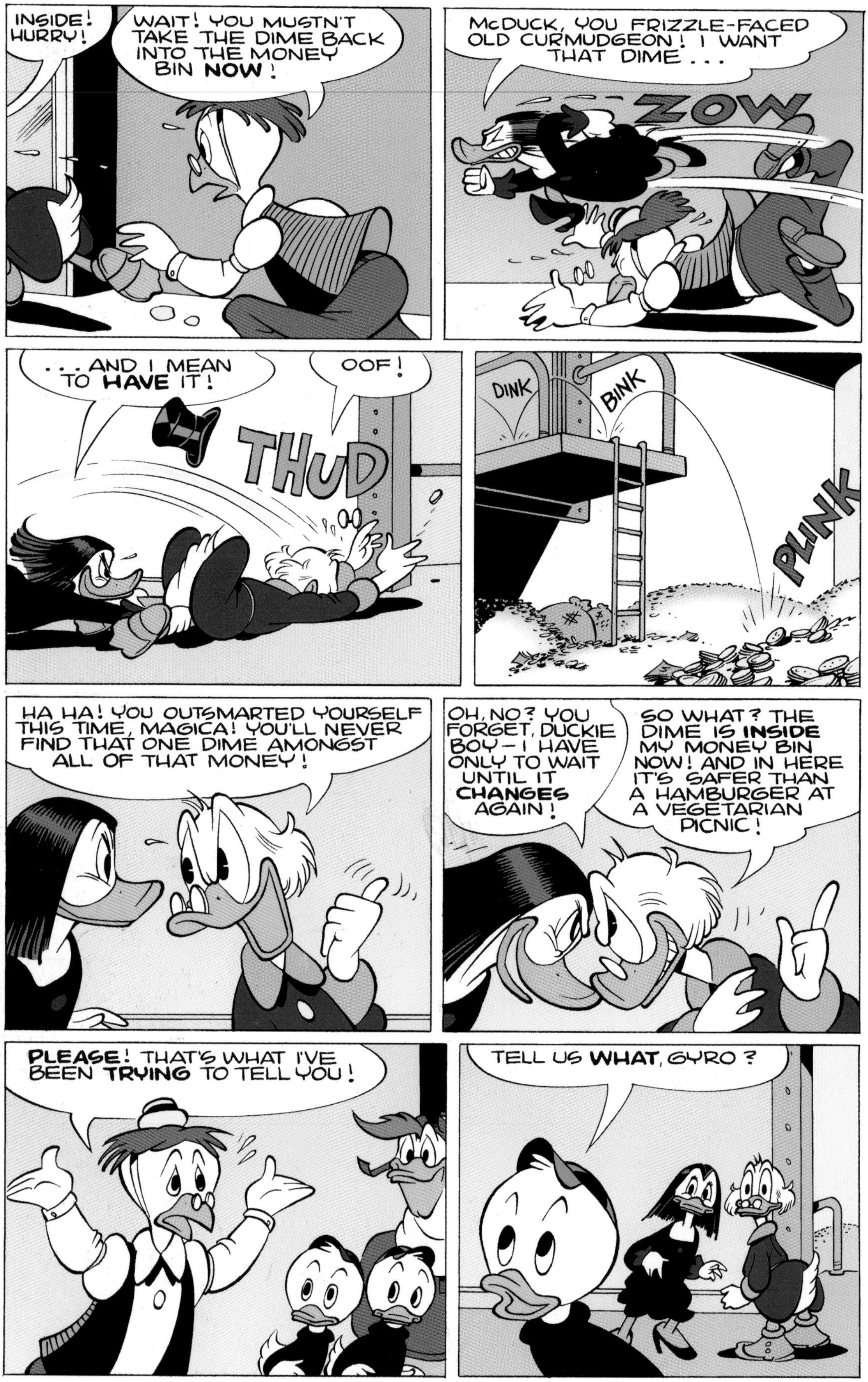
INSIDE! HURRY!
WAIT! YOU MUSTN'T TAKE THE DIME BACK INTO THE MONEY BIN **NOW**!
McDUCK, YOU FRIZZLE-FACED OLD CURMUDGEON! I WANT THAT DIME...
ZOW
...AND I MEAN TO **HAVE** IT!
OOF!
THUD
DINK
BINK
PLINK
HA HA! YOU OUTSMARTED YOURSELF THIS TIME, MAGICA! YOU'LL NEVER FIND THAT ONE DIME AMONGST ALL OF THAT MONEY!
OH, NO? YOU FORGET, DUCKIE BOY—I HAVE ONLY TO WAIT UNTIL IT **CHANGES** AGAIN!
SO WHAT? THE DIME IS **INSIDE** MY MONEY BIN NOW! AND IN HERE IT'S SAFER THAN A HAMBURGER AT A VEGETARIAN PICNIC!
PLEASE! THAT'S WHAT I'VE BEEN **TRYING** TO TELL YOU!
TELL US **WHAT**, GYRO?

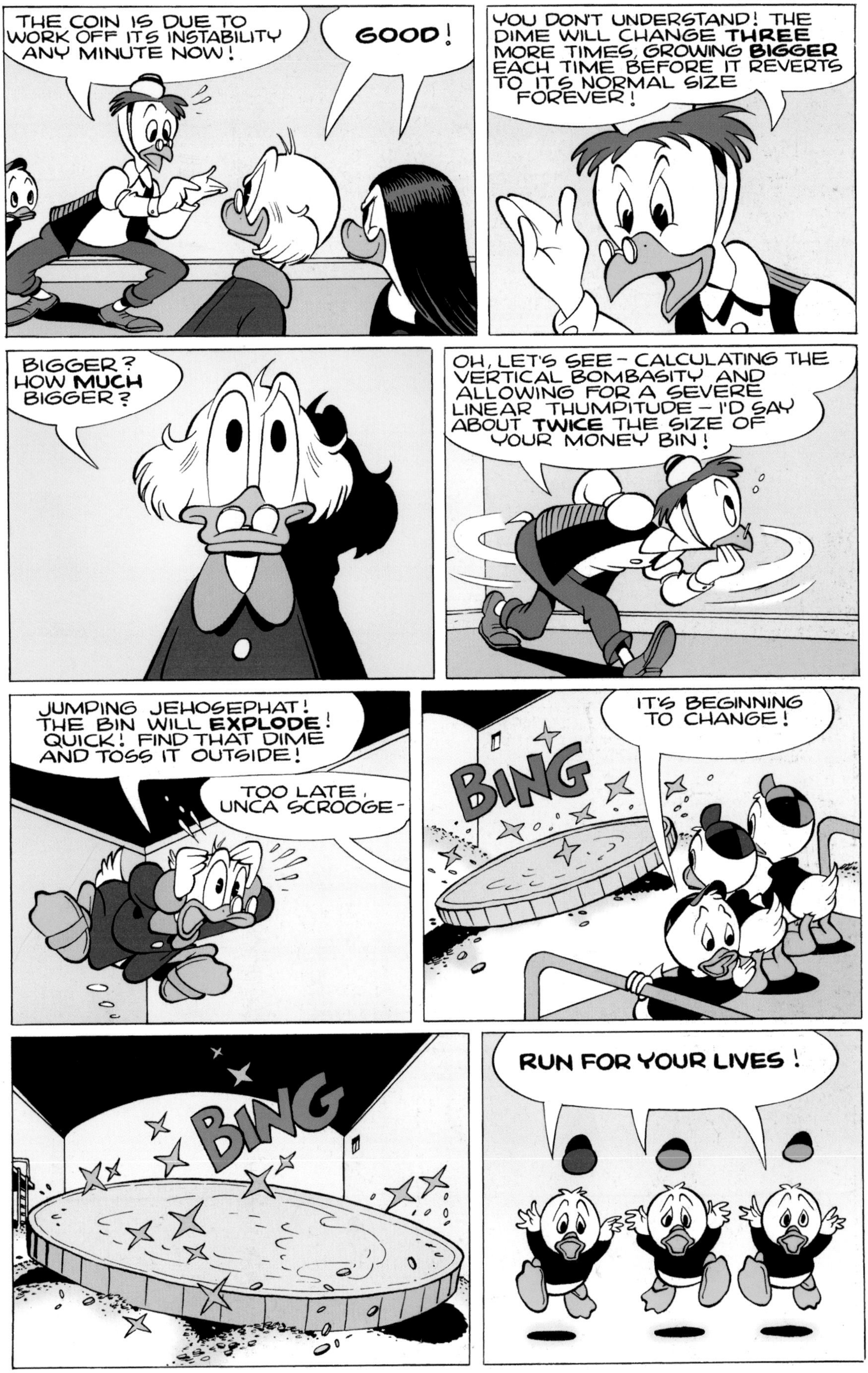

THE COIN IS DUE TO WORK OFF ITS INSTABILITY ANY MINUTE NOW!
GOOD!
YOU DON'T UNDERSTAND! THE DIME WILL CHANGE **THREE** MORE TIMES, GROWING **BIGGER** EACH TIME BEFORE IT REVERTS TO ITS NORMAL SIZE FOREVER!
BIGGER? HOW **MUCH** BIGGER?
OH, LET'S SEE – CALCULATING THE VERTICAL BOMBASITY AND ALLOWING FOR A SEVERE LINEAR THUMPITUDE – I'D SAY ABOUT **TWICE** THE SIZE OF YOUR MONEY BIN!
JUMPING JEHOSEPHAT! THE BIN WILL **EXPLODE**! QUICK! FIND THAT DIME AND TOSS IT OUTSIDE!
TOO LATE, UNCA SCROOGE –
IT'S BEGINNING TO CHANGE!
BING
BING
RUN FOR YOUR LIVES!

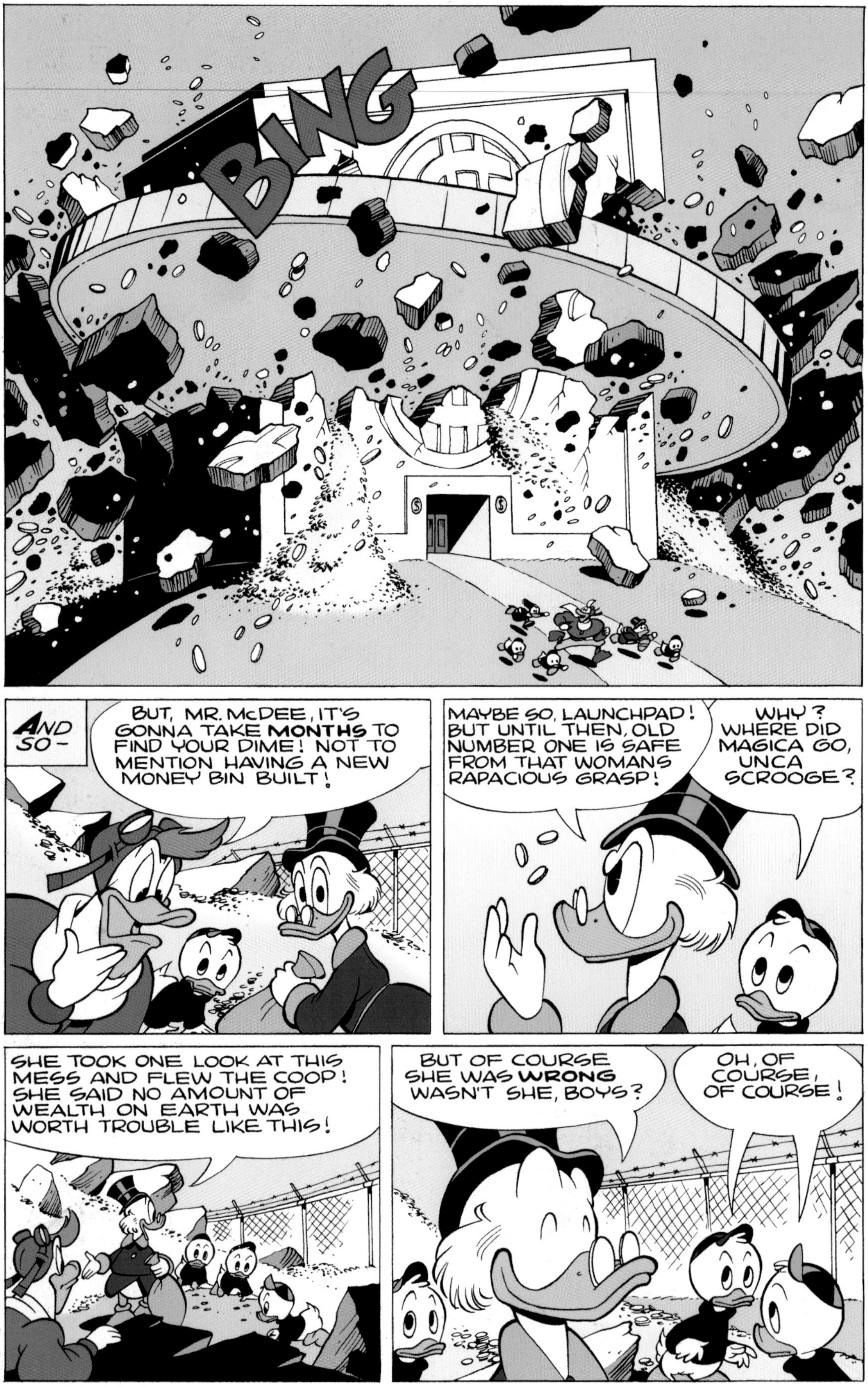
BING
AND SO–
BUT, MR. McDEE, IT'S GONNA TAKE MONTHS TO FIND YOUR DIME! NOT TO MENTION HAVING A NEW MONEY BIN BUILT!
MAYBE SO, LAUNCHPAD! BUT UNTIL THEN, OLD NUMBER ONE IS SAFE FROM THAT WOMANS RAPACIOUS GRASP!
WHY? WHERE DID MAGICA GO, UNCA SCROOGE?
SHE TOOK ONE LOOK AT THIS MESS AND FLEW THE COOP! SHE SAID NO AMOUNT OF WEALTH ON EARTH WAS WORTH TROUBLE LIKE THIS!
BUT OF COURSE SHE WAS WRONG WASN'T SHE, BOYS?
OH, OF COURSE, OF COURSE!

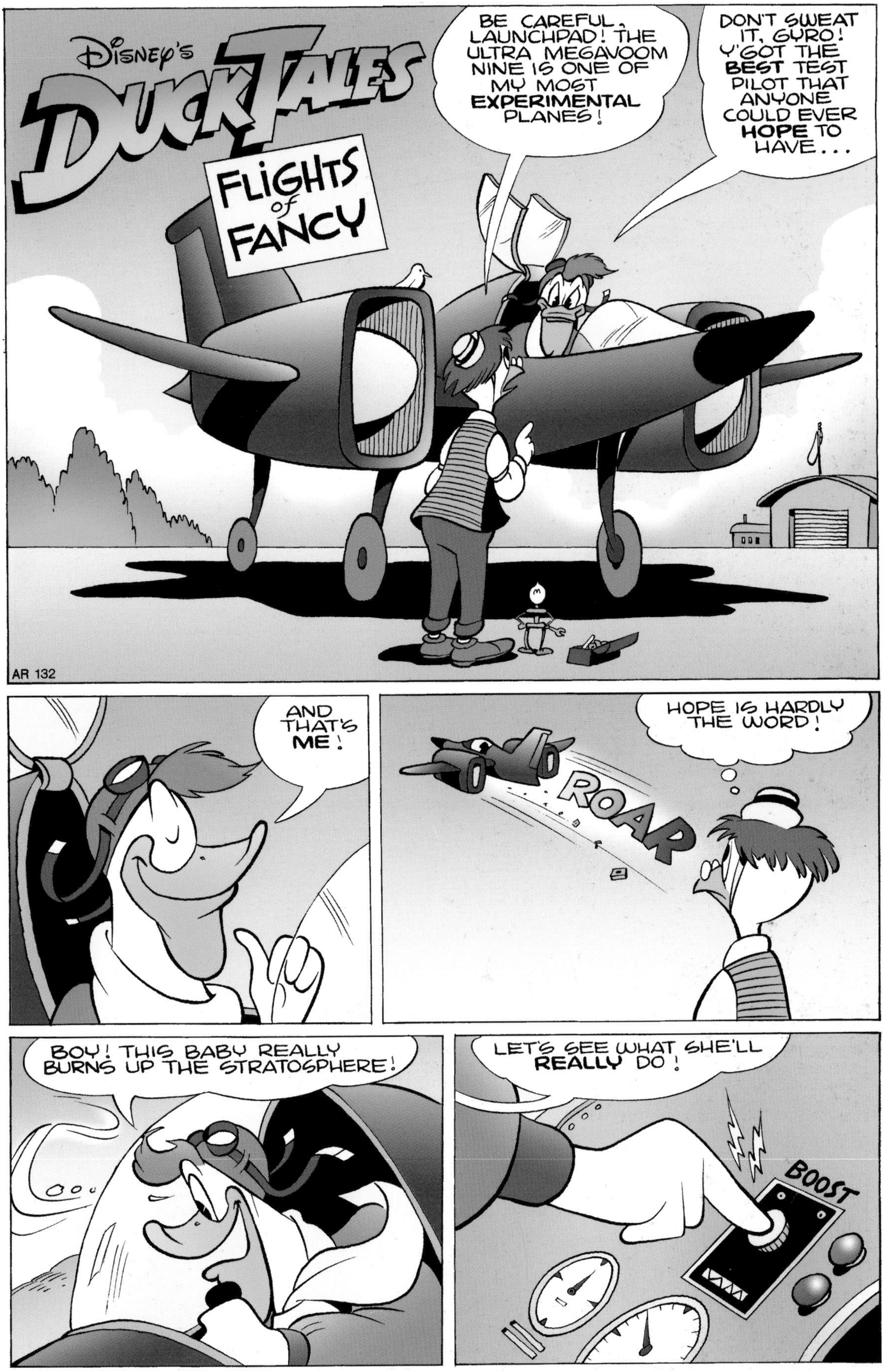
DISNEY'S DUCKTALES
FLIGHTS of FANCY
BE CAREFUL, LAUNCHPAD! THE ULTRA MEGAVOOM NINE IS ONE OF MY MOST EXPERIMENTAL PLANES!
DON'T SWEAT IT, GYRO! Y'GOT THE BEST TEST PILOT THAT ANYONE COULD EVER HOPE TO HAVE...
AR 132
AND THAT'S ME!
HOPE IS HARDLY THE WORD!
ROAR
BOY! THIS BABY REALLY BURNS UP THE STRATOSPHERE!
LET'S SEE WHAT SHE'LL REALLY DO!
BOOST

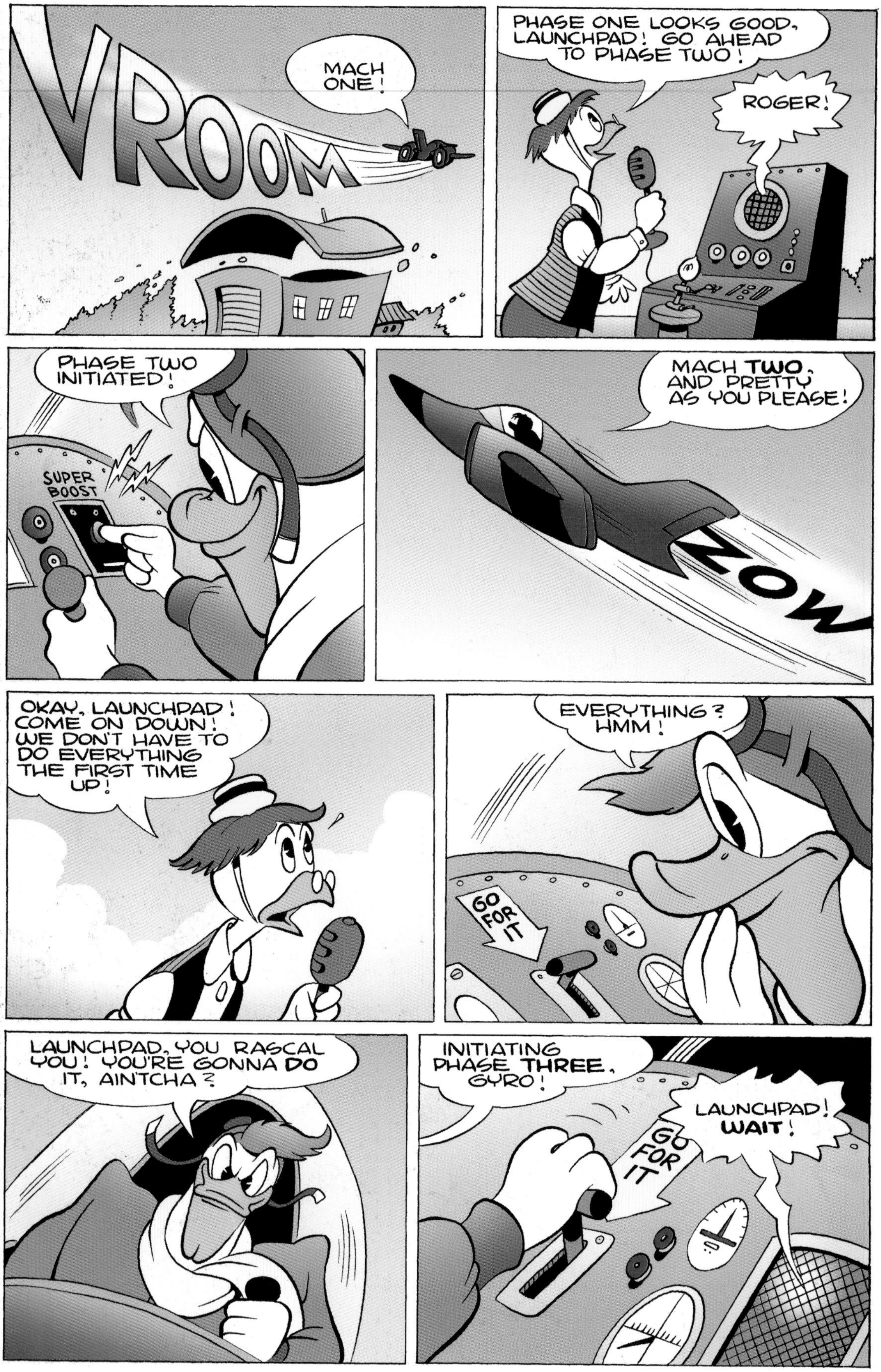
VROOM
MACH ONE!
PHASE ONE LOOKS GOOD, LAUNCHPAD! GO AHEAD TO PHASE TWO!
ROGER!
PHASE TWO INITIATED!
SUPER BOOST
MACH **TWO**, AND PRETTY AS YOU PLEASE!
ZOW
OKAY, LAUNCHPAD! COME ON DOWN! WE DON'T HAVE TO DO EVERYTHING THE FIRST TIME UP!
EVERYTHING? HMM!
GO FOR IT
LAUNCHPAD, YOU RASCAL YOU! YOU'RE GONNA **DO** IT, AIN'TCHA?
INITIATING PHASE **THREE**, GYRO!
GO FOR IT
LAUNCHPAD! **WAIT**!

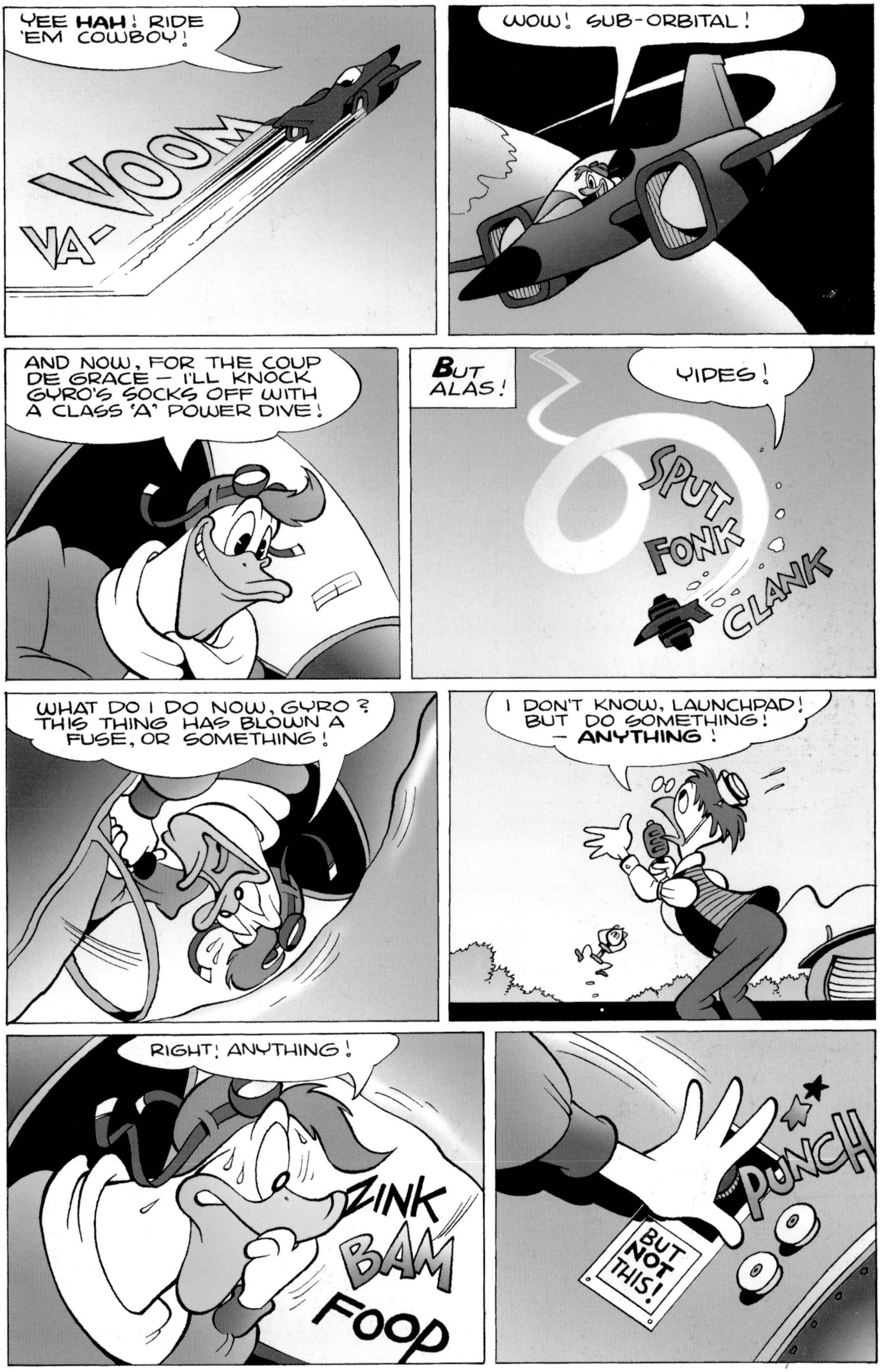

YEE HAH! RIDE 'EM COWBOY!
VA-VOOM
WOW! SUB-ORBITAL!
AND NOW, FOR THE COUP DE GRACE — I'LL KNOCK GYRO'S SOCKS OFF WITH A CLASS 'A' POWER DIVE!
BUT ALAS!
YIPES!
SPUT
FONK
CLANK
WHAT DO I DO NOW, GYRO? THIS THING HAS BLOWN A FUSE, OR SOMETHING!
I DON'T KNOW, LAUNCHPAD! BUT DO SOMETHING! — ANYTHING!
RIGHT! ANYTHING!
ZINK
BAM
FOOP
PUNCH
BUT NOT THIS!

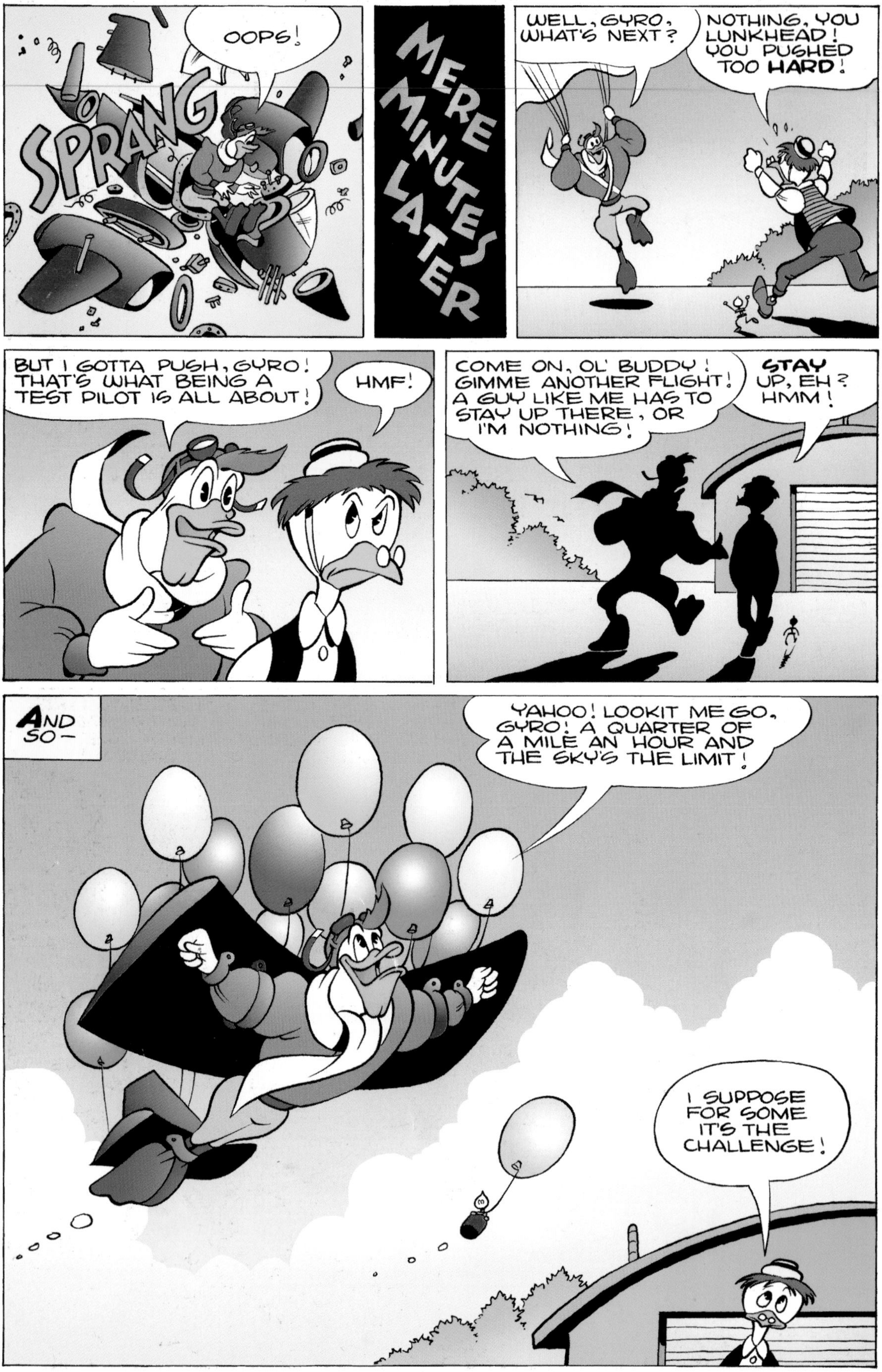
OOPS!
SPRANG
MERE MINUTES LATER
WELL, GYRO, WHAT'S NEXT?
NOTHING, YOU LUNKHEAD! YOU PUSHED TOO **HARD**!
BUT I GOTTA PUSH, GYRO! THAT'S WHAT BEING A TEST PILOT IS ALL ABOUT!
HMF!
COME ON, OL' BUDDY! GIMME ANOTHER FLIGHT! A GUY LIKE ME HAS TO STAY UP THERE, OR I'M NOTHING!
STAY UP, EH? HMM!
AND SO—
YAHOO! LOOKIT ME GO, GYRO! A QUARTER OF A MILE AN HOUR AND THE SKY'S THE LIMIT!
I SUPPOSE FOR SOME IT'S THE CHALLENGE!

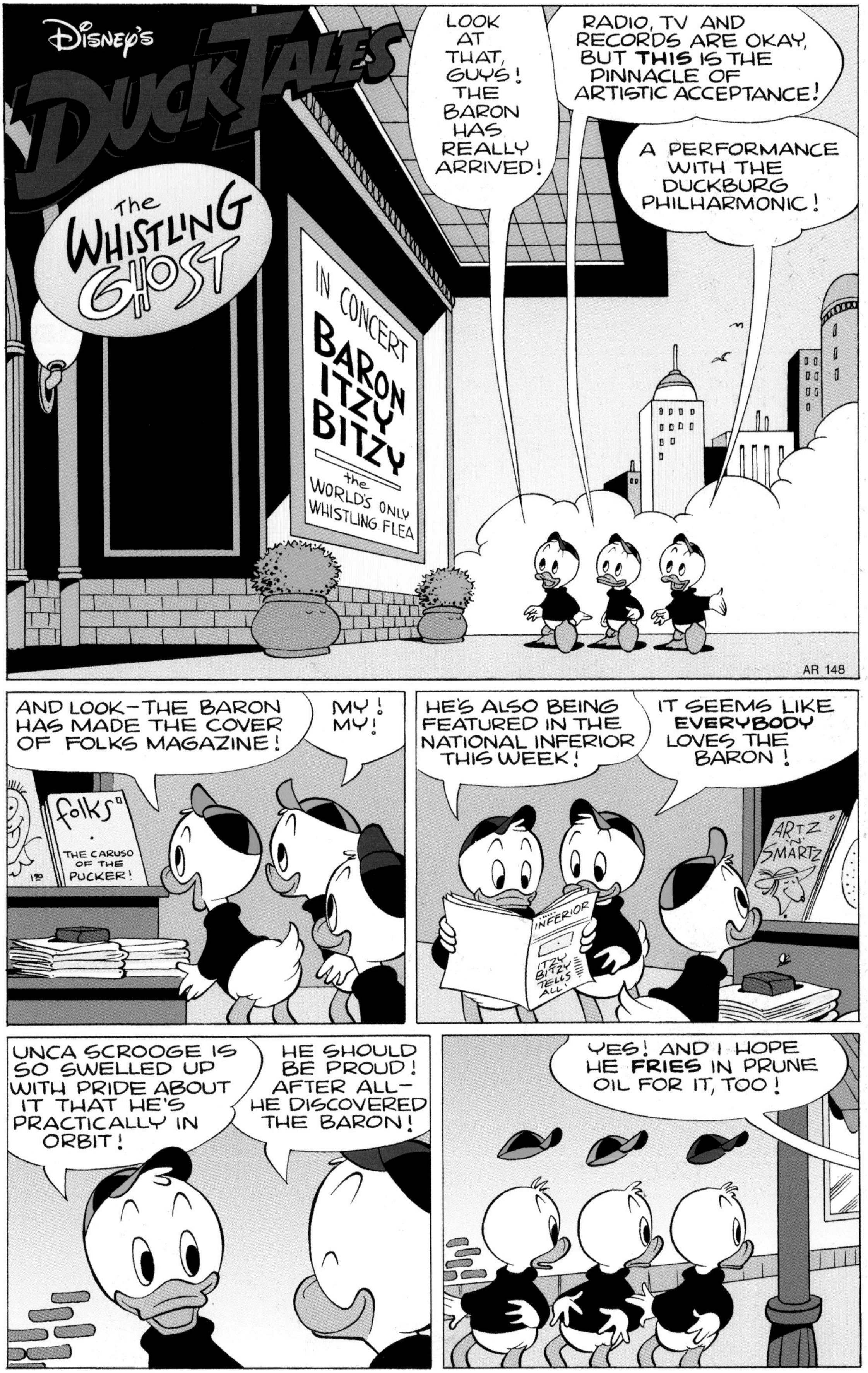

DISNEY'S
DUCKTALES
The WHISTLING GHOST
IN CONCERT BARON ITZY BITZY the WORLD'S ONLY WHISTLING FLEA
LOOK AT THAT, GUYS! THE BARON HAS REALLY ARRIVED!
RADIO, TV AND RECORDS ARE OKAY, BUT THIS IS THE PINNACLE OF ARTISTIC ACCEPTANCE!
A PERFORMANCE WITH THE DUCKBURG PHILHARMONIC!
AR 148
AND LOOK—THE BARON HAS MADE THE COVER OF FOLKS MAGAZINE!
MY! MY!
folks THE CARUSO OF THE PUCKER!
HE'S ALSO BEING FEATURED IN THE NATIONAL INFERIOR THIS WEEK!
IT SEEMS LIKE EVERYBODY LOVES THE BARON!
INFERIOR ITZY BITZY TELLS ALL!
ARTZ 'N' SMARTZ
UNCA SCROOGE IS SO SWELLED UP WITH PRIDE ABOUT IT THAT HE'S PRACTICALLY IN ORBIT!
HE SHOULD BE PROUD! AFTER ALL—HE DISCOVERED THE BARON!
YES! AND I HOPE HE FRIES IN PRUNE OIL FOR IT, TOO!

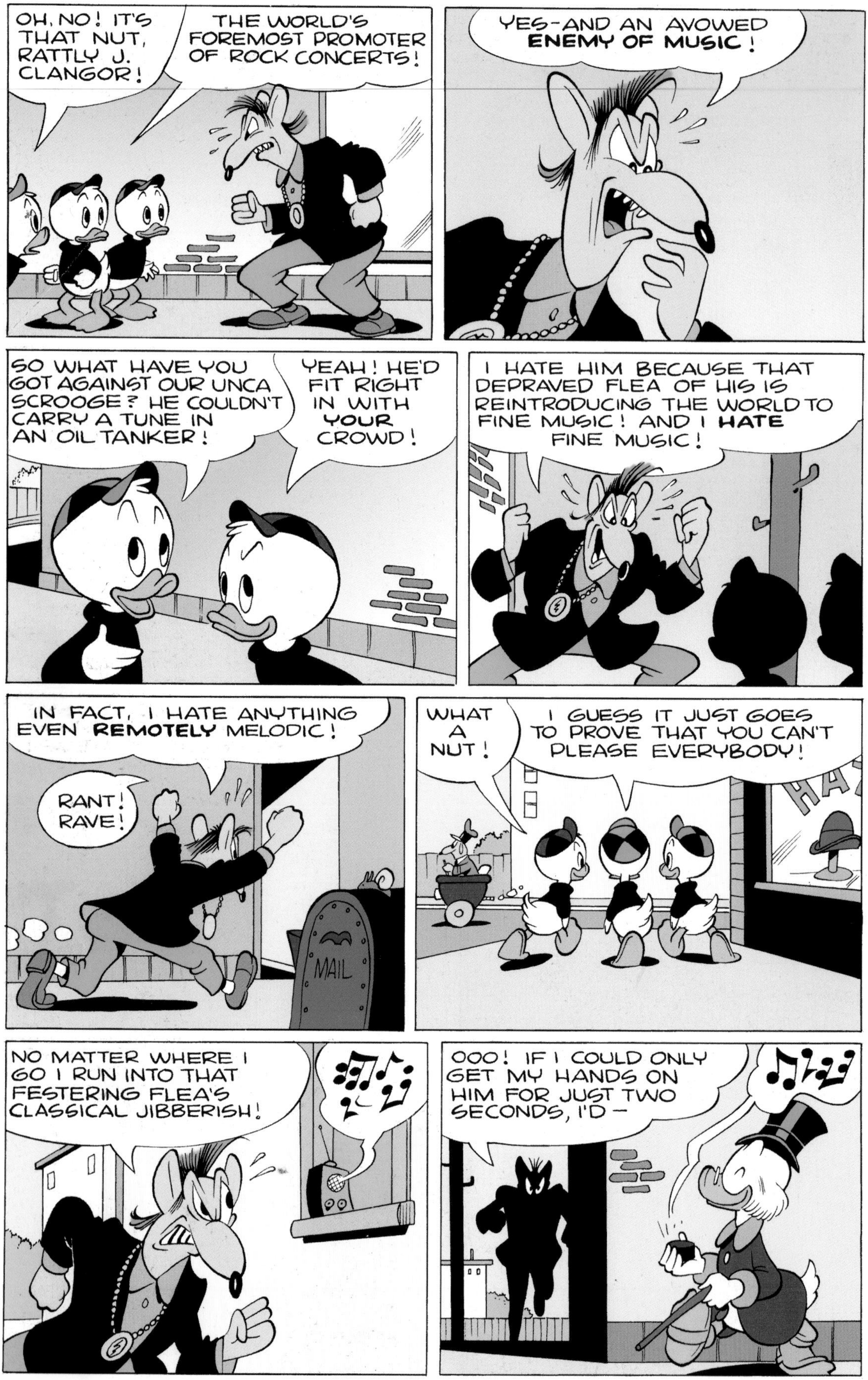

OH, NO! IT'S THAT NUT, RATTLY J. CLANGOR!
THE WORLD'S FOREMOST PROMOTER OF ROCK CONCERTS!
YES—AND AN AVOWED ENEMY OF MUSIC!
SO WHAT HAVE YOU GOT AGAINST OUR UNCA SCROOGE? HE COULDN'T CARRY A TUNE IN AN OIL TANKER!
YEAH! HE'D FIT RIGHT IN WITH YOUR CROWD!
I HATE HIM BECAUSE THAT DEPRAVED FLEA OF HIS IS REINTRODUCING THE WORLD TO FINE MUSIC! AND I HATE FINE MUSIC!
IN FACT, I HATE ANYTHING EVEN REMOTELY MELODIC!
RANT! RAVE!
MAIL
WHAT A NUT!
I GUESS IT JUST GOES TO PROVE THAT YOU CAN'T PLEASE EVERYBODY!
NO MATTER WHERE I GO I RUN INTO THAT FESTERING FLEA'S CLASSICAL JIBBERISH!
OOO! IF I COULD ONLY GET MY HANDS ON HIM FOR JUST TWO SECONDS, I'D—

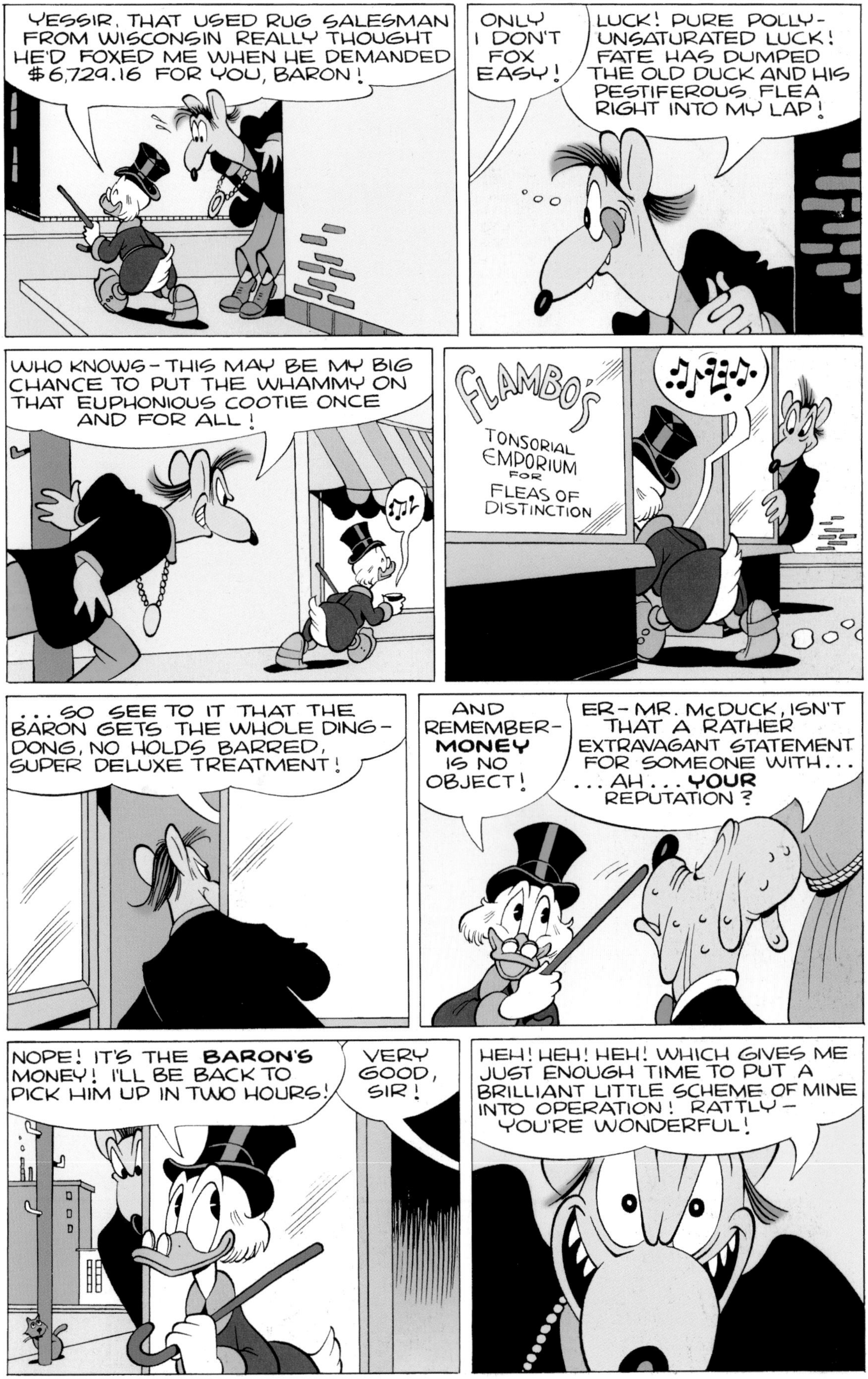
YESSIR, THAT USED RUG SALESMAN FROM WISCONSIN REALLY THOUGHT HE'D FOXED ME WHEN HE DEMANDED $6,729.16 FOR YOU, BARON!
ONLY I DON'T FOX EASY!
LUCK! PURE POLLY-UNSATURATED LUCK! FATE HAS DUMPED THE OLD DUCK AND HIS PESTIFEROUS FLEA RIGHT INTO MY LAP!
WHO KNOWS—THIS MAY BE MY BIG CHANCE TO PUT THE WHAMMY ON THAT EUPHONIOUS COOTIE ONCE AND FOR ALL!
FLAMBO'S
TONSORIAL EMPORIUM FOR FLEAS OF DISTINCTION
...SO SEE TO IT THAT THE BARON GETS THE WHOLE DING-DONG, NO HOLDS BARRED, SUPER DELUXE TREATMENT!
AND REMEMBER—**MONEY** IS NO OBJECT!
ER—MR. McDUCK, ISN'T THAT A RATHER EXTRAVAGANT STATEMENT FOR SOMEONE WITH... ...AH... **YOUR** REPUTATION?
NOPE! IT'S THE **BARON'S** MONEY! I'LL BE BACK TO PICK HIM UP IN TWO HOURS!
VERY GOOD, SIR!
HEH! HEH! HEH! WHICH GIVES ME JUST ENOUGH TIME TO PUT A BRILLIANT LITTLE SCHEME OF MINE INTO OPERATION! RATTLY—YOU'RE WONDERFUL!

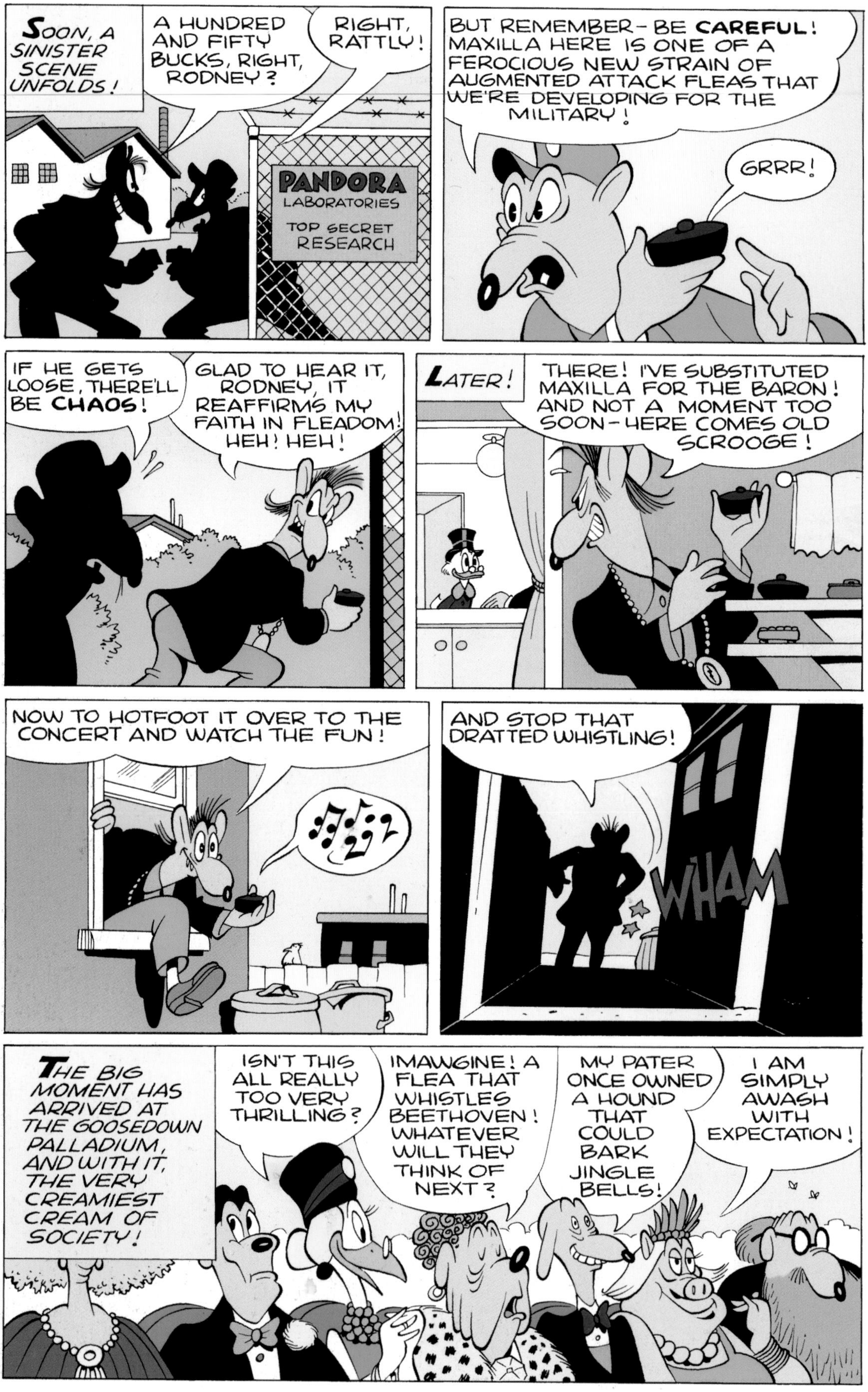
SOON, A SINISTER SCENE UNFOLDS!
A HUNDRED AND FIFTY BUCKS, RIGHT, RODNEY?
RIGHT, RATTLY!
PANDORA LABORATORIES
TOP SECRET RESEARCH
BUT REMEMBER – BE CAREFUL! MAXILLA HERE IS ONE OF A FEROCIOUS NEW STRAIN OF AUGMENTED ATTACK FLEAS THAT WE'RE DEVELOPING FOR THE MILITARY!
GRRR!
IF HE GETS LOOSE, THERE'LL BE CHAOS!
GLAD TO HEAR IT, RODNEY, IT REAFFIRMS MY FAITH IN FLEADOM! HEH! HEH!
LATER!
THERE! I'VE SUBSTITUTED MAXILLA FOR THE BARON! AND NOT A MOMENT TOO SOON – HERE COMES OLD SCROOGE!
NOW TO HOTFOOT IT OVER TO THE CONCERT AND WATCH THE FUN!
AND STOP THAT DRATTED WHISTLING!
WHAM
THE BIG MOMENT HAS ARRIVED AT THE GOOSEDOWN PALLADIUM, AND WITH IT, THE VERY CREAMIEST CREAM OF SOCIETY!
ISN'T THIS ALL REALLY TOO VERY THRILLING?
IMAWGINE! A FLEA THAT WHISTLES BEETHOVEN! WHATEVER WILL THEY THINK OF NEXT?
MY PATER ONCE OWNED A HOUND THAT COULD BARK JINGLE BELLS!
I AM SIMPLY AWASH WITH EXPECTATION!

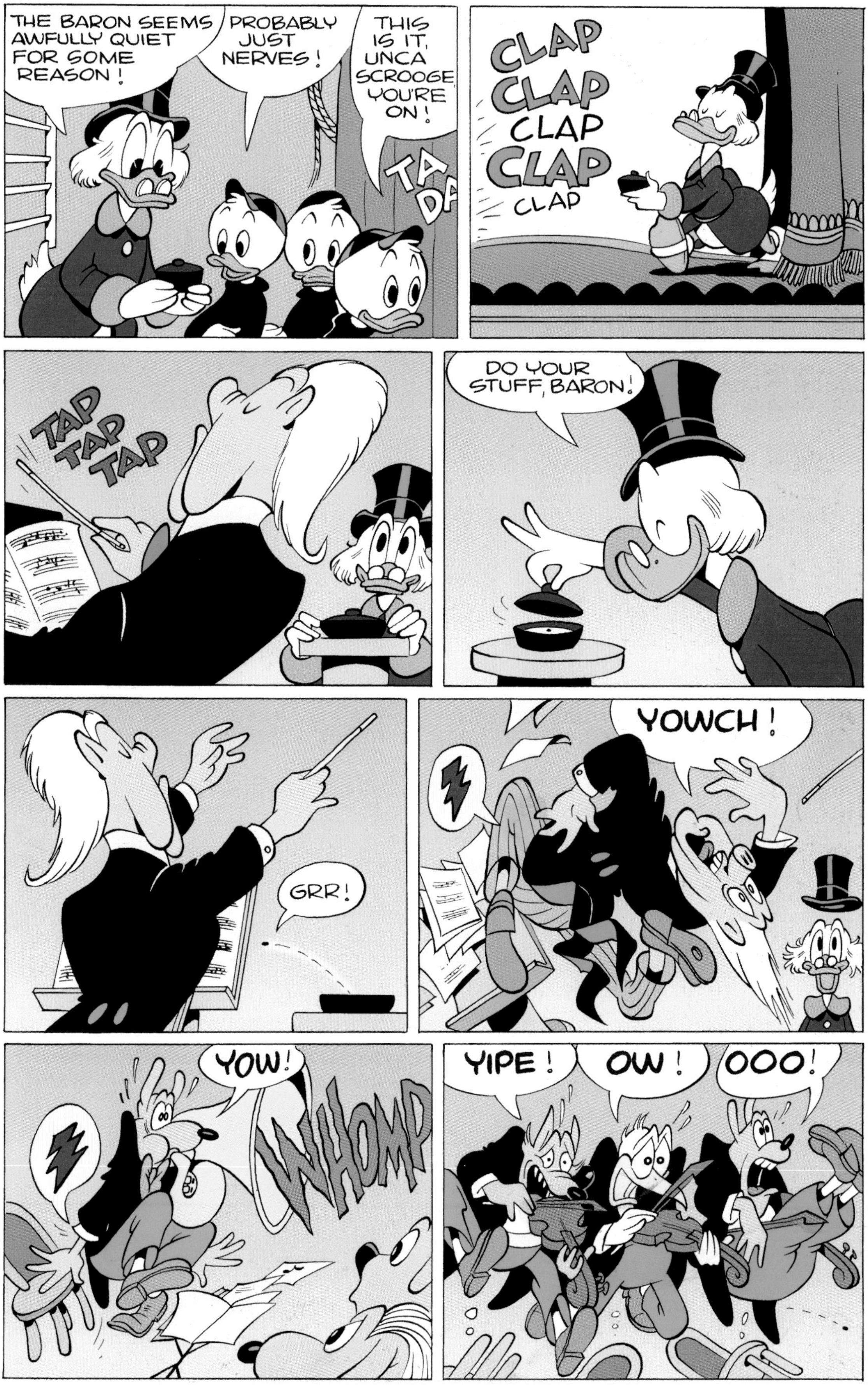
THE BARON SEEMS AWFULLY QUIET FOR SOME REASON!
PROBABLY JUST NERVES!
THIS IS IT, UNCA SCROOGE! YOU'RE ON!
TA DA
CLAP CLAP CLAP CLAP CLAP
TAP TAP TAP
DO YOUR STUFF, BARON!
GRR!
YOWCH!
YOW!
WHOMP
YIPE!
OW!
OOO!

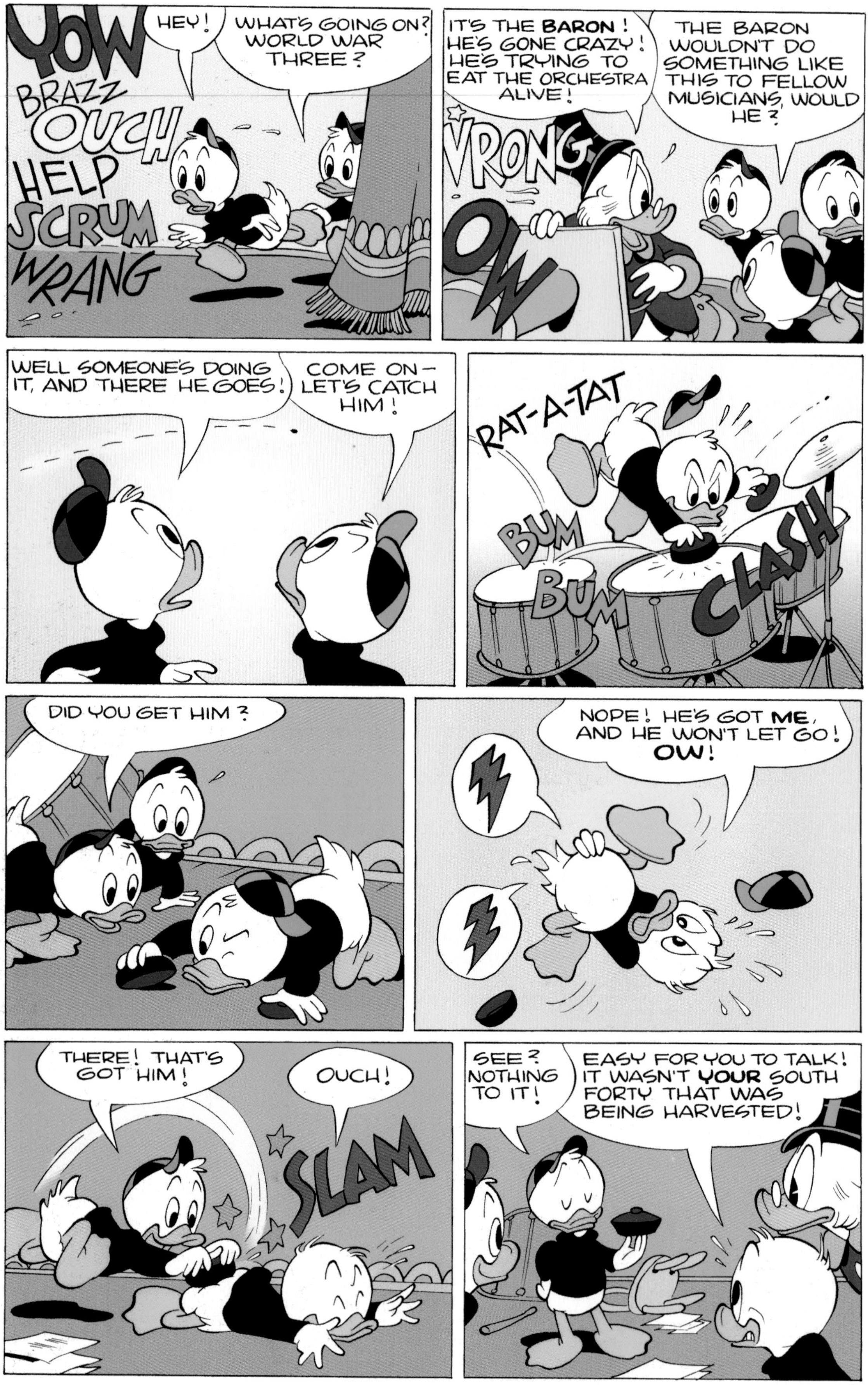

YOW
BRAZZ
OUCH
HELP
SCRUM
WRANG
HEY!
WHAT'S GOING ON? WORLD WAR THREE?
IT'S THE BARON! HE'S GONE CRAZY! HE'S TRYING TO EAT THE ORCHESTRA ALIVE!
THE BARON WOULDN'T DO SOMETHING LIKE THIS TO FELLOW MUSICIANS, WOULD HE?
VRONG
OW
WELL SOMEONE'S DOING IT, AND THERE HE GOES!
COME ON— LET'S CATCH HIM!
RAT-A-TAT
BUM
BUM
CLASH
DID YOU GET HIM?
NOPE! HE'S GOT ME, AND HE WON'T LET GO! OW!
THERE! THAT'S GOT HIM!
OUCH!
SLAM
SEE? NOTHING TO IT!
EASY FOR YOU TO TALK! IT WASN'T YOUR SOUTH FORTY THAT WAS BEING HARVESTED!

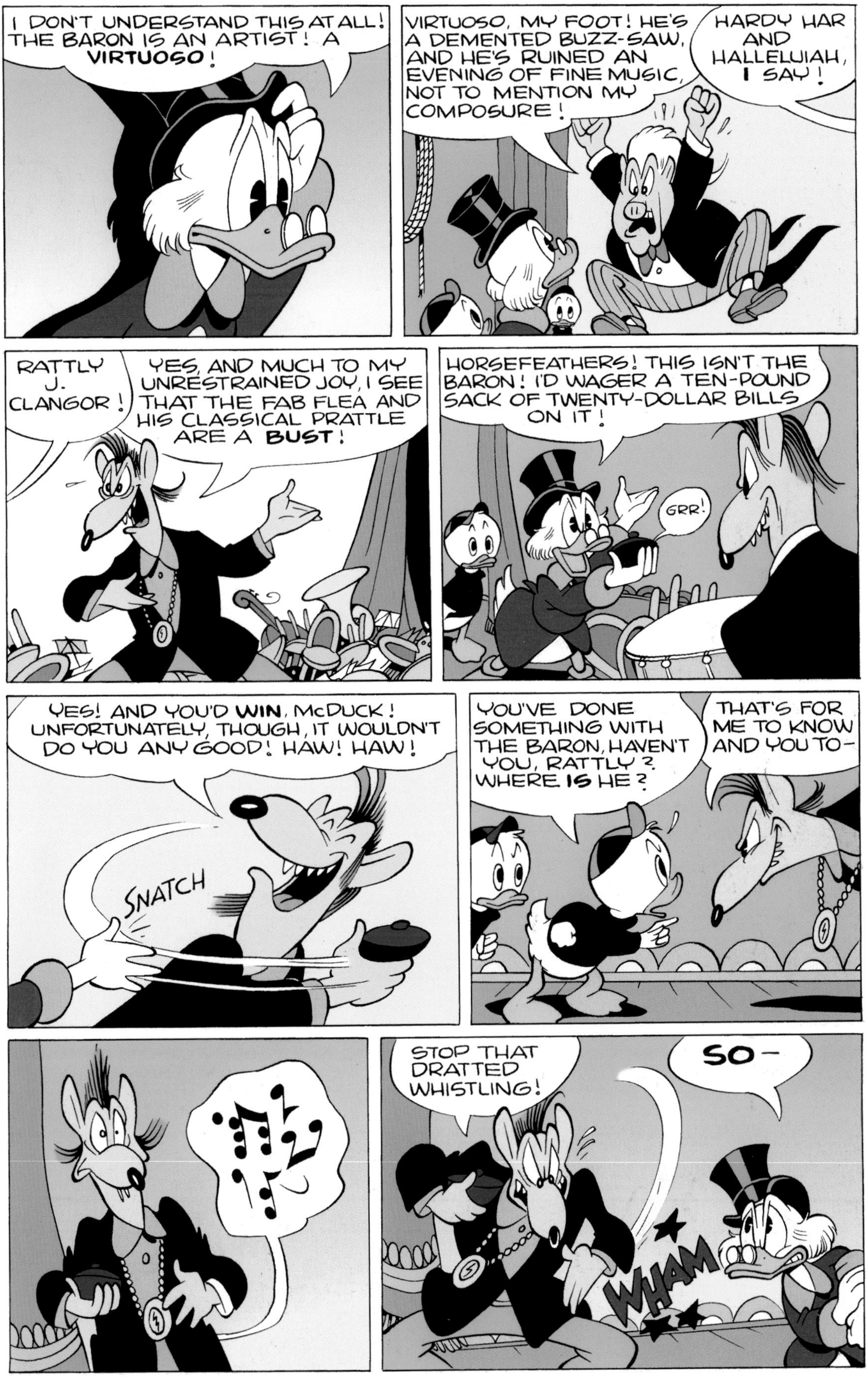
I DON'T UNDERSTAND THIS AT ALL! THE BARON IS AN ARTIST! A VIRTUOSO!
VIRTUOSO, MY FOOT! HE'S A DEMENTED BUZZ-SAW, AND HE'S RUINED AN EVENING OF FINE MUSIC, NOT TO MENTION MY COMPOSURE!
HARDY HAR AND HALLELUIAH, I SAY!
RATTLY J. CLANGOR!
YES, AND MUCH TO MY UNRESTRAINED JOY, I SEE THAT THE FAB FLEA AND HIS CLASSICAL PRATTLE ARE A BUST!
HORSEFEATHERS! THIS ISN'T THE BARON! I'D WAGER A TEN-POUND SACK OF TWENTY-DOLLAR BILLS ON IT!
GRR!
YES! AND YOU'D WIN, McDUCK! UNFORTUNATELY, THOUGH, IT WOULDN'T DO YOU ANY GOOD! HAW! HAW!
SNATCH
YOU'VE DONE SOMETHING WITH THE BARON, HAVEN'T YOU, RATTLY? WHERE IS HE?
THAT'S FOR ME TO KNOW AND YOU TO-
STOP THAT DRATTED WHISTLING!
SO-
WHAM

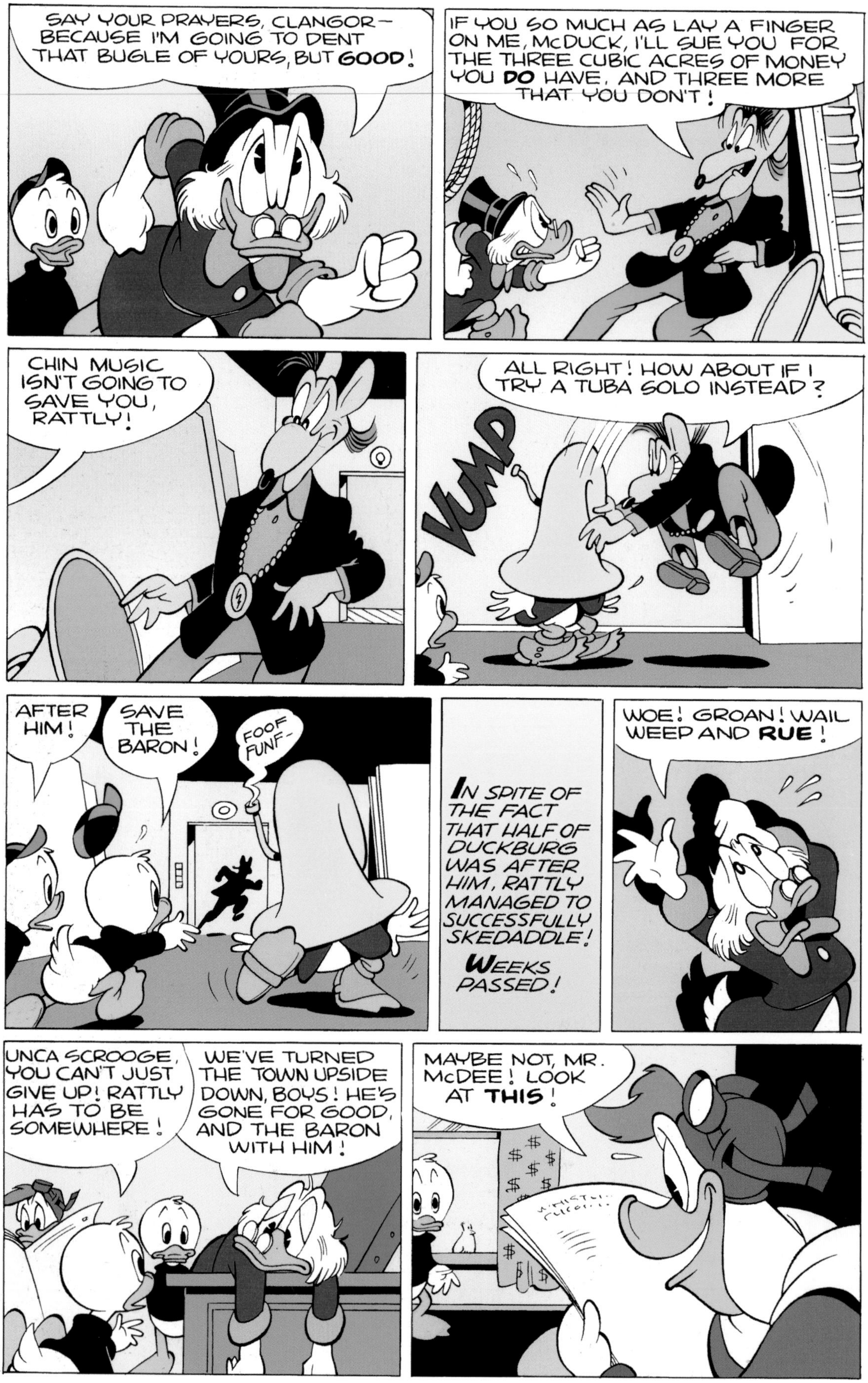
SAY YOUR PRAYERS, CLANGOR— BECAUSE I'M GOING TO DENT THAT BUGLE OF YOURS, BUT GOOD!
IF YOU SO MUCH AS LAY A FINGER ON ME, McDUCK, I'LL SUE YOU FOR THE THREE CUBIC ACRES OF MONEY YOU DO HAVE, AND THREE MORE THAT YOU DON'T!
CHIN MUSIC ISN'T GOING TO SAVE YOU, RATTLY!
ALL RIGHT! HOW ABOUT IF I TRY A TUBA SOLO INSTEAD?
VUMP
AFTER HIM!
SAVE THE BARON!
FOOF FUNF—
IN SPITE OF THE FACT THAT HALF OF DUCKBURG WAS AFTER HIM, RATTLY MANAGED TO SUCCESSFULLY SKEDADDLE!
WEEKS PASSED!
WOE! GROAN! WAIL WEEP AND RUE!
UNCA SCROOGE, YOU CAN'T JUST GIVE UP! RATTLY HAS TO BE SOMEWHERE!
WE'VE TURNED THE TOWN UPSIDE DOWN, BOYS! HE'S GONE FOR GOOD, AND THE BARON WITH HIM!
MAYBE NOT, MR. McDEE! LOOK AT THIS!

"WHISTLING GHOST SPOOKS NAVAHO NATION!" SO? IT'S JUST A LOT OF SUPERSTITIOUS NONSENSE! WHAT'S IT GOT TO DO WITH THE BARON?

DAILY PULP

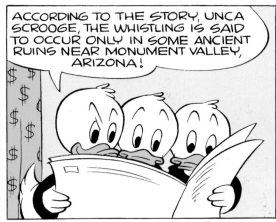

ACCORDING TO THE STORY, UNCA SCROOGE, THE WHISTLING IS SAID TO OCCUR ONLY IN SOME ANCIENT RUINS NEAR MONUMENT VALLEY, ARIZONA!

I REPEAT— SO?

SO IT SEEMS THAT THE GHOST HAS BEEN HEARD TO WHISTLE A MIGHTY INTERESTING LITTLE DITTY, MR. McDEE!

YEAH! A TUNE THAT WAS NOT EXACTLY NUMBER ONE ON THE ANCIENT NAVAHO HIT PARADE!

TUNE? **WHAT** TUNE?

BEETHOVEN'S SIXTH SYMPHONY!

THUS, IN A FLURRY OF NUTS AND BOLTS DOES A BRIEF BUT POIGNANT FLIGHT OCCUR!

THE COST OF THIS KITE IS COMING OUT OF **YOUR** PAY, LAUNCHPAD!

BUT AT MY SALARY IT'LL TAKE ME TWELVE HUNDRED YEARS TO PAY IT OFF!

TWELVE HUNDRED AND **ONE**! DON'T TRY TO CHISEL **ME**!

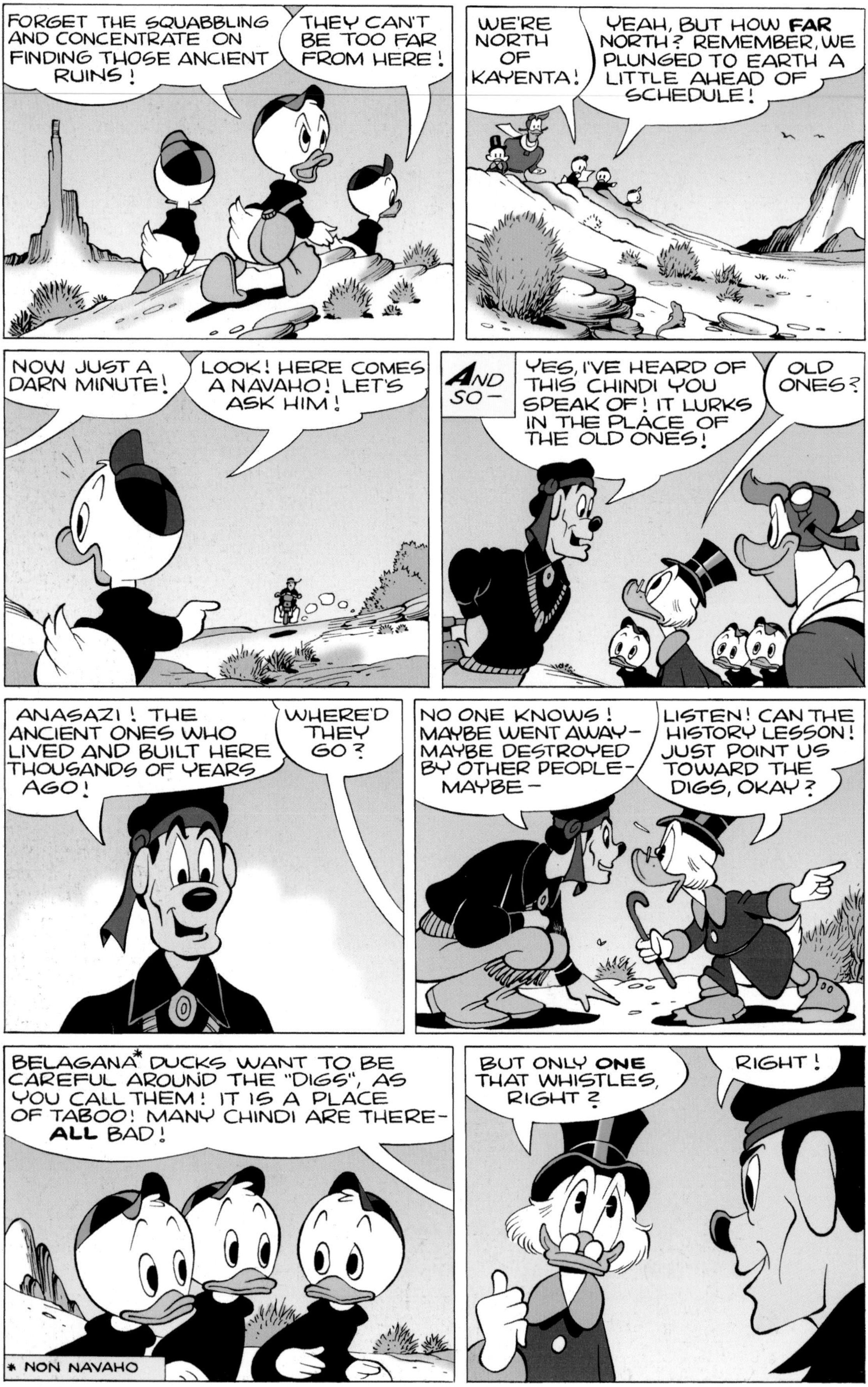
FORGET THE SQUABBLING AND CONCENTRATE ON FINDING THOSE ANCIENT RUINS!
THEY CAN'T BE TOO FAR FROM HERE!
WE'RE NORTH OF KAYENTA!
YEAH, BUT HOW **FAR** NORTH? REMEMBER, WE PLUNGED TO EARTH A LITTLE AHEAD OF SCHEDULE!
NOW JUST A DARN MINUTE!
LOOK! HERE COMES A NAVAHO! LET'S ASK HIM!
AND SO—
YES, I'VE HEARD OF THIS CHINDI YOU SPEAK OF! IT LURKS IN THE PLACE OF THE OLD ONES!
OLD ONES?
ANASAZI! THE ANCIENT ONES WHO LIVED AND BUILT HERE THOUSANDS OF YEARS AGO!
WHERE'D THEY GO?
NO ONE KNOWS! MAYBE WENT AWAY— MAYBE DESTROYED BY OTHER PEOPLE— MAYBE—
LISTEN! CAN THE HISTORY LESSON! JUST POINT US TOWARD THE DIGS, OKAY?
BELAGANA* DUCKS WANT TO BE CAREFUL AROUND THE "DIGS", AS YOU CALL THEM! IT IS A PLACE OF TABOO! MANY CHINDI ARE THERE— **ALL** BAD!
* NON NAVAHO
BUT ONLY **ONE** THAT WHISTLES, RIGHT?
RIGHT!

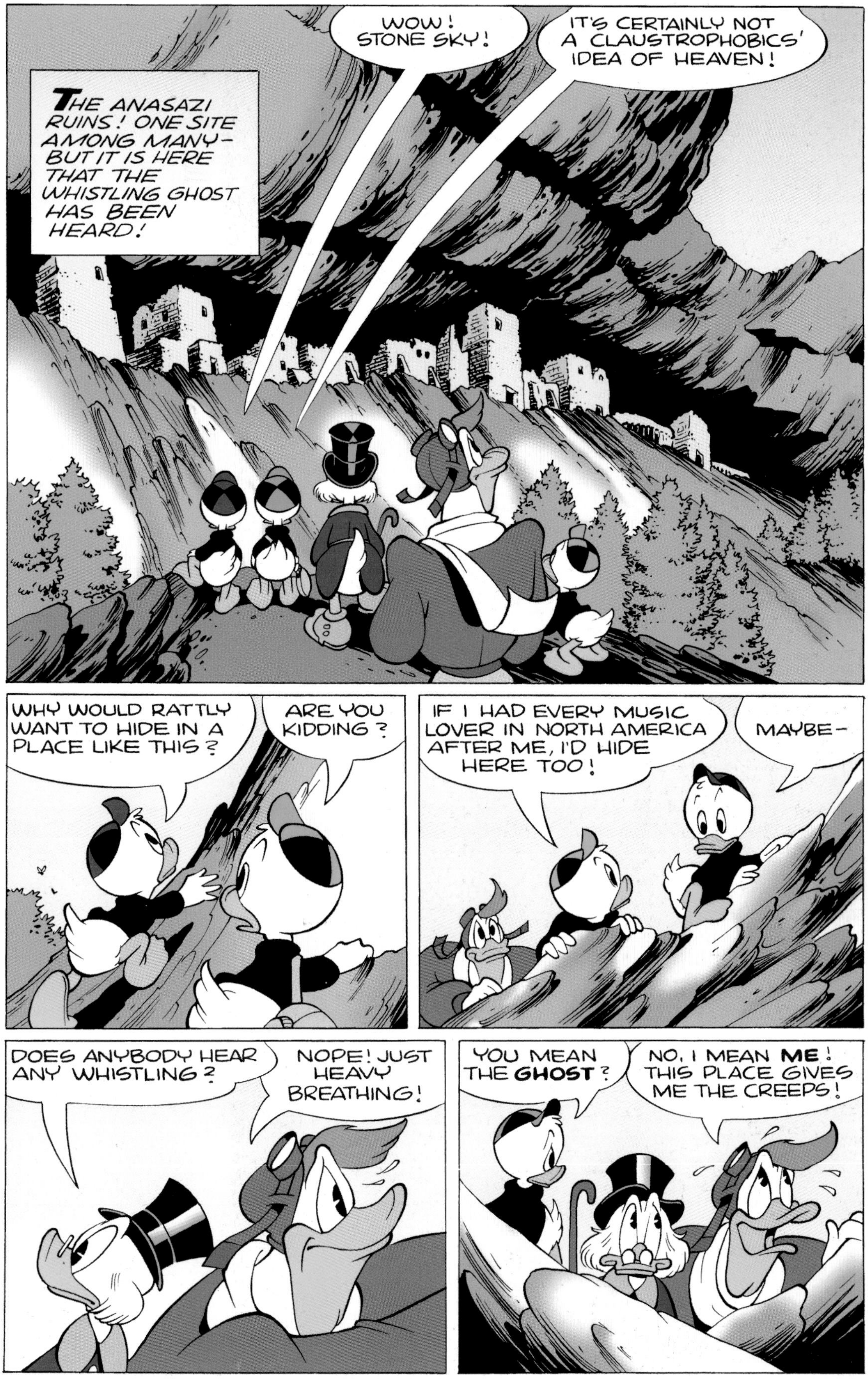
THE ANASAZI RUINS! ONE SITE AMONG MANY— BUT IT IS HERE THAT THE WHISTLING GHOST HAS BEEN HEARD!
WOW! STONE SKY!
IT'S CERTAINLY NOT A CLAUSTROPHOBICS' IDEA OF HEAVEN!
WHY WOULD RATTLY WANT TO HIDE IN A PLACE LIKE THIS?
ARE YOU KIDDING?
IF I HAD EVERY MUSIC LOVER IN NORTH AMERICA AFTER ME, I'D HIDE HERE TOO!
MAYBE—
DOES ANYBODY HEAR ANY WHISTLING?
NOPE! JUST HEAVY BREATHING!
YOU MEAN THE GHOST?
NO, I MEAN ME! THIS PLACE GIVES ME THE CREEPS!

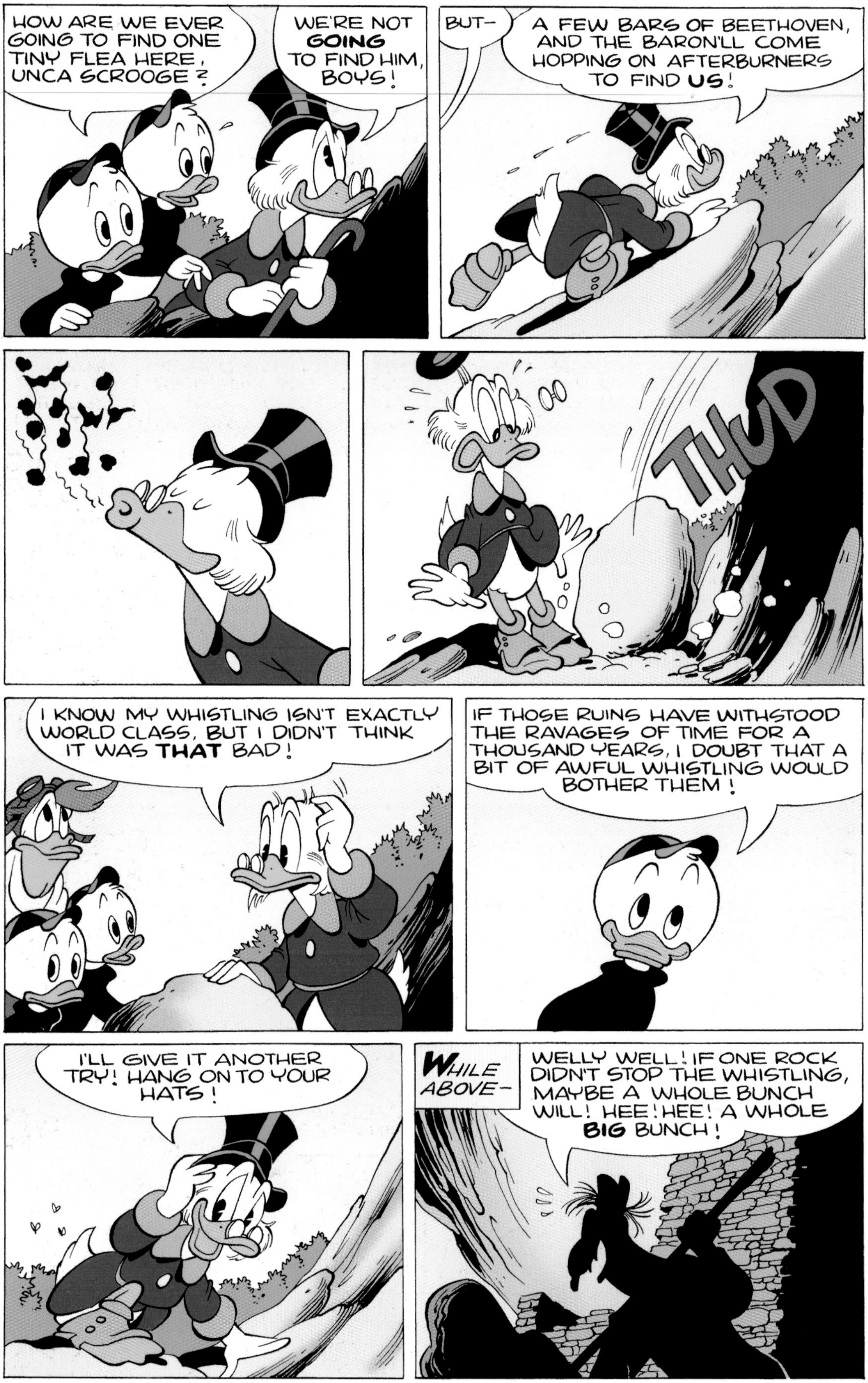
HOW ARE WE EVER GOING TO FIND ONE TINY FLEA HERE, UNCA SCROOGE?
WE'RE NOT **GOING** TO FIND HIM, BOYS!
BUT—
A FEW BARS OF BEETHOVEN, AND THE BARON'LL COME HOPPING ON AFTERBURNERS TO FIND **US**!
THUD
I KNOW MY WHISTLING ISN'T EXACTLY WORLD CLASS, BUT I DIDN'T THINK IT WAS **THAT** BAD!
IF THOSE RUINS HAVE WITHSTOOD THE RAVAGES OF TIME FOR A THOUSAND YEARS, I DOUBT THAT A BIT OF AWFUL WHISTLING WOULD BOTHER THEM!
I'LL GIVE IT ANOTHER TRY! HANG ON TO YOUR HATS!
WHILE ABOVE—
WELLY WELL! IF ONE ROCK DIDN'T STOP THE WHISTLING, MAYBE A WHOLE BUNCH WILL! HEE! HEE! A WHOLE **BIG** BUNCH!

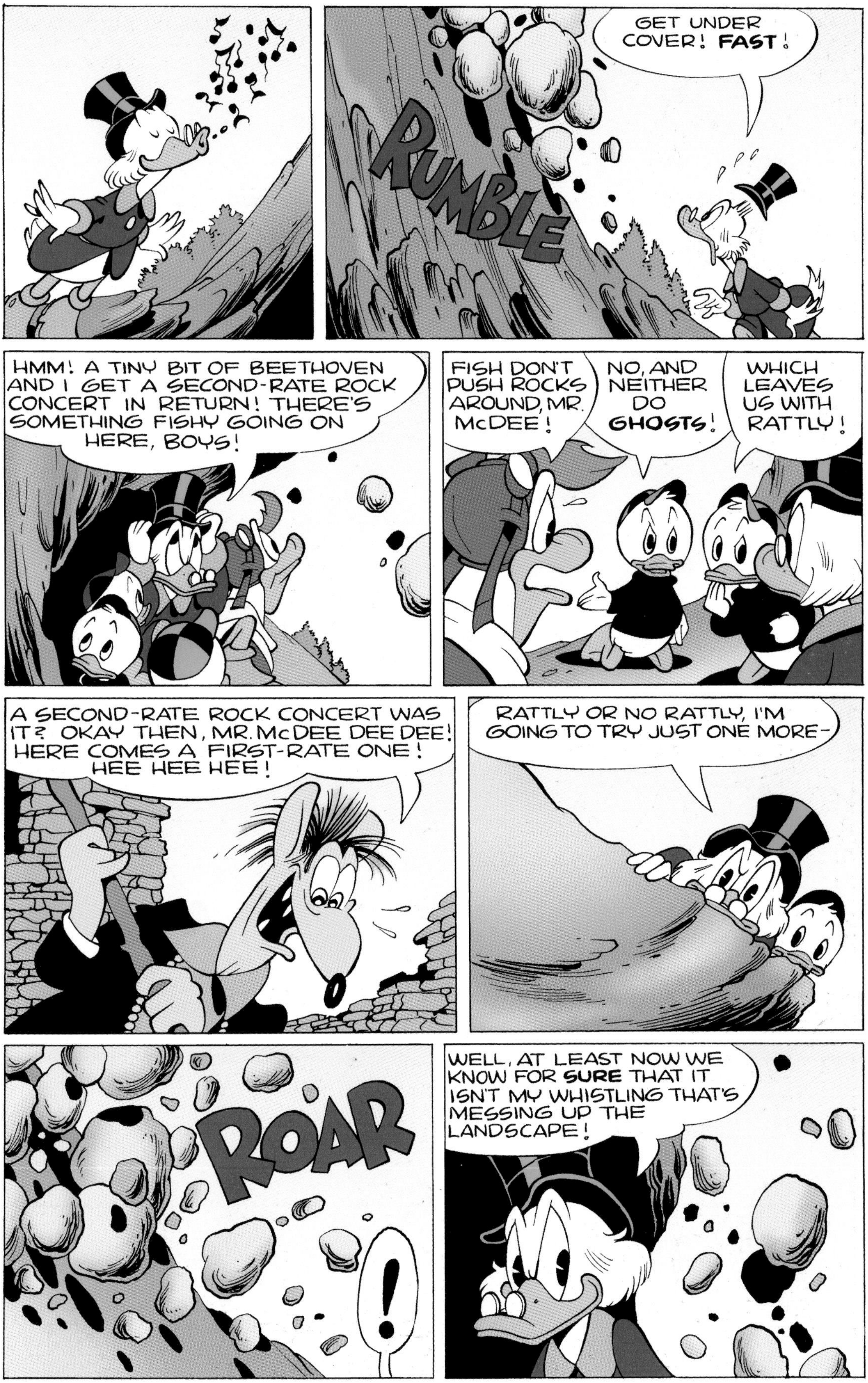
GET UNDER COVER! FAST!
RUMBLE
HMM! A TINY BIT OF BEETHOVEN AND I GET A SECOND-RATE ROCK CONCERT IN RETURN! THERE'S SOMETHING FISHY GOING ON HERE, BOYS!
FISH DON'T PUSH ROCKS AROUND, MR. McDEE!
NO, AND NEITHER DO GHOSTS!
WHICH LEAVES US WITH RATTLY!
A SECOND-RATE ROCK CONCERT WAS IT? OKAY THEN, MR. McDEE DEE DEE! HERE COMES A FIRST-RATE ONE! HEE HEE HEE!
RATTLY OR NO RATTLY, I'M GOING TO TRY JUST ONE MORE-
ROAR
!
WELL, AT LEAST NOW WE KNOW FOR SURE THAT IT ISN'T MY WHISTLING THAT'S MESSING UP THE LANDSCAPE!

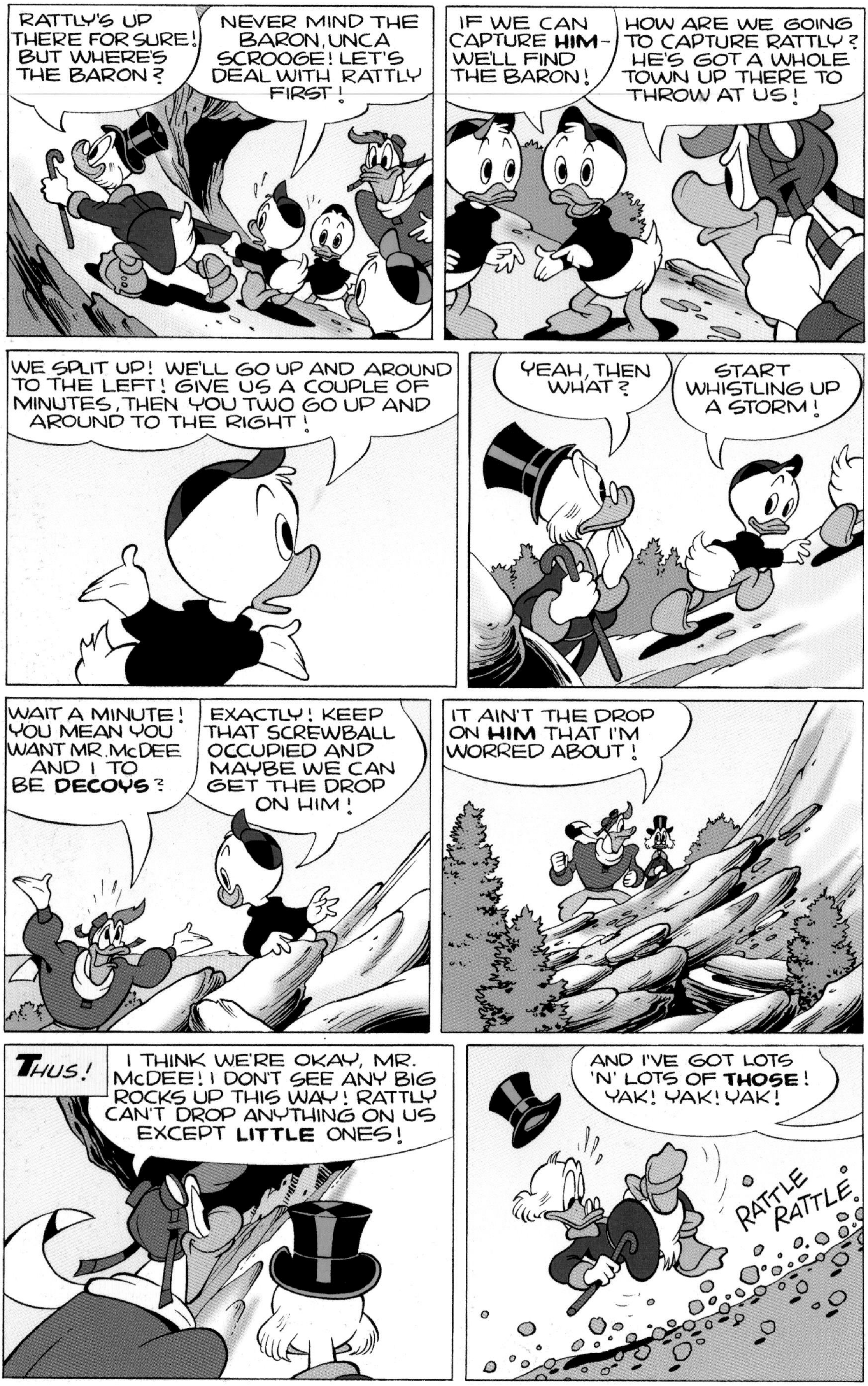
RATTLY'S UP THERE FOR SURE! BUT WHERE'S THE BARON?
NEVER MIND THE BARON, UNCA SCROOGE! LET'S DEAL WITH RATTLY FIRST!
IF WE CAN CAPTURE HIM - WE'LL FIND THE BARON!
HOW ARE WE GOING TO CAPTURE RATTLY? HE'S GOT A WHOLE TOWN UP THERE TO THROW AT US!
WE SPLIT UP! WE'LL GO UP AND AROUND TO THE LEFT! GIVE US A COUPLE OF MINUTES, THEN YOU TWO GO UP AND AROUND TO THE RIGHT!
YEAH, THEN WHAT?
START WHISTLING UP A STORM!
WAIT A MINUTE! YOU MEAN YOU WANT MR. McDEE AND I TO BE DECOYS?
EXACTLY! KEEP THAT SCREWBALL OCCUPIED AND MAYBE WE CAN GET THE DROP ON HIM!
IT AIN'T THE DROP ON HIM THAT I'M WORRED ABOUT!
THUS!
I THINK WE'RE OKAY, MR. McDEE! I DON'T SEE ANY BIG ROCKS UP THIS WAY! RATTLY CAN'T DROP ANYTHING ON US EXCEPT LITTLE ONES!
AND I'VE GOT LOTS 'N' LOTS OF THOSE! YAK! YAK! YAK!
RATTLE RATTLE

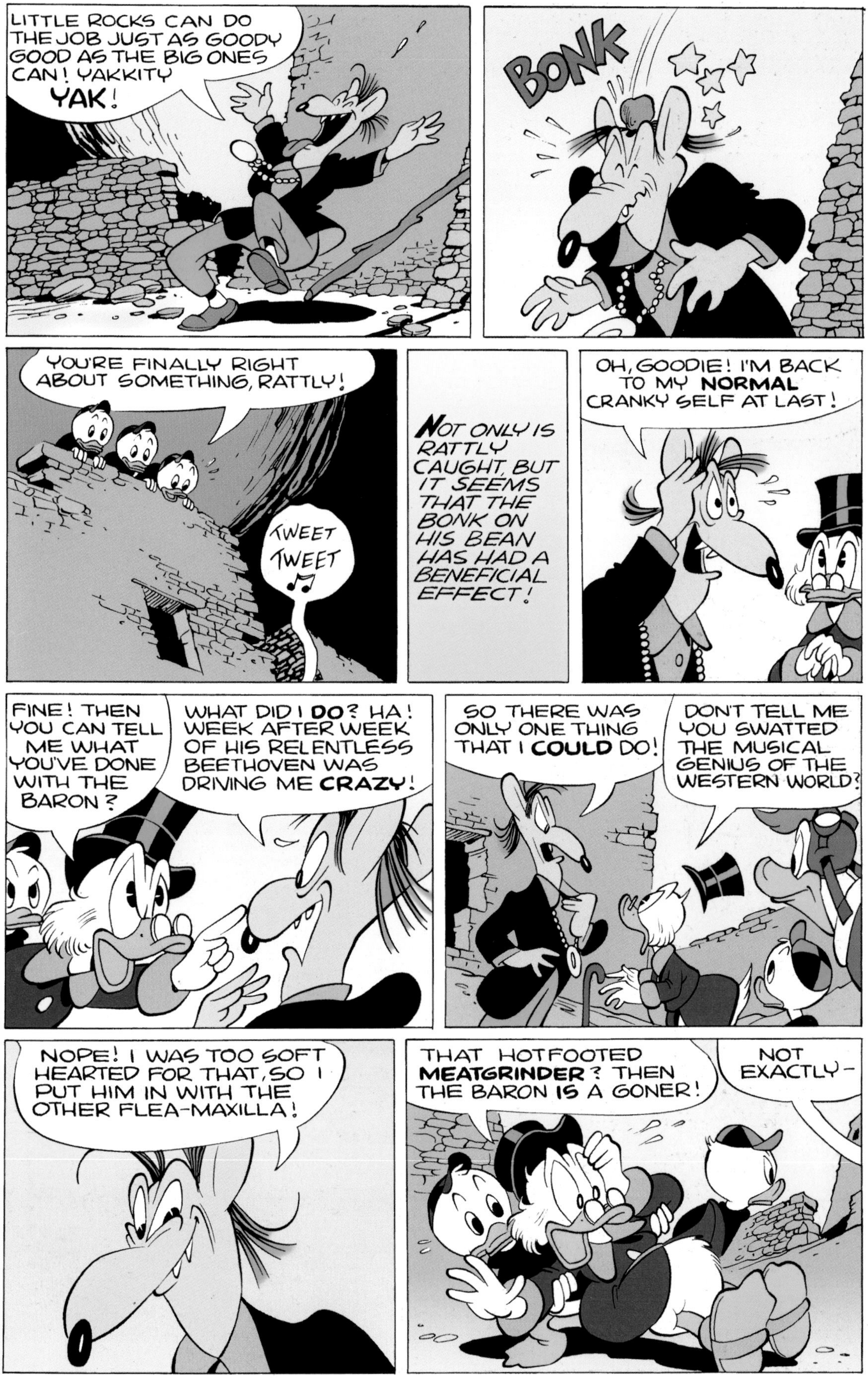

LITTLE ROCKS CAN DO THE JOB JUST AS GOODY GOOD AS THE BIG ONES CAN! YAKKITY **YAK**!
BONK
YOU'RE FINALLY RIGHT ABOUT SOMETHING, RATTLY!
TWEET TWEET
NOT ONLY IS RATTLY CAUGHT, BUT IT SEEMS THAT THE BONK ON HIS BEAN HAS HAD A BENEFICIAL EFFECT!
OH, GOODIE! I'M BACK TO MY **NORMAL** CRANKY SELF AT LAST!
FINE! THEN YOU CAN TELL ME WHAT YOU'VE DONE WITH THE BARON?
WHAT DID I **DO**? HA! WEEK AFTER WEEK OF HIS RELENTLESS BEETHOVEN WAS DRIVING ME **CRAZY**!
SO THERE WAS ONLY ONE THING THAT I **COULD** DO!
DON'T TELL ME YOU SWATTED THE MUSICAL GENIUS OF THE WESTERN WORLD?
NOPE! I WAS TOO SOFT HEARTED FOR THAT, SO I PUT HIM IN WITH THE OTHER FLEA-MAXILLA!
THAT HOTFOOTED **MEATGRINDER**? THEN THE BARON **IS** A GONER!
NOT EXACTLY–

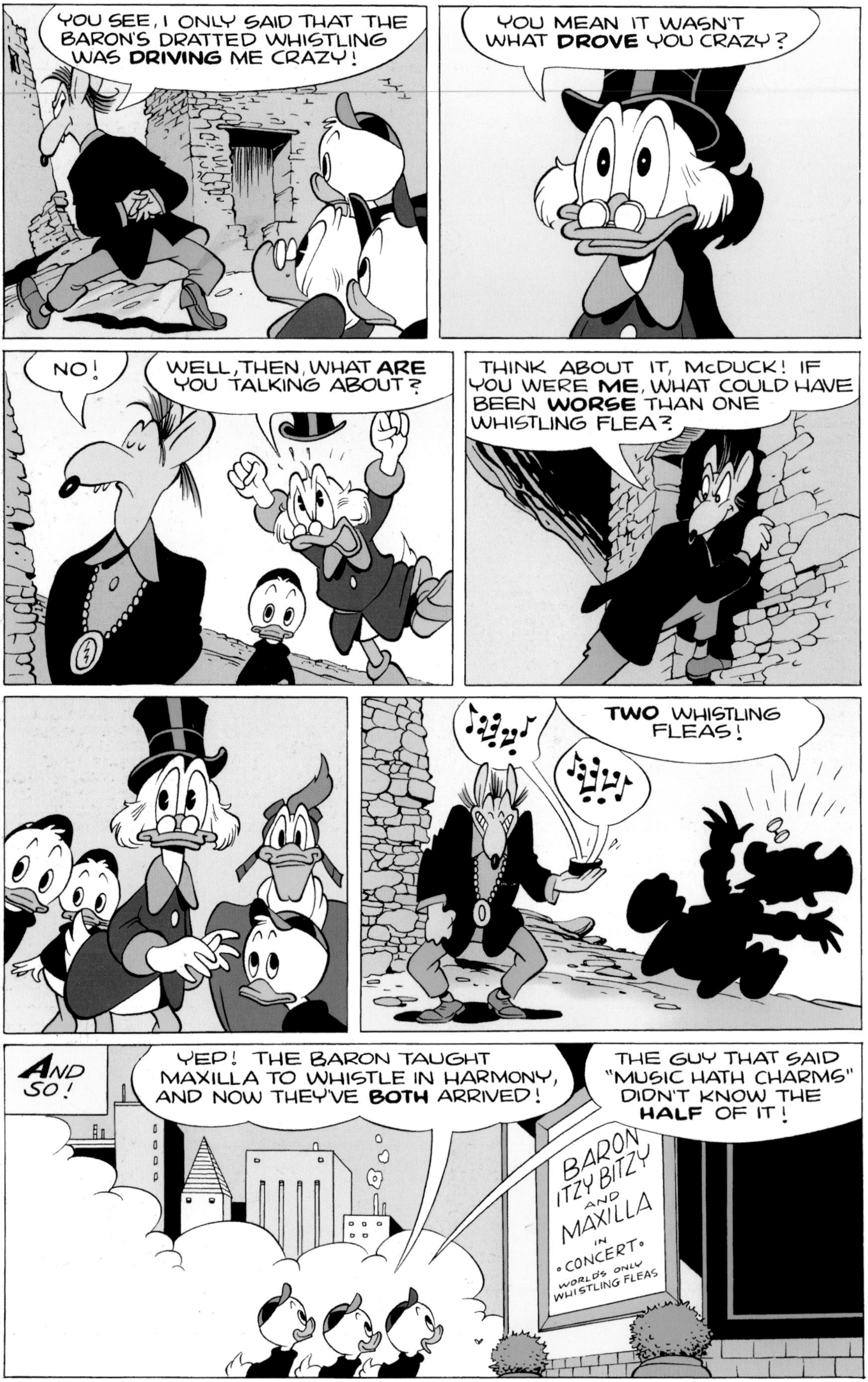
YOU SEE, I ONLY SAID THAT THE BARON'S DRATTED WHISTLING WAS DRIVING ME CRAZY!
YOU MEAN IT WASN'T WHAT DROVE YOU CRAZY?
NO!
WELL, THEN, WHAT ARE YOU TALKING ABOUT?
THINK ABOUT IT, McDUCK! IF YOU WERE ME, WHAT COULD HAVE BEEN WORSE THAN ONE WHISTLING FLEA?
TWO WHISTLING FLEAS!
AND SO!
YEP! THE BARON TAUGHT MAXILLA TO WHISTLE IN HARMONY, AND NOW THEY'VE BOTH ARRIVED!
THE GUY THAT SAID "MUSIC HATH CHARMS" DIDN'T KNOW THE HALF OF IT!
BARON ITZY BITZY AND MAXILLA IN CONCERT
WORLD'S ONLY WHISTLING FLEAS

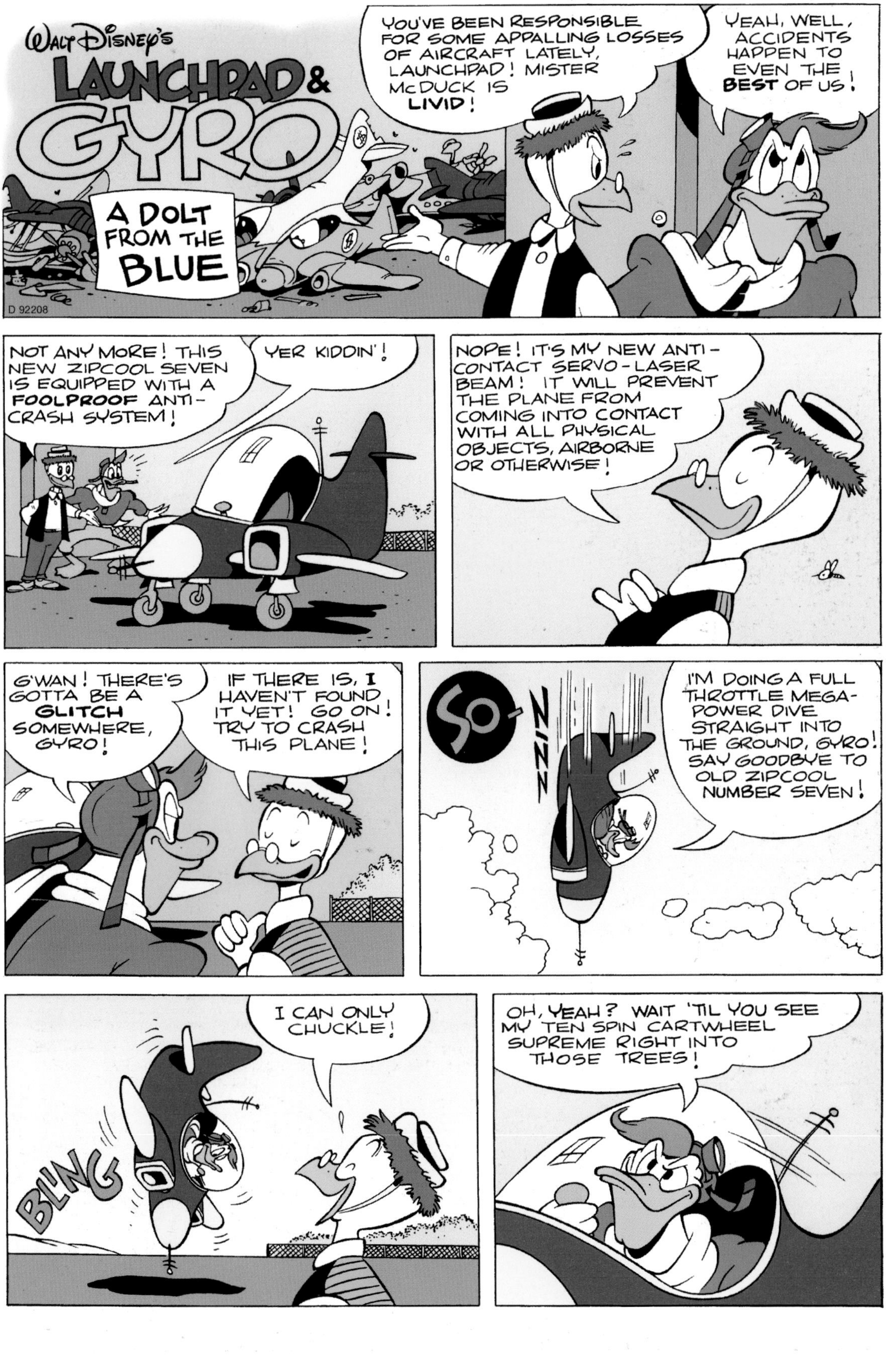
Walt Disney's
LAUNCHPAD & GYRO
A DOLT FROM THE BLUE
D 92208
YOU'VE BEEN RESPONSIBLE FOR SOME APPALLING LOSSES OF AIRCRAFT LATELY, LAUNCHPAD! MISTER McDUCK IS LIVID!
YEAH, WELL, ACCIDENTS HAPPEN TO EVEN THE BEST OF US!
NOT ANY MORE! THIS NEW ZIPCOOL SEVEN IS EQUIPPED WITH A FOOLPROOF ANTI-CRASH SYSTEM!
YER KIDDIN'!
NOPE! IT'S MY NEW ANTI-CONTACT SERVO-LASER BEAM! IT WILL PREVENT THE PLANE FROM COMING INTO CONTACT WITH ALL PHYSICAL OBJECTS, AIRBORNE OR OTHERWISE!
G'WAN! THERE'S GOTTA BE A GLITCH SOMEWHERE, GYRO!
IF THERE IS, I HAVEN'T FOUND IT YET! GO ON! TRY TO CRASH THIS PLANE!
SO-
NINN
I'M DOING A FULL THROTTLE MEGA-POWER DIVE STRAIGHT INTO THE GROUND, GYRO! SAY GOODBYE TO OLD ZIPCOOL NUMBER SEVEN!
BLING
I CAN ONLY CHUCKLE!
OH, YEAH? WAIT 'TIL YOU SEE MY TEN SPIN CARTWHEEL SUPREME RIGHT INTO THOSE TREES!

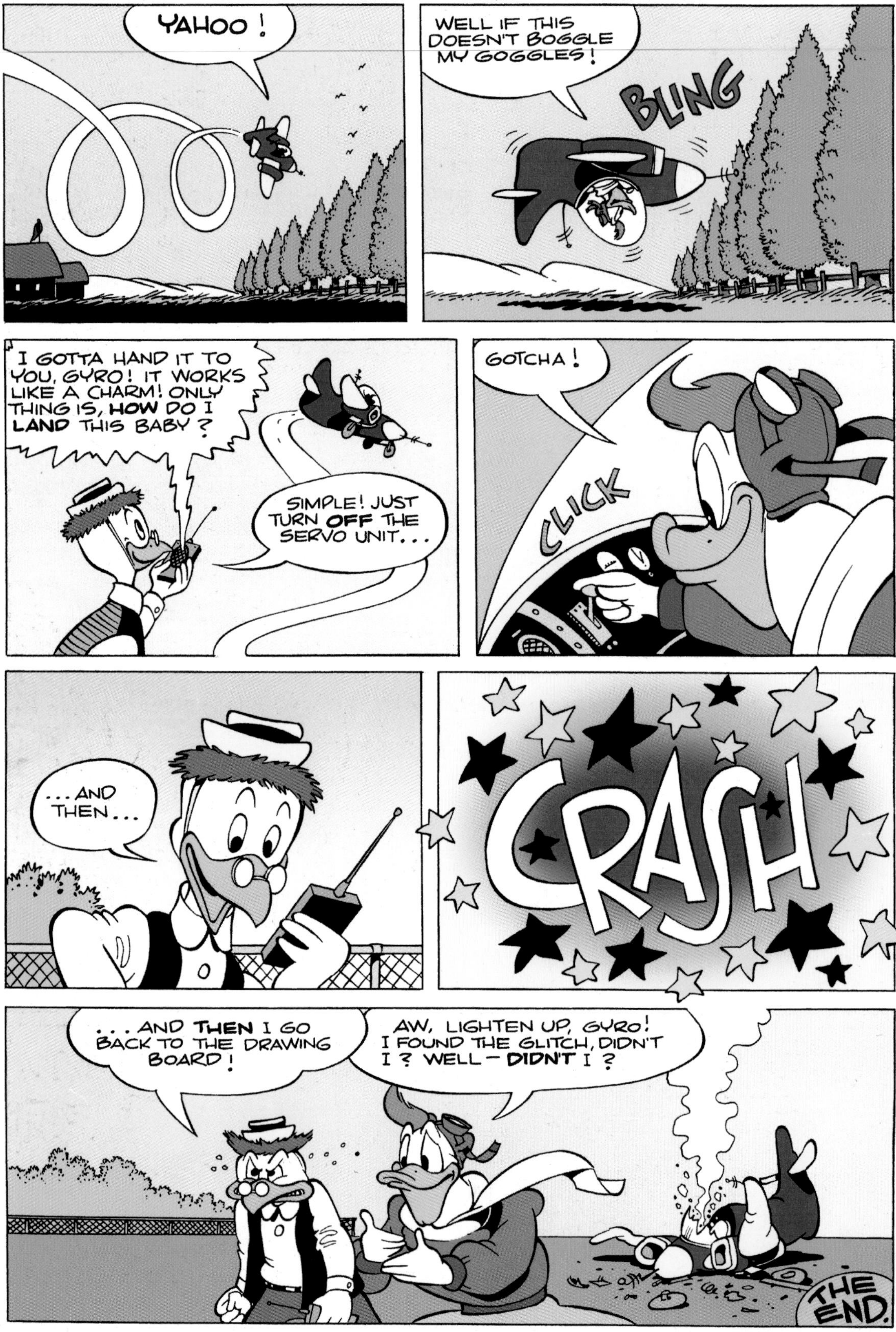
YAHOO!
WELL IF THIS DOESN'T BOGGLE MY GOGGLES!
BLING
I GOTTA HAND IT TO YOU, GYRO! IT WORKS LIKE A CHARM! ONLY THING IS, HOW DO I LAND THIS BABY?
SIMPLE! JUST TURN OFF THE SERVO UNIT...
GOTCHA!
CLICK
...AND THEN...
CRASH
...AND THEN I GO BACK TO THE DRAWING BOARD!
AW, LIGHTEN UP, GYRO! I FOUND THE GLITCH, DIDN'T I? WELL—DIDN'T I?
THE END.

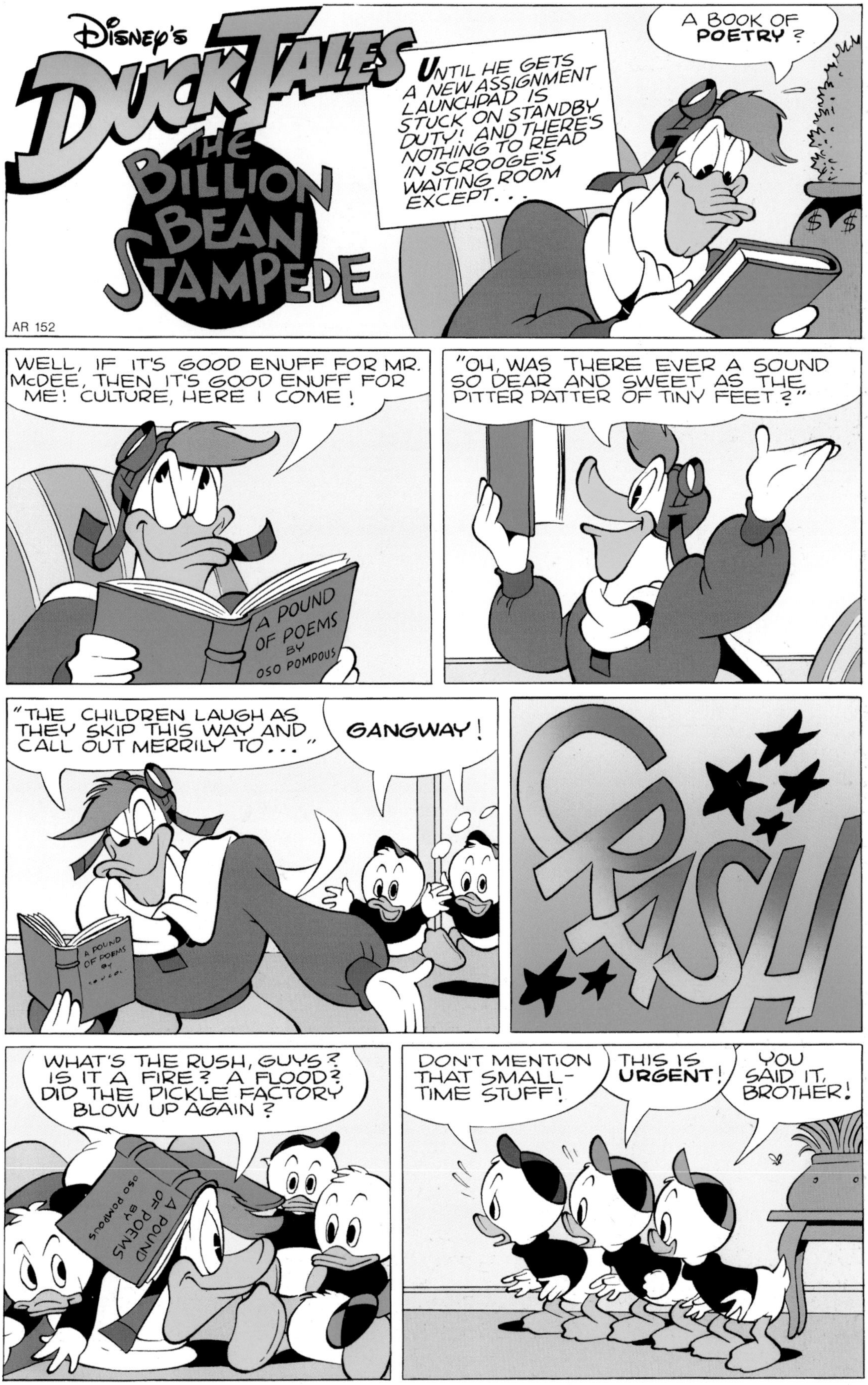
Disney's
DuckTales
The Billion Bean Stampede
UNTIL HE GETS A NEW ASSIGNMENT LAUNCHPAD IS STUCK ON STANDBY DUTY! AND THERE'S NOTHING TO READ IN SCROOGE'S WAITING ROOM EXCEPT. . .
A BOOK OF POETRY ?
AR 152
WELL, IF IT'S GOOD ENUFF FOR MR. McDEE, THEN IT'S GOOD ENUFF FOR ME! CULTURE, HERE I COME!
A POUND OF POEMS BY OSO POMPOUS
"OH, WAS THERE EVER A SOUND SO DEAR AND SWEET AS THE PITTER PATTER OF TINY FEET?"
"THE CHILDREN LAUGH AS THEY SKIP THIS WAY AND CALL OUT MERRILY TO . . ."
GANGWAY!
CRASH
WHAT'S THE RUSH, GUYS? IS IT A FIRE? A FLOOD? DID THE PICKLE FACTORY BLOW UP AGAIN?
DON'T MENTION THAT SMALL-TIME STUFF!
THIS IS URGENT!
YOU SAID IT, BROTHER!

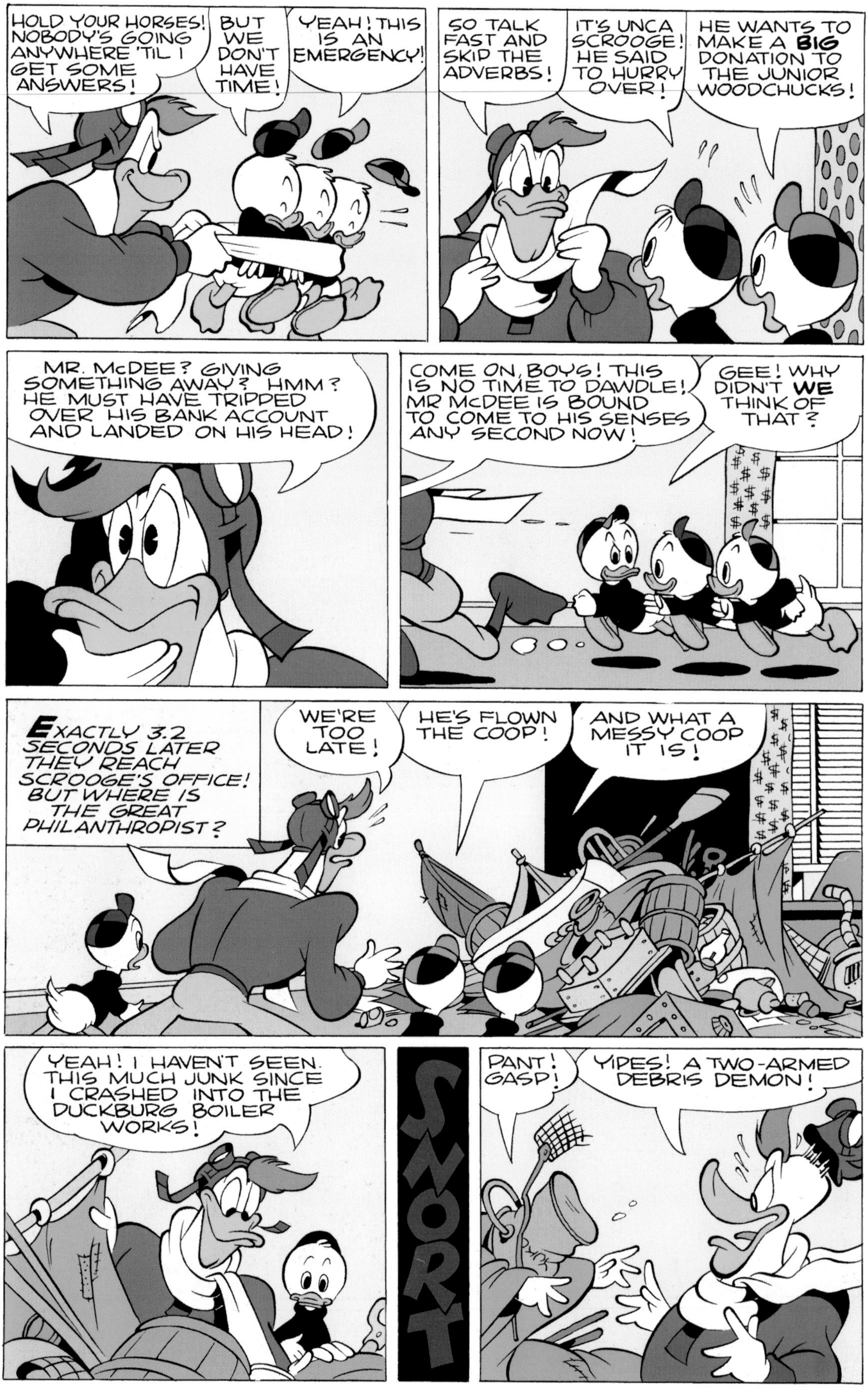
HOLD YOUR HORSES! NOBODY'S GOING ANYWHERE 'TIL I GET SOME ANSWERS!
BUT WE DON'T HAVE TIME!
YEAH! THIS IS AN EMERGENCY!
SO TALK FAST AND SKIP THE ADVERBS!
IT'S UNCA SCROOGE! HE SAID TO HURRY OVER!
HE WANTS TO MAKE A BIG DONATION TO THE JUNIOR WOODCHUCKS!
MR. McDEE? GIVING SOMETHING AWAY? HMM? HE MUST HAVE TRIPPED OVER HIS BANK ACCOUNT AND LANDED ON HIS HEAD!
COME ON, BOYS! THIS IS NO TIME TO DAWDLE! MR McDEE IS BOUND TO COME TO HIS SENSES ANY SECOND NOW!
GEE! WHY DIDN'T WE THINK OF THAT?
EXACTLY 3.2 SECONDS LATER THEY REACH SCROOGE'S OFFICE! BUT WHERE IS THE GREAT PHILANTHROPIST?
WE'RE TOO LATE!
HE'S FLOWN THE COOP!
AND WHAT A MESSY COOP IT IS!
YEAH! I HAVEN'T SEEN THIS MUCH JUNK SINCE I CRASHED INTO THE DUCKBURG BOILER WORKS!
SNORT
PANT! GASP!
YIPES! A TWO-ARMED DEBRIS DEMON!

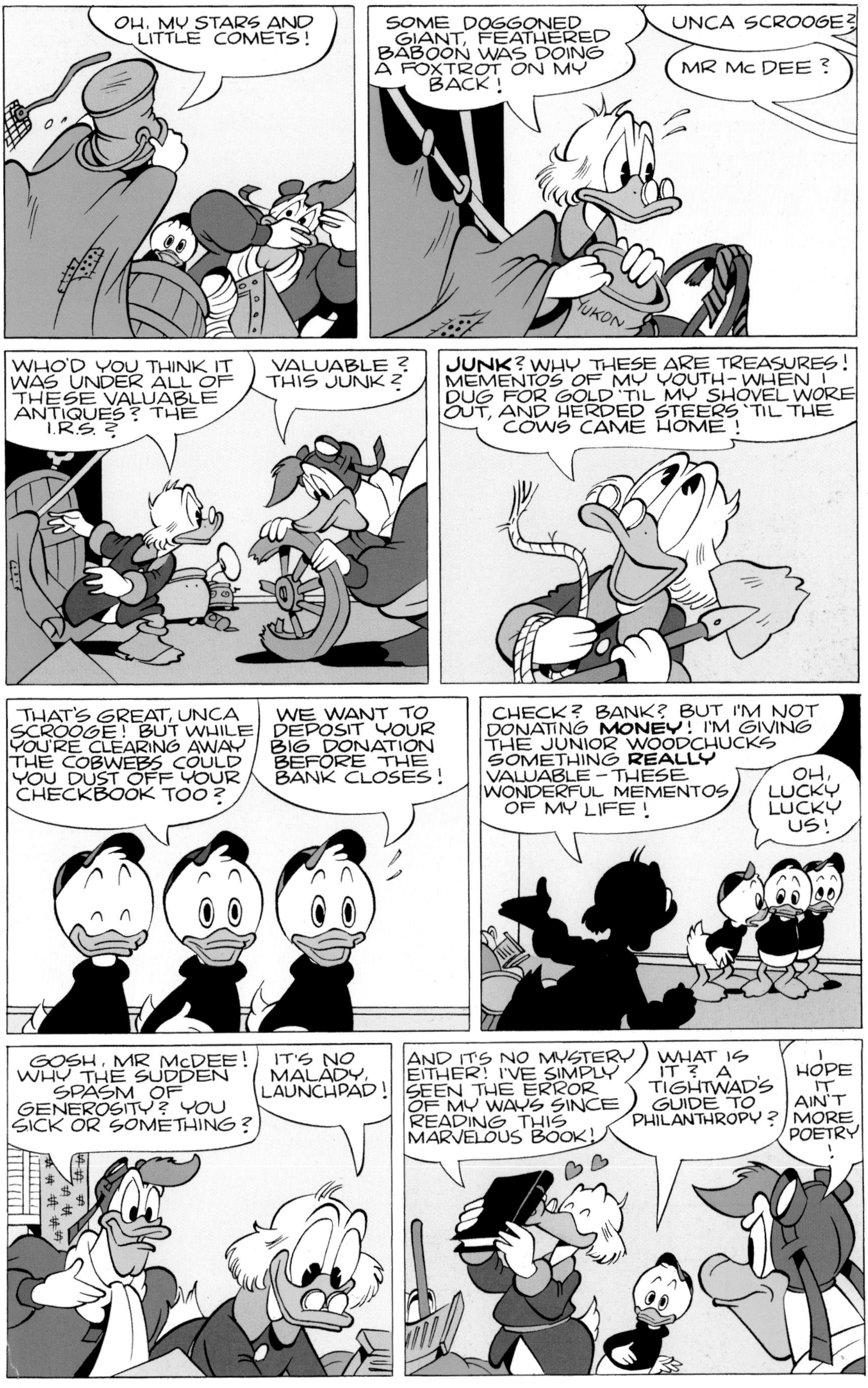
OH, MY STARS AND LITTLE COMETS!
SOME DOGGONED GIANT, FEATHERED BABOON WAS DOING A FOXTROT ON MY BACK!
UNCA SCROOGE?
MR McDEE?
YUKON
WHO'D YOU THINK IT WAS UNDER ALL OF THESE VALUABLE ANTIQUES? THE I.R.S.?
VALUABLE? THIS JUNK?
JUNK? WHY THESE ARE TREASURES! MEMENTOS OF MY YOUTH–WHEN I DUG FOR GOLD 'TIL MY SHOVEL WORE OUT, AND HERDED STEERS 'TIL THE COWS CAME HOME!
THAT'S GREAT, UNCA SCROOGE! BUT WHILE YOU'RE CLEARING AWAY THE COBWEBS COULD YOU DUST OFF YOUR CHECKBOOK TOO?
WE WANT TO DEPOSIT YOUR BIG DONATION BEFORE THE BANK CLOSES!
CHECK? BANK? BUT I'M NOT DONATING MONEY! I'M GIVING THE JUNIOR WOODCHUCKS SOMETHING REALLY VALUABLE–THESE WONDERFUL MEMENTOS OF MY LIFE!
OH, LUCKY LUCKY US!
GOSH, MR McDEE! WHY THE SUDDEN SPASM OF GENEROSITY? YOU SICK OR SOMETHING?
IT'S NO MALADY, LAUNCHPAD!
AND IT'S NO MYSTERY EITHER! I'VE SIMPLY SEEN THE ERROR OF MY WAYS SINCE READING THIS MARVELOUS BOOK!
WHAT IS IT? A TIGHTWAD'S GUIDE TO PHILANTHROPY?
I HOPE IT AIN'T MORE POETRY!

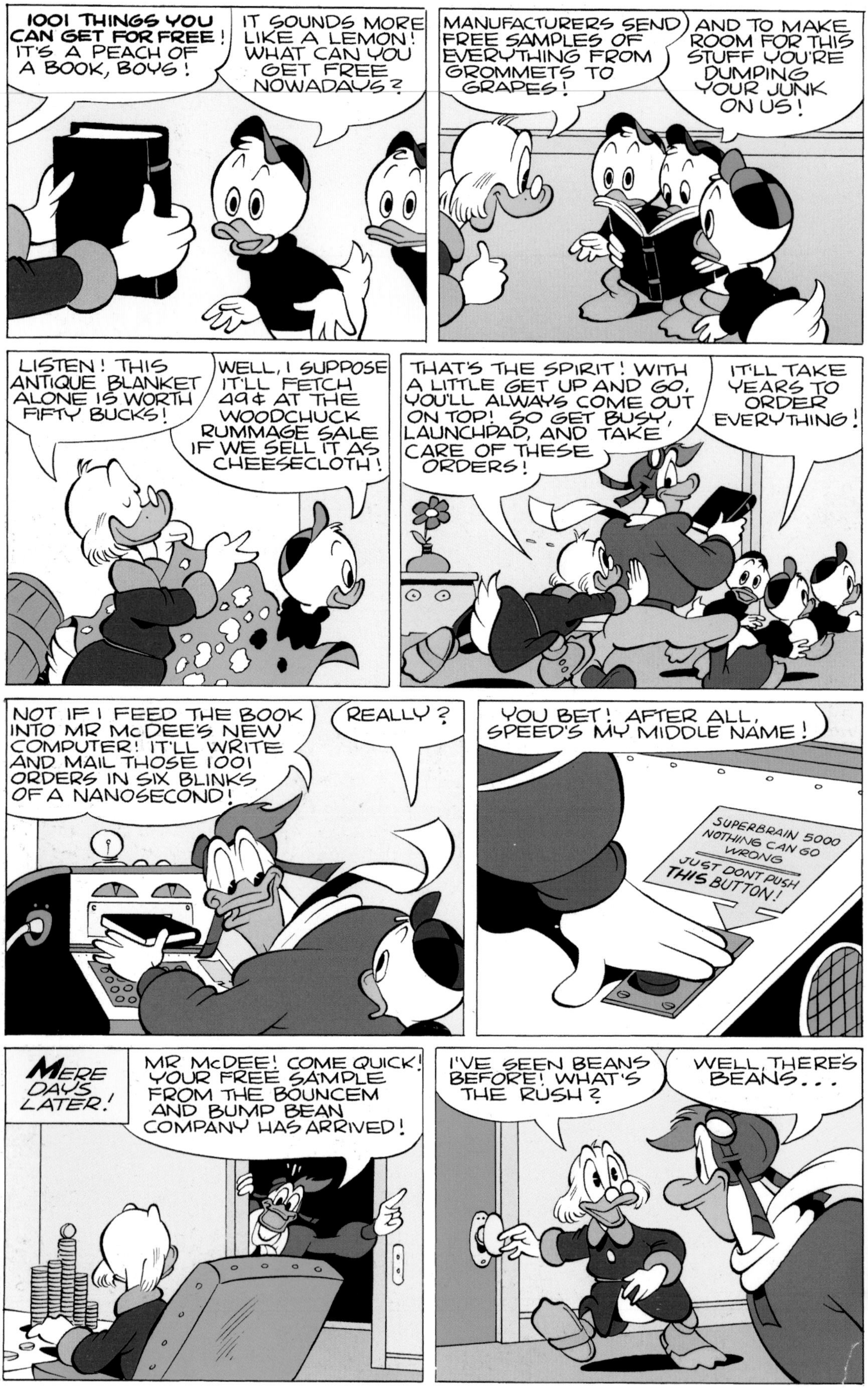
1001 THINGS YOU CAN GET FOR FREE! IT'S A PEACH OF A BOOK, BOYS!
IT SOUNDS MORE LIKE A LEMON! WHAT CAN YOU GET FREE NOWADAYS?
MANUFACTURERS SEND FREE SAMPLES OF EVERYTHING FROM GROMMETS TO GRAPES!
AND TO MAKE ROOM FOR THIS STUFF YOU'RE DUMPING YOUR JUNK ON US!
LISTEN! THIS ANTIQUE BLANKET ALONE IS WORTH FIFTY BUCKS!
WELL, I SUPPOSE IT'LL FETCH 49¢ AT THE WOODCHUCK RUMMAGE SALE IF WE SELL IT AS CHEESECLOTH!
THAT'S THE SPIRIT! WITH A LITTLE GET UP AND GO, YOU'LL ALWAYS COME OUT ON TOP! SO GET BUSY, LAUNCHPAD, AND TAKE CARE OF THESE ORDERS!
IT'LL TAKE YEARS TO ORDER EVERYTHING!
NOT IF I FEED THE BOOK INTO MR McDEE'S NEW COMPUTER! IT'LL WRITE AND MAIL THOSE 1001 ORDERS IN SIX BLINKS OF A NANOSECOND!
REALLY?
YOU BET! AFTER ALL, SPEED'S MY MIDDLE NAME!
SUPERBRAIN 5000
NOTHING CAN GO WRONG
JUST DONT PUSH THIS BUTTON!
MERE DAYS LATER!
MR McDEE! COME QUICK! YOUR FREE SAMPLE FROM THE BOUNCEM AND BUMP BEAN COMPANY HAS ARRIVED!
I'VE SEEN BEANS BEFORE! WHAT'S THE RUSH?
WELL, THERE'S BEANS...

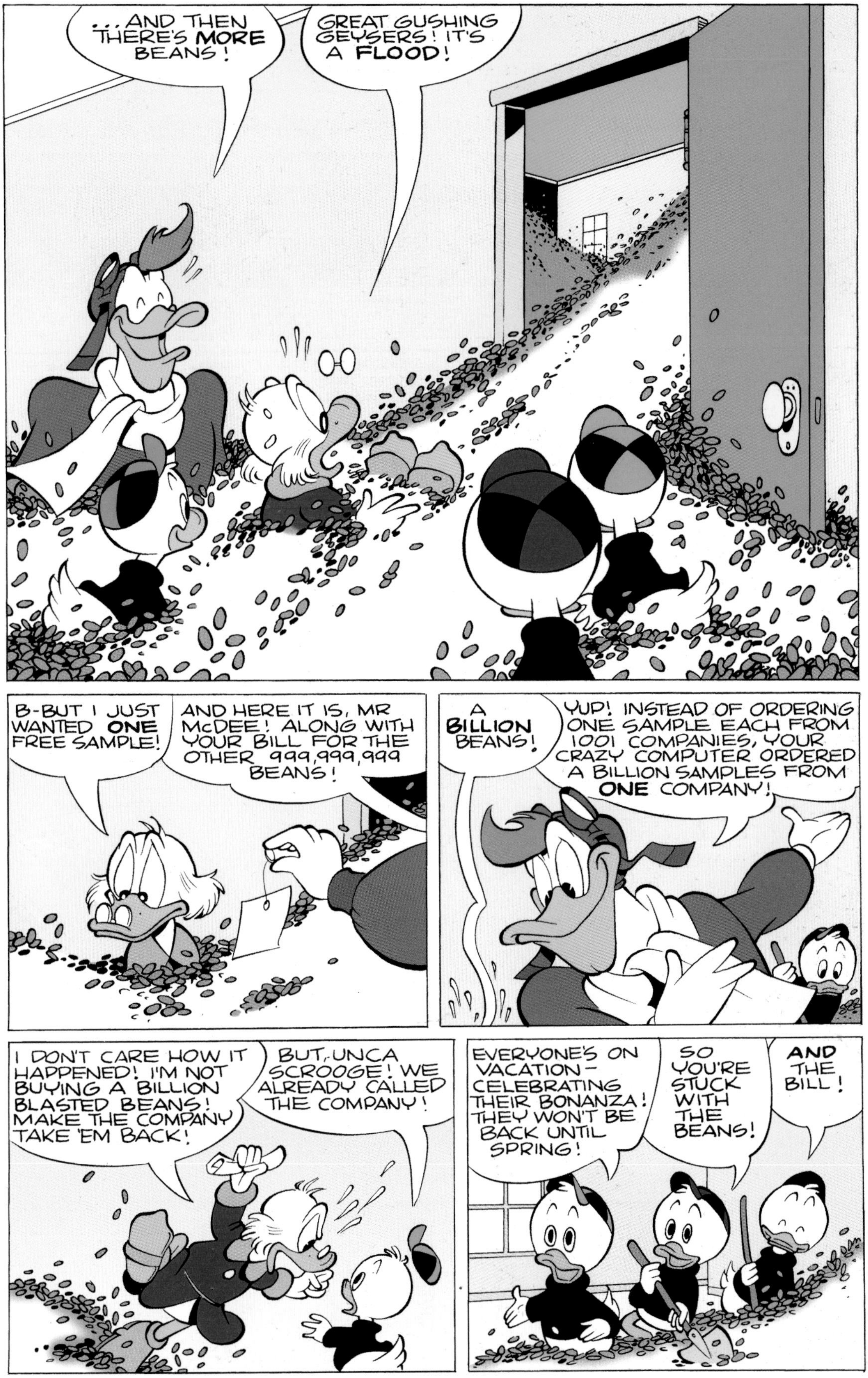

...AND THEN THERE'S **MORE** BEANS!
GREAT GUSHING GEYSERS! IT'S A **FLOOD**!
B-BUT I JUST WANTED **ONE** FREE SAMPLE!
AND HERE IT IS, MR McDEE! ALONG WITH YOUR BILL FOR THE OTHER 999,999,999 BEANS!
A **BILLION** BEANS!
YUP! INSTEAD OF ORDERING ONE SAMPLE EACH FROM 1001 COMPANIES, YOUR CRAZY COMPUTER ORDERED A BILLION SAMPLES FROM **ONE** COMPANY!
I DON'T CARE HOW IT HAPPENED! I'M NOT BUYING A BILLION BLASTED BEANS! MAKE THE COMPANY TAKE 'EM BACK!
BUT, UNCA SCROOGE! WE ALREADY CALLED THE COMPANY!
EVERYONE'S ON VACATION — CELEBRATING THEIR BONANZA! THEY WON'T BE BACK UNTIL SPRING!
SO YOU'RE STUCK WITH THE BEANS!
AND THE BILL!

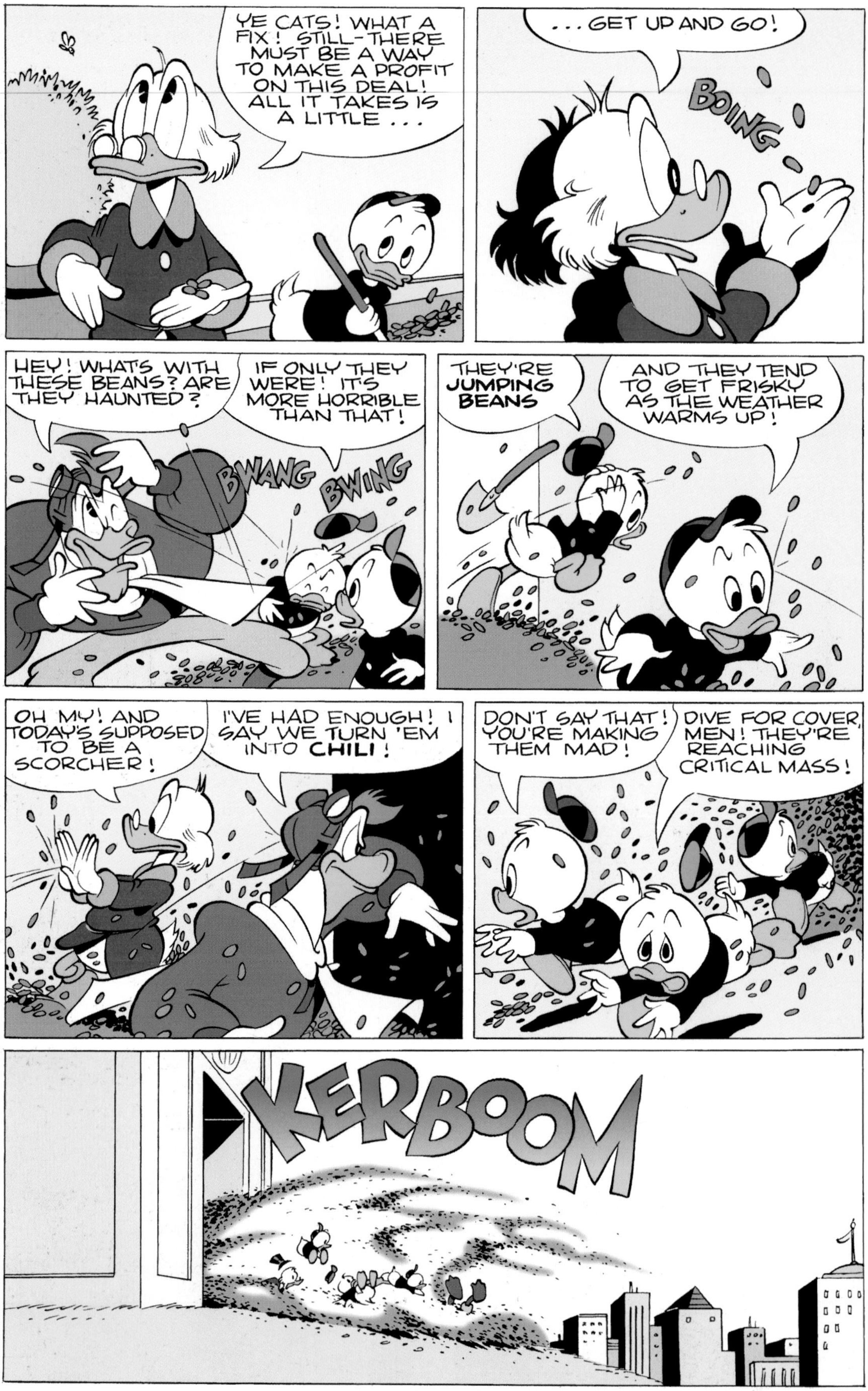
YE CATS! WHAT A FIX! STILL-THERE MUST BE A WAY TO MAKE A PROFIT ON THIS DEAL! ALL IT TAKES IS A LITTLE . . .
. . . GET UP AND GO!
BOING
HEY! WHAT'S WITH THESE BEANS? ARE THEY HAUNTED?
IF ONLY THEY WERE! IT'S MORE HORRIBLE THAN THAT!
BWANG
BWING
THEY'RE JUMPING BEANS
AND THEY TEND TO GET FRISKY AS THE WEATHER WARMS UP!
OH MY! AND TODAY'S SUPPOSED TO BE A SCORCHER!
I'VE HAD ENOUGH! I SAY WE TURN 'EM INTO CHILI!
DON'T SAY THAT! YOU'RE MAKING THEM MAD!
DIVE FOR COVER, MEN! THEY'RE REACHING CRITICAL MASS!
KERBOOM

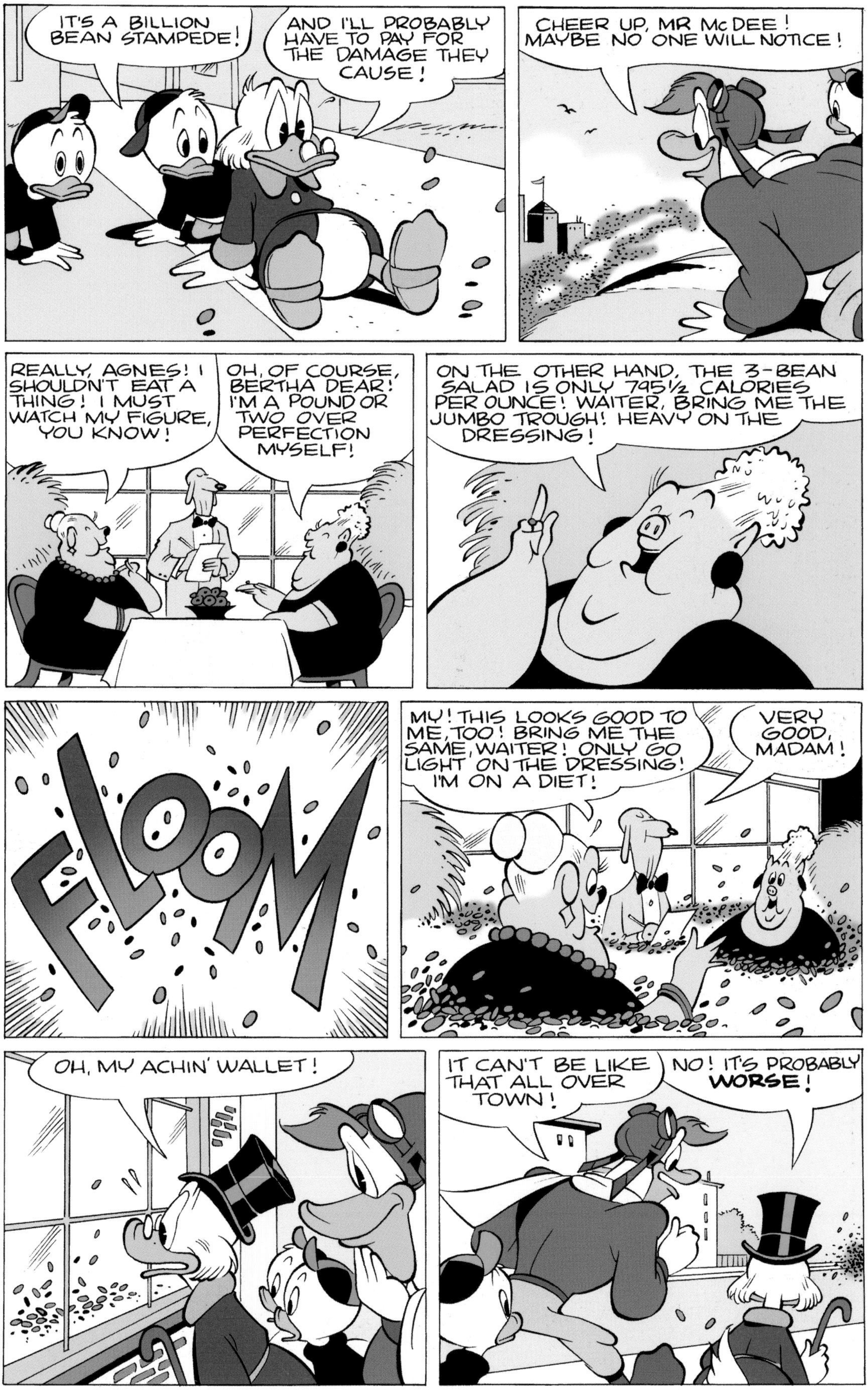
IT'S A BILLION BEAN STAMPEDE!
AND I'LL PROBABLY HAVE TO PAY FOR THE DAMAGE THEY CAUSE!
CHEER UP, MR McDEE! MAYBE NO ONE WILL NOTICE!
REALLY, AGNES! I SHOULDN'T EAT A THING! I MUST WATCH MY FIGURE, YOU KNOW!
OH, OF COURSE, BERTHA DEAR! I'M A POUND OR TWO OVER PERFECTION MYSELF!
ON THE OTHER HAND, THE 3-BEAN SALAD IS ONLY 795½ CALORIES PER OUNCE! WAITER, BRING ME THE JUMBO TROUGH! HEAVY ON THE DRESSING!
FLOOM
MY! THIS LOOKS GOOD TO ME, TOO! BRING ME THE SAME, WAITER! ONLY GO LIGHT ON THE DRESSING! I'M ON A DIET!
VERY GOOD, MADAM!
OH, MY ACHIN' WALLET!
IT CAN'T BE LIKE THAT ALL OVER TOWN!
NO! IT'S PROBABLY **WORSE**!

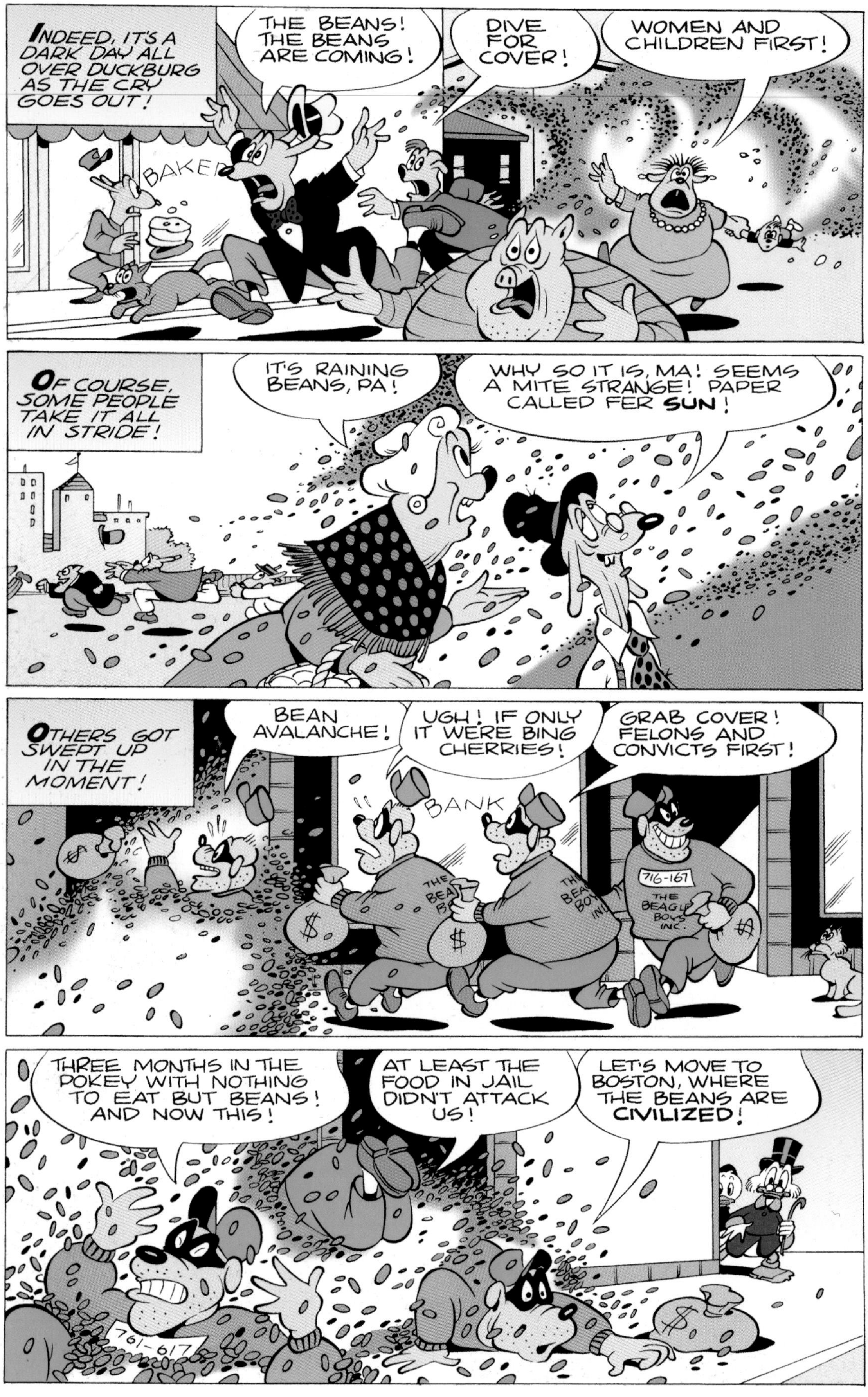
INDEED, IT'S A DARK DAY ALL OVER DUCKBURG AS THE CRY GOES OUT!
THE BEANS! THE BEANS ARE COMING!
DIVE FOR COVER!
WOMEN AND CHILDREN FIRST!
OF COURSE, SOME PEOPLE TAKE IT ALL IN STRIDE!
IT'S RAINING BEANS, PA!
WHY SO IT IS, MA! SEEMS A MITE STRANGE! PAPER CALLED FER **SUN**!
OTHERS GOT SWEPT UP IN THE MOMENT!
BEAN AVALANCHE!
UGH! IF ONLY IT WERE BING CHERRIES!
GRAB COVER! FELONS AND CONVICTS FIRST!
BANK
716-167
THREE MONTHS IN THE POKEY WITH NOTHING TO EAT BUT BEANS! AND NOW THIS!
AT LEAST THE FOOD IN JAIL DIDN'T ATTACK US!
LET'S MOVE TO BOSTON, WHERE THE BEANS ARE **CIVILIZED**!
761-617

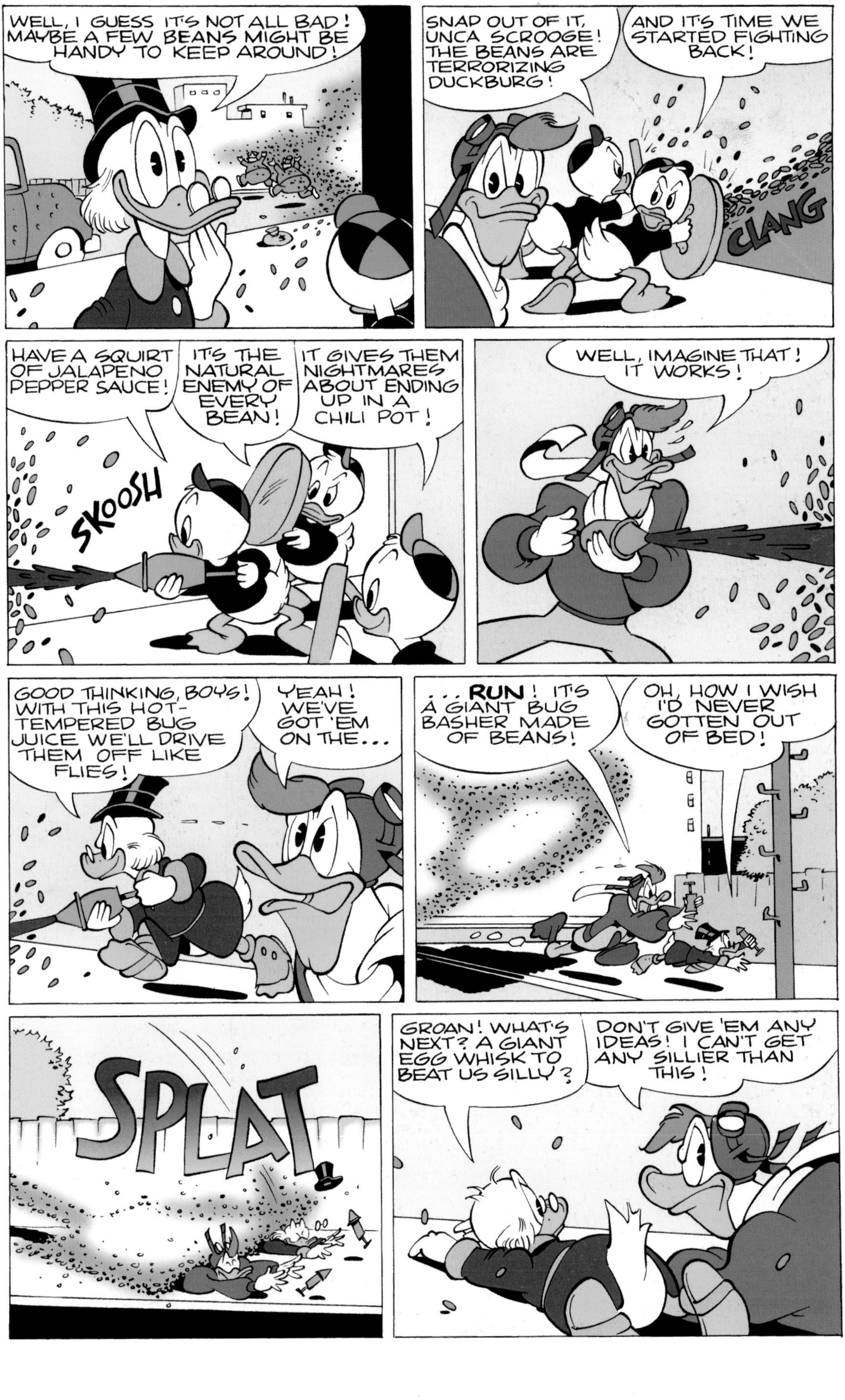
WELL, I GUESS IT'S NOT ALL BAD! MAYBE A FEW BEANS MIGHT BE HANDY TO KEEP AROUND!
SNAP OUT OF IT, UNCA SCROOGE! THE BEANS ARE TERRORIZING DUCKBURG!
AND IT'S TIME WE STARTED FIGHTING BACK!
CLANG
HAVE A SQUIRT OF JALAPENO PEPPER SAUCE!
IT'S THE NATURAL ENEMY OF EVERY BEAN!
IT GIVES THEM NIGHTMARES ABOUT ENDING UP IN A CHILI POT!
SKOOSH
WELL, IMAGINE THAT! IT WORKS!
GOOD THINKING, BOYS! WITH THIS HOT-TEMPERED BUG JUICE WE'LL DRIVE THEM OFF LIKE FLIES!
YEAH! WE'VE GOT 'EM ON THE...
...RUN! IT'S A GIANT BUG BASHER MADE OF BEANS!
OH, HOW I WISH I'D NEVER GOTTEN OUT OF BED!
SPLAT
GROAN! WHAT'S NEXT? A GIANT EGG WHISK TO BEAT US SILLY?
DON'T GIVE 'EM ANY IDEAS! I CAN'T GET ANY SILLIER THAN THIS!

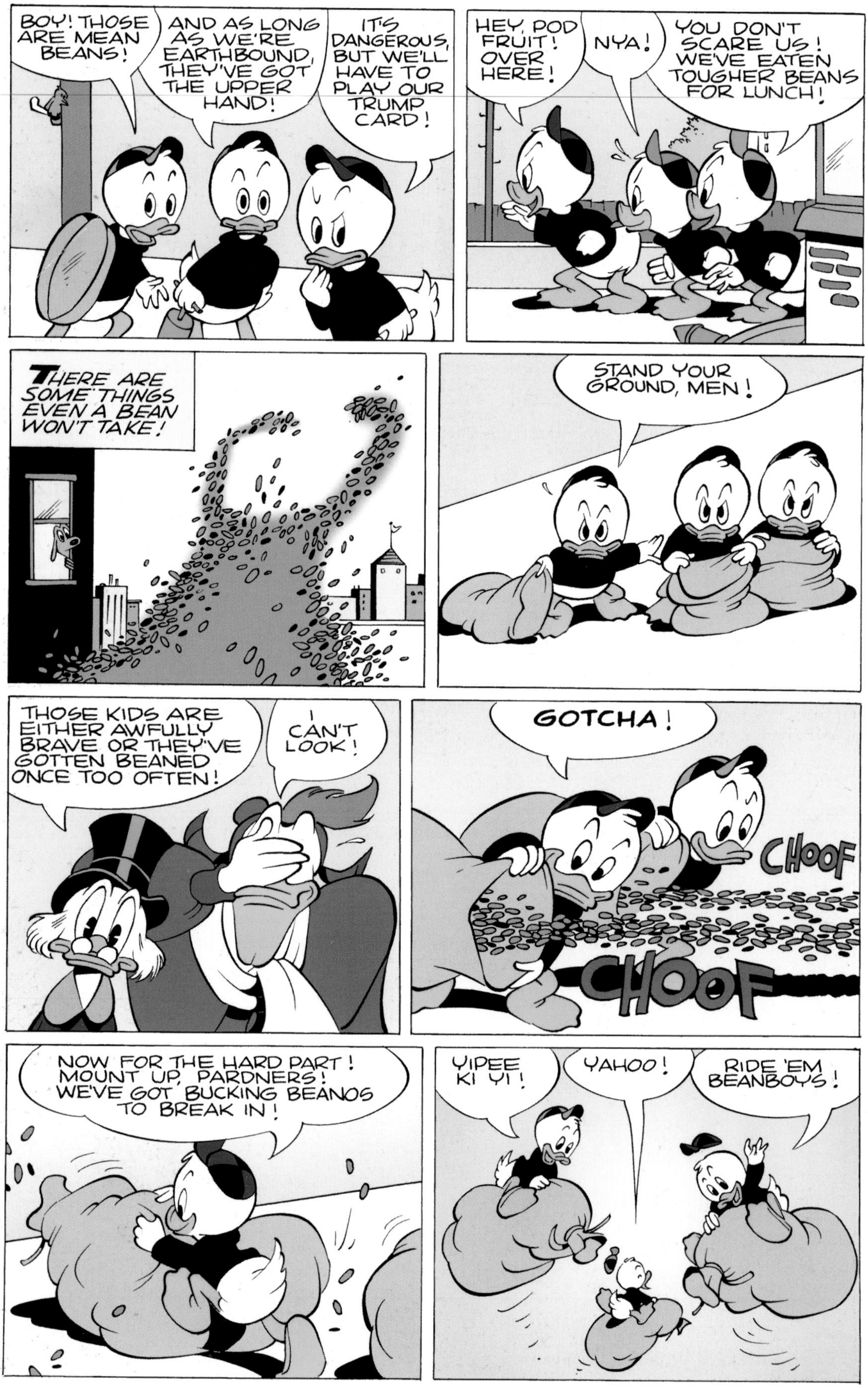
BOY! THOSE ARE MEAN BEANS!
AND AS LONG AS WE'RE EARTHBOUND, THEY'VE GOT THE UPPER HAND!
IT'S DANGEROUS, BUT WE'LL HAVE TO PLAY OUR TRUMP CARD!
HEY, POD FRUIT! OVER HERE!
NYA!
YOU DON'T SCARE US! WE'VE EATEN TOUGHER BEANS FOR LUNCH!
THERE ARE SOME THINGS EVEN A BEAN WON'T TAKE!
STAND YOUR GROUND, MEN!
THOSE KIDS ARE EITHER AWFULLY BRAVE OR THEY'VE GOTTEN BEANED ONCE TOO OFTEN!
I CAN'T LOOK!
GOTCHA!
CHOOF
CHOOF
NOW FOR THE HARD PART! MOUNT UP, PARDNERS! WE'VE GOT BUCKING BEANOS TO BREAK IN!
YIPEE KI YI!
YAHOO!
RIDE 'EM BEANBOYS!

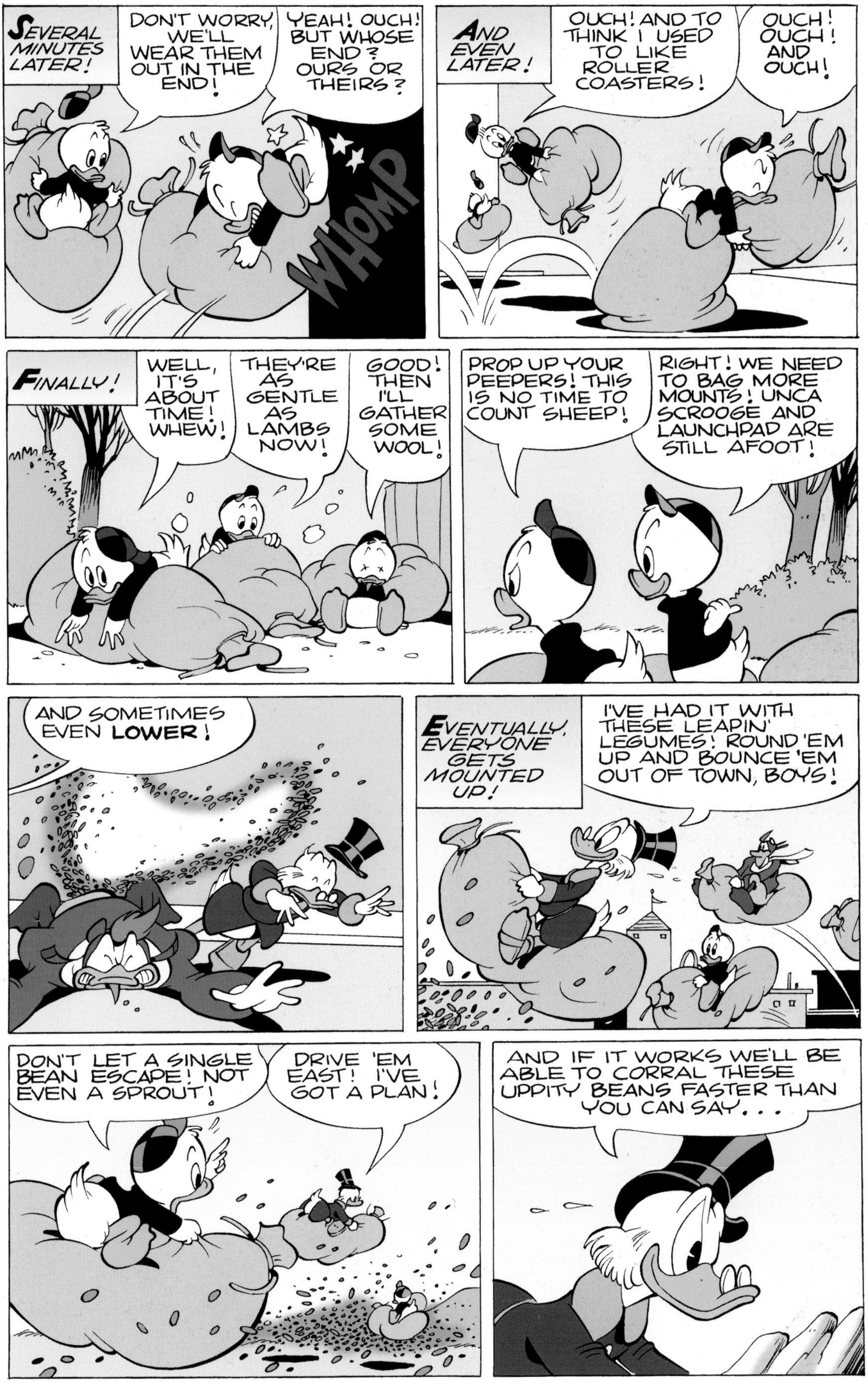
SEVERAL MINUTES LATER!
DON'T WORRY, WE'LL WEAR THEM OUT IN THE END!
YEAH! OUCH! BUT WHOSE END? OURS OR THEIRS?
WHOMP
AND EVEN LATER!
OUCH! AND TO THINK I USED TO LIKE ROLLER COASTERS!
OUCH! OUCH! AND OUCH!
FINALLY!
WELL, IT'S ABOUT TIME! WHEW!
THEY'RE AS GENTLE AS LAMBS NOW!
GOOD! THEN I'LL GATHER SOME WOOL!
PROP UP YOUR PEEPERS! THIS IS NO TIME TO COUNT SHEEP!
RIGHT! WE NEED TO BAG MORE MOUNTS! UNCA SCROOGE AND LAUNCHPAD ARE STILL AFOOT!
AND SOMETIMES EVEN **LOWER**!
EVENTUALLY, EVERYONE GETS MOUNTED UP!
I'VE HAD IT WITH THESE LEAPIN' LEGUMES! ROUND 'EM UP AND BOUNCE 'EM OUT OF TOWN, BOYS!
DON'T LET A SINGLE BEAN ESCAPE! NOT EVEN A SPROUT!
DRIVE 'EM EAST! I'VE GOT A PLAN!
AND IF IT WORKS WE'LL BE ABLE TO CORRAL THESE UPPITY BEANS FASTER THAN YOU CAN SAY...

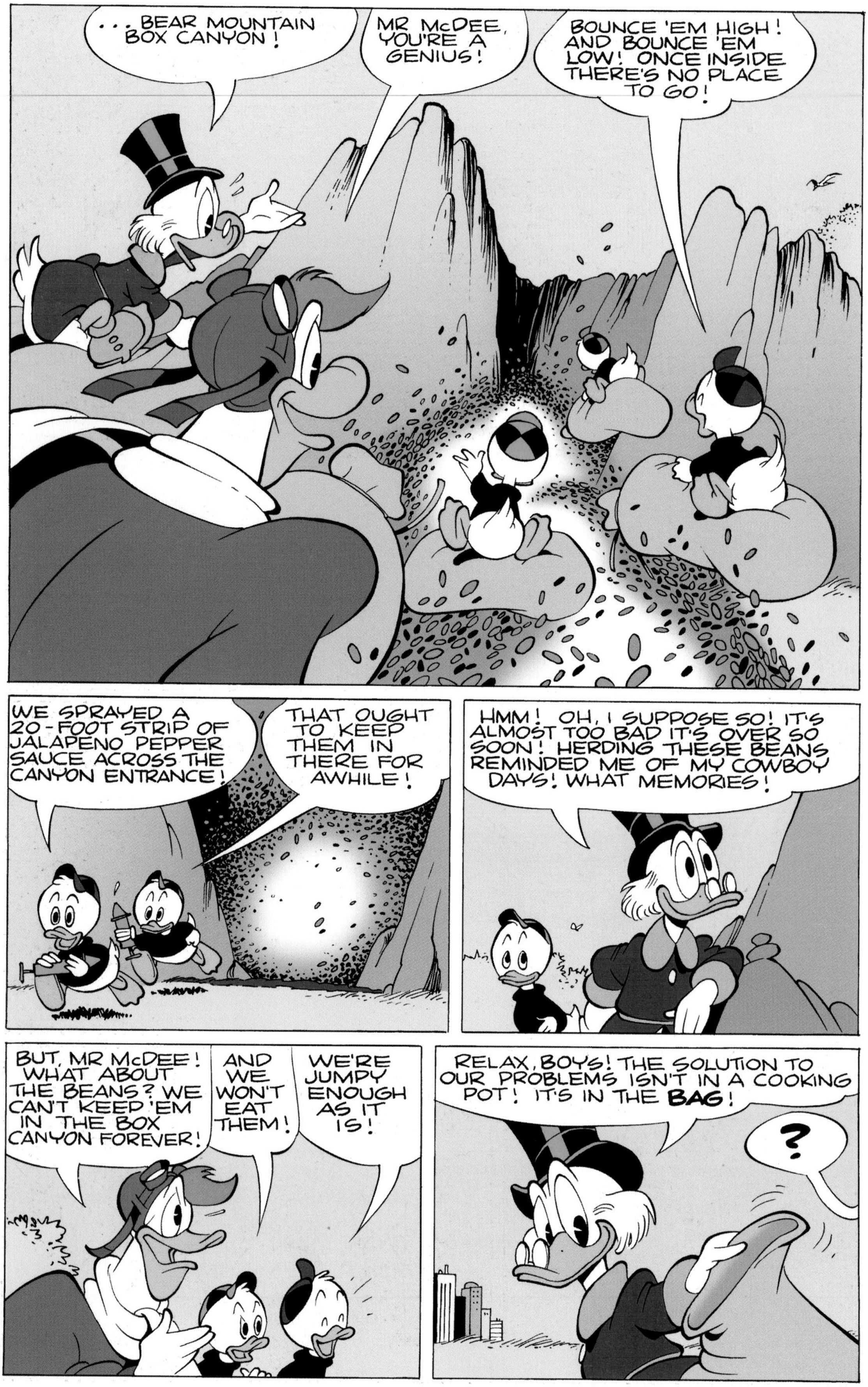
. . . BEAR MOUNTAIN BOX CANYON!
MR McDEE, YOU'RE A GENIUS!
BOUNCE 'EM HIGH! AND BOUNCE 'EM LOW! ONCE INSIDE THERE'S NO PLACE TO GO!
WE SPRAYED A 20-FOOT STRIP OF JALAPENO PEPPER SAUCE ACROSS THE CANYON ENTRANCE!
THAT OUGHT TO KEEP THEM IN THERE FOR AWHILE!
HMM! OH, I SUPPOSE SO! IT'S ALMOST TOO BAD IT'S OVER SO SOON! HERDING THESE BEANS REMINDED ME OF MY COWBOY DAYS! WHAT MEMORIES!
BUT, MR McDEE! WHAT ABOUT THE BEANS? WE CAN'T KEEP 'EM IN THE BOX CANYON FOREVER!
AND WE WON'T EAT THEM!
WE'RE JUMPY ENOUGH AS IT IS!
RELAX, BOYS! THE SOLUTION TO OUR PROBLEMS ISN'T IN A COOKING POT! IT'S IN THE **BAG**!
?

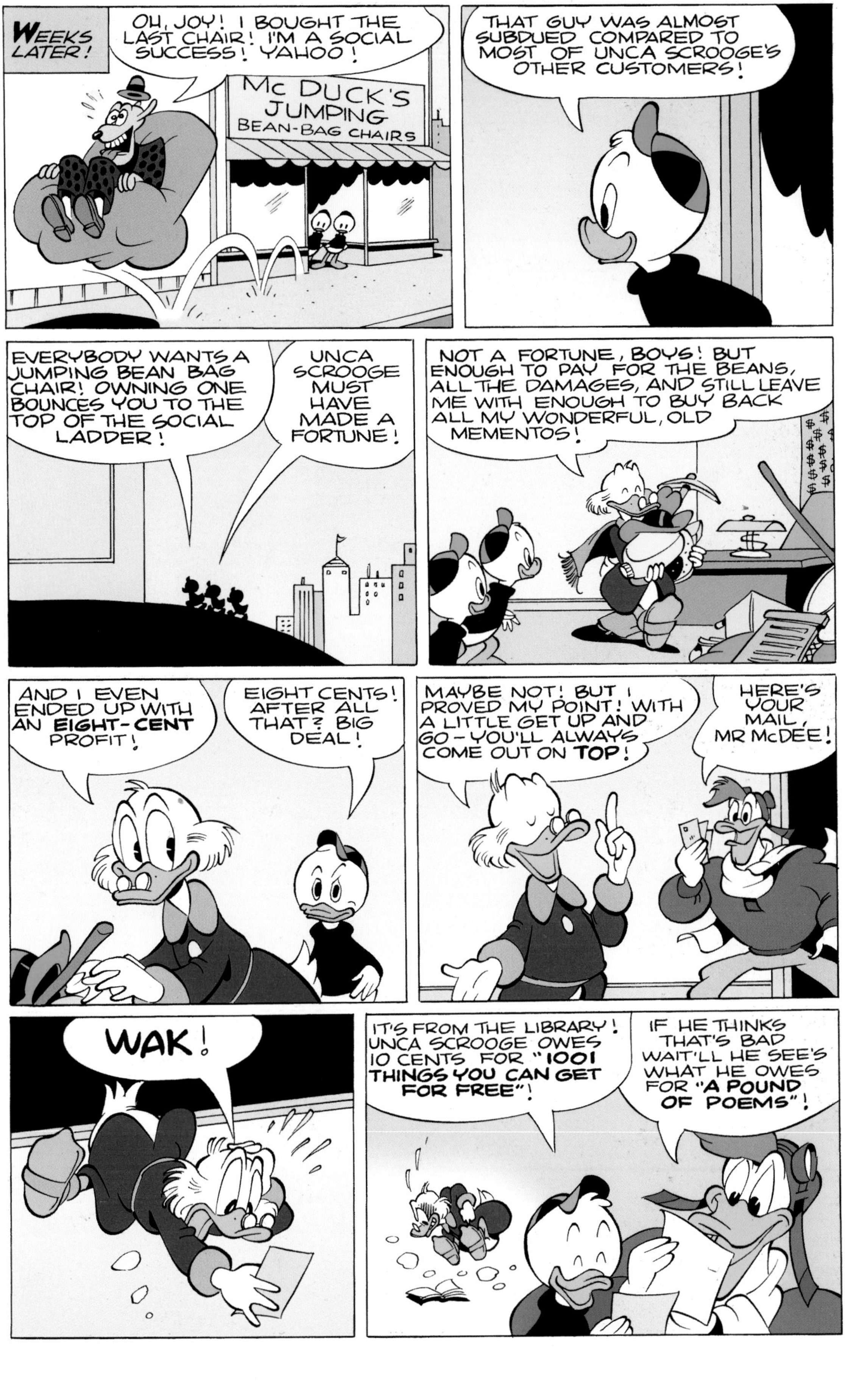
WEEKS LATER!
OH, JOY! I BOUGHT THE LAST CHAIR! I'M A SOCIAL SUCCESS! YAHOO!
McDUCK'S JUMPING BEAN-BAG CHAIRS
THAT GUY WAS ALMOST SUBDUED COMPARED TO MOST OF UNCA SCROOGE'S OTHER CUSTOMERS!
EVERYBODY WANTS A JUMPING BEAN BAG CHAIR! OWNING ONE BOUNCES YOU TO THE TOP OF THE SOCIAL LADDER!
UNCA SCROOGE MUST HAVE MADE A FORTUNE!
NOT A FORTUNE, BOYS! BUT ENOUGH TO PAY FOR THE BEANS, ALL THE DAMAGES, AND STILL LEAVE ME WITH ENOUGH TO BUY BACK ALL MY WONDERFUL, OLD MEMENTOS!
AND I EVEN ENDED UP WITH AN EIGHT-CENT PROFIT!
EIGHT CENTS! AFTER ALL THAT? BIG DEAL!
MAYBE NOT! BUT I PROVED MY POINT! WITH A LITTLE GET UP AND GO - YOU'LL ALWAYS COME OUT ON TOP!
HERE'S YOUR MAIL, MR McDEE!
WAK!
IT'S FROM THE LIBRARY! UNCA SCROOGE OWES 10 CENTS FOR "1001 THINGS YOU CAN GET FOR FREE"!
IF HE THINKS THAT'S BAD WAIT'LL HE SEE'S WHAT HE OWES FOR "A POUND OF POEMS"!

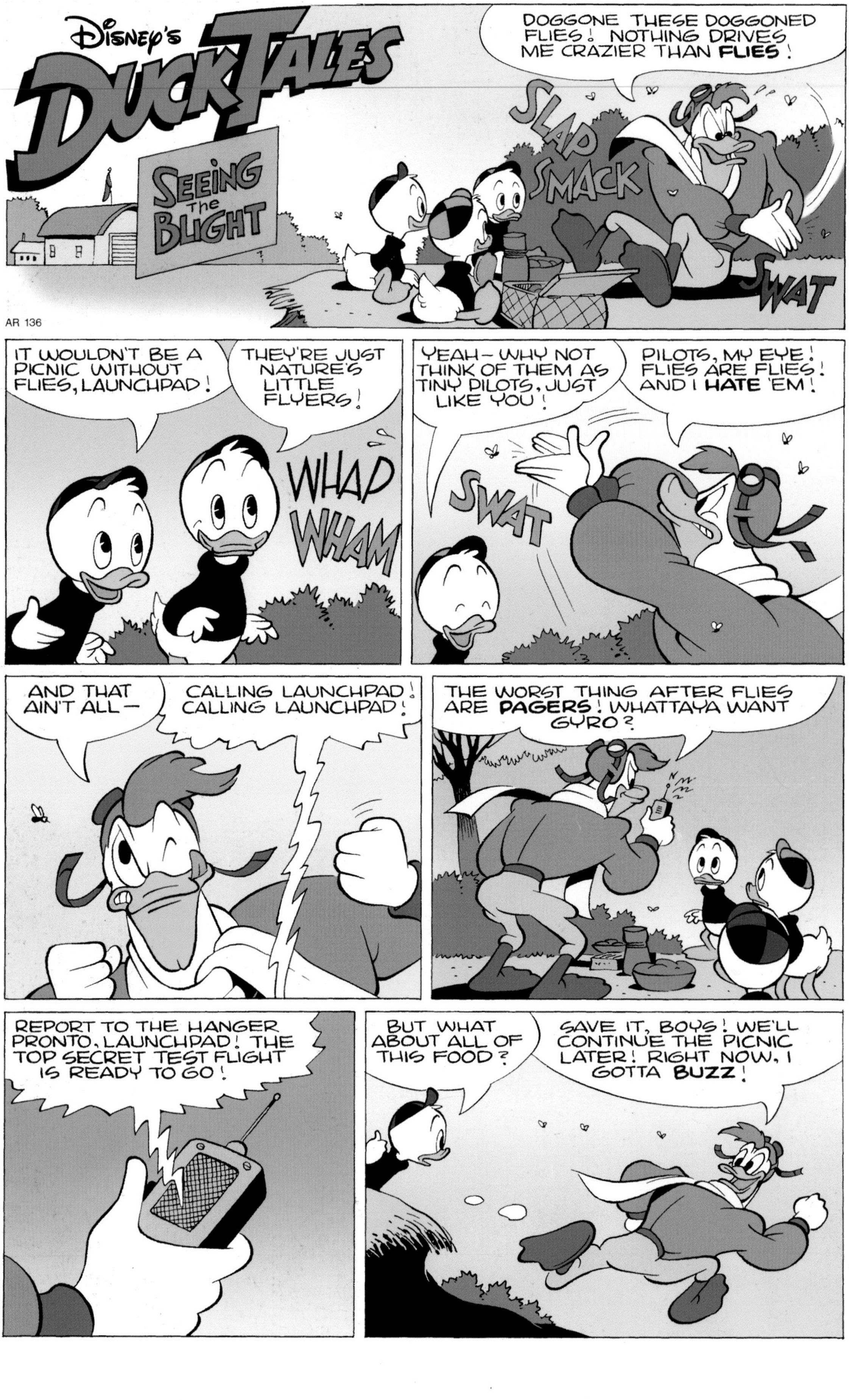

DISNEY'S DUCKTALES
SEEING The BLIGHT
DOGGONE THESE DOGGONED FLIES! NOTHING DRIVES ME CRAZIER THAN **FLIES**!
SLAP
SMACK
SWAT
AR 136
IT WOULDN'T BE A PICNIC WITHOUT FLIES, LAUNCHPAD!
THEY'RE JUST NATURE'S LITTLE FLYERS!
WHAP
WHAM
YEAH— WHY NOT THINK OF THEM AS TINY PILOTS, JUST LIKE YOU!
PILOTS, MY EYE! FLIES ARE FLIES! AND I **HATE** 'EM!
SWAT
AND THAT AIN'T ALL—
CALLING LAUNCHPAD! CALLING LAUNCHPAD!
THE WORST THING AFTER FLIES ARE **PAGERS**! WHATTAYA WANT GYRO?
REPORT TO THE HANGER PRONTO, LAUNCHPAD! THE TOP SECRET TEST FLIGHT IS READY TO GO!
BUT WHAT ABOUT ALL OF THIS FOOD?
SAVE IT, BOYS! WE'LL CONTINUE THE PICNIC LATER! RIGHT NOW, I GOTTA **BUZZ**!

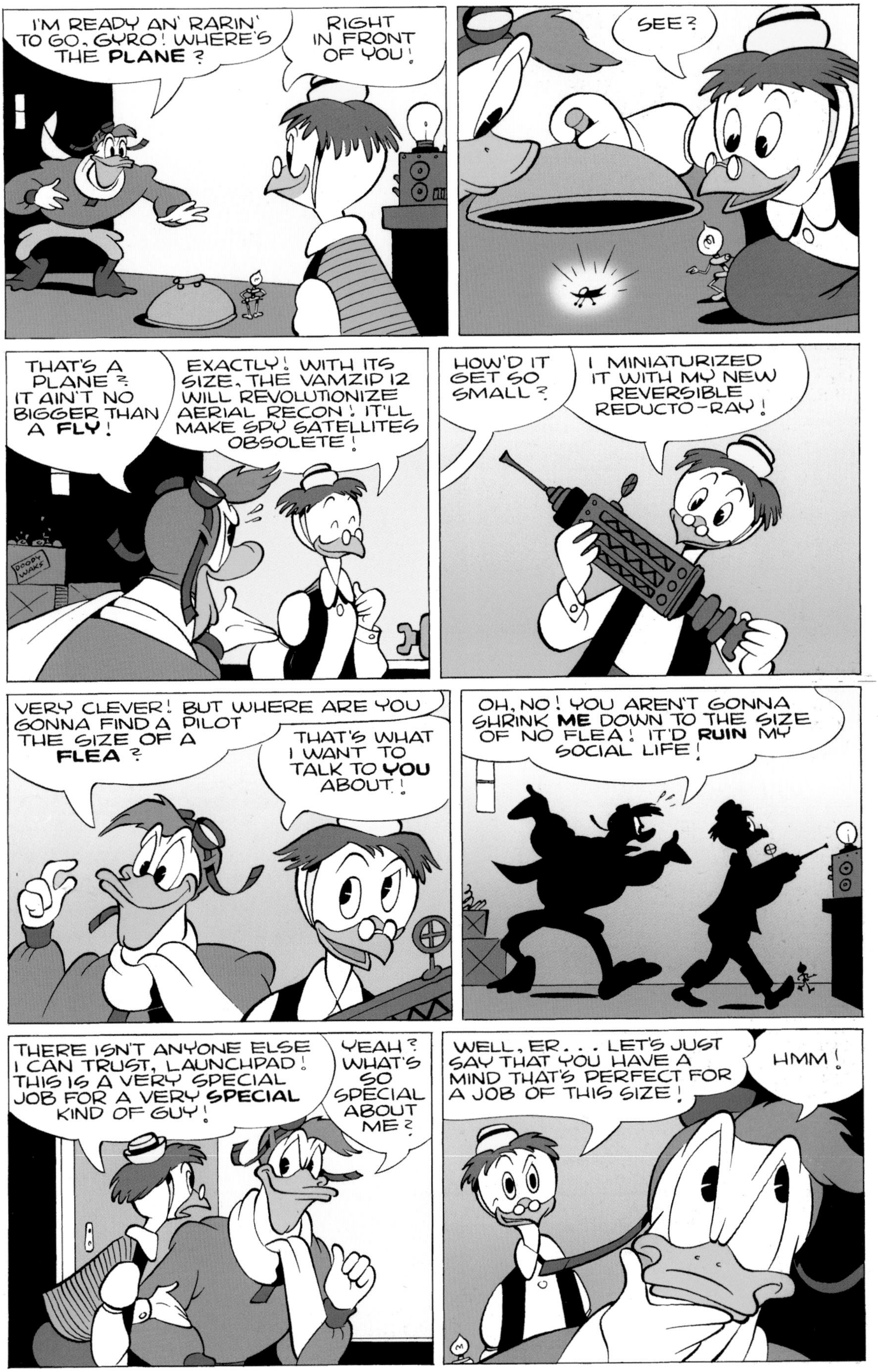
I'M READY AN' RARIN' TO GO, GYRO! WHERE'S THE PLANE?
RIGHT IN FRONT OF YOU!
SEE?
THAT'S A PLANE? IT AIN'T NO BIGGER THAN A FLY!
EXACTLY! WITH ITS SIZE, THE VAMZIP 12 WILL REVOLUTIONIZE AERIAL RECON! IT'LL MAKE SPY SATELLITES OBSOLETE!
DOODY WAKS
HOW'D IT GET SO SMALL?
I MINIATURIZED IT WITH MY NEW REVERSIBLE REDUCTO-RAY!
VERY CLEVER! BUT WHERE ARE YOU GONNA FIND A PILOT THE SIZE OF A FLEA?
THAT'S WHAT I WANT TO TALK TO YOU ABOUT!
OH, NO! YOU AREN'T GONNA SHRINK ME DOWN TO THE SIZE OF NO FLEA! IT'D RUIN MY SOCIAL LIFE!
THERE ISN'T ANYONE ELSE I CAN TRUST, LAUNCHPAD! THIS IS A VERY SPECIAL JOB FOR A VERY SPECIAL KIND OF GUY!
YEAH? WHAT'S SO SPECIAL ABOUT ME?
WELL, ER... LET'S JUST SAY THAT YOU HAVE A MIND THAT'S PERFECT FOR A JOB OF THIS SIZE!
HMM!

AND SO! YOU'RE DOING GREAT, LAUNCHPAD! TRY A FEW LOOPS!

NO SWEAT, GYRO! THIS THING EVEN **FLIES** LIKE A FLY! WATCH THIS!

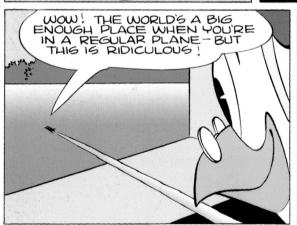

WAHOO!

ZIP
ZIP
ZIP

OPEN THE WINDOW, GYRO! I WANT TO PUT THIS BABY THROUGH HER PACES OUT IN THE WILD BLUE!

ALRIGHT— BUT WATCH OUT FOR SPIDER WEBS!

WOW! THE WORLD'S A BIG ENOUGH PLACE WHEN YOU'RE IN A REGULAR PLANE— BUT THIS IS RIDICULOUS!

HA! THERE'S THE BOYS! HEH HEH! WHAT BETTER PLACE TO TEST A 'FLY' PLANE THAN AT A PICNIC?

I WONDER WHAT SORT OF PLANE LAUNCHPAD IS TESTING? I DON'T SEE ANYTHING AIR-BORNE, DO YOU?

NOPE! EVEN THE FLIES ARE GONE!

BZIZZ

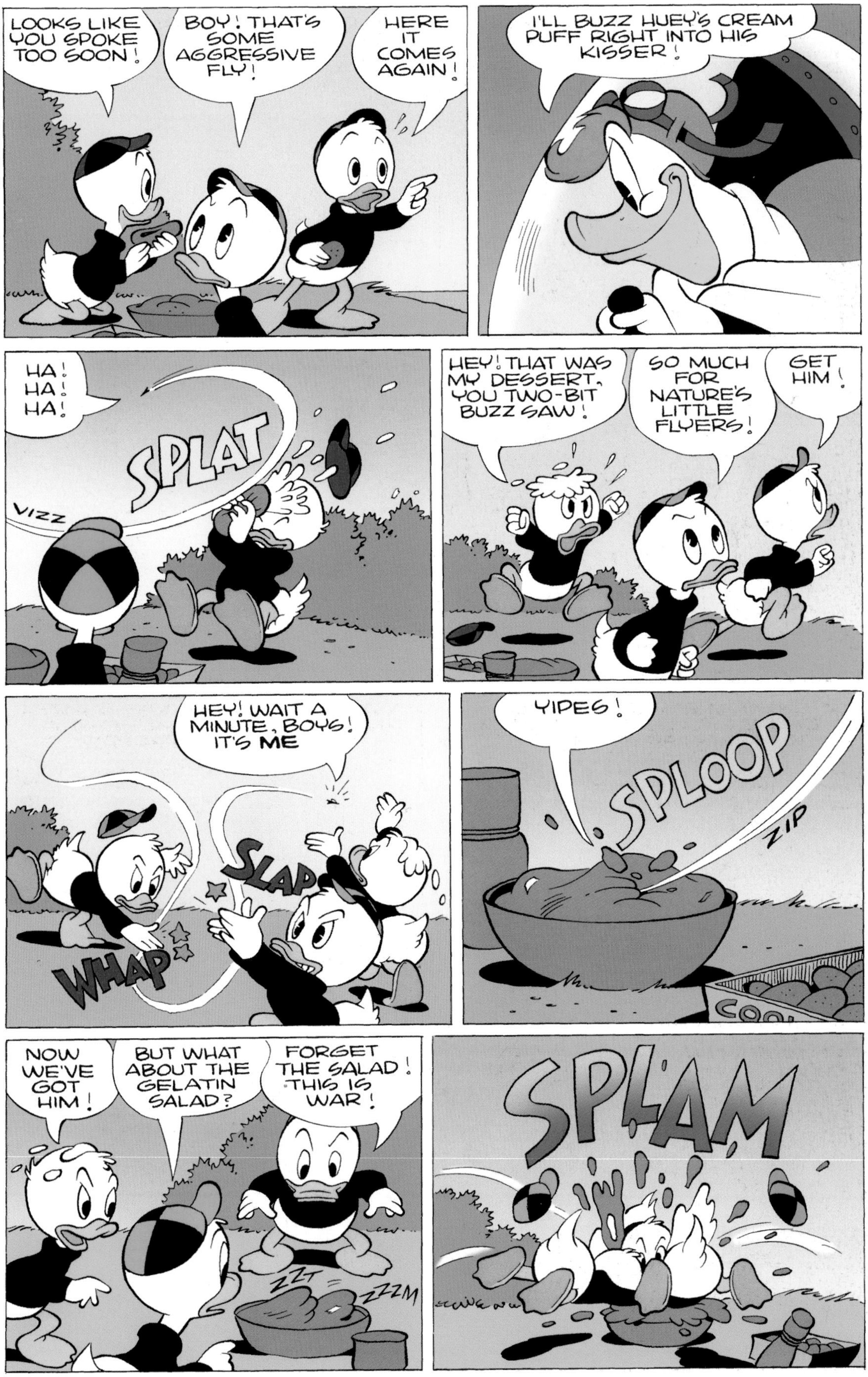
LOOKS LIKE YOU SPOKE TOO SOON!
BOY! THAT'S SOME AGGRESSIVE FLY!
HERE IT COMES AGAIN!
I'LL BUZZ HUEY'S CREAM PUFF RIGHT INTO HIS KISSER!
HA! HA! HA!
SPLAT
VIZZ
HEY! THAT WAS MY DESSERT, YOU TWO-BIT BUZZ SAW!
SO MUCH FOR NATURE'S LITTLE FLYERS!
GET HIM!
HEY! WAIT A MINUTE, BOYS! IT'S ME
SLAP
WHAP
YIPES!
SPLOOP
ZIP
NOW WE'VE GOT HIM!
BUT WHAT ABOUT THE GELATIN SALAD?
FORGET THE SALAD! THIS IS WAR!
ZZT
ZZZM
SPLAM

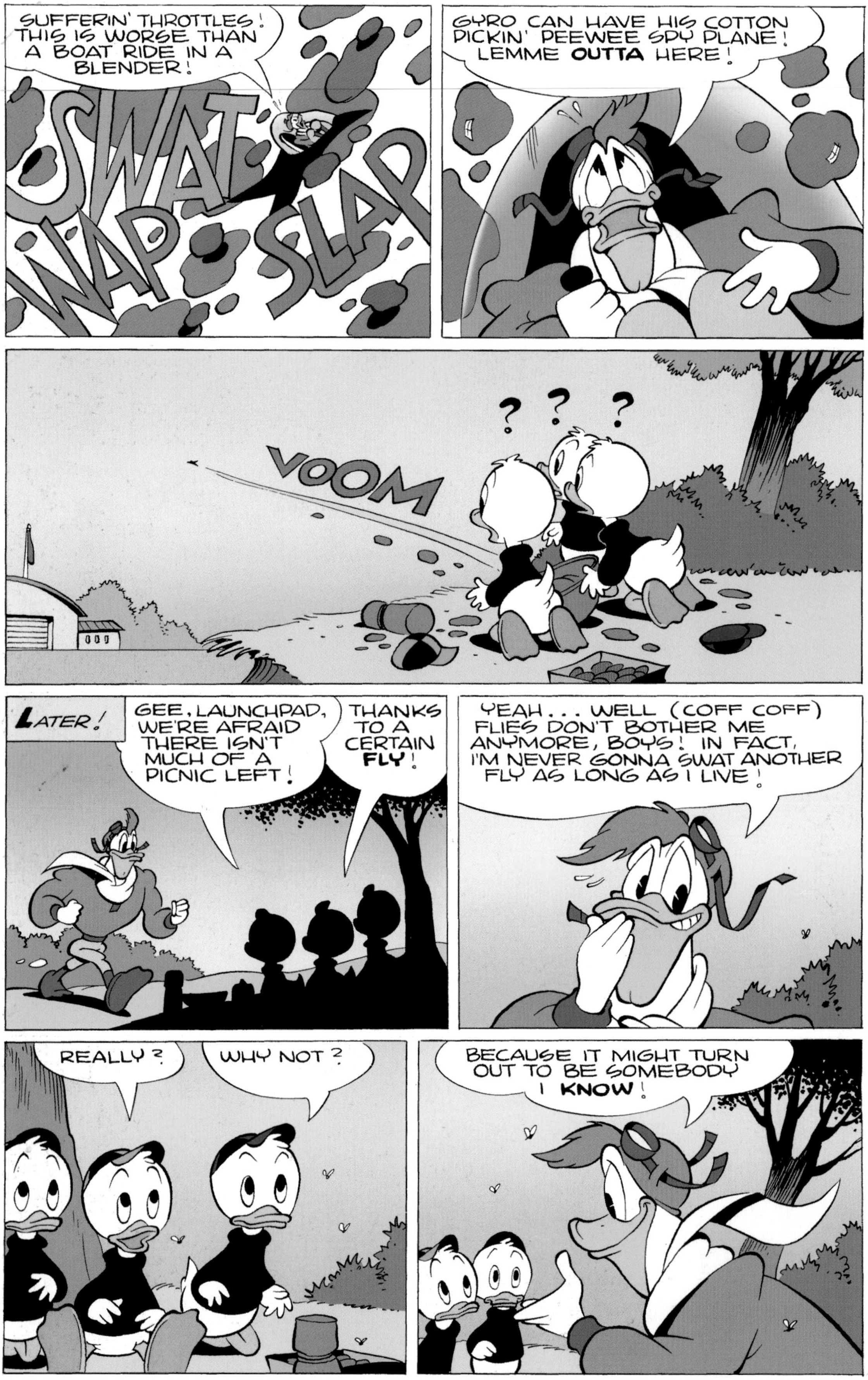

SUFFERIN' THROTTLES! THIS IS WORSE THAN A BOAT RIDE IN A BLENDER!
SWAT
WAP
SLAP
GYRO CAN HAVE HIS COTTON PICKIN' PEEWEE SPY PLANE! LEMME OUTTA HERE!
? ? ?
VOOM
LATER!
GEE, LAUNCHPAD, WE'RE AFRAID THERE ISN'T MUCH OF A PICNIC LEFT!
THANKS TO A CERTAIN FLY!
YEAH... WELL (COFF COFF) FLIES DON'T BOTHER ME ANYMORE, BOYS! IN FACT, I'M NEVER GONNA SWAT ANOTHER FLY AS LONG AS I LIVE!
REALLY?
WHY NOT?
BECAUSE IT MIGHT TURN OUT TO BE SOMEBODY I KNOW!

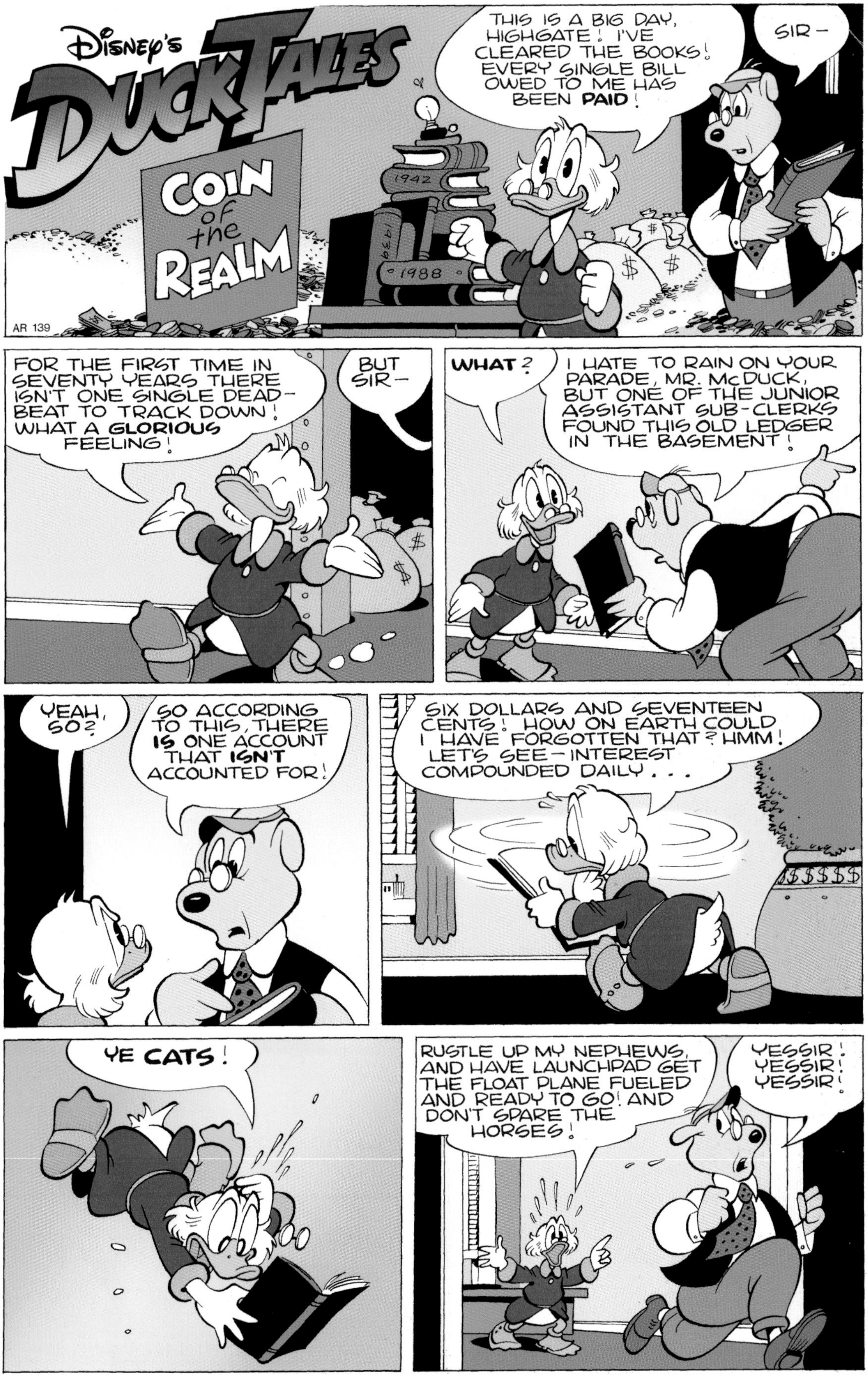

DISNEY'S
DUCKTALES
COIN of the REALM
1942
1939
1988
AR 139
THIS IS A BIG DAY, HIGHGATE! I'VE CLEARED THE BOOKS! EVERY SINGLE BILL OWED TO ME HAS BEEN PAID!
SIR—
FOR THE FIRST TIME IN SEVENTY YEARS THERE ISN'T ONE SINGLE DEAD-BEAT TO TRACK DOWN! WHAT A GLORIOUS FEELING!
BUT SIR—
WHAT?
I HATE TO RAIN ON YOUR PARADE, MR. McDUCK, BUT ONE OF THE JUNIOR ASSISTANT SUB-CLERKS FOUND THIS OLD LEDGER IN THE BASEMENT!
YEAH, SO?
SO ACCORDING TO THIS, THERE IS ONE ACCOUNT THAT ISN'T ACCOUNTED FOR!
SIX DOLLARS AND SEVENTEEN CENTS! HOW ON EARTH COULD I HAVE FORGOTTEN THAT? HMM! LET'S SEE—INTEREST COMPOUNDED DAILY . . .
YE CATS!
RUSTLE UP MY NEPHEWS, AND HAVE LAUNCHPAD GET THE FLOAT PLANE FUELED AND READY TO GO! AND DON'T SPARE THE HORSES!
YESSIR! YESSIR! YESSIR!

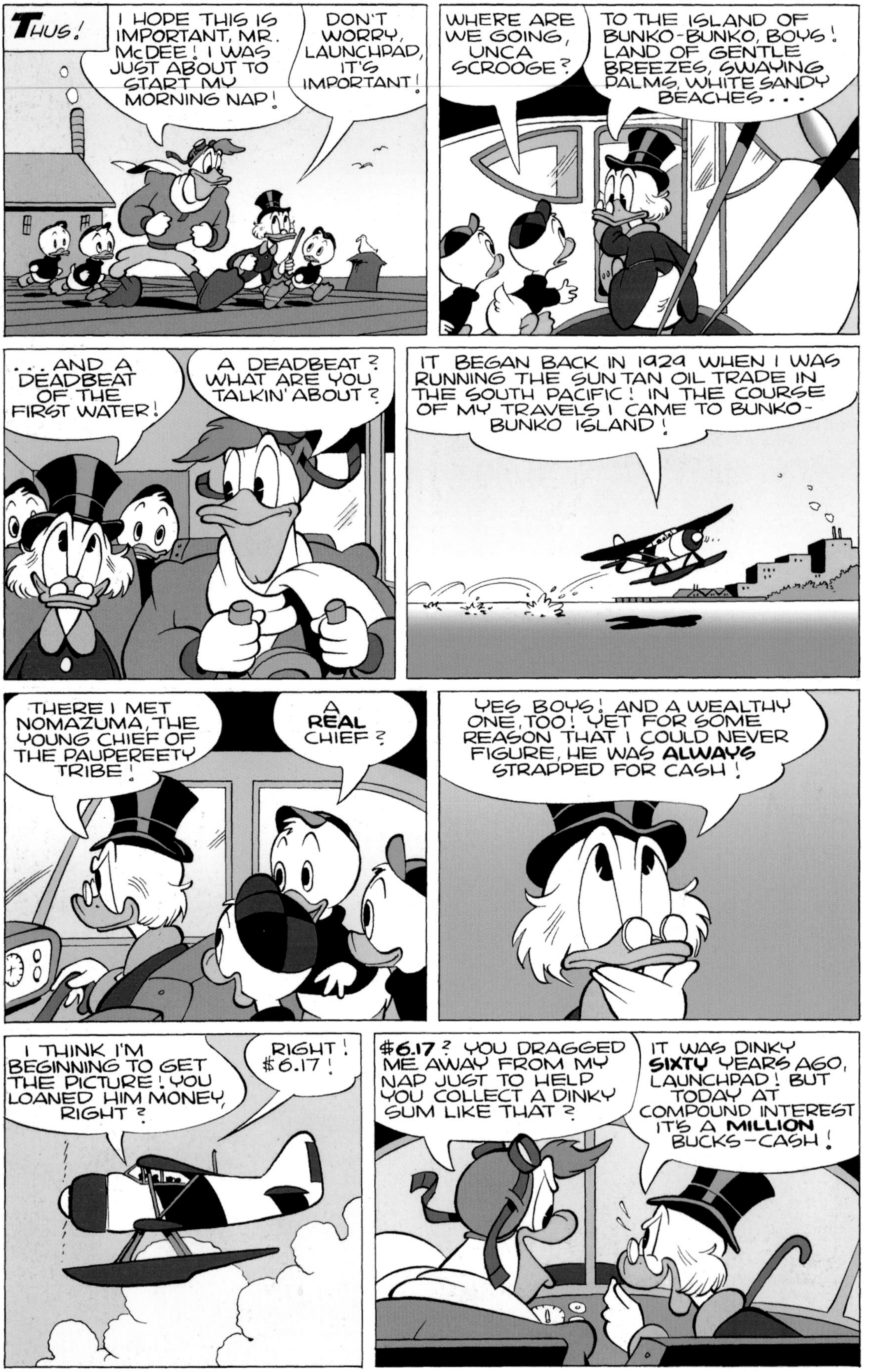
THUS!
I HOPE THIS IS IMPORTANT, MR. McDEE! I WAS JUST ABOUT TO START MY MORNING NAP!
DON'T WORRY, LAUNCHPAD, IT'S IMPORTANT!
WHERE ARE WE GOING, UNCA SCROOGE?
TO THE ISLAND OF BUNKO-BUNKO, BOYS! LAND OF GENTLE BREEZES, SWAYING PALMS, WHITE SANDY BEACHES...
...AND A DEADBEAT OF THE FIRST WATER!
A DEADBEAT? WHAT ARE YOU TALKIN' ABOUT?
IT BEGAN BACK IN 1929 WHEN I WAS RUNNING THE SUN TAN OIL TRADE IN THE SOUTH PACIFIC! IN THE COURSE OF MY TRAVELS I CAME TO BUNKO-BUNKO ISLAND!
THERE I MET NOMAZUMA, THE YOUNG CHIEF OF THE PAUPEREETY TRIBE!
A **REAL** CHIEF?
YES BOYS! AND A WEALTHY ONE, TOO! YET FOR SOME REASON THAT I COULD NEVER FIGURE, HE WAS **ALWAYS** STRAPPED FOR CASH!
I THINK I'M BEGINNING TO GET THE PICTURE! YOU LOANED HIM MONEY, RIGHT?
RIGHT! $6.17!
$6.17? YOU DRAGGED ME AWAY FROM MY NAP JUST TO HELP YOU COLLECT A DINKY SUM LIKE THAT?
IT WAS DINKY **SIXTY** YEARS AGO, LAUNCHPAD! BUT TODAY AT COMPOUND INTEREST IT'S A **MILLION** BUCKS—CASH!

OKAY, SO IT'S BIG MONEY! BUT WHAT IF OLD NOMAZUMA CAN'T **PAY** CASH?

I DON'T EXPECT HIM TO!

AND WHEN HE DOESN'T, HEH HEH! OUR AGREEMENT STATES THAT HE WILL TURN OVER **ALL** OF HIS ANCIENT ANCESTRAL WEALTH TO YOU KNOW WHO!

AND THAT WILL TRANSLATE INTO EVEN **BIGGER** MONEY!

*L*ATER—

BUNKO-BUNKO ISLAND COMING UP!

*N*EWS OF SCROOGE'S ARRIVAL TRAVELS FAST!

CHIEF! CHIEF! A GREAT METAL BIRD HAS LANDED ON LAGOON!

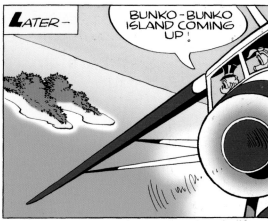

COME ON WITH THAT GREAT METAL BIRD STUFF! YOU MEAN A SEA-PLANE, DON'T YOU?

WELL, YEAH...

HEH-HEH! PROBABLY A BUNCH OF WELL-HEELED TOURISTS, WOULDN'T YOU SAY?

DEFINITELY, CHIEF! THE HEAD MAN IS A RITZY-LOOKING OLD DUCK IN A TOP HAT!

A DUCK IN A **TOP HAT**!

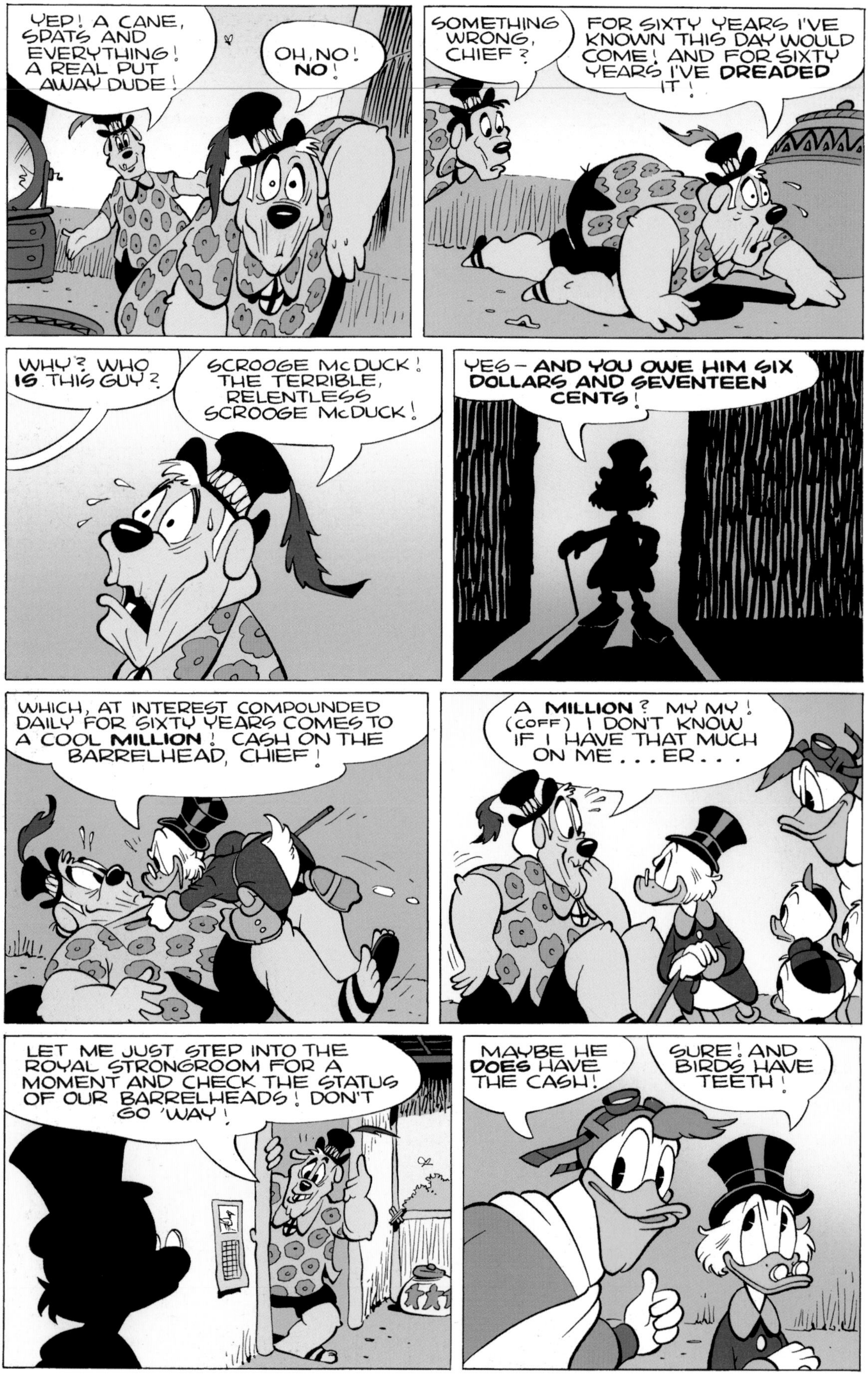
YEP! A CANE, SPATS AND EVERYTHING! A REAL PUT AWAY DUDE!
OH, NO! **NO**!
SOMETHING WRONG, CHIEF?
FOR SIXTY YEARS I'VE KNOWN THIS DAY WOULD COME! AND FOR SIXTY YEARS I'VE **DREADED** IT!
WHY? WHO **IS** THIS GUY?
SCROOGE McDUCK! THE TERRIBLE, RELENTLESS SCROOGE McDUCK!
YES— **AND YOU OWE HIM SIX DOLLARS AND SEVENTEEN CENTS**!
WHICH, AT INTEREST COMPOUNDED DAILY FOR SIXTY YEARS COMES TO A COOL **MILLION**! CASH ON THE BARRELHEAD, CHIEF!
A **MILLION**? MY MY! (COFF) I DON'T KNOW IF I HAVE THAT MUCH ON ME . . . ER . . .
LET ME JUST STEP INTO THE ROYAL STRONGROOM FOR A MOMENT AND CHECK THE STATUS OF OUR BARRELHEADS! DON'T GO 'WAY!
MAYBE HE **DOES** HAVE THE CASH!
SURE! AND BIRDS HAVE TEETH!

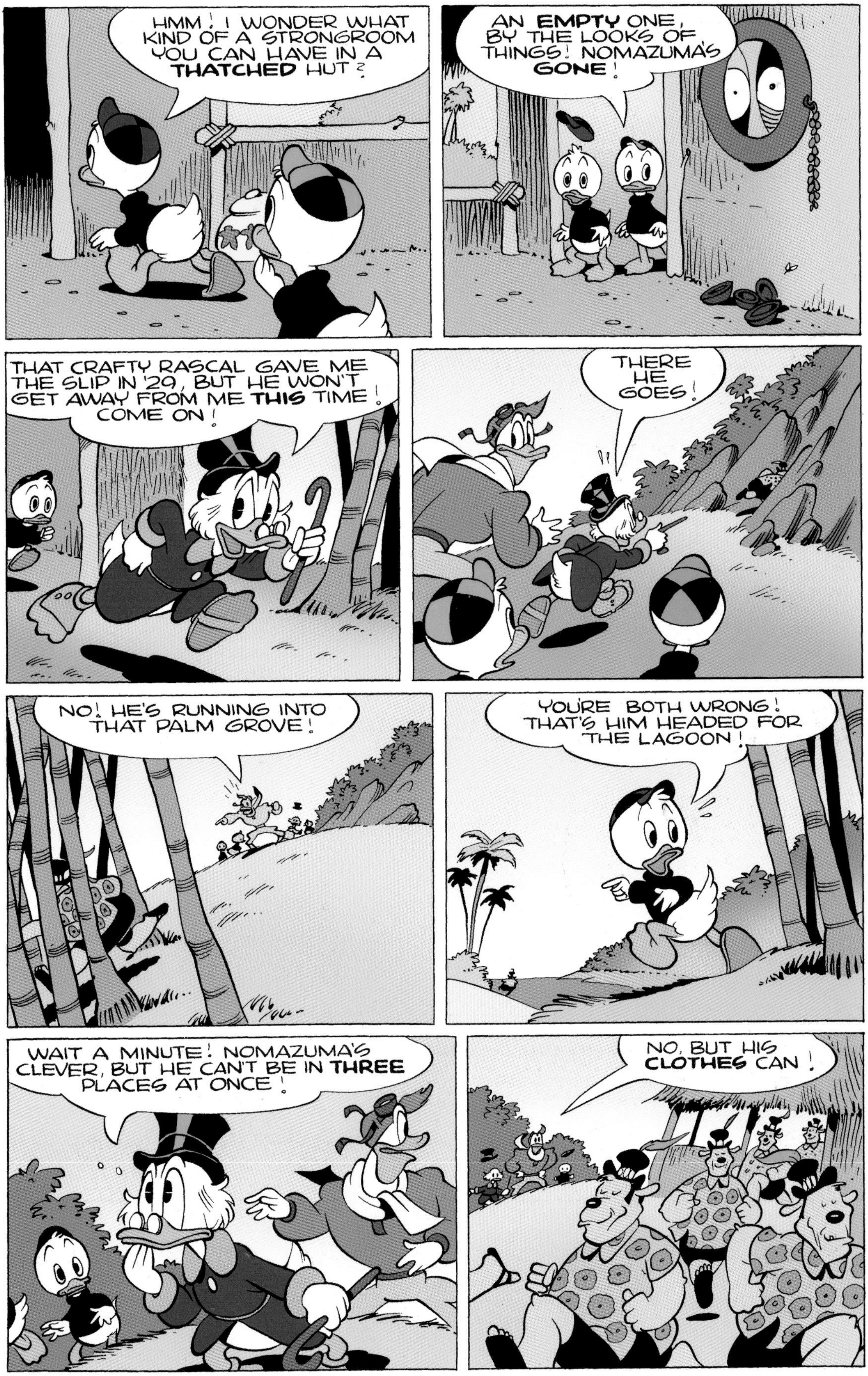

HMM! I WONDER WHAT KIND OF A STRONGROOM YOU CAN HAVE IN A **THATCHED** HUT?
AN **EMPTY** ONE, BY THE LOOKS OF THINGS! NOMAZUMA'S **GONE**!
THAT CRAFTY RASCAL GAVE ME THE SLIP IN '29, BUT HE WON'T GET AWAY FROM ME **THIS** TIME! COME ON!
THERE HE GOES!
NO! HE'S RUNNING INTO THAT PALM GROVE!
YOU'RE BOTH WRONG! THAT'S HIM HEADED FOR THE LAGOON!
WAIT A MINUTE! NOMAZUMA'S CLEVER, BUT HE CAN'T BE IN **THREE** PLACES AT ONCE!
NO, BUT HIS **CLOTHES** CAN!

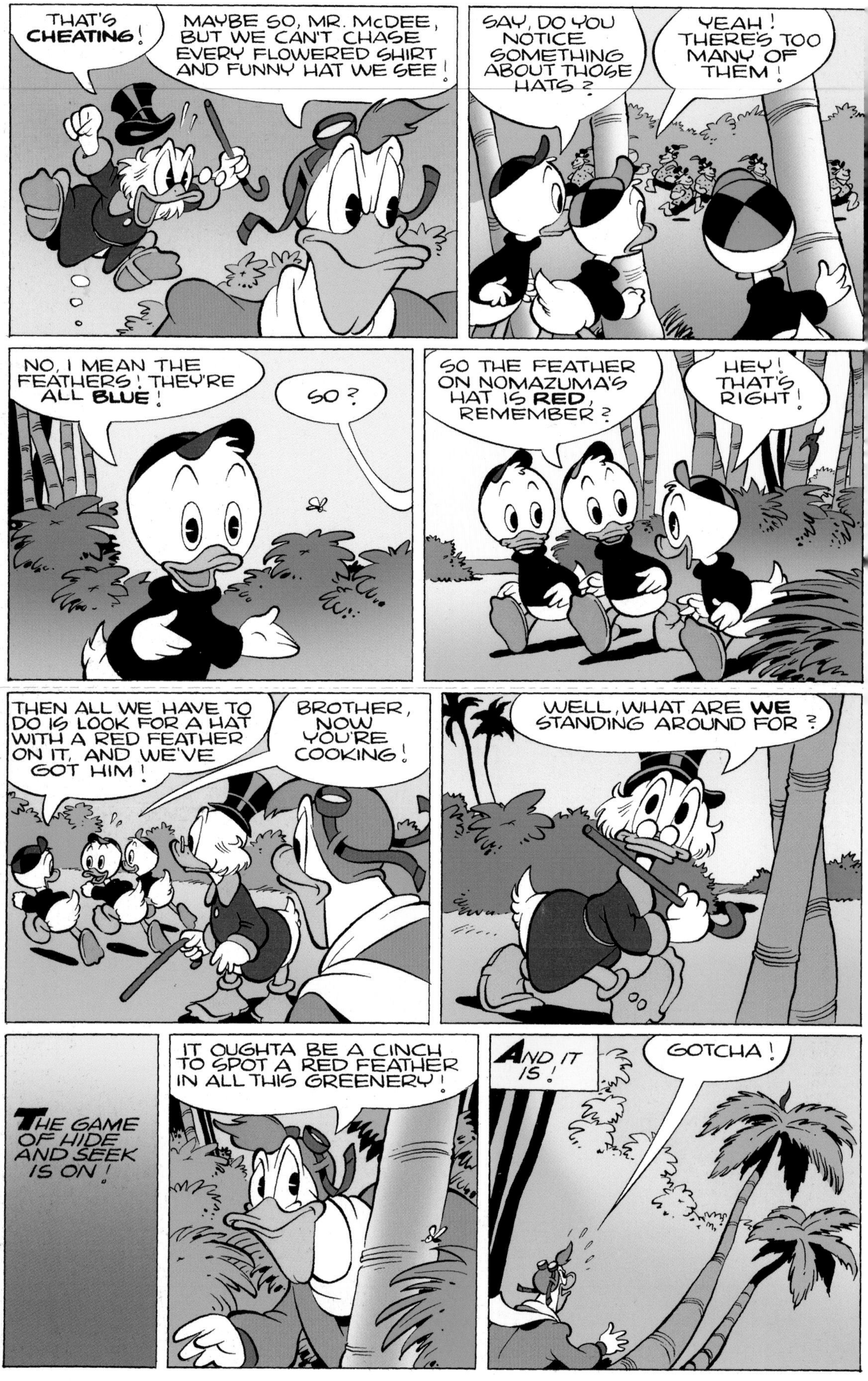
THAT'S CHEATING!
MAYBE SO, MR. McDEE, BUT WE CAN'T CHASE EVERY FLOWERED SHIRT AND FUNNY HAT WE SEE!
SAY, DO YOU NOTICE SOMETHING ABOUT THOSE HATS?
YEAH! THERE'S TOO MANY OF THEM!
NO, I MEAN THE FEATHERS! THEY'RE ALL BLUE!
SO?
SO THE FEATHER ON NOMAZUMA'S HAT IS RED, REMEMBER?
HEY! THAT'S RIGHT!
THEN ALL WE HAVE TO DO IS LOOK FOR A HAT WITH A RED FEATHER ON IT, AND WE'VE GOT HIM!
BROTHER, NOW YOU'RE COOKING!
WELL, WHAT ARE WE STANDING AROUND FOR?
THE GAME OF HIDE AND SEEK IS ON!
IT OUGHTA BE A CINCH TO SPOT A RED FEATHER IN ALL THIS GREENERY!
AND IT IS!
GOTCHA!

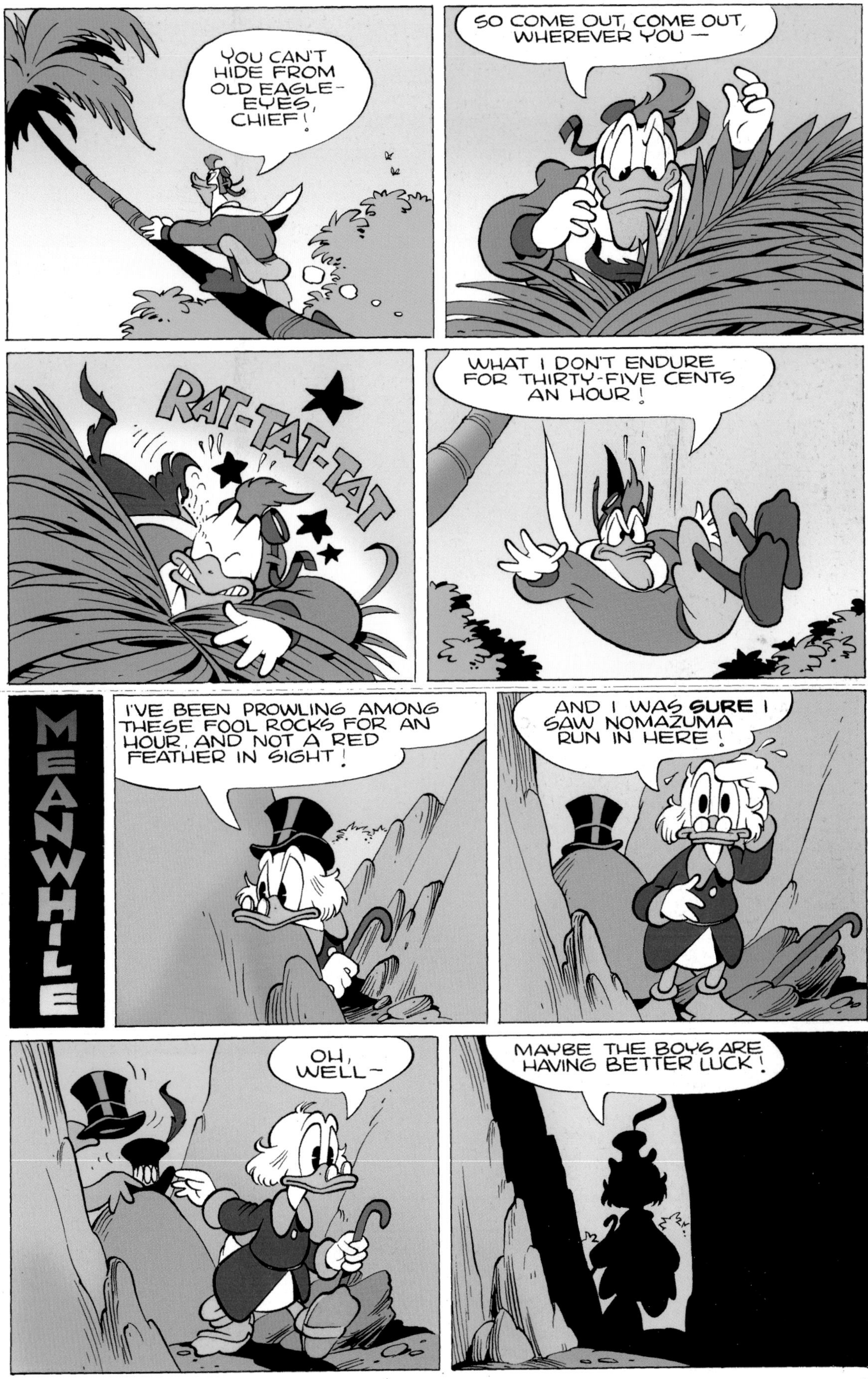
YOU CAN'T HIDE FROM OLD EAGLE-EYES, CHIEF!
SO COME OUT, COME OUT, WHEREVER YOU —
RAT-TAT-TAT
WHAT I DON'T ENDURE FOR THIRTY-FIVE CENTS AN HOUR!
MEANWHILE
I'VE BEEN PROWLING AMONG THESE FOOL ROCKS FOR AN HOUR, AND NOT A RED FEATHER IN SIGHT!
AND I WAS **SURE** I SAW NOMAZUMA RUN IN HERE!
OH, WELL—
MAYBE THE BOYS ARE HAVING BETTER LUCK!

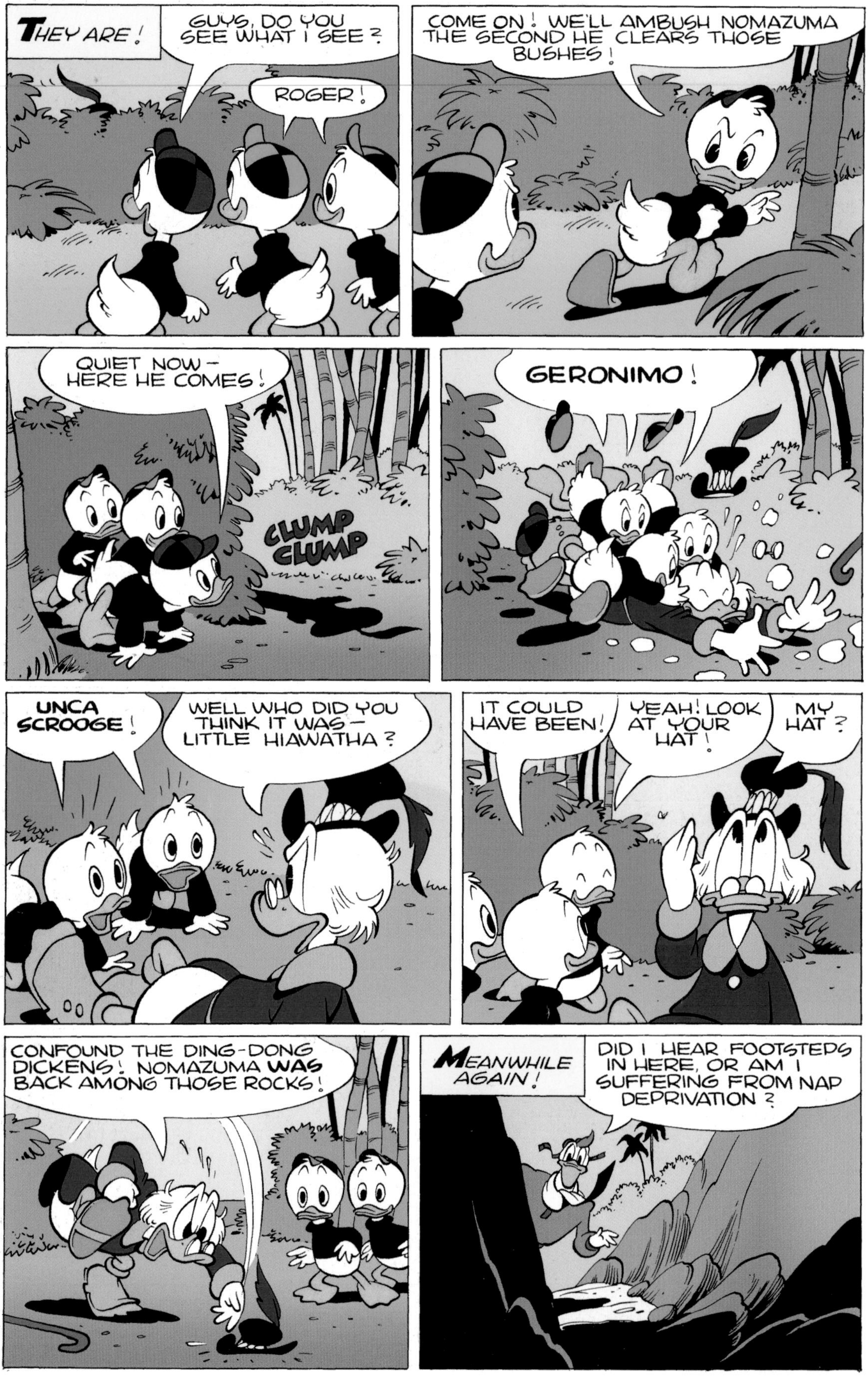
THEY ARE!
GUYS, DO YOU SEE WHAT I SEE?
ROGER!
COME ON! WE'LL AMBUSH NOMAZUMA THE SECOND HE CLEARS THOSE BUSHES!
QUIET NOW— HERE HE COMES!
CLUMP CLUMP
GERONIMO!
UNCA SCROOGE!
WELL WHO DID YOU THINK IT WAS— LITTLE HIAWATHA?
IT COULD HAVE BEEN!
YEAH! LOOK AT YOUR HAT!
MY HAT?
CONFOUND THE DING-DONG DICKENS! NOMAZUMA WAS BACK AMONG THOSE ROCKS!
MEANWHILE AGAIN!
DID I HEAR FOOTSTEPS IN HERE, OR AM I SUFFERING FROM NAP DEPRIVATION?

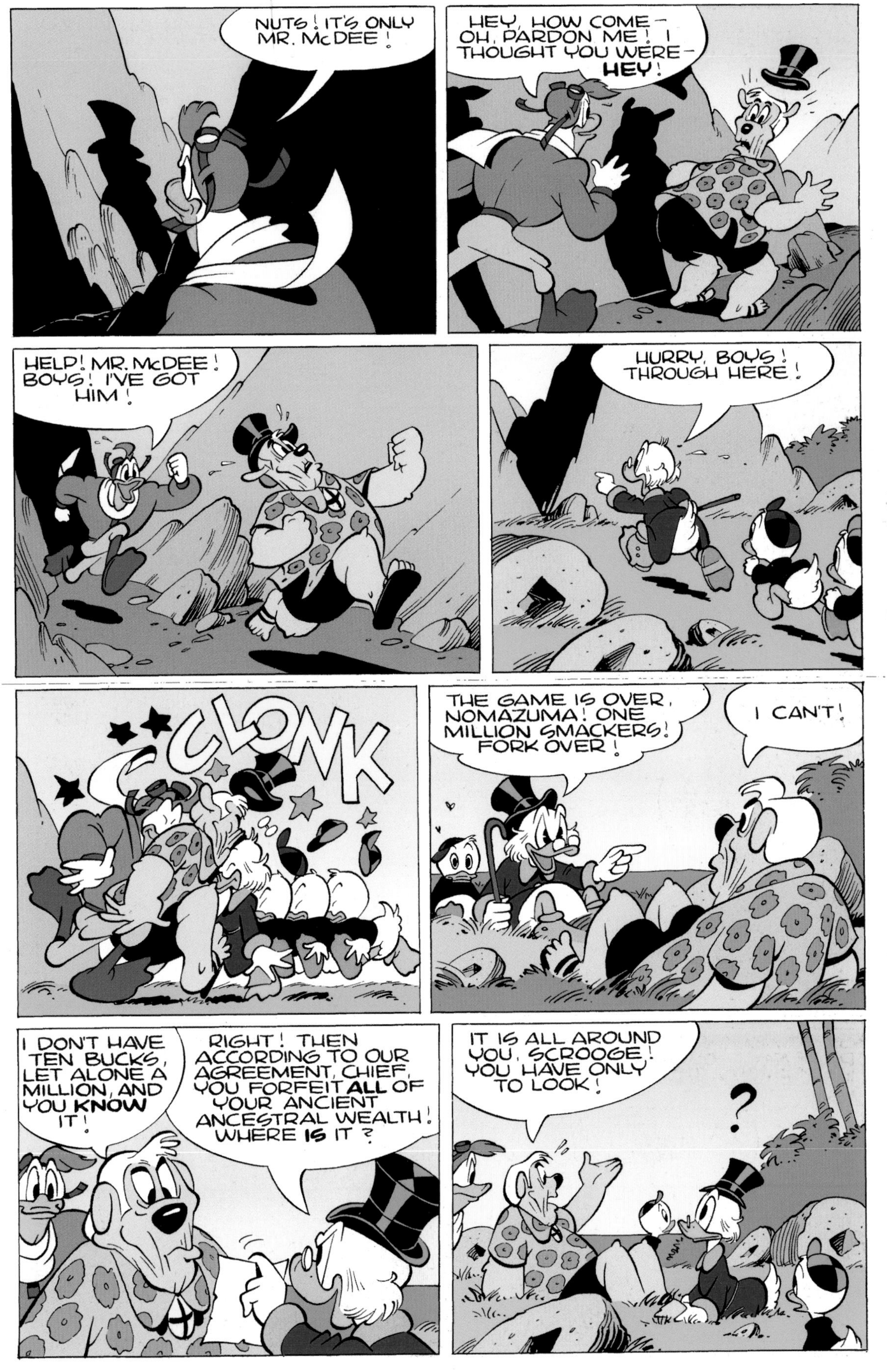

NUTS! IT'S ONLY MR. McDEE!
HEY, HOW COME— OH, PARDON ME! I THOUGHT YOU WERE— HEY!
HELP! MR. McDEE! BOYS! I'VE GOT HIM!
HURRY, BOYS! THROUGH HERE!
CLONK
THE GAME IS OVER, NOMAZUMA! ONE MILLION SMACKERS! FORK OVER!
I CAN'T!
I DON'T HAVE TEN BUCKS, LET ALONE A MILLION, AND YOU KNOW IT!
RIGHT! THEN ACCORDING TO OUR AGREEMENT, CHIEF, YOU FORFEIT ALL OF YOUR ANCIENT ANCESTRAL WEALTH! WHERE IS IT?
IT IS ALL AROUND YOU, SCROOGE! YOU HAVE ONLY TO LOOK!
?

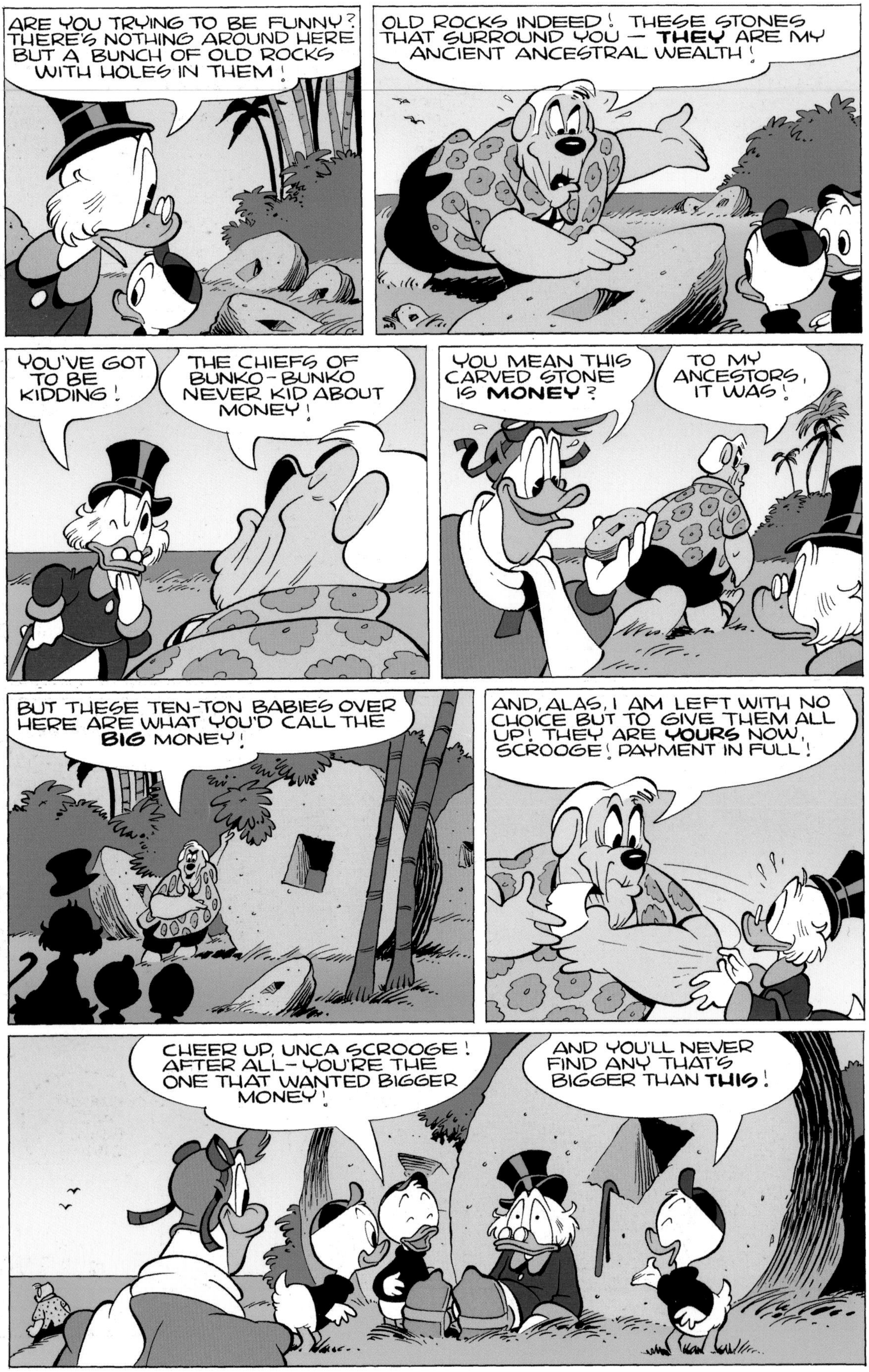

ARE YOU TRYING TO BE FUNNY? THERE'S NOTHING AROUND HERE BUT A BUNCH OF OLD ROCKS WITH HOLES IN THEM!
OLD ROCKS INDEED! THESE STONES THAT SURROUND YOU — THEY ARE MY ANCIENT ANCESTRAL WEALTH!
YOU'VE GOT TO BE KIDDING!
THE CHIEFS OF BUNKO-BUNKO NEVER KID ABOUT MONEY!
YOU MEAN THIS CARVED STONE IS MONEY?
TO MY ANCESTORS, IT WAS!
BUT THESE TEN-TON BABIES OVER HERE ARE WHAT YOU'D CALL THE BIG MONEY!
AND, ALAS, I AM LEFT WITH NO CHOICE BUT TO GIVE THEM ALL UP! THEY ARE YOURS NOW, SCROOGE! PAYMENT IN FULL!
CHEER UP, UNCA SCROOGE! AFTER ALL–YOU'RE THE ONE THAT WANTED BIGGER MONEY!
AND YOU'LL NEVER FIND ANY THAT'S BIGGER THAN THIS!

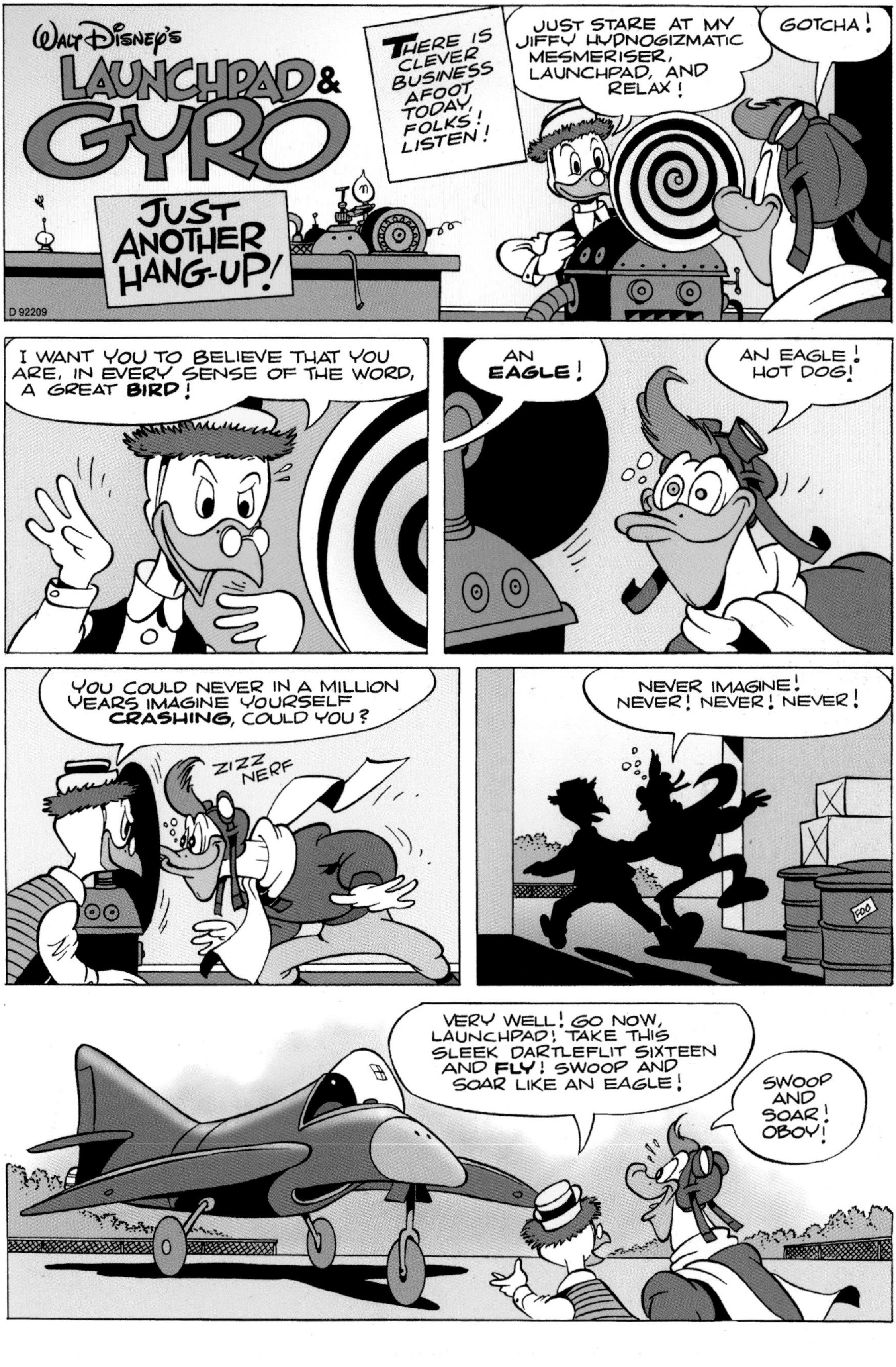

WALT DISNEY'S
LAUNCHPAD & GYRO
JUST ANOTHER HANG-UP!
D 92209
THERE IS CLEVER BUSINESS AFOOT TODAY, FOLKS! LISTEN!
JUST STARE AT MY JIFFY HYPNOGIZMATIC MESMERISER, LAUNCHPAD, AND RELAX!
GOTCHA!
I WANT YOU TO BELIEVE THAT YOU ARE, IN EVERY SENSE OF THE WORD, A GREAT BIRD!
AN EAGLE!
AN EAGLE! HOT DOG!
YOU COULD NEVER IN A MILLION YEARS IMAGINE YOURSELF CRASHING, COULD YOU?
ZIZZ NERF
NEVER IMAGINE! NEVER! NEVER! NEVER!
VERY WELL! GO NOW, LAUNCHPAD! TAKE THIS SLEEK DARTLEFLIT SIXTEEN AND FLY! SWOOP AND SOAR LIKE AN EAGLE!
SWOOP AND SOAR! OBOY!

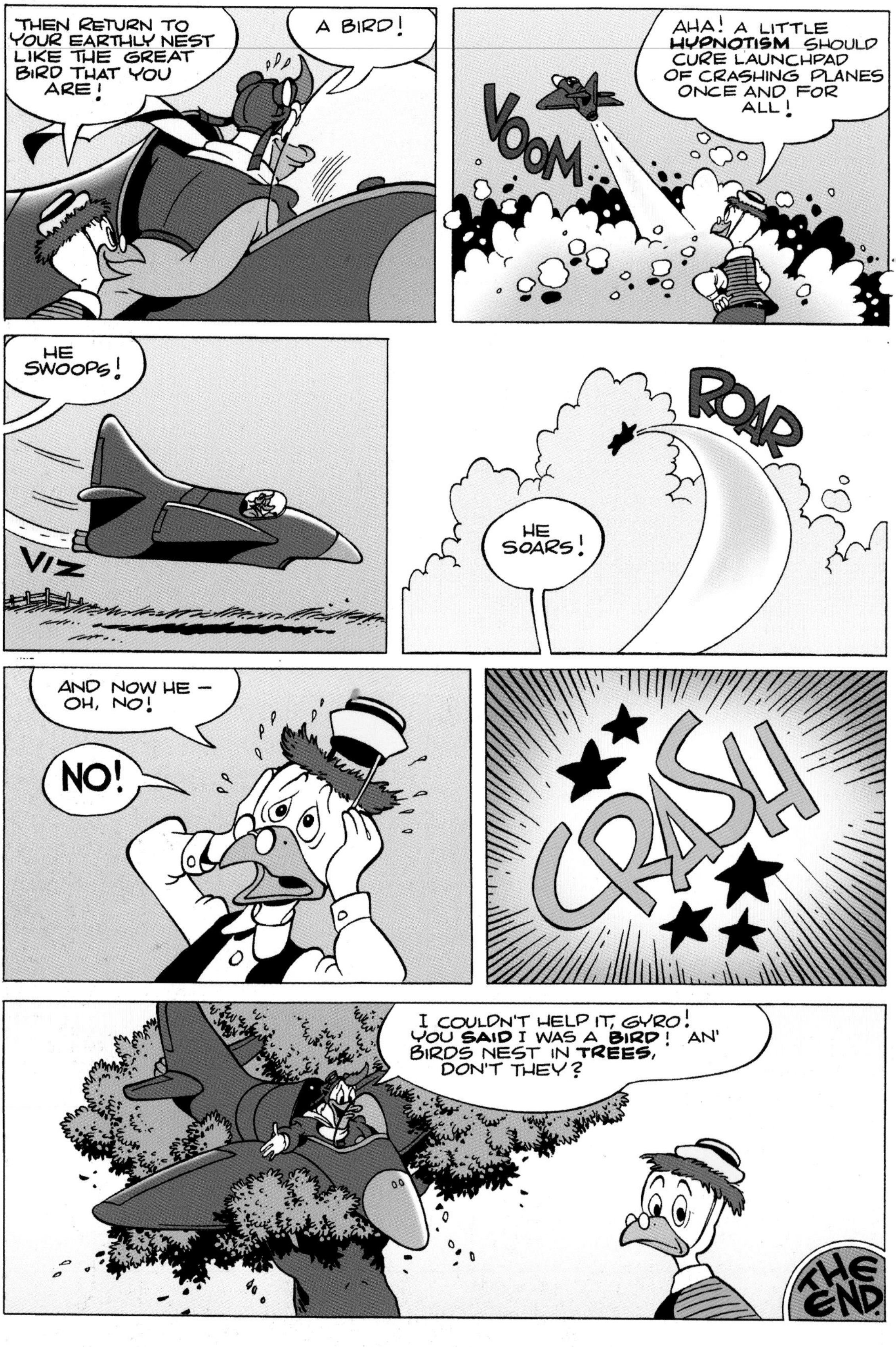
THEN RETURN TO YOUR EARTHLY NEST LIKE THE GREAT BIRD THAT YOU ARE!
A BIRD!
AHA! A LITTLE HYPNOTISM SHOULD CURE LAUNCHPAD OF CRASHING PLANES ONCE AND FOR ALL!
VOOM
HE SWOOPS!
VIZ
ROAR
HE SOARS!
AND NOW HE — OH, NO!
NO!
CRASH
I COULDN'T HELP IT, GYRO! YOU SAID I WAS A BIRD! AN' BIRDS NEST IN TREES, DON'T THEY?
THE END.

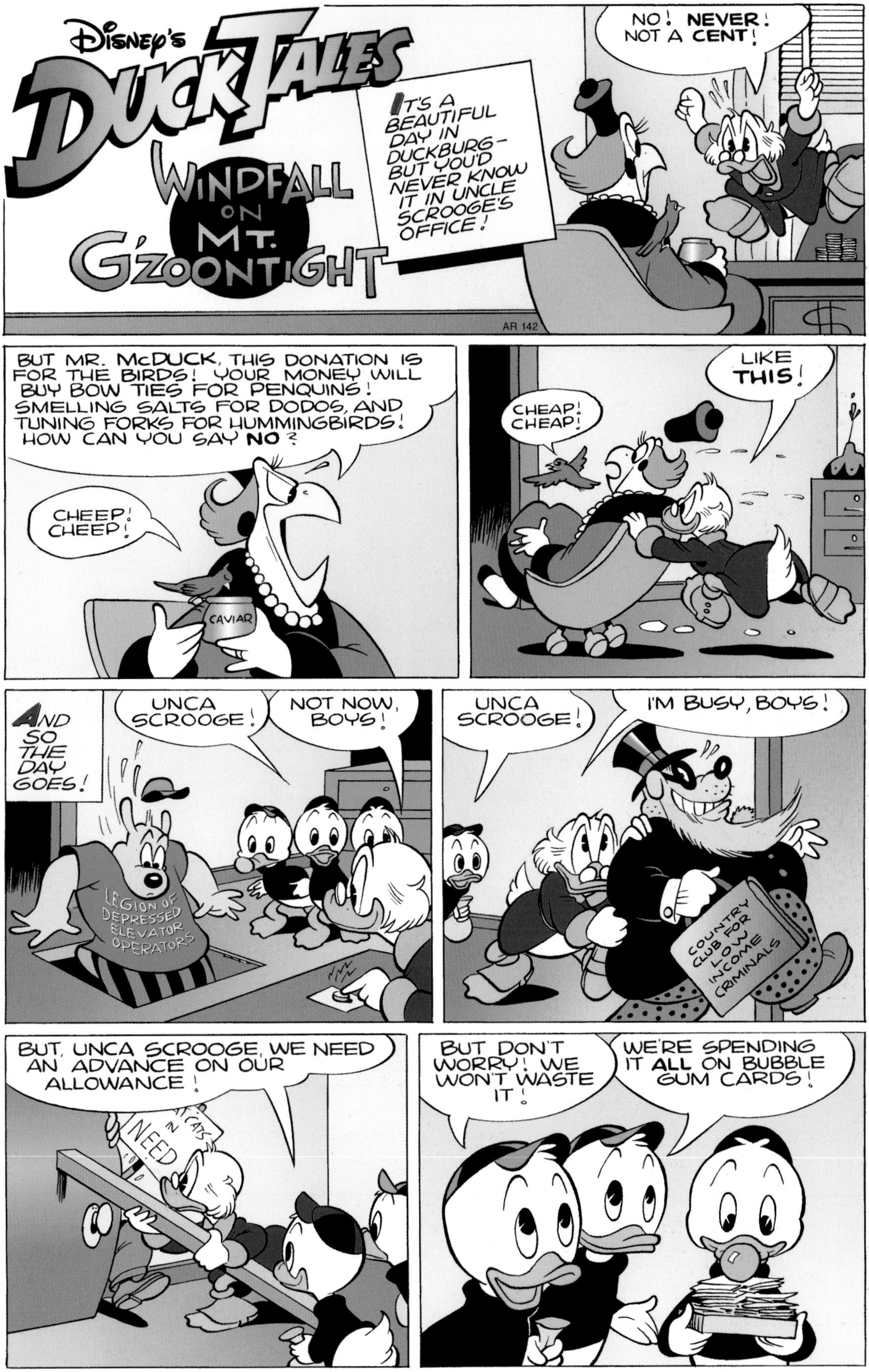
Disney's
DuckTales
Windfall on Mt. G'zoontight
It's a beautiful day in Duckburg— but you'd never know it in Uncle Scrooge's office!
No! Never! Not a cent!
AR 142
But Mr. McDuck, this donation is for the birds! Your money will buy bow ties for penguins! Smelling salts for dodos, and tuning forks for hummingbirds! How can you say no?
Cheep! Cheep!
Caviar
Cheap! Cheap!
Like this!
And so the day goes!
Unca Scrooge!
Not now, boys!
Legion of Depressed Elevator Operators
Unca Scrooge!
I'm busy, boys!
Country Club for Low Income Criminals
But, Unca Scrooge, we need an advance on our allowance!
Need
But don't worry! We won't waste it!
We're spending it all on bubble gum cards!

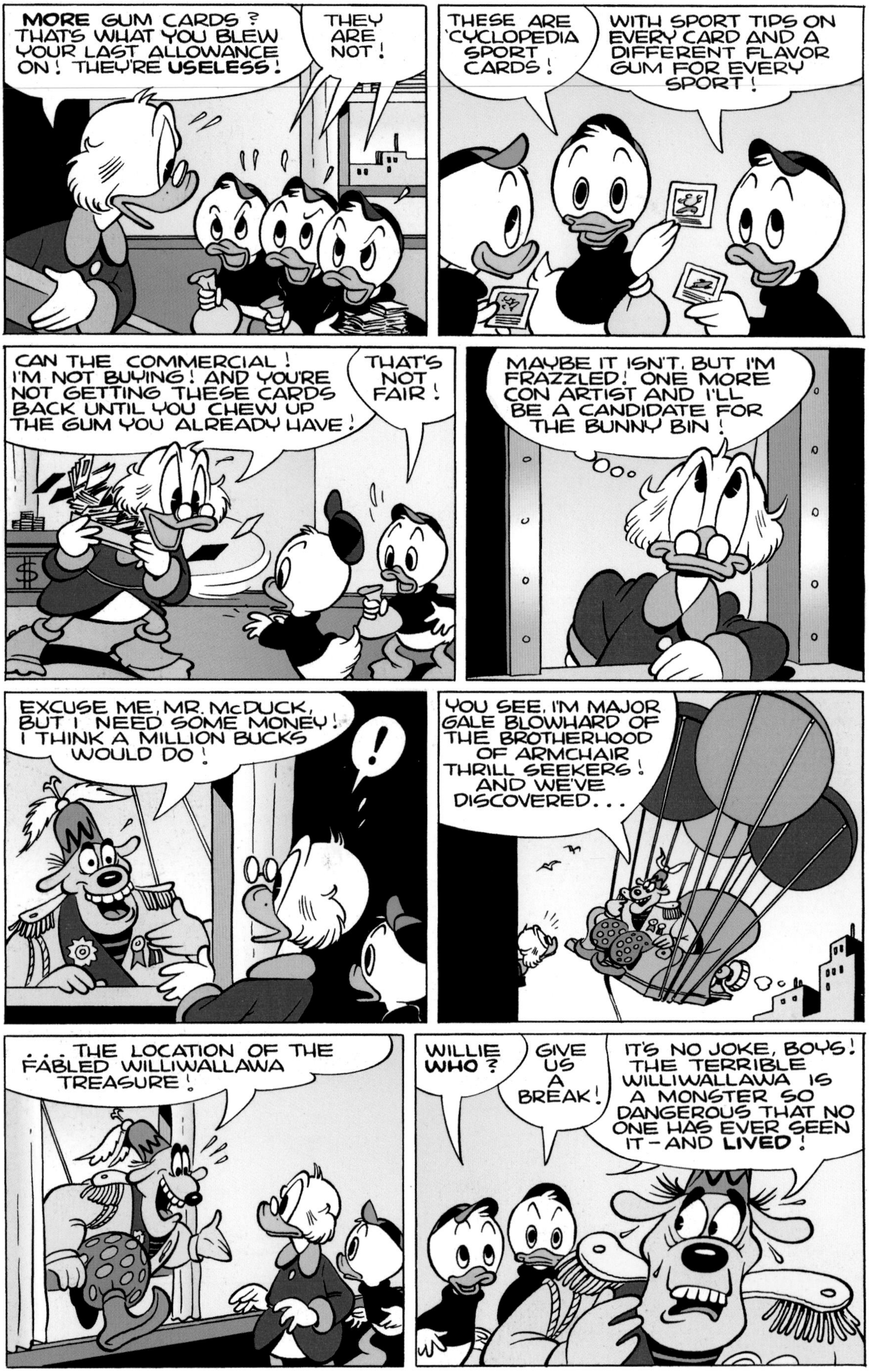
MORE GUM CARDS? THAT'S WHAT YOU BLEW YOUR LAST ALLOWANCE ON! THEY'RE USELESS!
THEY ARE NOT!
THESE ARE 'CYCLOPEDIA SPORT CARDS!
WITH SPORT TIPS ON EVERY CARD AND A DIFFERENT FLAVOR GUM FOR EVERY SPORT!
CAN THE COMMERCIAL! I'M NOT BUYING! AND YOU'RE NOT GETTING THESE CARDS BACK UNTIL YOU CHEW UP THE GUM YOU ALREADY HAVE!
THAT'S NOT FAIR!
MAYBE IT ISN'T, BUT I'M FRAZZLED! ONE MORE CON ARTIST AND I'LL BE A CANDIDATE FOR THE BUNNY BIN!
EXCUSE ME, MR. McDUCK, BUT I NEED SOME MONEY! I THINK A MILLION BUCKS WOULD DO!
!
YOU SEE, I'M MAJOR GALE BLOWHARD OF THE BROTHERHOOD OF ARMCHAIR THRILL SEEKERS! AND WE'VE DISCOVERED...
... THE LOCATION OF THE FABLED WILLIWALLAWA TREASURE!
WILLIE WHO?
GIVE US A BREAK!
IT'S NO JOKE, BOYS! THE TERRIBLE WILLIWALLAWA IS A MONSTER SO DANGEROUS THAT NO ONE HAS EVER SEEN IT—AND LIVED!

YES, I KNOW! IT CONTROLS THE WIND AND CAN WHIP UP A GUST SO FIERCE IT'LL TURN A MAN TO **STONE**! QUITE A FAIRY TALE!

BUT IT'S TRUE! WE'VE TRACED THE WILLIWALLIWA TO MT. G'ZOONTIGHT— THE STORMIEST SPOT ON EARTH!

FIDDLESTICKS AND PITCHFORKS! I DON'T BELIEVE A WORD OF IT!

STILL, THOUGH, I'D RATHER GO TREASURE HUNTING FOR A PIG IN A POKE THAN STAY HERE AND DEAL WITH THESE MONEY MOOCHERS!

EXCELLENT! NOW, WE'LL NEED ONE MILLION DOLLARS TO FORM A COMMITTEE— TO SELECT A TASK FORCE— AND PLAN THE EXPIDITION! IF WE HURRY, IT'LL ONLY TAKE **THIRTEEN** YEARS!

WE'RE GOING **TODAY**, MAJOR!

T-**TODAY**? OURSELVES? B-BUT THAT COULD BE **DANGEROUS**!

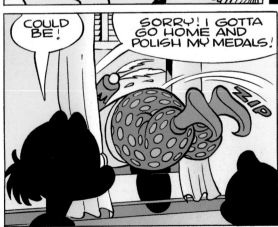

COULD BE!

SORRY! I GOTTA GO HOME AND POLISH MY MEDALS!

ZIP

TSK! TSK! HE SHOULD'VE BENT HIS KNEES LIKE HARRY LEEPUR ON CARD NUMBER 59!

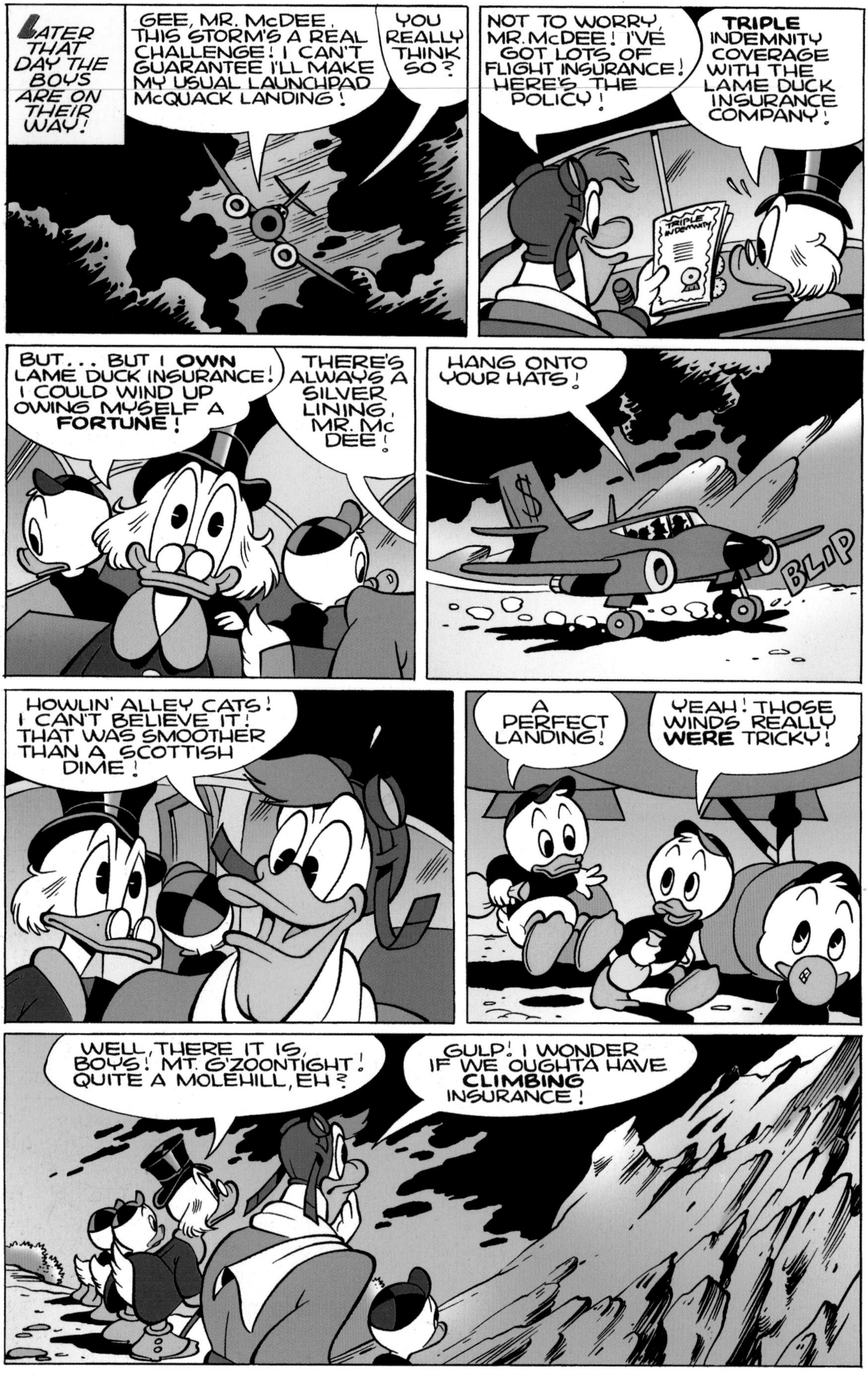
LATER THAT DAY THE BOYS ARE ON THEIR WAY!
GEE, MR. McDEE, THIS STORM'S A REAL CHALLENGE! I CAN'T GUARANTEE I'LL MAKE MY USUAL LAUNCHPAD McQUACK LANDING!
YOU REALLY THINK SO?
NOT TO WORRY, MR. McDEE! I'VE GOT LOTS OF FLIGHT INSURANCE! HERE'S THE POLICY!
TRIPLE INDEMNITY COVERAGE WITH THE LAME DUCK INSURANCE COMPANY!
TRIPLE INDEMNITY
BUT... BUT I OWN LAME DUCK INSURANCE! I COULD WIND UP OWING MYSELF A FORTUNE!
THERE'S ALWAYS A SILVER LINING, MR. Mc DEE!
HANG ONTO YOUR HATS!
BLIP
HOWLIN' ALLEY CATS! I CAN'T BELIEVE IT! THAT WAS SMOOTHER THAN A SCOTTISH DIME!
A PERFECT LANDING!
YEAH! THOSE WINDS REALLY WERE TRICKY!
WELL, THERE IT IS, BOYS! MT. G'ZOONTIGHT! QUITE A MOLEHILL, EH?
GULP! I WONDER IF WE OUGHTA HAVE CLIMBING INSURANCE!

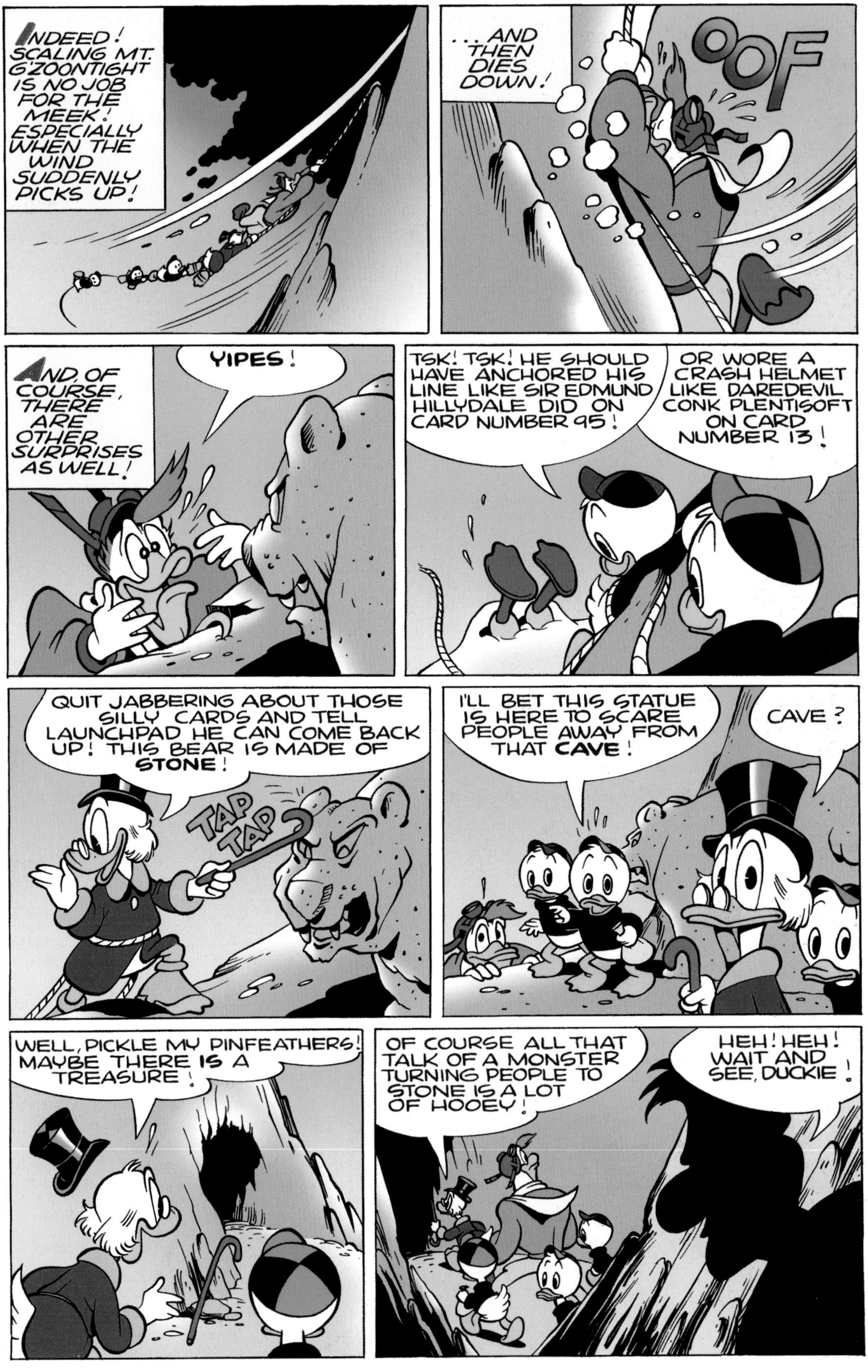
INDEED! SCALING MT. G'ZOONTIGHT IS NO JOB FOR THE MEEK! ESPECIALLY WHEN THE WIND SUDDENLY PICKS UP!
...AND THEN DIES DOWN!
OOF
AND, OF COURSE, THERE ARE OTHER SURPRISES AS WELL!
YIPES!
TSK! TSK! HE SHOULD HAVE ANCHORED HIS LINE LIKE SIR EDMUND HILLYDALE DID ON CARD NUMBER 95!
OR WORE A CRASH HELMET LIKE DAREDEVIL CONK PLENTISOFT ON CARD NUMBER 13!
QUIT JABBERING ABOUT THOSE SILLY CARDS AND TELL LAUNCHPAD HE CAN COME BACK UP! THIS BEAR IS MADE OF STONE!
TAP TAP
I'LL BET THIS STATUE IS HERE TO SCARE PEOPLE AWAY FROM THAT CAVE!
CAVE?
WELL, PICKLE MY PINFEATHERS! MAYBE THERE IS A TREASURE!
OF COURSE ALL THAT TALK OF A MONSTER TURNING PEOPLE TO STONE IS A LOT OF HOOEY!
HEH! HEH! WAIT AND SEE, DUCKIE!

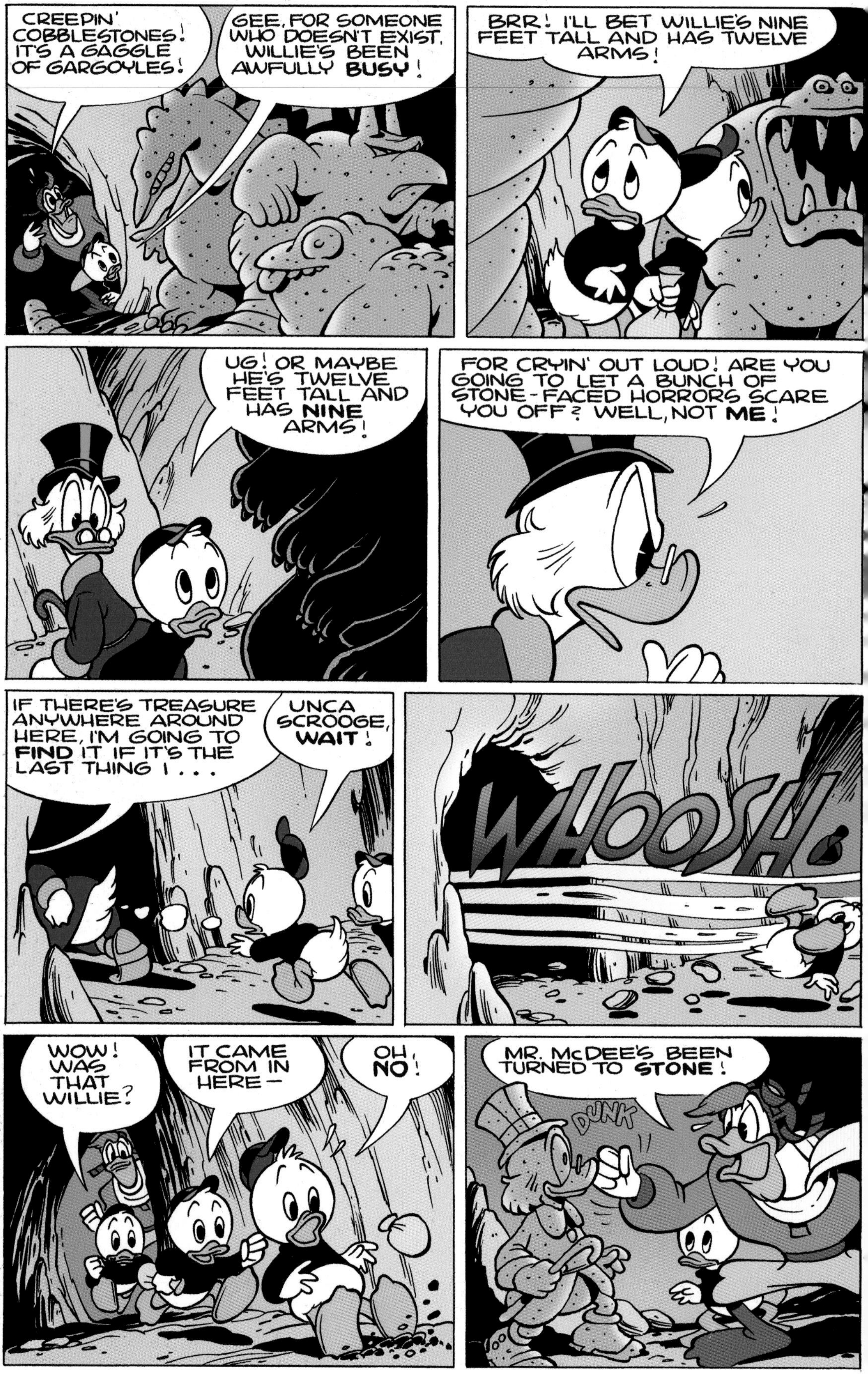
CREEPIN' COBBLESTONES! IT'S A GAGGLE OF GARGOYLES!
GEE, FOR SOMEONE WHO DOESN'T EXIST, WILLIE'S BEEN AWFULLY BUSY!
BRR! I'LL BET WILLIE'S NINE FEET TALL AND HAS TWELVE ARMS!
UG! OR MAYBE HE'S TWELVE FEET TALL AND HAS NINE ARMS!
FOR CRYIN' OUT LOUD! ARE YOU GOING TO LET A BUNCH OF STONE-FACED HORRORS SCARE YOU OFF? WELL, NOT ME!
IF THERE'S TREASURE ANYWHERE AROUND HERE, I'M GOING TO FIND IT IF IT'S THE LAST THING I . . .
UNCA SCROOGE, WAIT!
WHOOSH!
WOW! WAS THAT WILLIE?
IT CAME FROM IN HERE—
OH NO!
MR. McDEE'S BEEN TURNED TO STONE!
DUNK

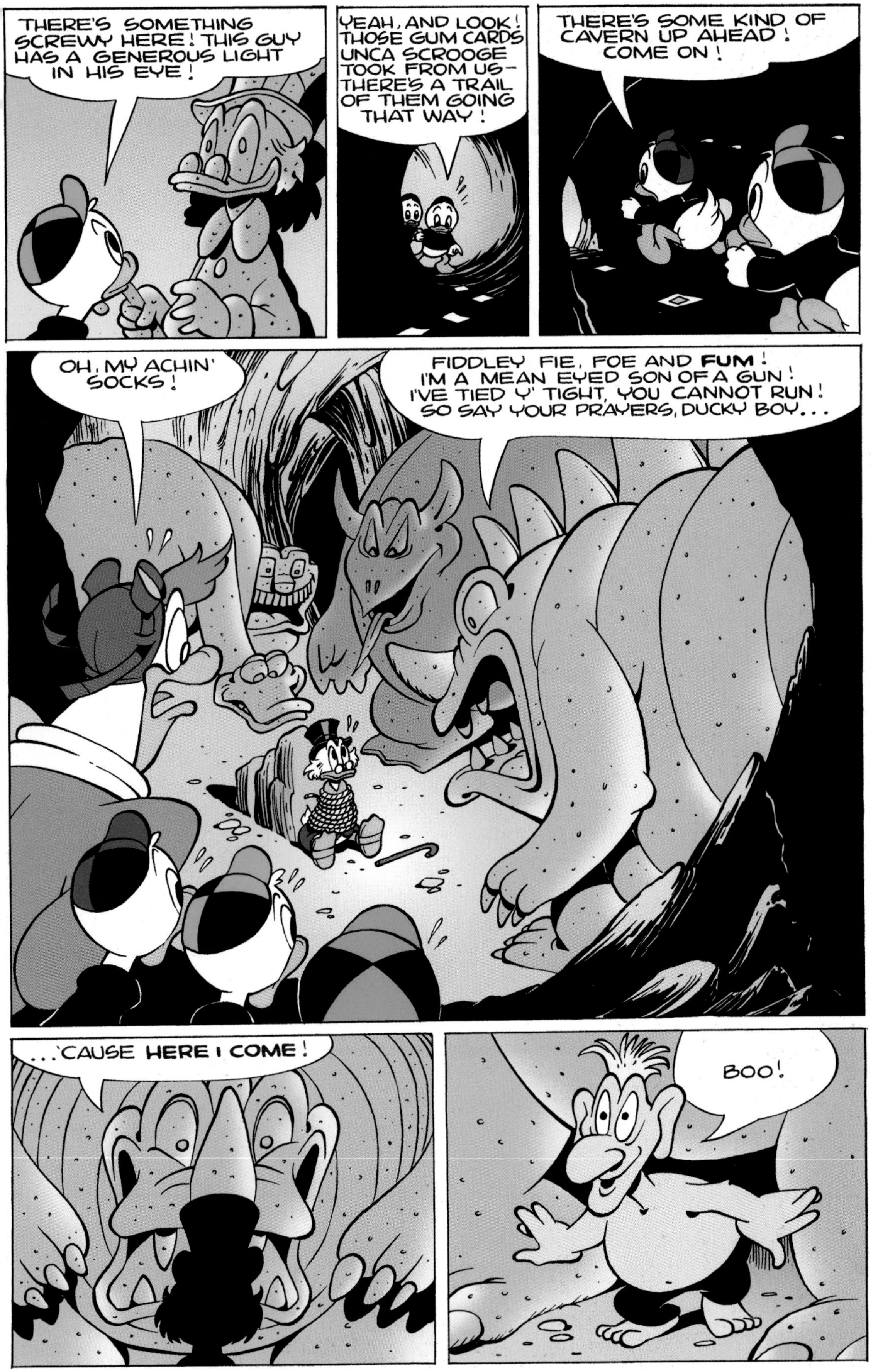
THERE'S SOMETHING SCREWY HERE! THIS GUY HAS A GENEROUS LIGHT IN HIS EYE!
YEAH, AND LOOK! THOSE GUM CARDS UNCA SCROOGE TOOK FROM US– THERE'S A TRAIL OF THEM GOING THAT WAY!
THERE'S SOME KIND OF CAVERN UP AHEAD! COME ON!
OH, MY ACHIN' SOCKS!
FIDDLEY FIE, FOE AND FUM! I'M A MEAN EYED SON OF A GUN! I'VE TIED Y' TIGHT, YOU CANNOT RUN! SO SAY YOUR PRAYERS, DUCKY BOY...
...'CAUSE HERE I COME!
BOO!

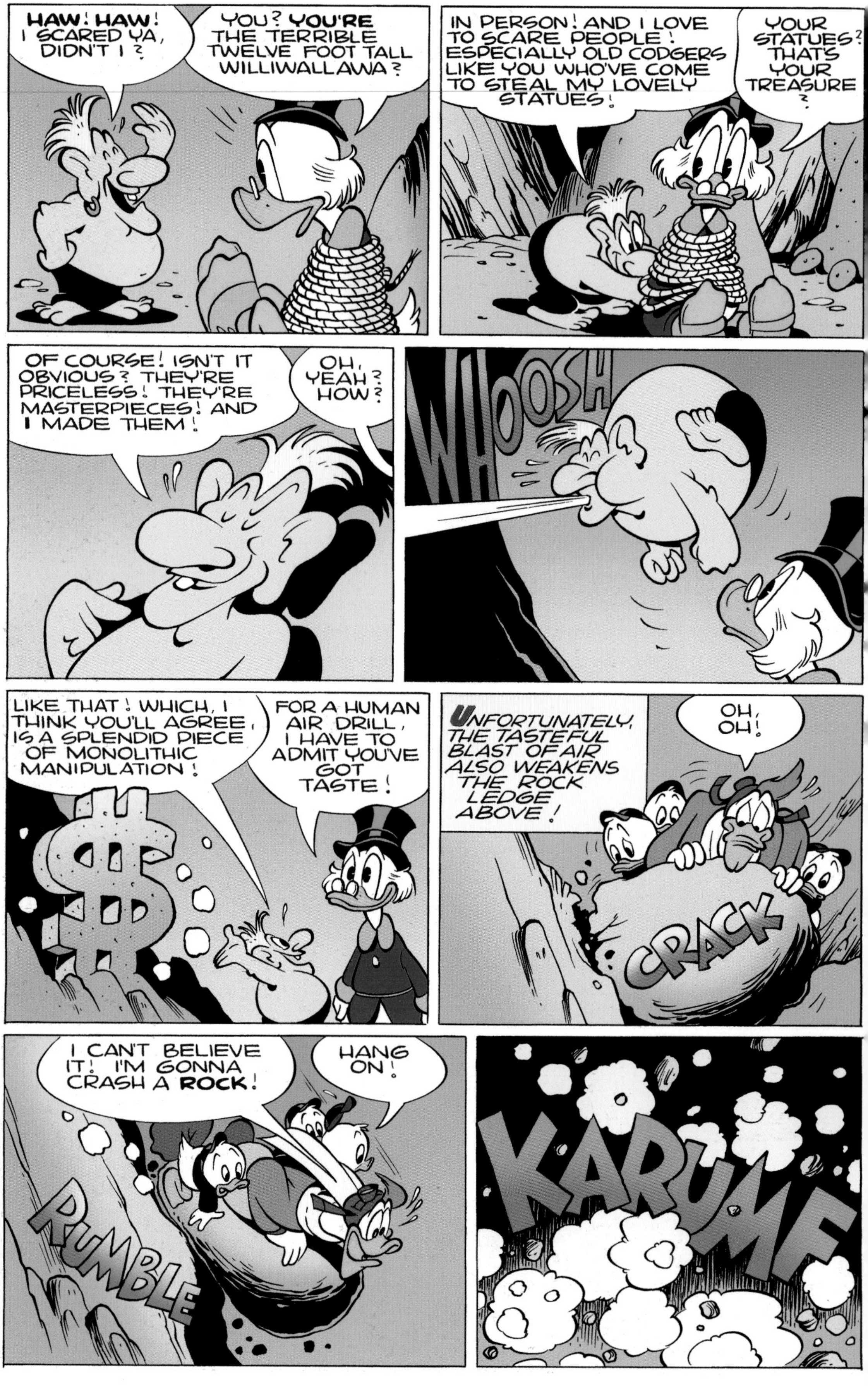
HAW! HAW! I SCARED YA, DIDN'T I?
YOU? YOU'RE THE TERRIBLE TWELVE FOOT TALL WILLIWALLAWA?
IN PERSON! AND I LOVE TO SCARE PEOPLE! ESPECIALLY OLD CODGERS LIKE YOU WHO'VE COME TO STEAL MY LOVELY STATUES!
YOUR STATUES? THAT'S YOUR TREASURE?
OF COURSE! ISN'T IT OBVIOUS? THEY'RE PRICELESS! THEY'RE MASTERPIECES! AND I MADE THEM!
OH, YEAH? HOW?
WHOOSH
LIKE THAT! WHICH, I THINK YOU'LL AGREE, IS A SPLENDID PIECE OF MONOLITHIC MANIPULATION!
FOR A HUMAN AIR DRILL, I HAVE TO ADMIT YOU'VE GOT TASTE!
UNFORTUNATELY, THE TASTEFUL BLAST OF AIR ALSO WEAKENS THE ROCK LEDGE ABOVE!
OH, OH!
CRACK
I CAN'T BELIEVE IT! I'M GONNA CRASH A ROCK!
HANG ON!
RUMBLE
KARUMF

SO!

THIEVES! THIEVES! AND **MORE** THIEVES! WELL, DUCKY BOYS, I'M GONNA HUFF— AND I'M GONNA PUFF— AND I'M GONNA BLOW YOU GUYS ALL THE WAY TO DING DONG **BOMBAY**!

HEY! OUR BUBBLE GUM!

HoOOOF

FOOP

SNORFT

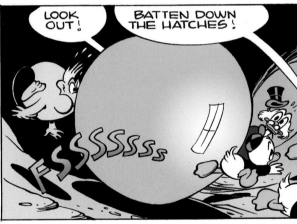

LOOK OUT!

BATTEN DOWN THE HATCHES!

FSSSSSSS

PLAM

BOY! THAT WAS BETTER THAN COSMO SWELLPOP'S CHAMPIONSHIP BUBBLE ON CARD 38!

HA! I EVEN SCARED MYSELF! I HAVEN'T HAD THIS MUCH FUN IN CENTURIES!

REALLY?

WELL, IF **THAT'S** YOUR IDEA OF FUN, MR. WILLIWALLAWA, THEN BOY, HAVE WE GOT A **DEAL** FOR **YOU**!

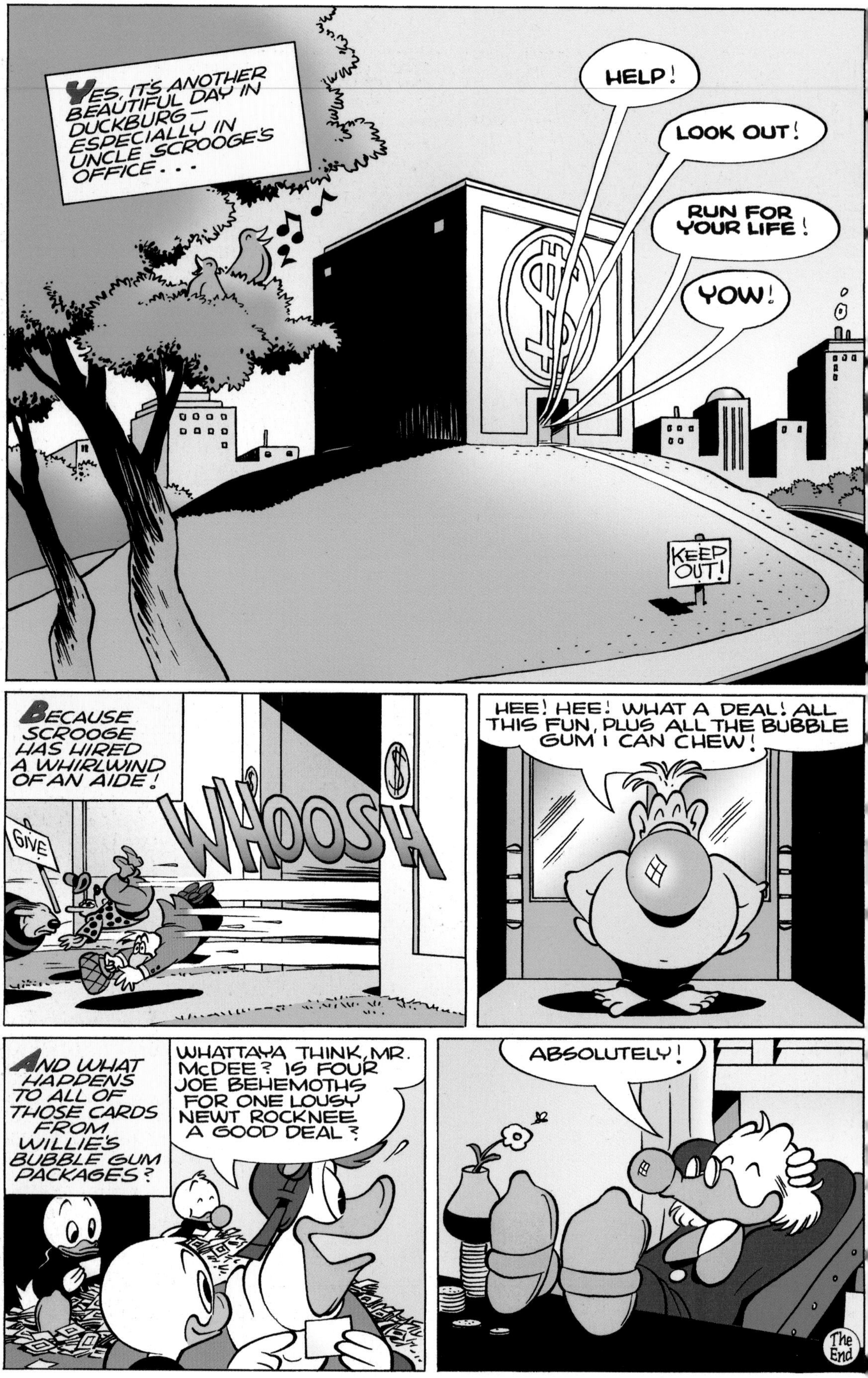
YES, IT'S ANOTHER BEAUTIFUL DAY IN DUCKBURG— ESPECIALLY IN UNCLE SCROOGE'S OFFICE . . .
HELP!
LOOK OUT!
RUN FOR YOUR LIFE!
YOW!
KEEP OUT!
BECAUSE SCROOGE HAS HIRED A WHIRLWIND OF AN AIDE!
GIVE
WHOOSH
HEE! HEE! WHAT A DEAL! ALL THIS FUN, PLUS ALL THE BUBBLE GUM I CAN CHEW!
AND WHAT HAPPENS TO ALL OF THOSE CARDS FROM WILLIE'S BUBBLE GUM PACKAGES?
WHATTAYA THINK, MR. McDEE? IS FOUR JOE BEHEMOTHS FOR ONE LOUSY NEWT ROCKNEE A GOOD DEAL?
ABSOLUTELY!
The End

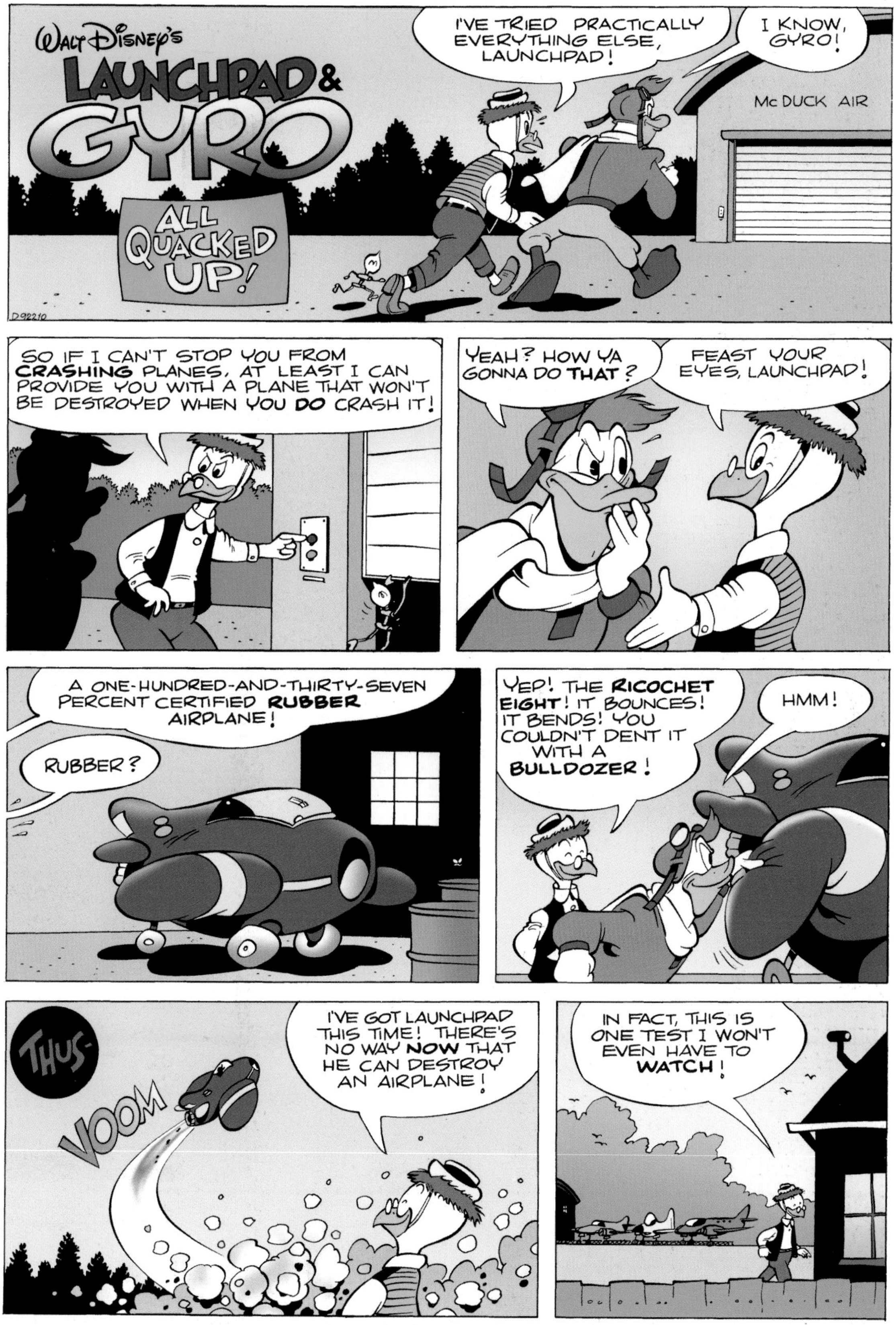

WALT DISNEY'S
LAUNCHPAD & GYRO
ALL QUACKED UP!
I'VE TRIED PRACTICALLY EVERYTHING ELSE, LAUNCHPAD!
I KNOW, GYRO!
McDUCK AIR
D92210
SO IF I CAN'T STOP YOU FROM CRASHING PLANES, AT LEAST I CAN PROVIDE YOU WITH A PLANE THAT WON'T BE DESTROYED WHEN YOU DO CRASH IT!
YEAH? HOW YA GONNA DO THAT?
FEAST YOUR EYES, LAUNCHPAD!
A ONE-HUNDRED-AND-THIRTY-SEVEN PERCENT CERTIFIED RUBBER AIRPLANE!
RUBBER?
YEP! THE RICOCHET EIGHT! IT BOUNCES! IT BENDS! YOU COULDN'T DENT IT WITH A BULLDOZER!
HMM!
THUS-
VOOM
I'VE GOT LAUNCHPAD THIS TIME! THERE'S NO WAY NOW THAT HE CAN DESTROY AN AIRPLANE!
IN FACT, THIS IS ONE TEST I WON'T EVEN HAVE TO WATCH!

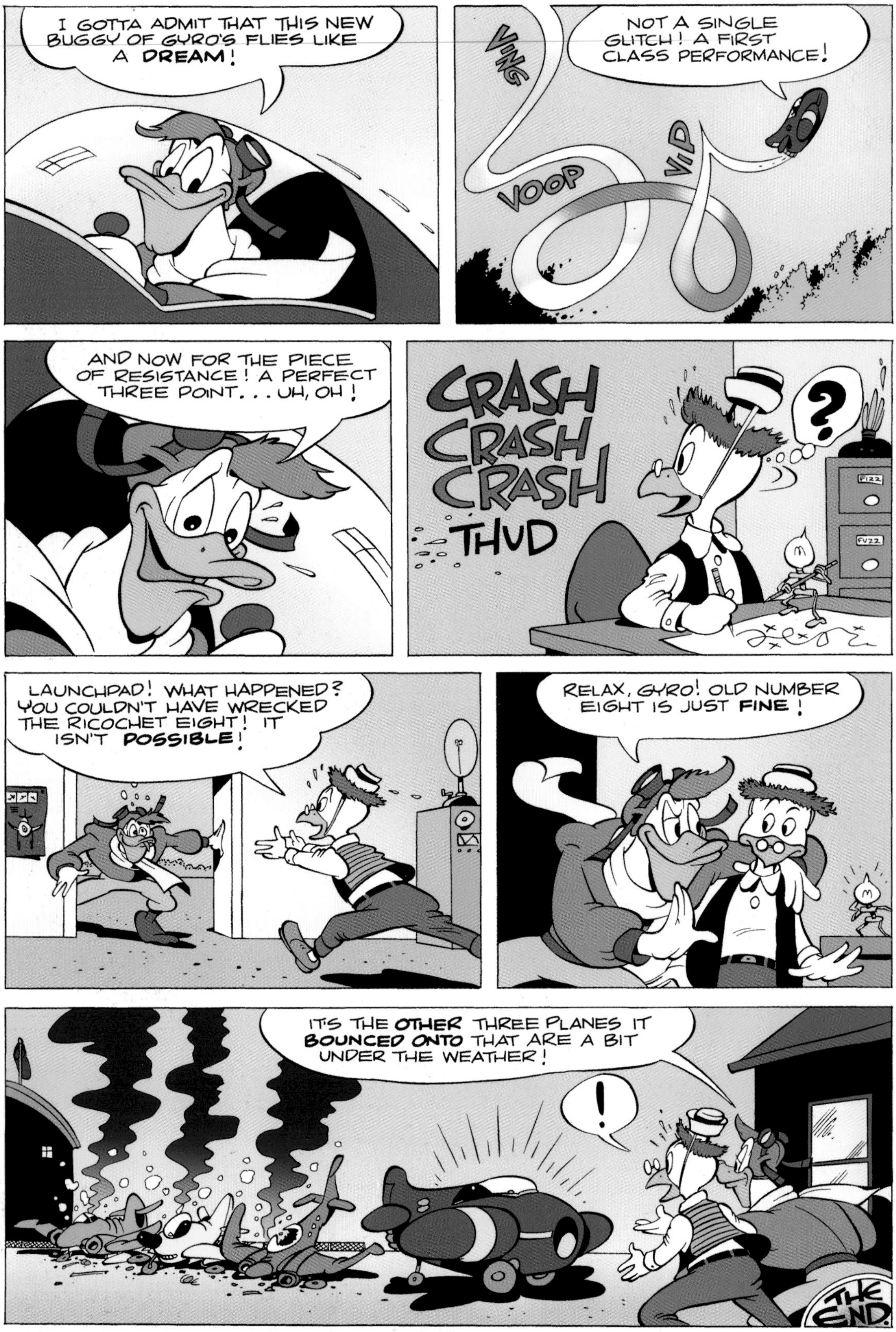
I GOTTA ADMIT THAT THIS NEW BUGGY OF GYRO'S FLIES LIKE A **DREAM**!
VING
NOT A SINGLE GLITCH! A FIRST CLASS PERFORMANCE!
VOOP
VIP
AND NOW FOR THE PIECE OF RESISTANCE! A PERFECT THREE POINT... UH, OH!
CRASH
CRASH
CRASH
THUD
?
FIZZ
FUZZ
LAUNCHPAD! WHAT HAPPENED? YOU COULDN'T HAVE WRECKED THE RICOCHET EIGHT! IT ISN'T **POSSIBLE**!
RELAX, GYRO! OLD NUMBER EIGHT IS JUST **FINE**!
IT'S THE **OTHER** THREE PLANES IT **BOUNCED ONTO** THAT ARE A BIT UNDER THE WEATHER!
!
THE END.

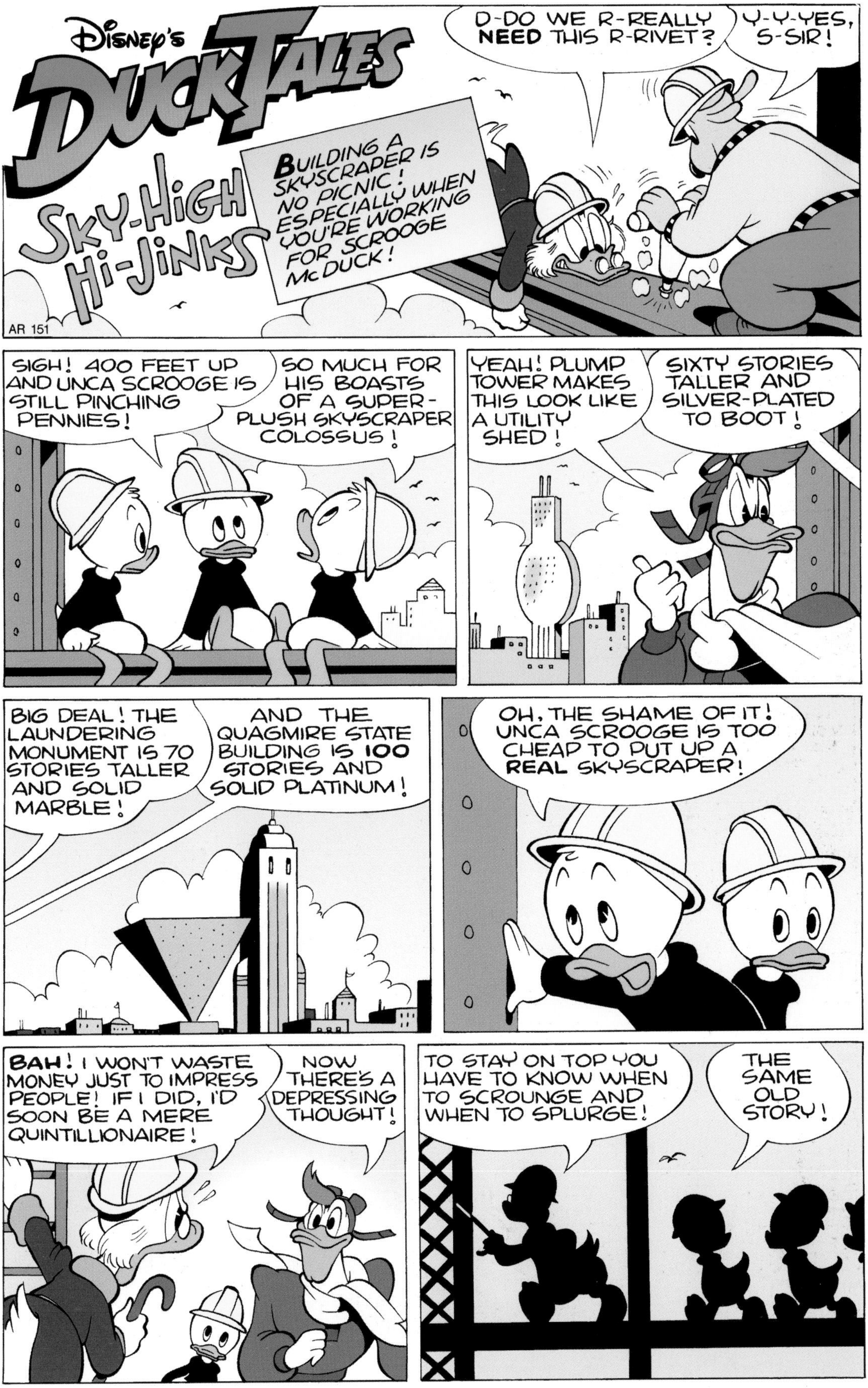
Disney's
DuckTales
Sky-High Hi-Jinks
BUILDING A SKYSCRAPER IS NO PICNIC! ESPECIALLY WHEN YOU'RE WORKING FOR SCROOGE McDUCK!
D-DO WE R-REALLY NEED THIS R-RIVET?
Y-Y-YES, S-SIR!
AR 151
SIGH! 400 FEET UP AND UNCA SCROOGE IS STILL PINCHING PENNIES!
SO MUCH FOR HIS BOASTS OF A SUPER-PLUSH SKYSCRAPER COLOSSUS!
YEAH! PLUMP TOWER MAKES THIS LOOK LIKE A UTILITY SHED!
SIXTY STORIES TALLER AND SILVER-PLATED TO BOOT!
BIG DEAL! THE LAUNDERING MONUMENT IS 70 STORIES TALLER AND SOLID MARBLE!
AND THE QUAGMIRE STATE BUILDING IS 100 STORIES AND SOLID PLATINUM!
OH, THE SHAME OF IT! UNCA SCROOGE IS TOO CHEAP TO PUT UP A REAL SKYSCRAPER!
BAH! I WON'T WASTE MONEY JUST TO IMPRESS PEOPLE! IF I DID, I'D SOON BE A MERE QUINTILLIONAIRE!
NOW THERE'S A DEPRESSING THOUGHT!
TO STAY ON TOP YOU HAVE TO KNOW WHEN TO SCROUNGE AND WHEN TO SPLURGE!
THE SAME OLD STORY!

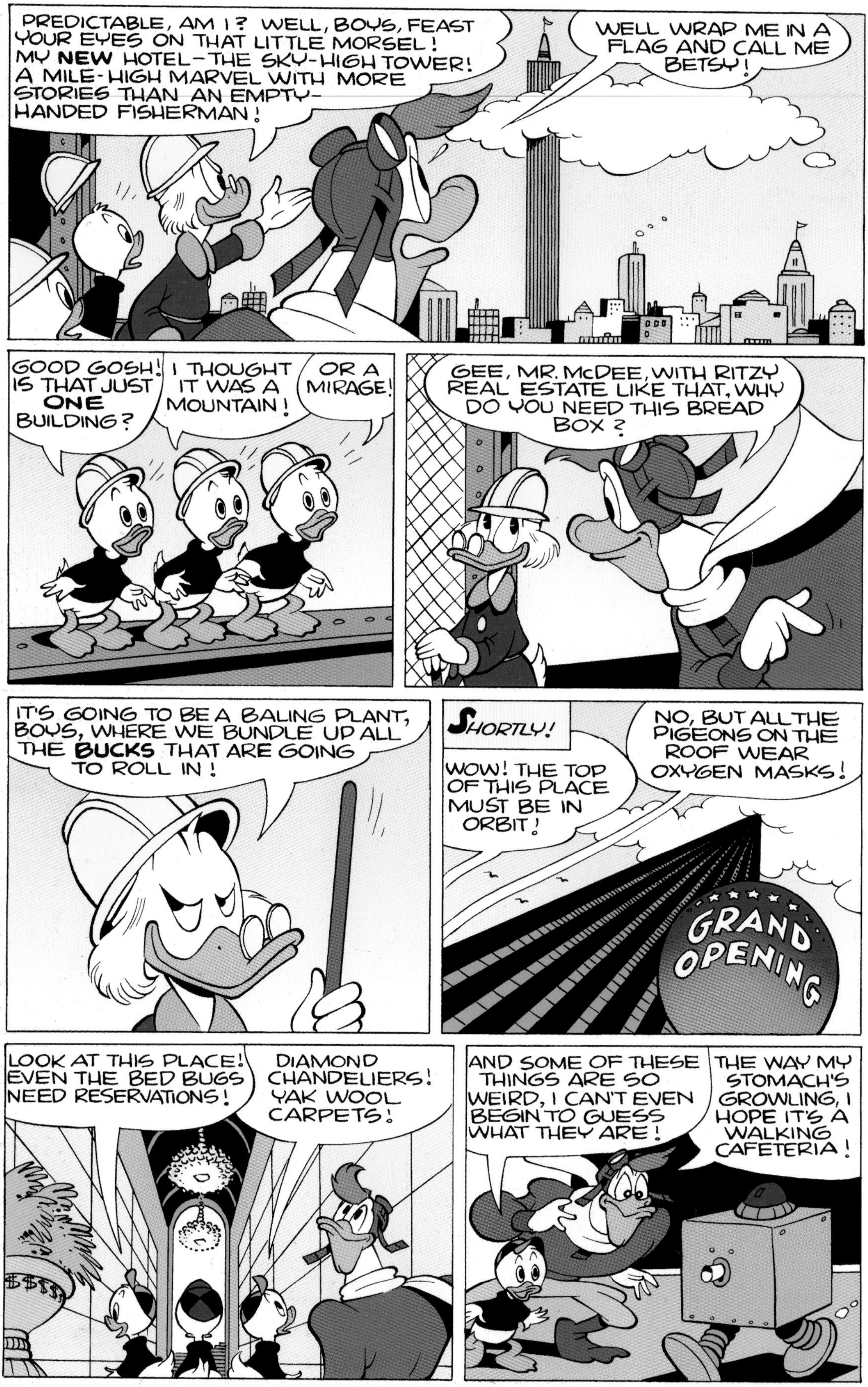

PREDICTABLE, AM I? WELL, BOYS, FEAST YOUR EYES ON THAT LITTLE MORSEL! MY **NEW** HOTEL—THE SKY-HIGH TOWER! A MILE-HIGH MARVEL WITH MORE STORIES THAN AN EMPTY-HANDED FISHERMAN!
WELL WRAP ME IN A FLAG AND CALL ME BETSY!
GOOD GOSH! IS THAT JUST **ONE** BUILDING?
I THOUGHT IT WAS A MOUNTAIN!
OR A MIRAGE!
GEE, MR. McDEE, WITH RITZY REAL ESTATE LIKE THAT, WHY DO YOU NEED THIS BREAD BOX?
IT'S GOING TO BE A BALING PLANT, BOYS, WHERE WE BUNDLE UP ALL THE **BUCKS** THAT ARE GOING TO ROLL IN!
SHORTLY!
WOW! THE TOP OF THIS PLACE MUST BE IN ORBIT!
NO, BUT ALL THE PIGEONS ON THE ROOF WEAR OXYGEN MASKS!
GRAND OPENING
LOOK AT THIS PLACE! EVEN THE BED BUGS NEED RESERVATIONS!
DIAMOND CHANDELIERS! YAK WOOL CARPETS!
AND SOME OF THESE THINGS ARE SO WEIRD, I CAN'T EVEN BEGIN TO GUESS WHAT THEY ARE!
THE WAY MY STOMACH'S GROWLING, I HOPE IT'S A WALKING CAFETERIA!

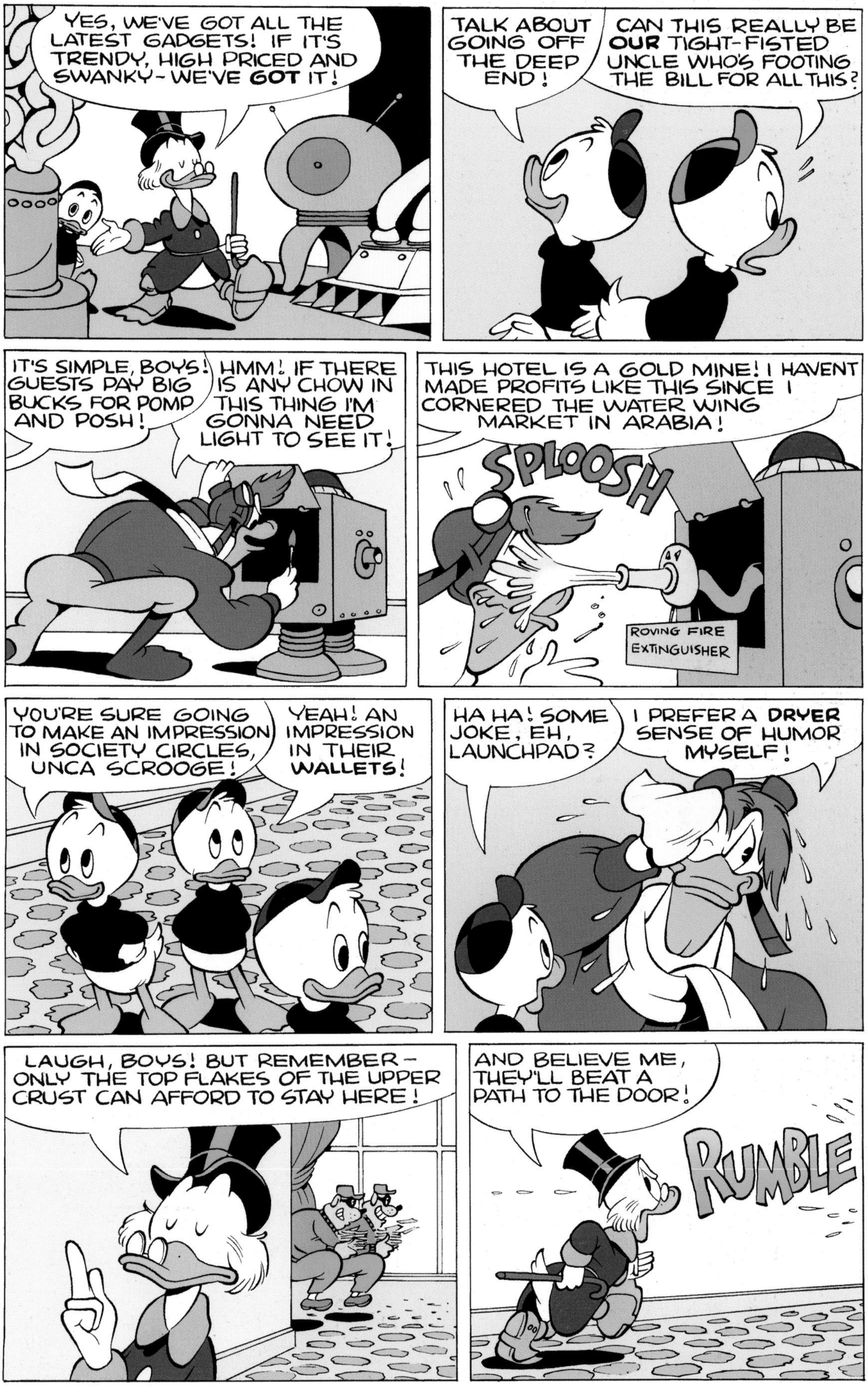
YES, WE'VE GOT ALL THE LATEST GADGETS! IF IT'S TRENDY, HIGH PRICED AND SWANKY- WE'VE **GOT** IT!
TALK ABOUT GOING OFF THE DEEP END!
CAN THIS REALLY BE **OUR** TIGHT-FISTED UNCLE WHO'S FOOTING THE BILL FOR ALL THIS?
IT'S SIMPLE, BOYS! GUESTS PAY BIG BUCKS FOR POMP AND POSH!
HMM! IF THERE IS ANY CHOW IN THIS THING I'M GONNA NEED LIGHT TO SEE IT!
THIS HOTEL IS A GOLD MINE! I HAVENT MADE PROFITS LIKE THIS SINCE I CORNERED THE WATER WING MARKET IN ARABIA!
SPLOOSH
ROVING FIRE EXTINGUISHER
YOU'RE SURE GOING TO MAKE AN IMPRESSION IN SOCIETY CIRCLES, UNCA SCROOGE!
YEAH! AN IMPRESSION IN THEIR **WALLETS**!
HA HA! SOME JOKE, EH, LAUNCHPAD?
I PREFER A **DRYER** SENSE OF HUMOR MYSELF!
LAUGH, BOYS! BUT REMEMBER- ONLY THE TOP FLAKES OF THE UPPER CRUST CAN AFFORD TO STAY HERE!
AND BELIEVE ME, THEY'LL BEAT A PATH TO THE DOOR!
RUMBLE

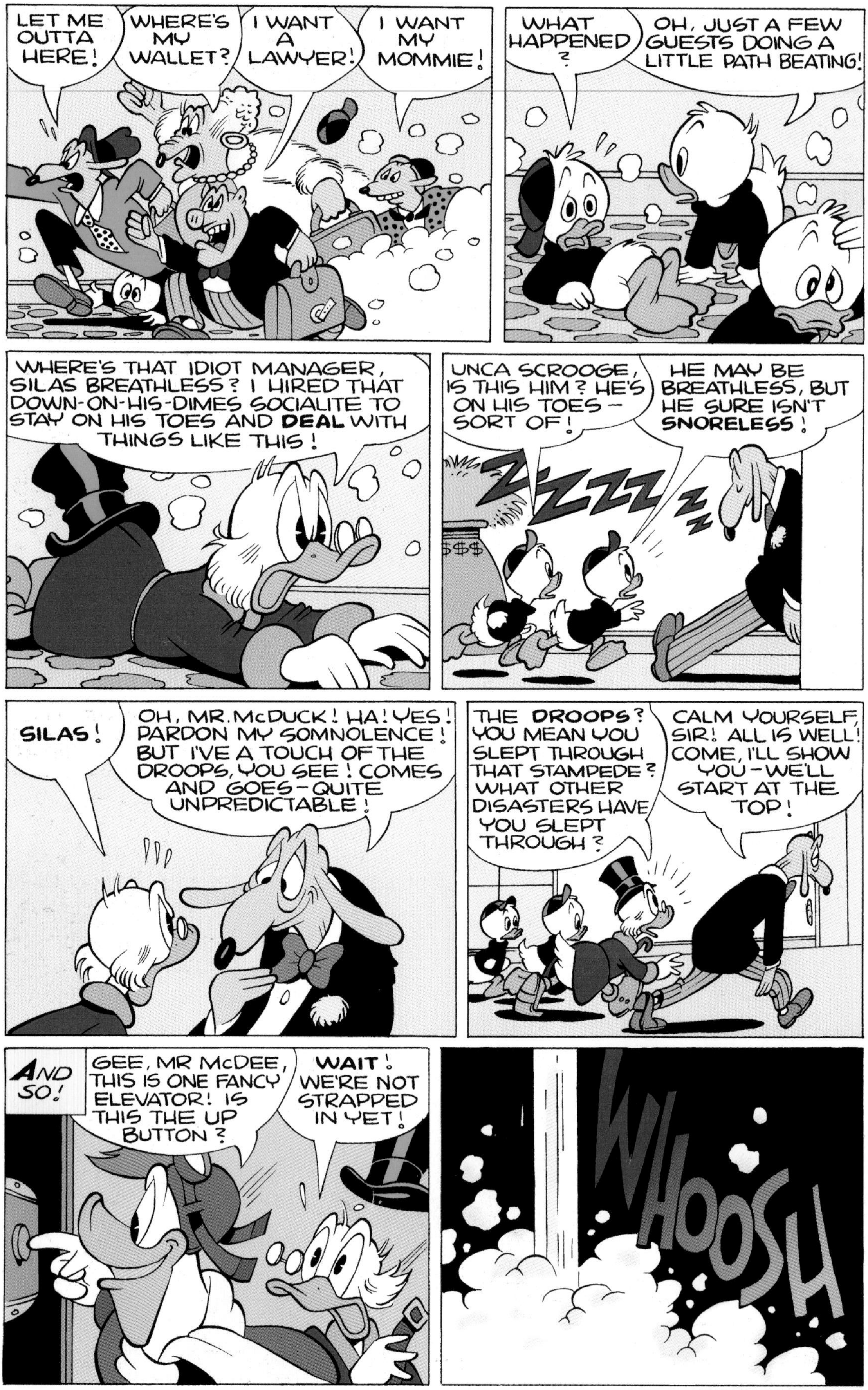
LET ME OUTTA HERE!
WHERE'S MY WALLET?
I WANT A LAWYER!
I WANT MY MOMMIE!
WHAT HAPPENED?
OH, JUST A FEW GUESTS DOING A LITTLE PATH BEATING!
WHERE'S THAT IDIOT MANAGER, SILAS BREATHLESS? I HIRED THAT DOWN-ON-HIS-DIMES SOCIALITE TO STAY ON HIS TOES AND DEAL WITH THINGS LIKE THIS!
UNCA SCROOGE, IS THIS HIM? HE'S ON HIS TOES — SORT OF!
HE MAY BE BREATHLESS, BUT HE SURE ISN'T SNORELESS!
ZZZZZ
ZZ
$$$
SILAS!
OH, MR. McDUCK! HA! YES! PARDON MY SOMNOLENCE! BUT I'VE A TOUCH OF THE DROOPS, YOU SEE! COMES AND GOES—QUITE UNPREDICTABLE!
THE DROOPS? YOU MEAN YOU SLEPT THROUGH THAT STAMPEDE? WHAT OTHER DISASTERS HAVE YOU SLEPT THROUGH?
CALM YOURSELF, SIR! ALL IS WELL! COME, I'LL SHOW YOU—WE'LL START AT THE TOP!
AND SO!
GEE, MR McDEE, THIS IS ONE FANCY ELEVATOR! IS THIS THE UP BUTTON?
WAIT! WE'RE NOT STRAPPED IN YET!
WHOOSH

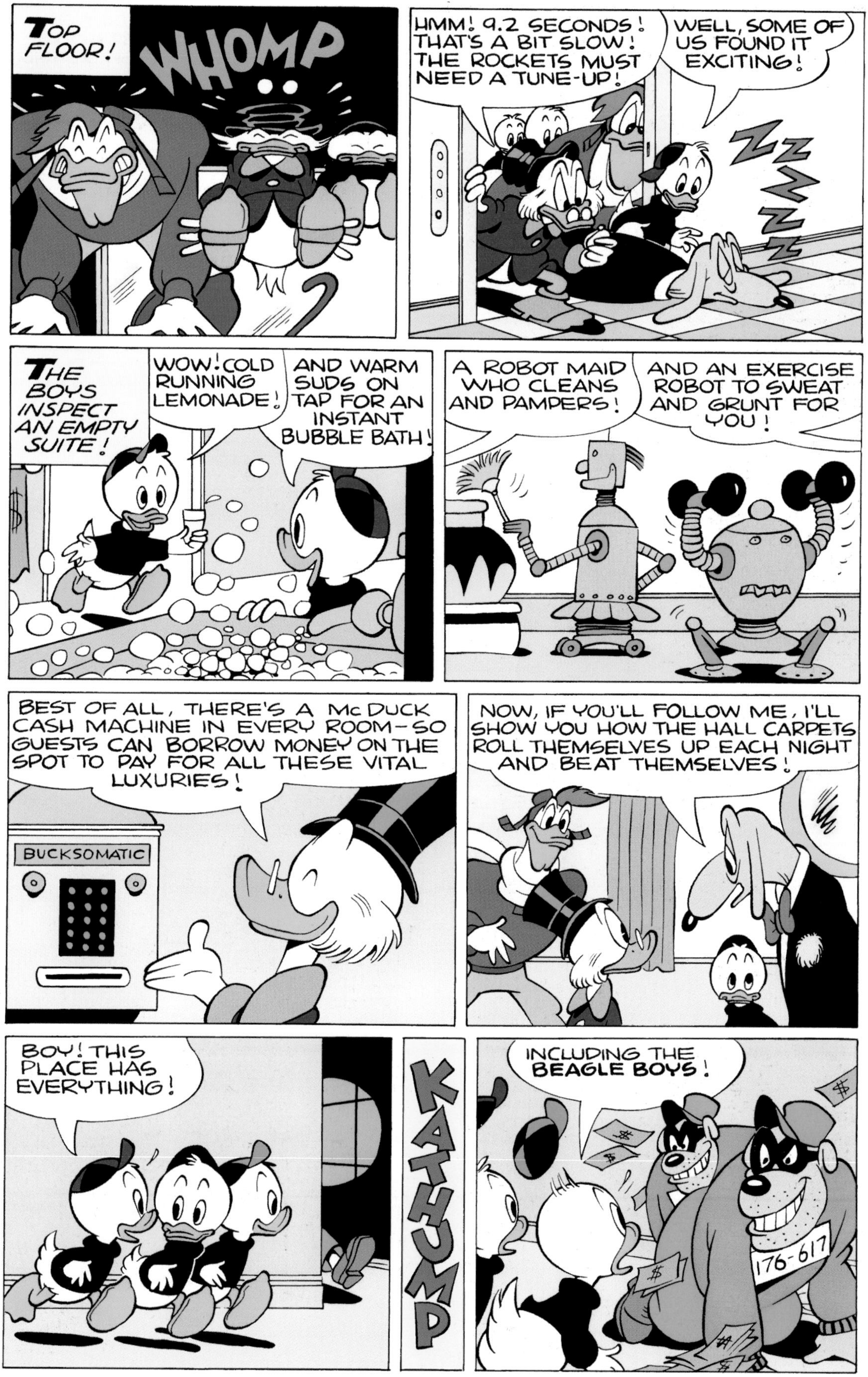
TOP FLOOR!
WHOMP
HMM! 9.2 SECONDS! THAT'S A BIT SLOW! THE ROCKETS MUST NEED A TUNE-UP!
WELL, SOME OF US FOUND IT EXCITING!
THE BOYS INSPECT AN EMPTY SUITE!
WOW! COLD RUNNING LEMONADE!
AND WARM SUDS ON TAP FOR AN INSTANT BUBBLE BATH!
A ROBOT MAID WHO CLEANS AND PAMPERS!
AND AN EXERCISE ROBOT TO SWEAT AND GRUNT FOR YOU!
BEST OF ALL, THERE'S A McDUCK CASH MACHINE IN EVERY ROOM—SO GUESTS CAN BORROW MONEY ON THE SPOT TO PAY FOR ALL THESE VITAL LUXURIES!
BUCKSOMATIC
NOW, IF YOU'LL FOLLOW ME, I'LL SHOW YOU HOW THE HALL CARPETS ROLL THEMSELVES UP EACH NIGHT AND BEAT THEMSELVES!
BOY! THIS PLACE HAS EVERYTHING!
KATHUMP
INCLUDING THE **BEAGLE BOYS**!
176-617

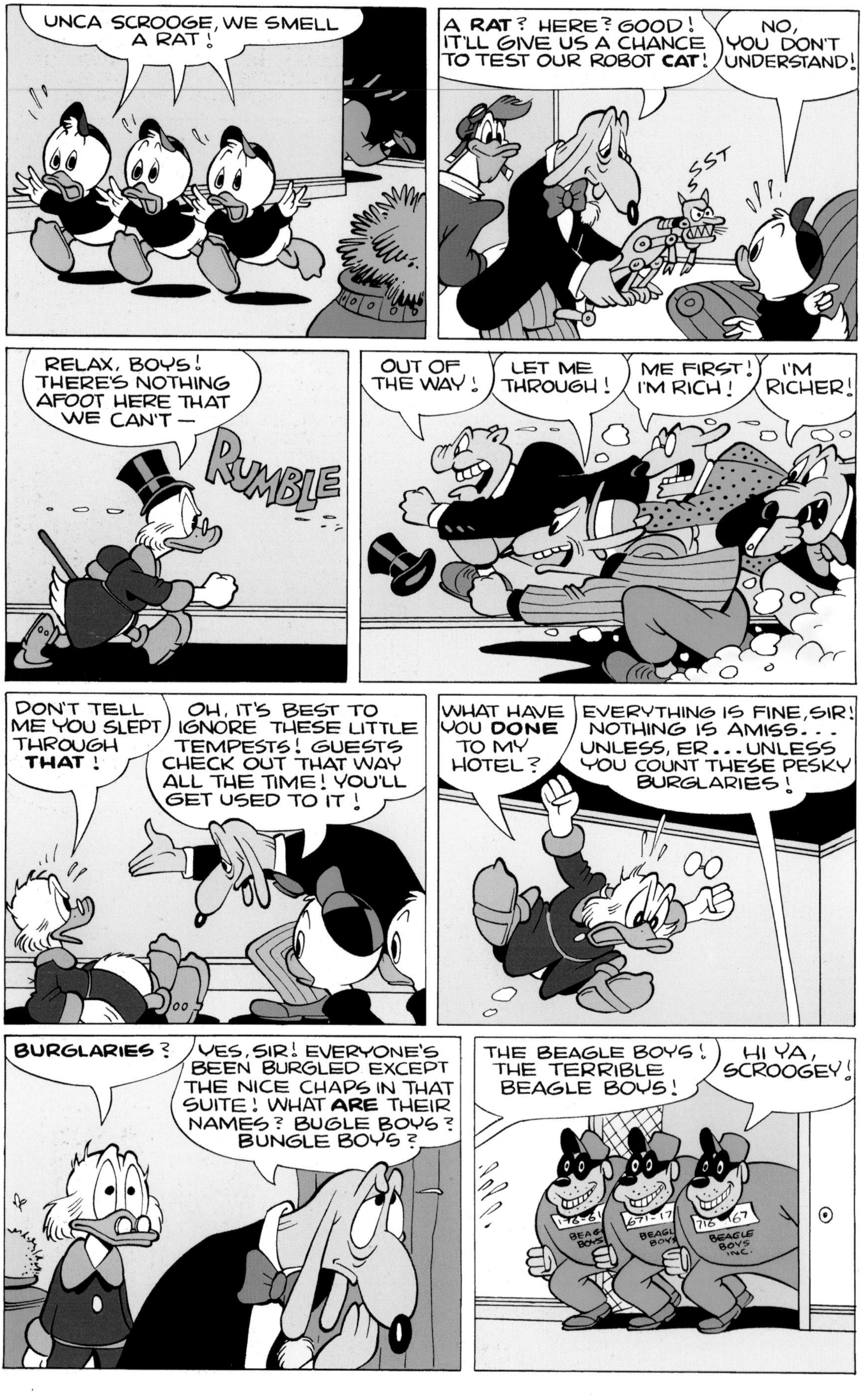
UNCA SCROOGE, WE SMELL A RAT!
A RAT? HERE? GOOD! IT'LL GIVE US A CHANCE TO TEST OUR ROBOT CAT!
NO, YOU DON'T UNDERSTAND!
SST
RELAX, BOYS! THERE'S NOTHING AFOOT HERE THAT WE CAN'T —
RUMBLE
OUT OF THE WAY!
LET ME THROUGH!
ME FIRST! I'M RICH!
I'M RICHER!
DON'T TELL ME YOU SLEPT THROUGH THAT!
OH, IT'S BEST TO IGNORE THESE LITTLE TEMPESTS! GUESTS CHECK OUT THAT WAY ALL THE TIME! YOU'LL GET USED TO IT!
WHAT HAVE YOU DONE TO MY HOTEL?
EVERYTHING IS FINE, SIR! NOTHING IS AMISS... UNLESS, ER... UNLESS YOU COUNT THESE PESKY BURGLARIES!
BURGLARIES?
YES, SIR! EVERYONE'S BEEN BURGLED EXCEPT THE NICE CHAPS IN THAT SUITE! WHAT ARE THEIR NAMES? BUGLE BOYS? BUNGLE BOYS?
THE BEAGLE BOYS! THE TERRIBLE BEAGLE BOYS!
HI YA, SCROOGEY!
716-167
BEAGLE BOYS INC.

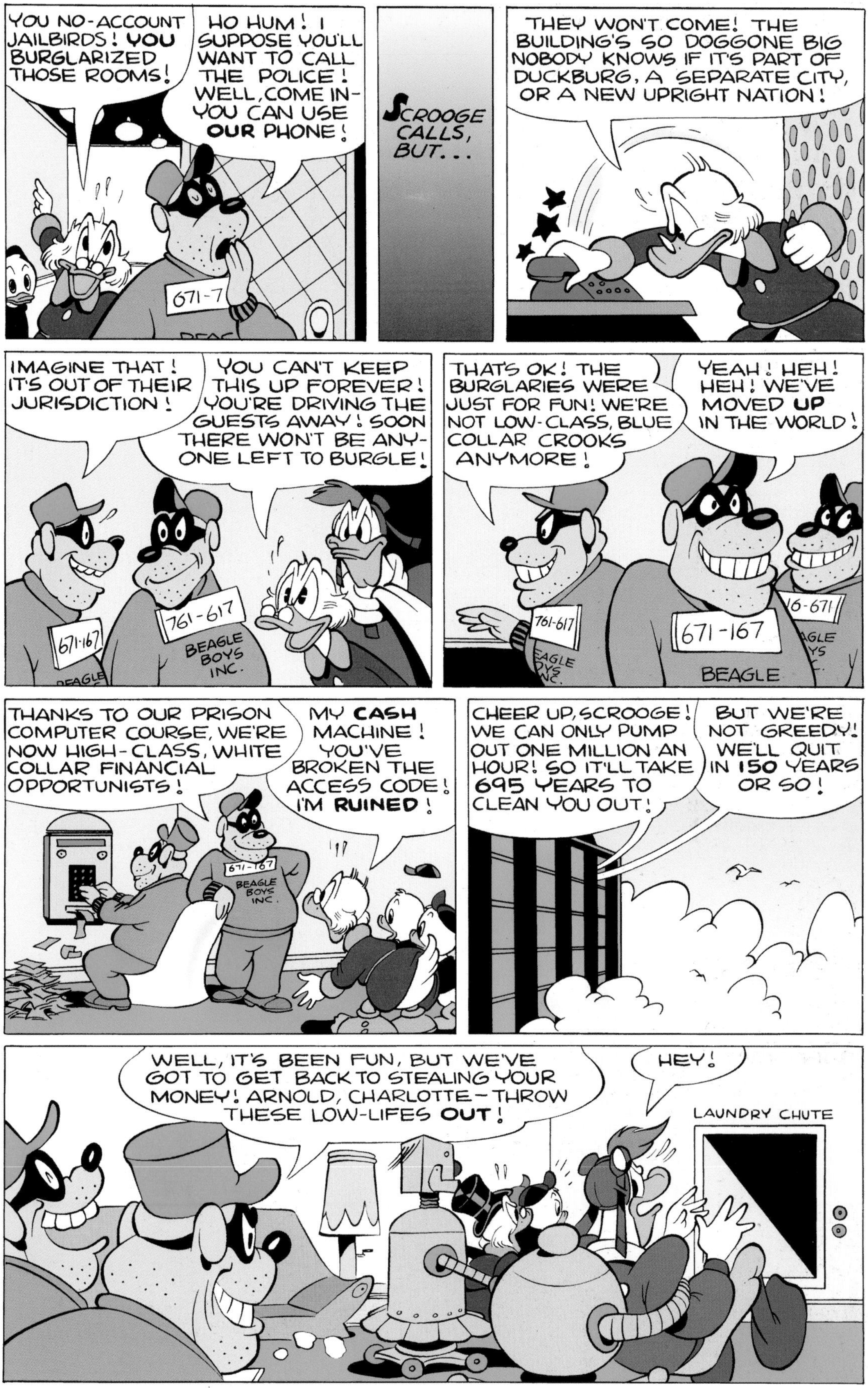
YOU NO-ACCOUNT JAILBIRDS! **YOU** BURGLARIZED THOSE ROOMS!
HO HUM! I SUPPOSE YOU'LL WANT TO CALL THE POLICE! WELL, COME IN- YOU CAN USE **OUR** PHONE!
671-7
SCROOGE CALLS, BUT...
THEY WON'T COME! THE BUILDING'S SO DOGGONE BIG NOBODY KNOWS IF IT'S PART OF DUCKBURG, A SEPARATE CITY, OR A NEW UPRIGHT NATION!
IMAGINE THAT! IT'S OUT OF THEIR JURISDICTION!
YOU CAN'T KEEP THIS UP FOREVER! YOU'RE DRIVING THE GUESTS AWAY! SOON THERE WON'T BE ANY-ONE LEFT TO BURGLE!
671-167
761-617
BEAGLE BOYS INC.
THAT'S OK! THE BURGLARIES WERE JUST FOR FUN! WE'RE NOT LOW-CLASS, BLUE COLLAR CROOKS ANYMORE!
YEAH! HEH! HEH! WE'VE MOVED **UP** IN THE WORLD!
761-617
671-167
16-671
BEAGLE
THANKS TO OUR PRISON COMPUTER COURSE, WE'RE NOW HIGH-CLASS, WHITE COLLAR FINANCIAL OPPORTUNISTS!
MY **CASH** MACHINE! YOU'VE BROKEN THE ACCESS CODE! I'M **RUINED**!
671-167
BEAGLE BOYS INC.
CHEER UP, SCROOGE! WE CAN ONLY PUMP OUT ONE MILLION AN HOUR! SO IT'LL TAKE **695** YEARS TO CLEAN YOU OUT!
BUT WE'RE NOT GREEDY! WE'LL QUIT IN **150** YEARS OR SO!
WELL, IT'S BEEN FUN, BUT WE'VE GOT TO GET BACK TO STEALING YOUR MONEY! ARNOLD, CHARLOTTE—THROW THESE LOW-LIFES **OUT**!
HEY!
LAUNDRY CHUTE

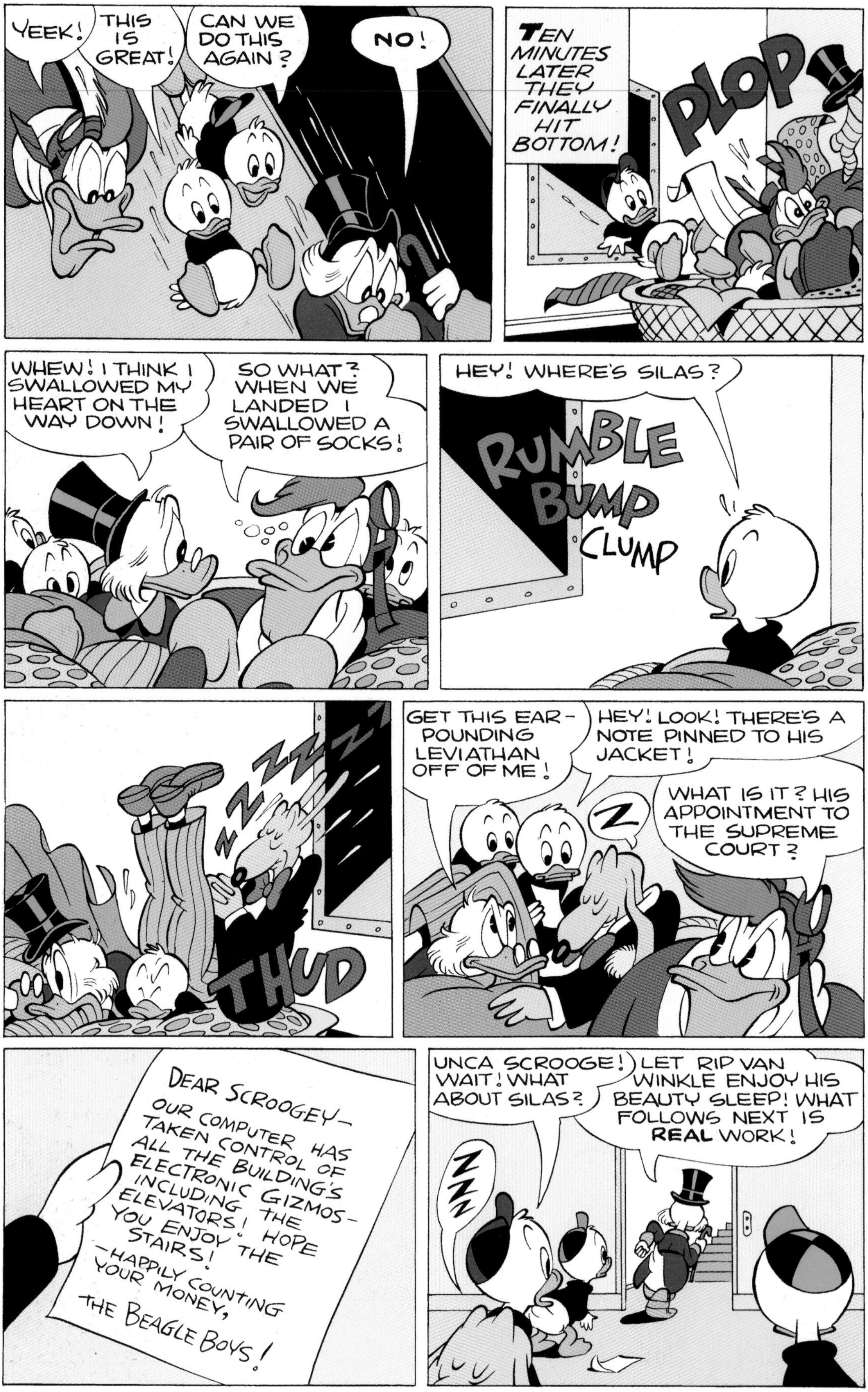
YEEK!
THIS IS GREAT!
CAN WE DO THIS AGAIN?
NO!
TEN MINUTES LATER THEY FINALLY HIT BOTTOM!
PLOP
WHEW! I THINK I SWALLOWED MY HEART ON THE WAY DOWN!
SO WHAT? WHEN WE LANDED I SWALLOWED A PAIR OF SOCKS!
HEY! WHERE'S SILAS?
RUMBLE
BUMP
CLUMP
ZZZZZ
THUD
GET THIS EAR-POUNDING LEVIATHAN OFF OF ME!
HEY! LOOK! THERE'S A NOTE PINNED TO HIS JACKET!
Z
WHAT IS IT? HIS APPOINTMENT TO THE SUPREME COURT?
DEAR SCROOGEY— OUR COMPUTER HAS TAKEN CONTROL OF ALL THE BUILDING'S ELECTRONIC GIZMOS-INCLUDING THE ELEVATORS! HOPE YOU ENJOY THE STAIRS! —HAPPILY COUNTING YOUR MONEY, THE BEAGLE BOYS!
UNCA SCROOGE! WAIT! WHAT ABOUT SILAS?
LET RIP VAN WINKLE ENJOY HIS BEAUTY SLEEP! WHAT FOLLOWS NEXT IS **REAL** WORK!
ZZZ

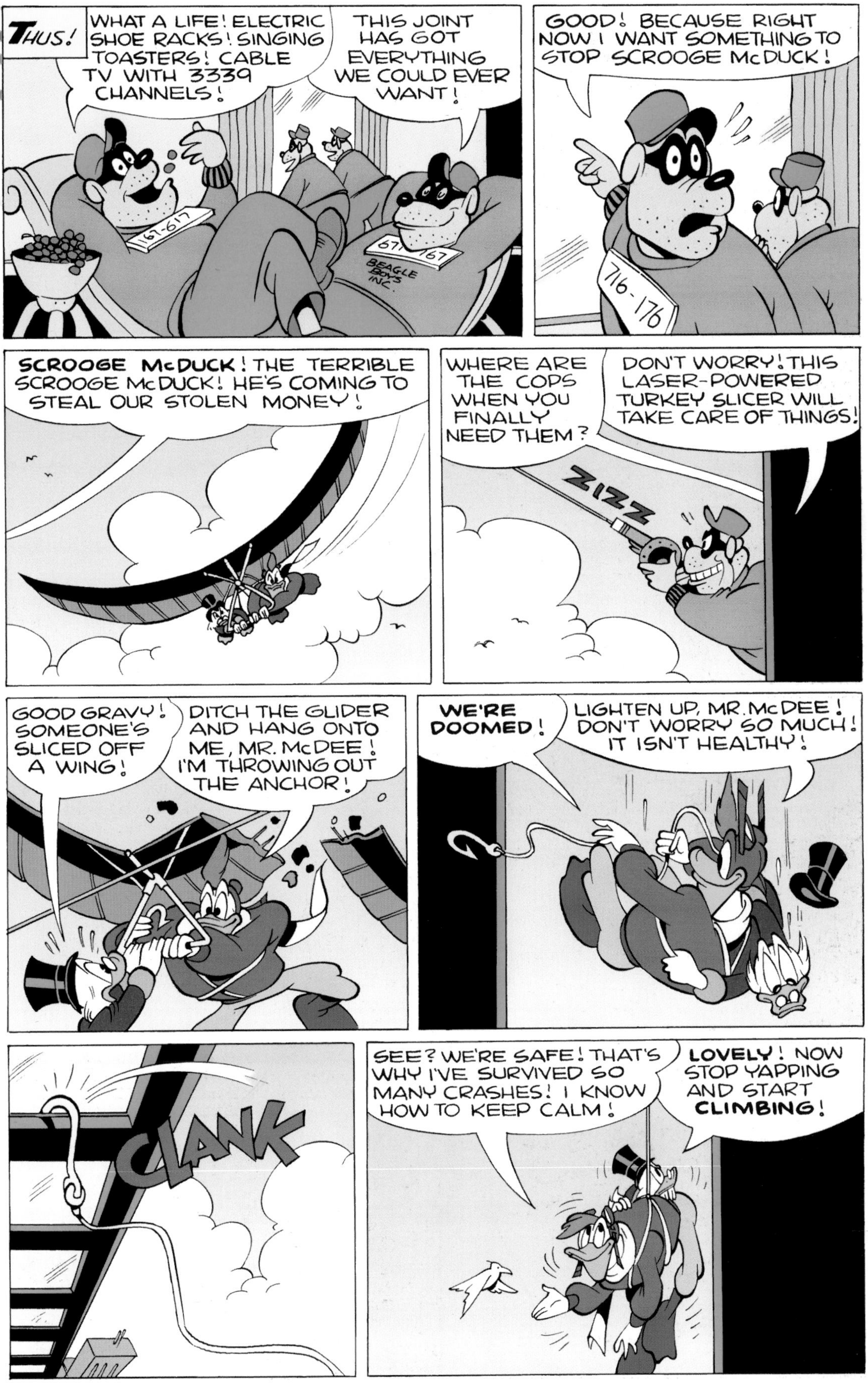
THUS!
WHAT A LIFE! ELECTRIC SHOE RACKS! SINGING TOASTERS! CABLE TV WITH 3339 CHANNELS!
THIS JOINT HAS GOT EVERYTHING WE COULD EVER WANT!
167-617
671-167
BEAGLE BOYS INC.
GOOD! BECAUSE RIGHT NOW I WANT SOMETHING TO STOP SCROOGE McDUCK!
716-176
SCROOGE McDUCK! THE TERRIBLE SCROOGE McDUCK! HE'S COMING TO STEAL OUR STOLEN MONEY!
WHERE ARE THE COPS WHEN YOU FINALLY NEED THEM?
DON'T WORRY! THIS LASER-POWERED TURKEY SLICER WILL TAKE CARE OF THINGS!
ZIZZ
GOOD GRAVY! SOMEONE'S SLICED OFF A WING!
DITCH THE GLIDER AND HANG ONTO ME, MR. McDEE! I'M THROWING OUT THE ANCHOR!
WE'RE DOOMED!
LIGHTEN UP, MR. McDEE! DON'T WORRY SO MUCH! IT ISN'T HEALTHY!
CLANK
SEE? WE'RE SAFE! THAT'S WHY I'VE SURVIVED SO MANY CRASHES! I KNOW HOW TO KEEP CALM!
LOVELY! NOW STOP YAPPING AND START CLIMBING!

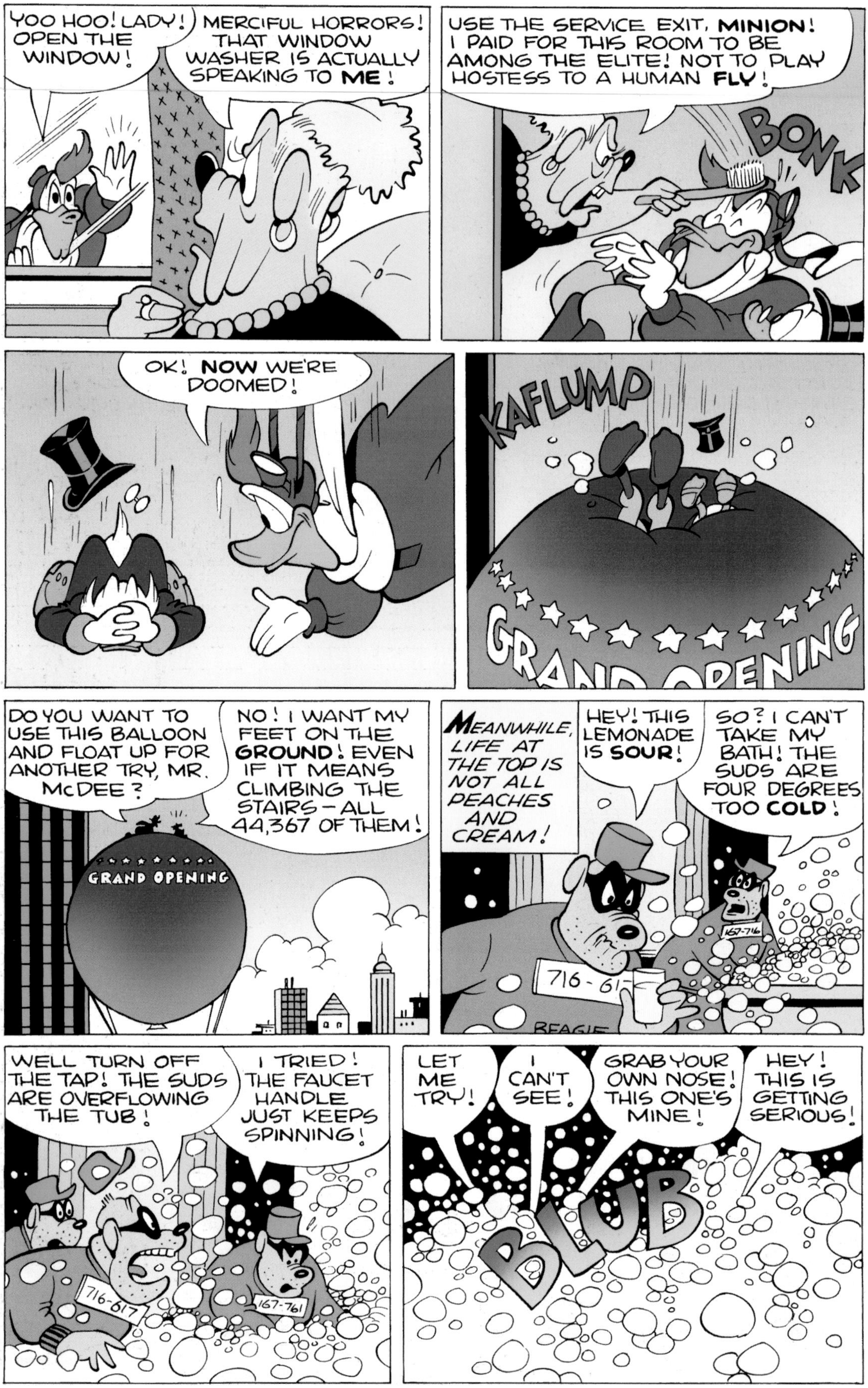
YOO HOO! LADY! OPEN THE WINDOW!
MERCIFUL HORRORS! THAT WINDOW WASHER IS ACTUALLY SPEAKING TO ME!
USE THE SERVICE EXIT, MINION! I PAID FOR THIS ROOM TO BE AMONG THE ELITE! NOT TO PLAY HOSTESS TO A HUMAN FLY!
BONK
OK! NOW WE'RE DOOMED!
KAFLUMP
GRAND OPENING
DO YOU WANT TO USE THIS BALLOON AND FLOAT UP FOR ANOTHER TRY, MR. McDEE?
NO! I WANT MY FEET ON THE GROUND! EVEN IF IT MEANS CLIMBING THE STAIRS—ALL 44,367 OF THEM!
GRAND OPENING
MEANWHILE, LIFE AT THE TOP IS NOT ALL PEACHES AND CREAM!
HEY! THIS LEMONADE IS SOUR!
SO? I CAN'T TAKE MY BATH! THE SUDS ARE FOUR DEGREES TOO COLD!
716-61
167-716
WELL TURN OFF THE TAP! THE SUDS ARE OVERFLOWING THE TUB!
I TRIED! THE FAUCET HANDLE JUST KEEPS SPINNING!
716-617
167-761
LET ME TRY!
I CAN'T SEE!
GRAB YOUR OWN NOSE! THIS ONE'S MINE!
HEY! THIS IS GETTING SERIOUS!
BLUB

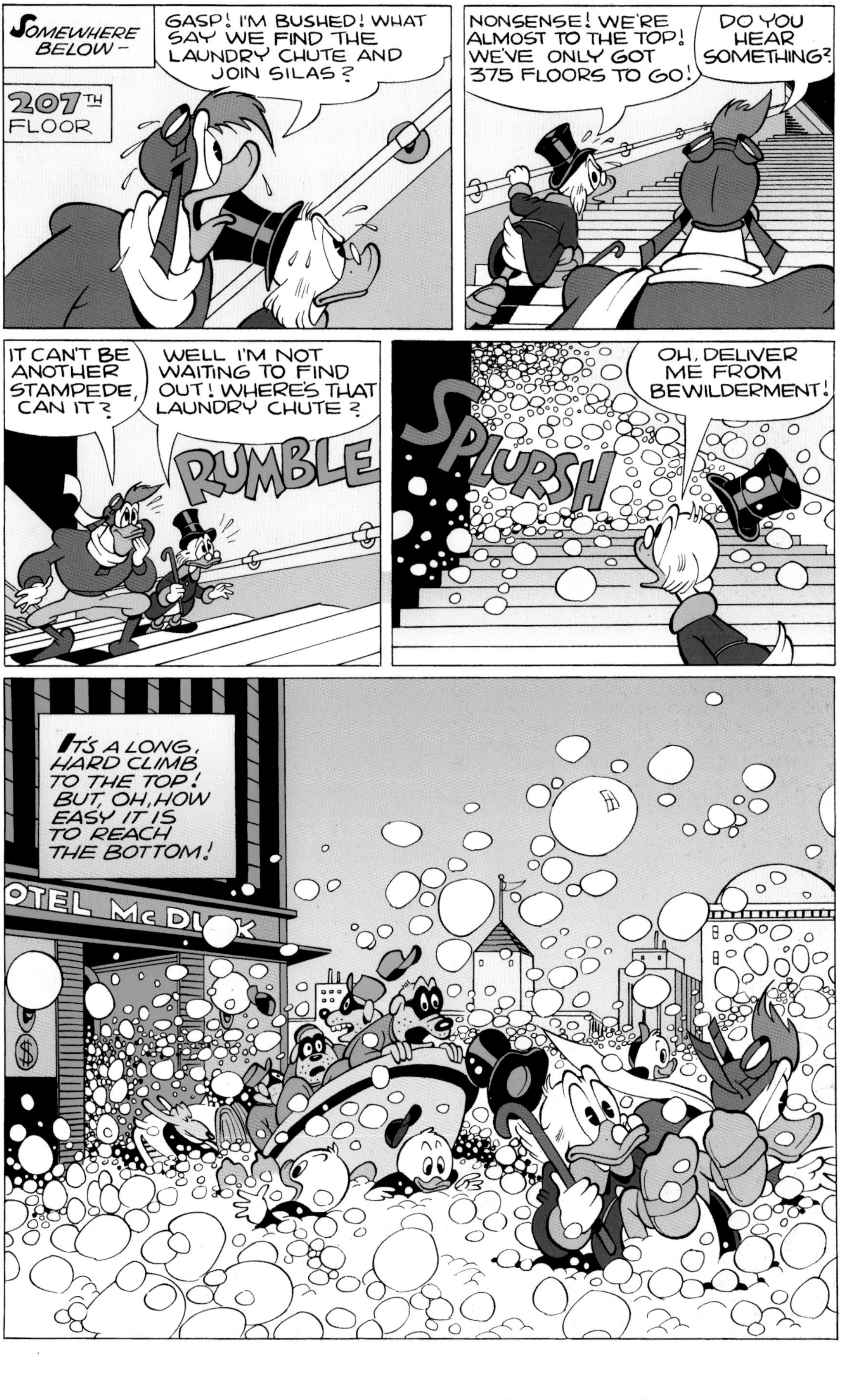
SOMEWHERE BELOW -
207TH FLOOR
GASP! I'M BUSHED! WHAT SAY WE FIND THE LAUNDRY CHUTE AND JOIN SILAS?
NONSENSE! WE'RE ALMOST TO THE TOP! WE'VE ONLY GOT 375 FLOORS TO GO!
DO YOU HEAR SOMETHING?
IT CAN'T BE ANOTHER STAMPEDE, CAN IT?
WELL I'M NOT WAITING TO FIND OUT! WHERE'S THAT LAUNDRY CHUTE?
RUMBLE
SPLURSH
OH, DELIVER ME FROM BEWILDERMENT!
IT'S A LONG, HARD CLIMB TO THE TOP! BUT, OH, HOW EASY IT IS TO REACH THE BOTTOM!
OTEL McDU K

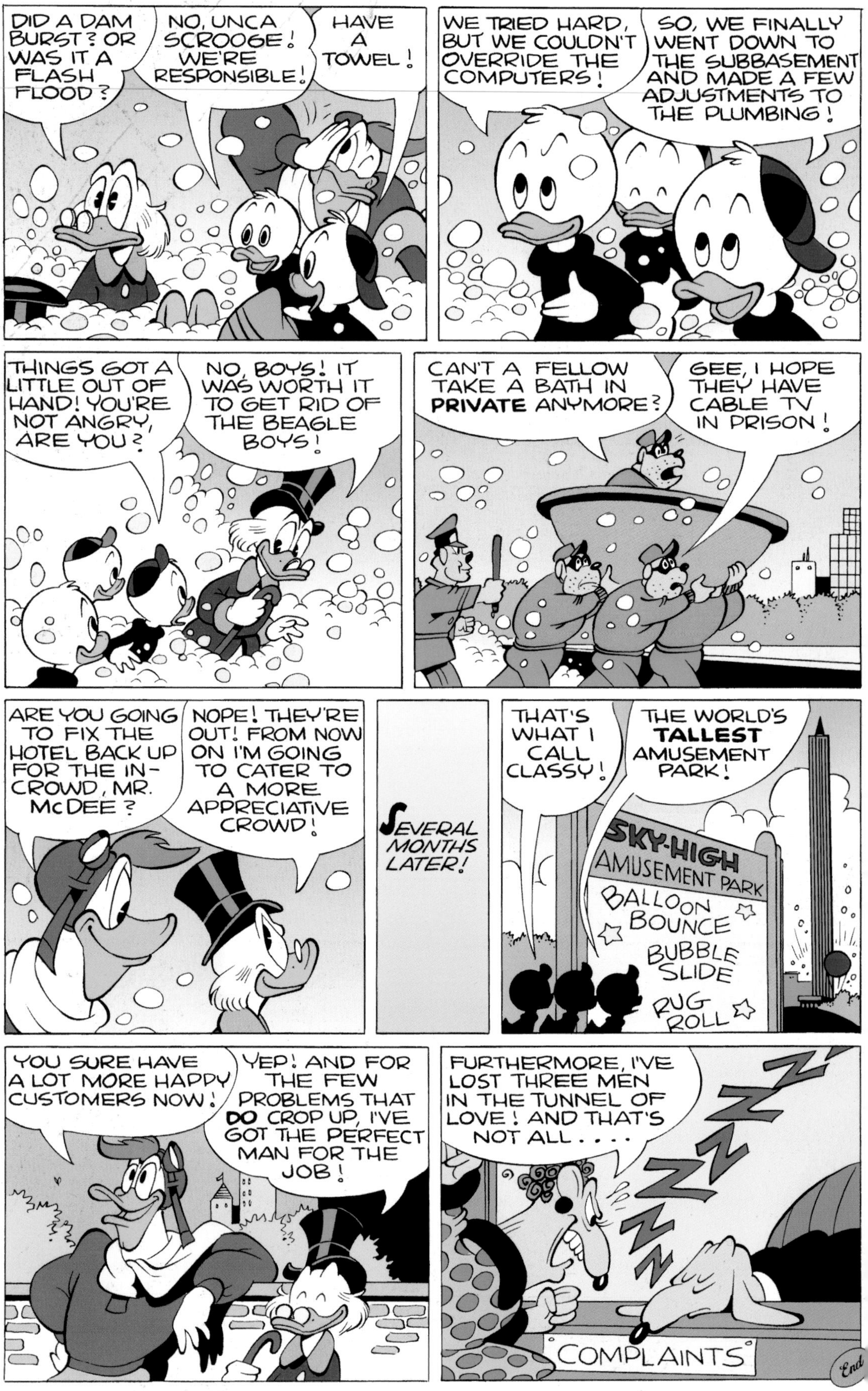
DID A DAM BURST? OR WAS IT A FLASH FLOOD?
NO, UNCA SCROOGE! WE'RE RESPONSIBLE!
HAVE A TOWEL!
WE TRIED HARD, BUT WE COULDN'T OVERRIDE THE COMPUTERS!
SO, WE FINALLY WENT DOWN TO THE SUBBASEMENT AND MADE A FEW ADJUSTMENTS TO THE PLUMBING!
THINGS GOT A LITTLE OUT OF HAND! YOU'RE NOT ANGRY, ARE YOU?
NO, BOYS! IT WAS WORTH IT TO GET RID OF THE BEAGLE BOYS!
CAN'T A FELLOW TAKE A BATH IN PRIVATE ANYMORE?
GEE, I HOPE THEY HAVE CABLE TV IN PRISON!
ARE YOU GOING TO FIX THE HOTEL BACK UP FOR THE IN-CROWD, MR. McDEE?
NOPE! THEY'RE OUT! FROM NOW ON I'M GOING TO CATER TO A MORE APPRECIATIVE CROWD!
SEVERAL MONTHS LATER!
THAT'S WHAT I CALL CLASSY!
THE WORLD'S TALLEST AMUSEMENT PARK!
SKY-HIGH AMUSEMENT PARK
BALLOON BOUNCE
BUBBLE SLIDE
RUG ROLL
YOU SURE HAVE A LOT MORE HAPPY CUSTOMERS NOW!
YEP! AND FOR THE FEW PROBLEMS THAT DO CROP UP, I'VE GOT THE PERFECT MAN FOR THE JOB!
FURTHERMORE, I'VE LOST THREE MEN IN THE TUNNEL OF LOVE! AND THAT'S NOT ALL....
ZZZZZZ
COMPLAINTS
End

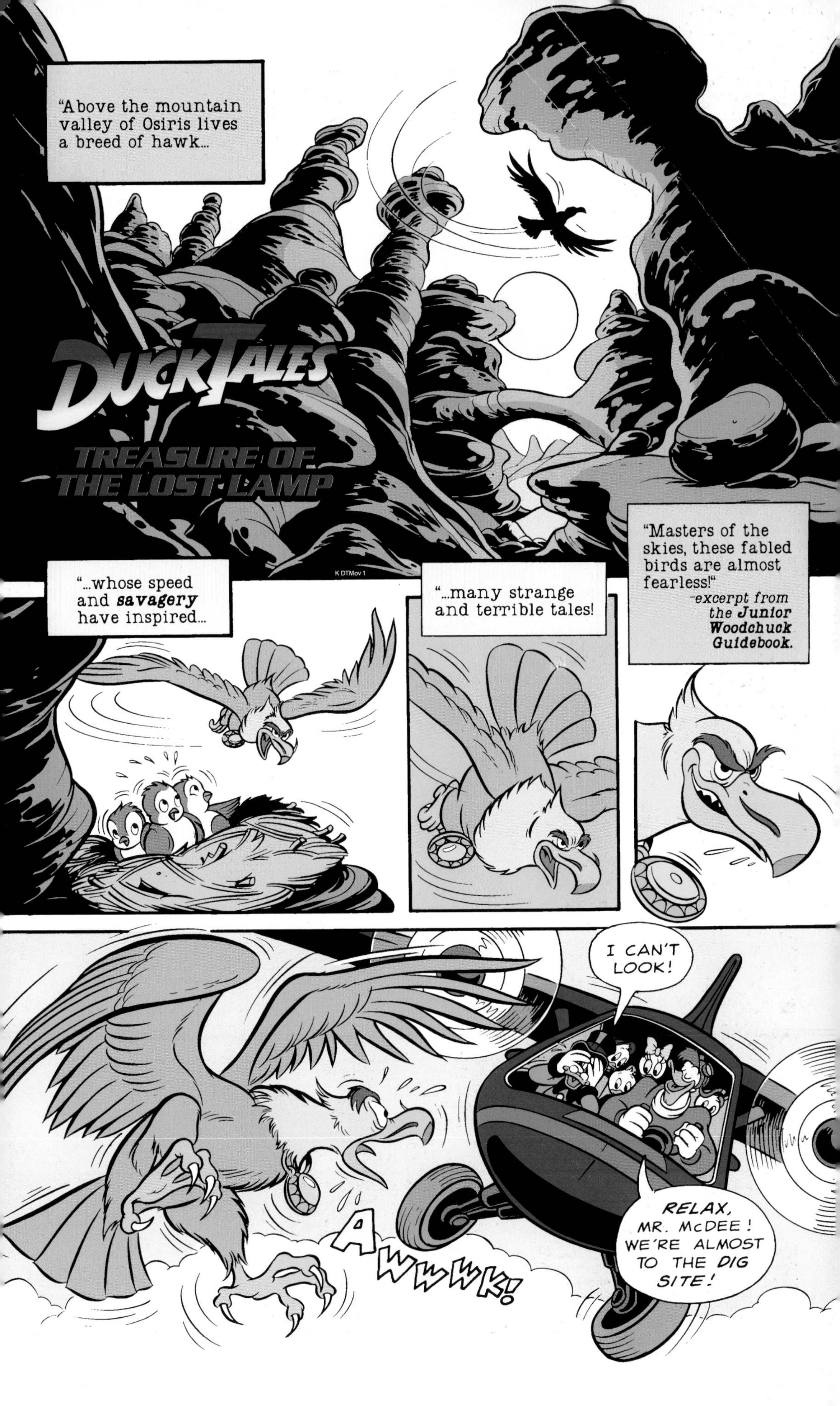
"Above the mountain valley of Osiris lives a breed of hawk...
DUCKTALES
TREASURE OF THE LOST LAMP
K DTMov 1
"...whose speed and savagery have inspired...
"...many strange and terrible tales!
"Masters of the skies, these fabled birds are almost fearless!"
–excerpt from the Junior Woodchuck Guidebook.
I CAN'T LOOK!
RELAX, MR. McDEE! WE'RE ALMOST TO THE DIG SITE!
AWWWK!

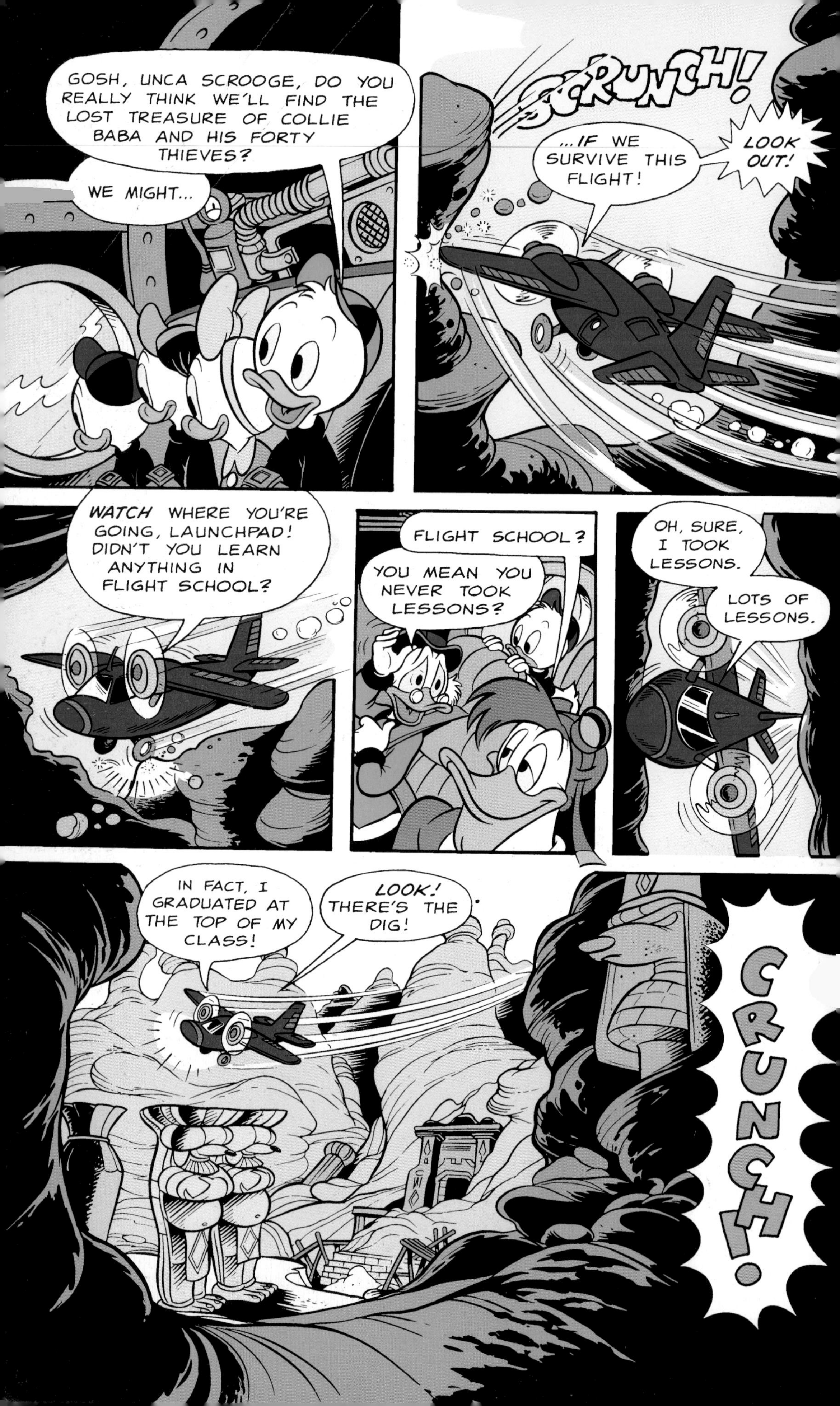
GOSH, UNCA SCROOGE, DO YOU REALLY THINK WE'LL FIND THE LOST TREASURE OF COLLIE BABA AND HIS FORTY THIEVES?
WE MIGHT...
SCRUNCH!
...IF WE SURVIVE THIS FLIGHT!
LOOK OUT!
WATCH WHERE YOU'RE GOING, LAUNCHPAD! DIDN'T YOU LEARN ANYTHING IN FLIGHT SCHOOL?
FLIGHT SCHOOL?
YOU MEAN YOU NEVER TOOK LESSONS?
OH, SURE, I TOOK LESSONS.
LOTS OF LESSONS.
IN FACT, I GRADUATED AT THE TOP OF MY CLASS!
LOOK! THERE'S THE DIG!
CRUNCH!

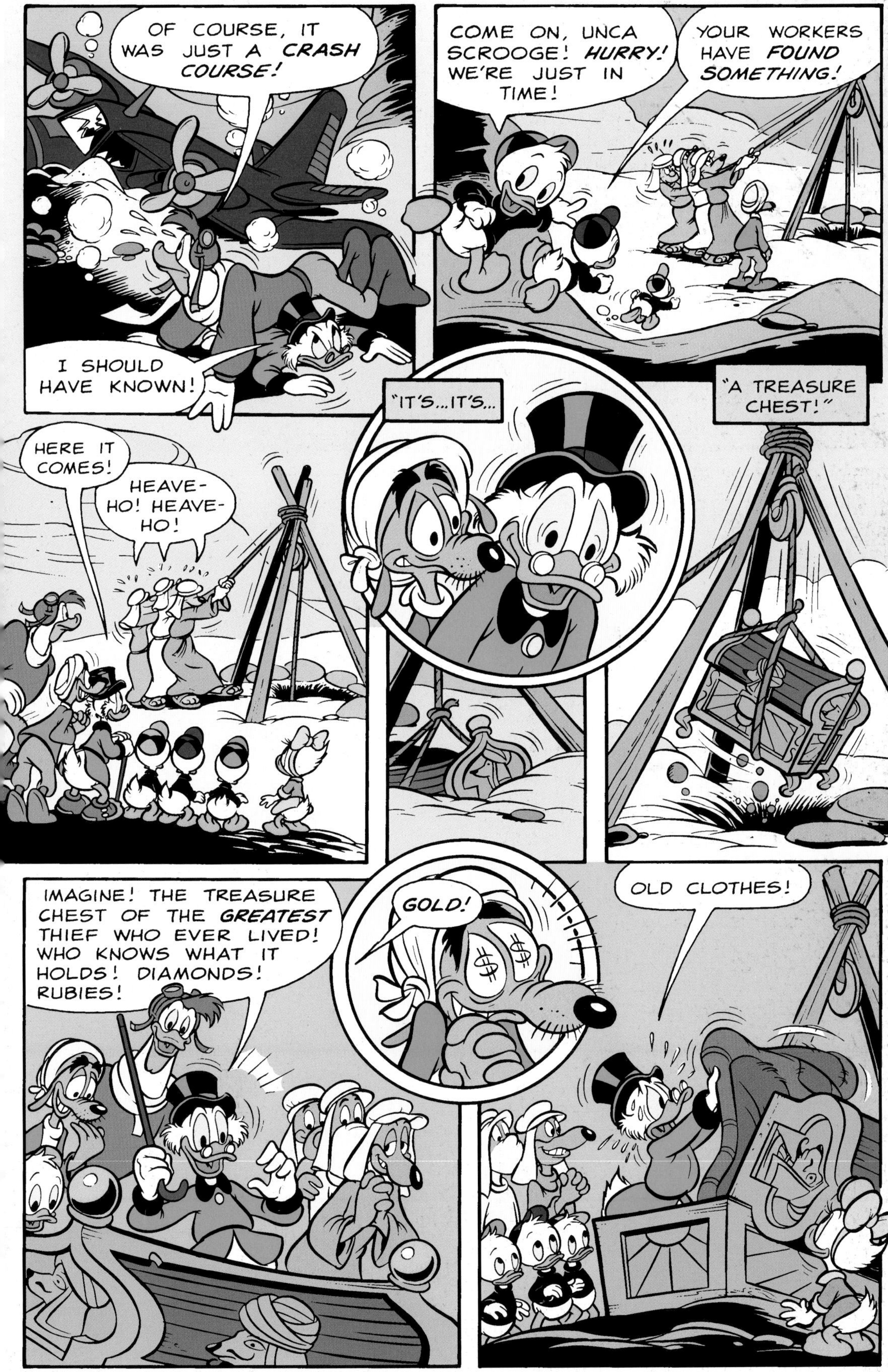
OF COURSE, IT WAS JUST A CRASH COURSE!
I SHOULD HAVE KNOWN!
COME ON, UNCA SCROOGE! HURRY! WE'RE JUST IN TIME!
YOUR WORKERS HAVE FOUND SOMETHING!
HERE IT COMES!
HEAVE-HO! HEAVE-HO!
"IT'S...IT'S...
"A TREASURE CHEST!"
IMAGINE! THE TREASURE CHEST OF THE GREATEST THIEF WHO EVER LIVED! WHO KNOWS WHAT IT HOLDS! DIAMONDS! RUBIES!
GOLD!
OLD CLOTHES!

ROBES! SHEETS! TURBANS!

FORTY YEARS OF SEARCHING AND I END UP WITH...

...COLLIE BABA'S DIRTY LAUNDRY!

YES! BUT LOOK WHAT WAS IN THE *POCKET* OF ONE OF THOSE ROBES!

A SCROLL WITH THE SEA OF *COLLIE BABA!*

WELL, SCRAPE ME BARNACLES AND CALL ME A BUCCANEER!

IT'S A *MAP!*

OOOOH!

"YES, A TREASURE MAP LEADING INTO THE DESERT..."

...AND IT'S WRITTEN IN COLLIE BABA'S OWN HAND!

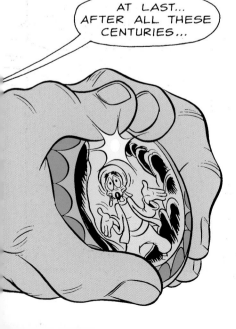

AT LAST... AFTER ALL THESE CENTURIES...

...THE POWER OF THE MAGIC LAMP WILL BE *MINE* AGAIN!

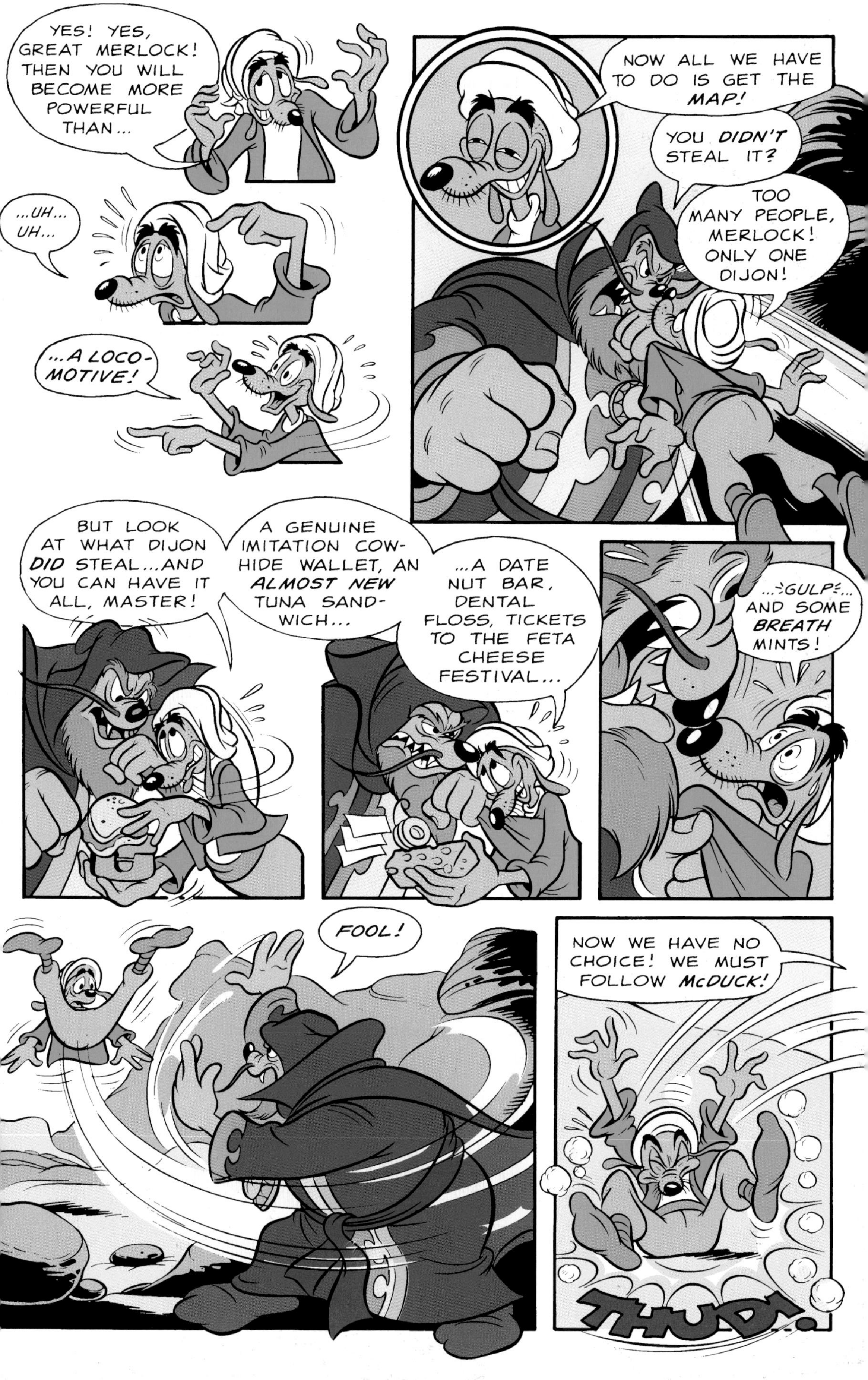

YES! YES, GREAT MERLOCK! THEN YOU WILL BECOME MORE POWERFUL THAN...
...UH... UH...
...A LOCO-MOTIVE!
NOW ALL WE HAVE TO DO IS GET THE MAP!
YOU DIDN'T STEAL IT?
TOO MANY PEOPLE, MERLOCK! ONLY ONE DIJON!
BUT LOOK AT WHAT DIJON DID STEAL...AND YOU CAN HAVE IT ALL, MASTER!
A GENUINE IMITATION COW-HIDE WALLET, AN ALMOST NEW TUNA SAND-WICH...
...A DATE NUT BAR, DENTAL FLOSS, TICKETS TO THE FETA CHEESE FESTIVAL...
...GULP... AND SOME BREATH MINTS!
FOOL!
NOW WE HAVE NO CHOICE! WE MUST FOLLOW McDUCK!
THUD!

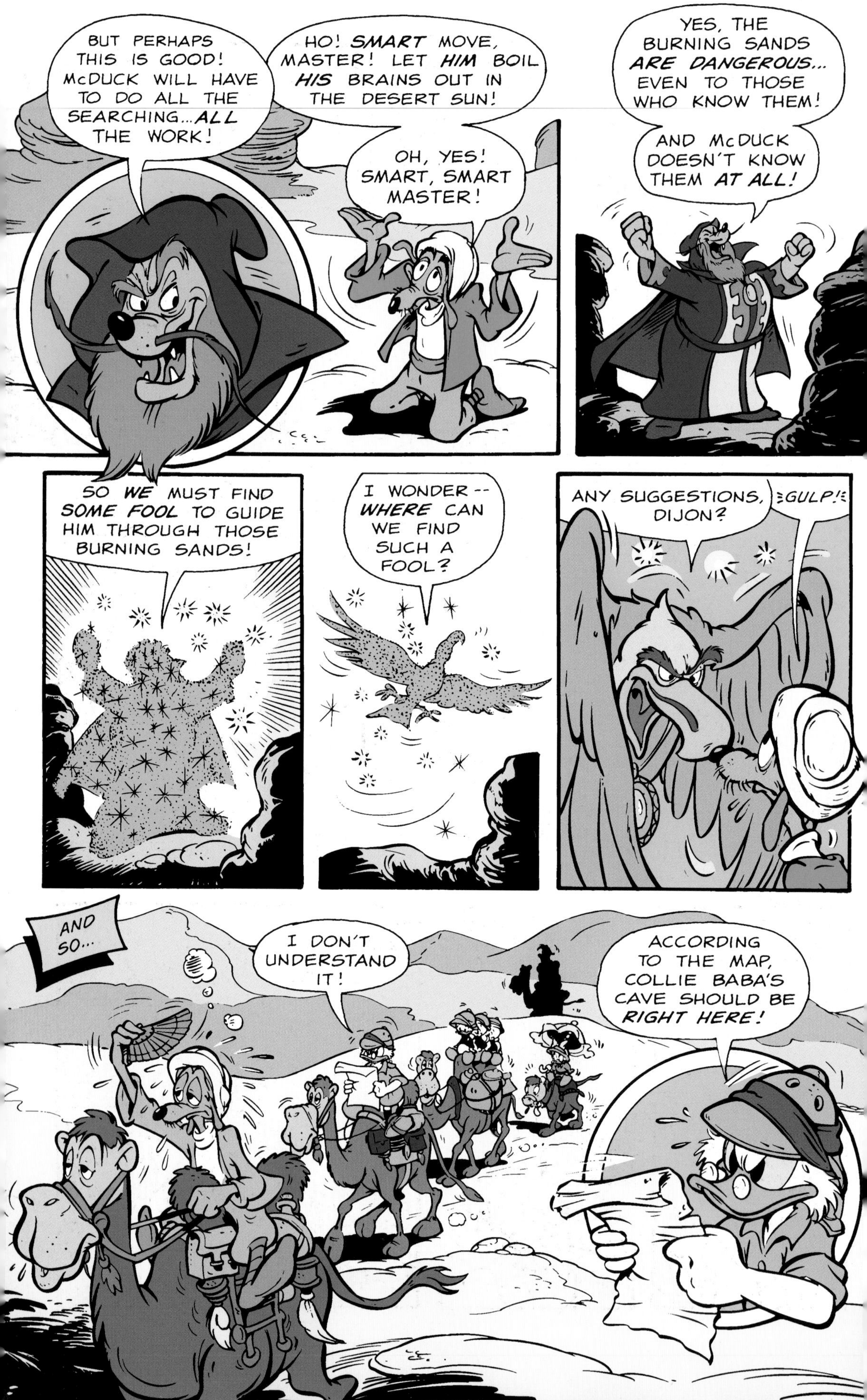
BUT PERHAPS THIS IS GOOD! McDUCK WILL HAVE TO DO ALL THE SEARCHING... ALL THE WORK!
HO! SMART MOVE, MASTER! LET HIM BOIL HIS BRAINS OUT IN THE DESERT SUN!
OH, YES! SMART, SMART MASTER!
YES, THE BURNING SANDS ARE DANGEROUS... EVEN TO THOSE WHO KNOW THEM!
AND McDUCK DOESN'T KNOW THEM AT ALL!
SO WE MUST FIND SOME FOOL TO GUIDE HIM THROUGH THOSE BURNING SANDS!
I WONDER -- WHERE CAN WE FIND SUCH A FOOL?
ANY SUGGESTIONS, DIJON?
GULP!
AND SO...
I DON'T UNDERSTAND IT!
ACCORDING TO THE MAP, COLLIE BABA'S CAVE SHOULD BE RIGHT HERE!

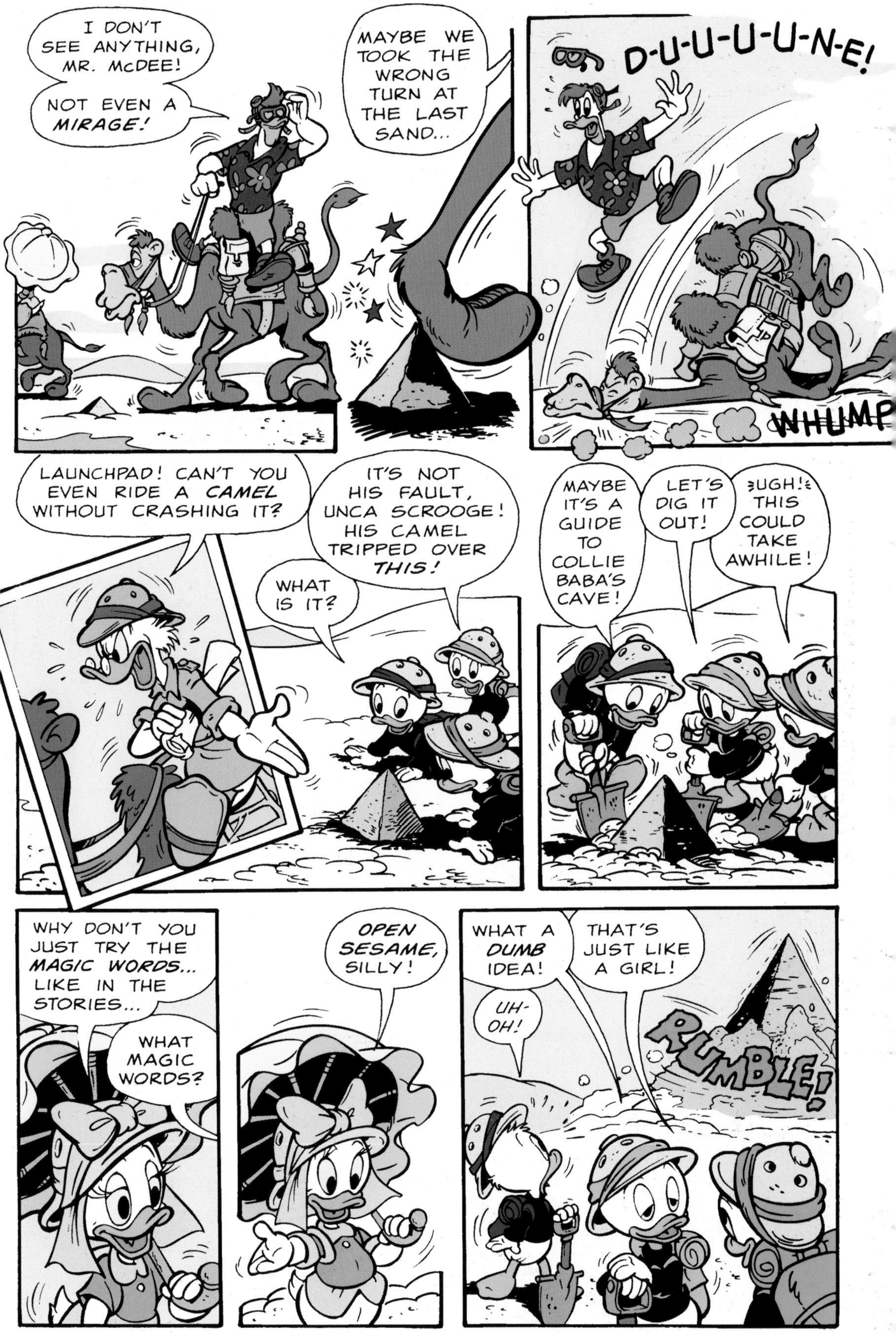

I DON'T SEE ANYTHING, MR. McDEE!
NOT EVEN A *MIRAGE!*
MAYBE WE TOOK THE WRONG TURN AT THE LAST SAND...
D-U-U-U-U-N-E!
WHUMP
LAUNCHPAD! CAN'T YOU EVEN RIDE A *CAMEL* WITHOUT CRASHING IT?
IT'S NOT HIS FAULT, UNCA SCROOGE! HIS CAMEL TRIPPED OVER *THIS!*
WHAT IS IT?
MAYBE IT'S A GUIDE TO COLLIE BABA'S CAVE!
LET'S DIG IT OUT!
UGH! THIS COULD TAKE AWHILE!
WHY DON'T YOU JUST TRY THE *MAGIC WORDS*... LIKE IN THE STORIES...
WHAT MAGIC WORDS?
OPEN SESAME, SILLY!
WHAT A *DUMB* IDEA!
THAT'S JUST LIKE A GIRL!
UH-OH!
RUMBLE!

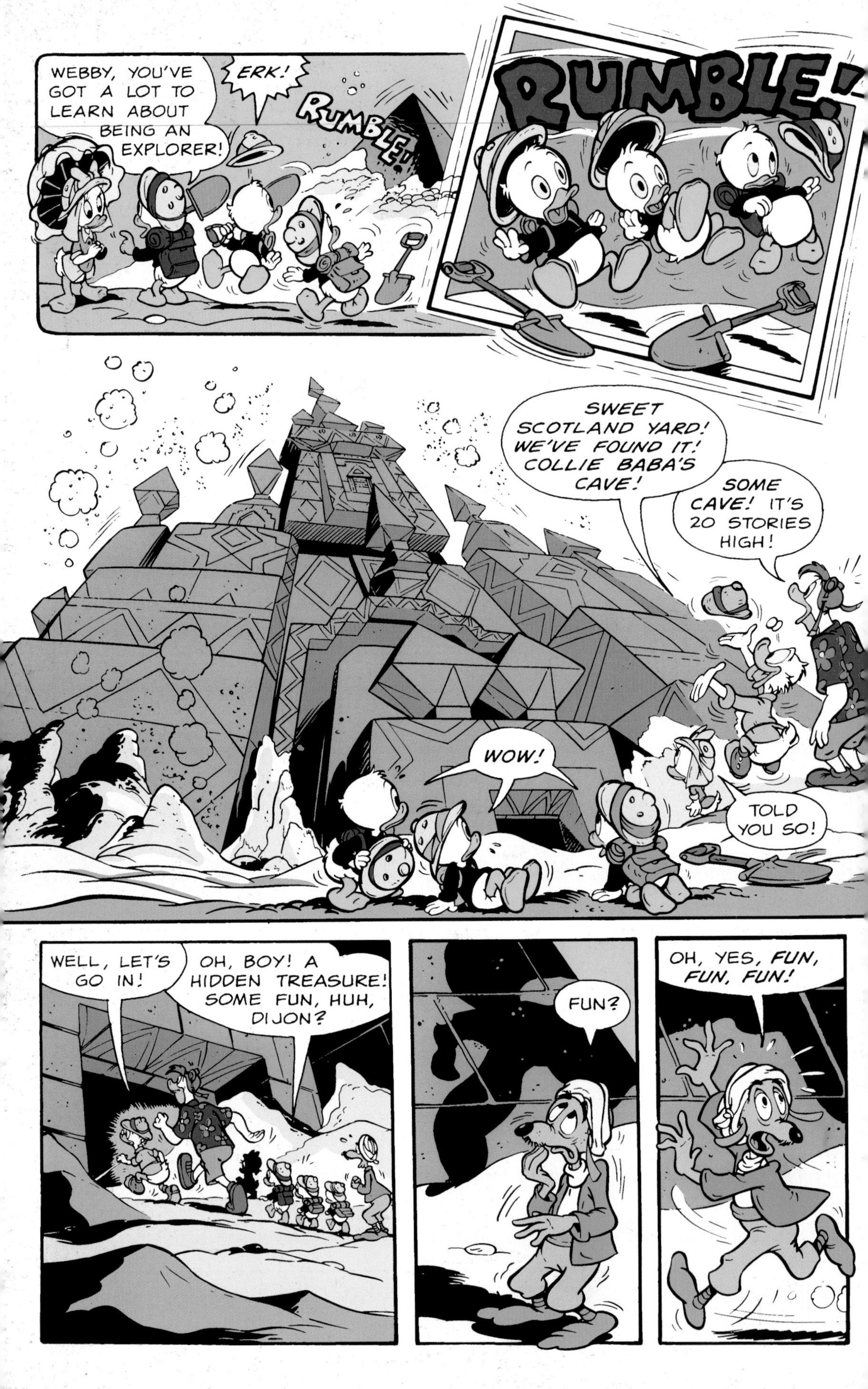
WEBBY, YOU'VE GOT A LOT TO LEARN ABOUT BEING AN EXPLORER!
ERK!
RUMBLE!
RUMBLE!
SWEET SCOTLAND YARD! WE'VE FOUND IT! COLLIE BABA'S CAVE!
SOME CAVE! IT'S 20 STORIES HIGH!
WOW!
TOLD YOU SO!
WELL, LET'S GO IN!
OH, BOY! A HIDDEN TREASURE! SOME FUN, HUH, DIJON?
FUN?
OH, YES, FUN, FUN, FUN!

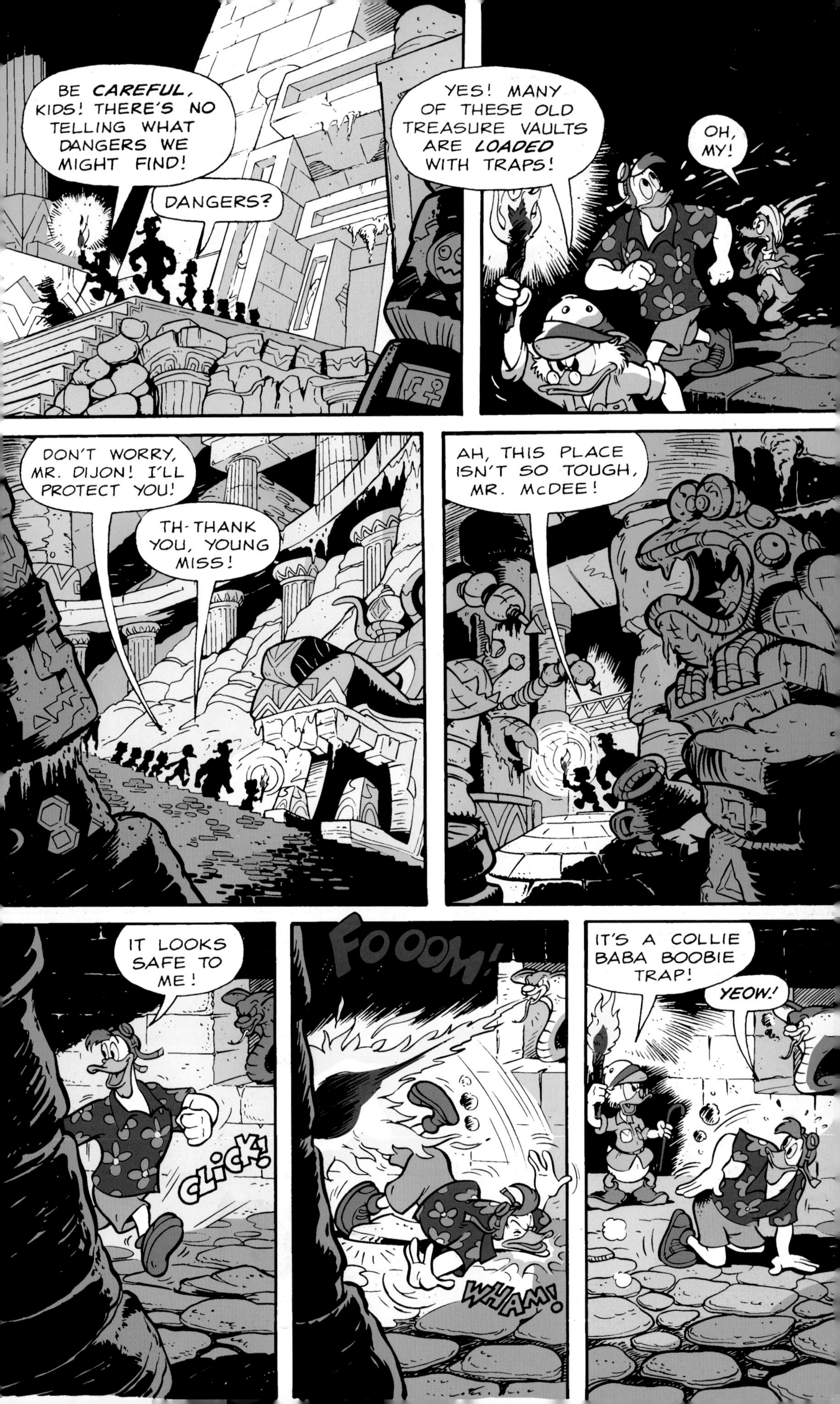
BE CAREFUL, KIDS! THERE'S NO TELLING WHAT DANGERS WE MIGHT FIND!
DANGERS?
YES! MANY OF THESE OLD TREASURE VAULTS ARE LOADED WITH TRAPS!
OH, MY!
DON'T WORRY, MR. DIJON! I'LL PROTECT YOU!
TH-THANK YOU, YOUNG MISS!
AH, THIS PLACE ISN'T SO TOUGH, MR. McDEE!
IT LOOKS SAFE TO ME!
CLICK!
FOOOM!
WHAM!
IT'S A COLLIE BABA BOOBIE TRAP!
YEOW!

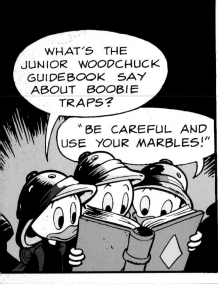

WHAT'S THE JUNIOR WOODCHUCK GUIDEBOOK SAY ABOUT BOOBIE TRAPS?

"BE CAREFUL AND USE YOUR MARBLES!"

IT'S A GOOD THING WE BROUGHT SOME!

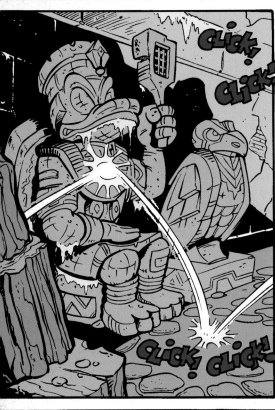

CLICK!

CLICK!

CLICK! CLICK!

WHOOSH!

WHIRR!

FOOM!

SCREECH!

I THINK WE GOT THEM ALL, UNCA SCROOGE!

BOYS, I DON'T KNOW WHAT I'D DO WITHOUT YOU!

GOOD! NOW DIJON IS SAFE!

CLICK!

YEOOOW!

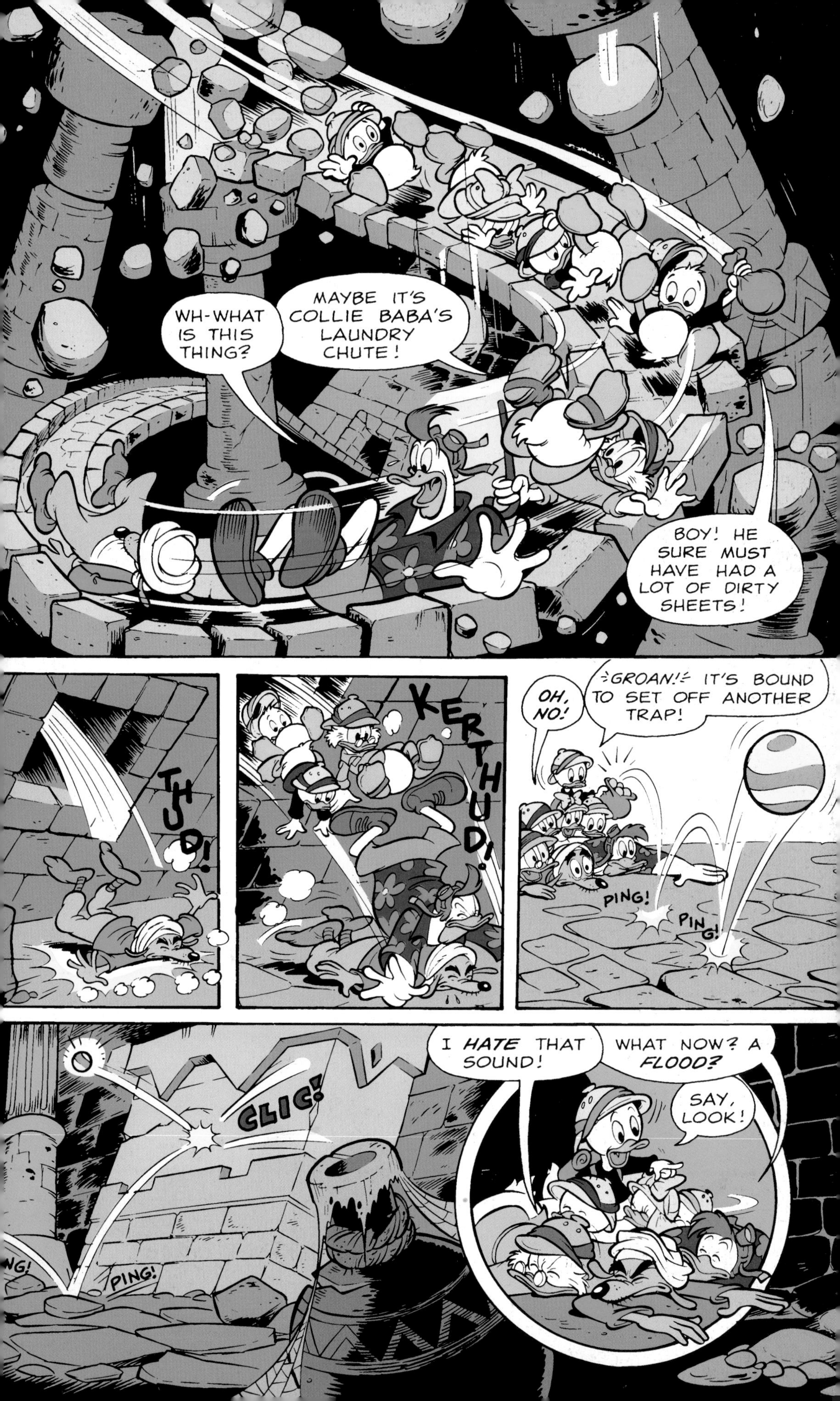

WH-WHAT IS THIS THING?
MAYBE IT'S COLLIE BABA'S LAUNDRY CHUTE!
BOY! HE SURE MUST HAVE HAD A LOT OF DIRTY SHEETS!
THUD!
KERTHUD!
OH, NO!
GROAN! IT'S BOUND TO SET OFF ANOTHER TRAP!
PING!
PING!
CLIC!
NG!
PING!
I HATE THAT SOUND!
WHAT NOW? A FLOOD?
SAY, LOOK!

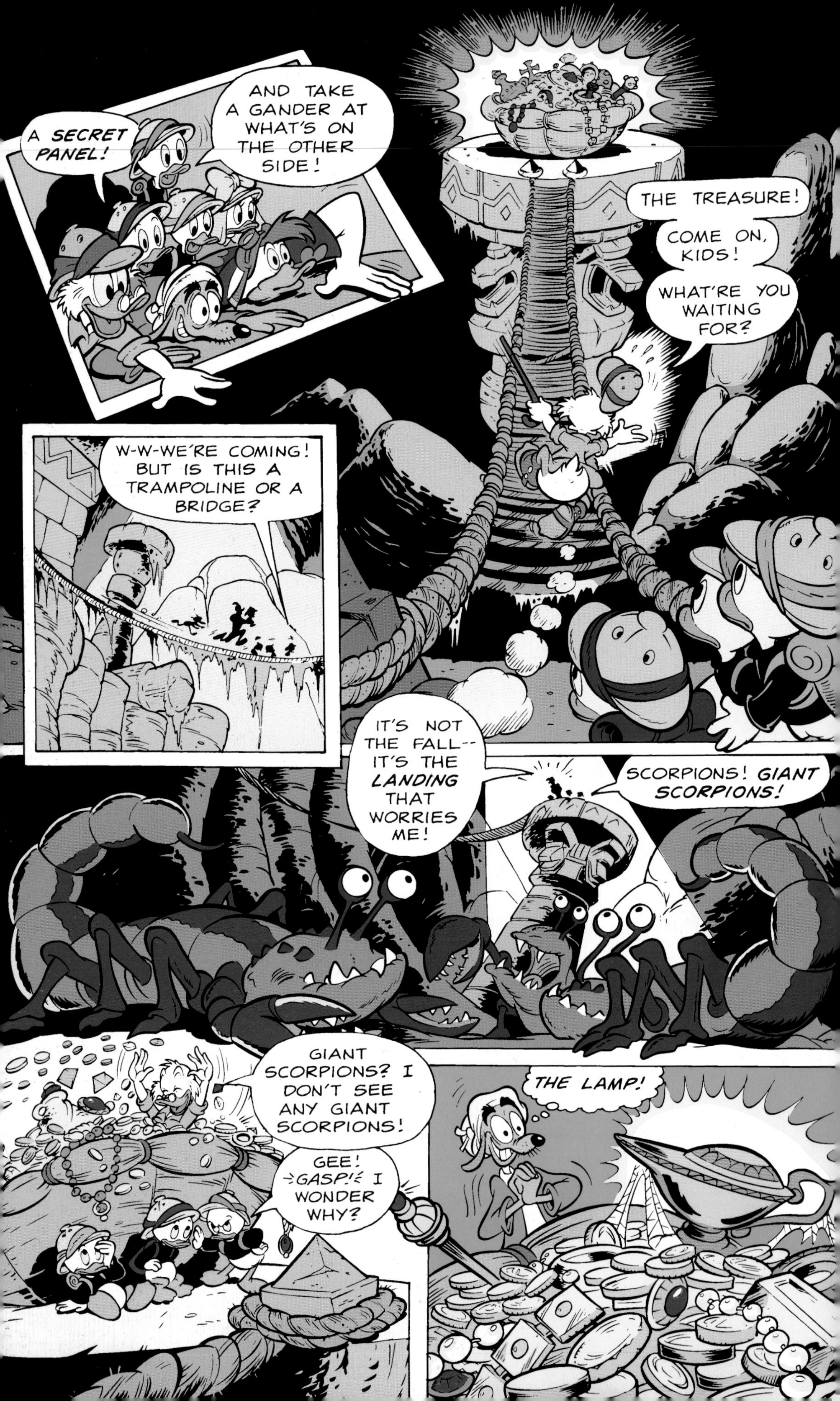
A SECRET PANEL!
AND TAKE A GANDER AT WHAT'S ON THE OTHER SIDE!
THE TREASURE!
COME ON, KIDS!
WHAT'RE YOU WAITING FOR?
W-W-WE'RE COMING! BUT IS THIS A TRAMPOLINE OR A BRIDGE?
IT'S NOT THE FALL-- IT'S THE LANDING THAT WORRIES ME!
SCORPIONS! GIANT SCORPIONS!
GIANT SCORPIONS? I DON'T SEE ANY GIANT SCORPIONS!
GEE! *GASP!* I WONDER WHY?
THE LAMP!

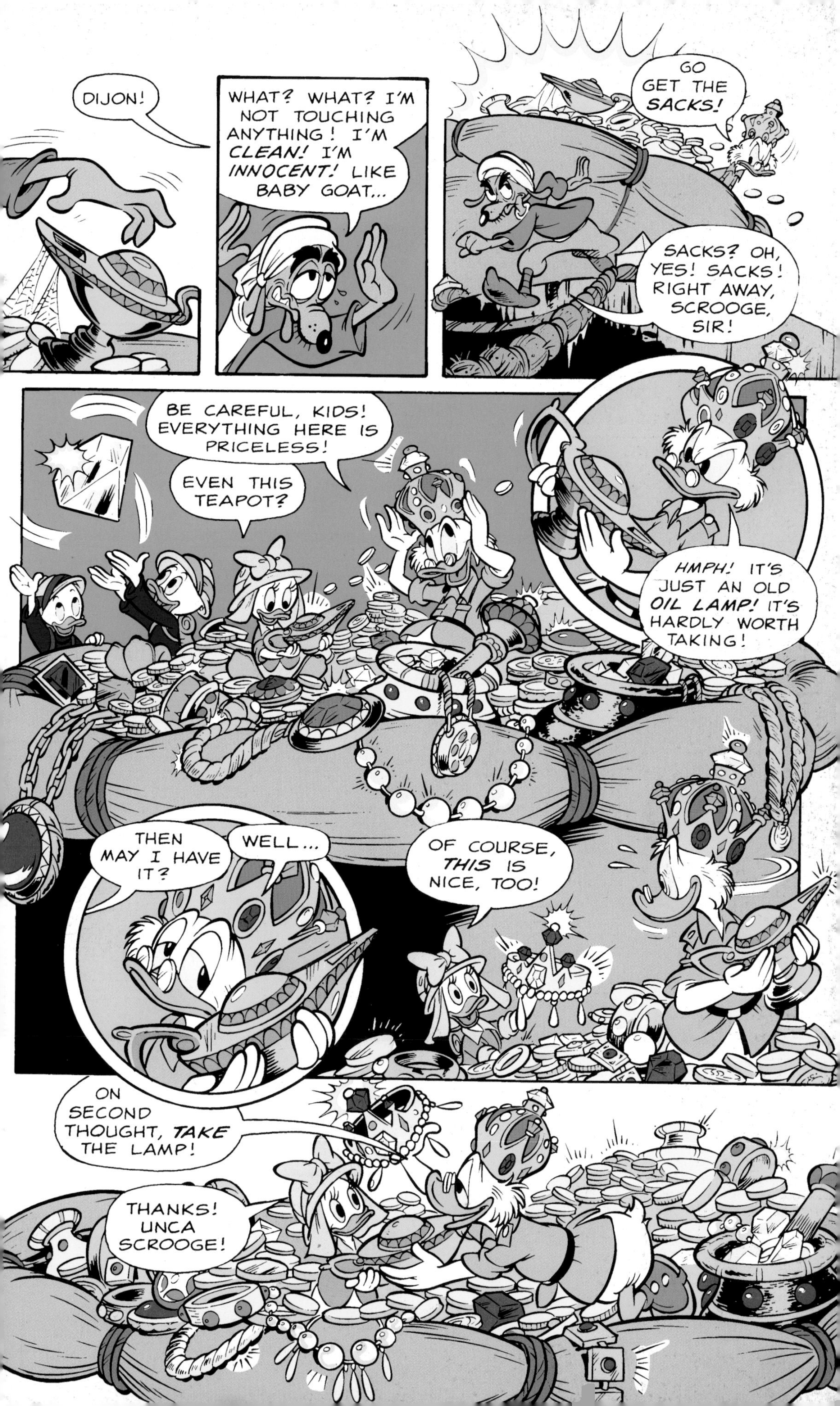
DIJON!
WHAT? WHAT? I'M NOT TOUCHING ANYTHING! I'M CLEAN! I'M INNOCENT! LIKE BABY GOAT...
GO GET THE SACKS!
SACKS? OH, YES! SACKS! RIGHT AWAY, SCROOGE, SIR!
BE CAREFUL, KIDS! EVERYTHING HERE IS PRICELESS!
EVEN THIS TEAPOT?
HMPH! IT'S JUST AN OLD OIL LAMP! IT'S HARDLY WORTH TAKING!
THEN MAY I HAVE IT?
WELL...
OF COURSE, THIS IS NICE, TOO!
ON SECOND THOUGHT, TAKE THE LAMP!
THANKS! UNCA SCROOGE!

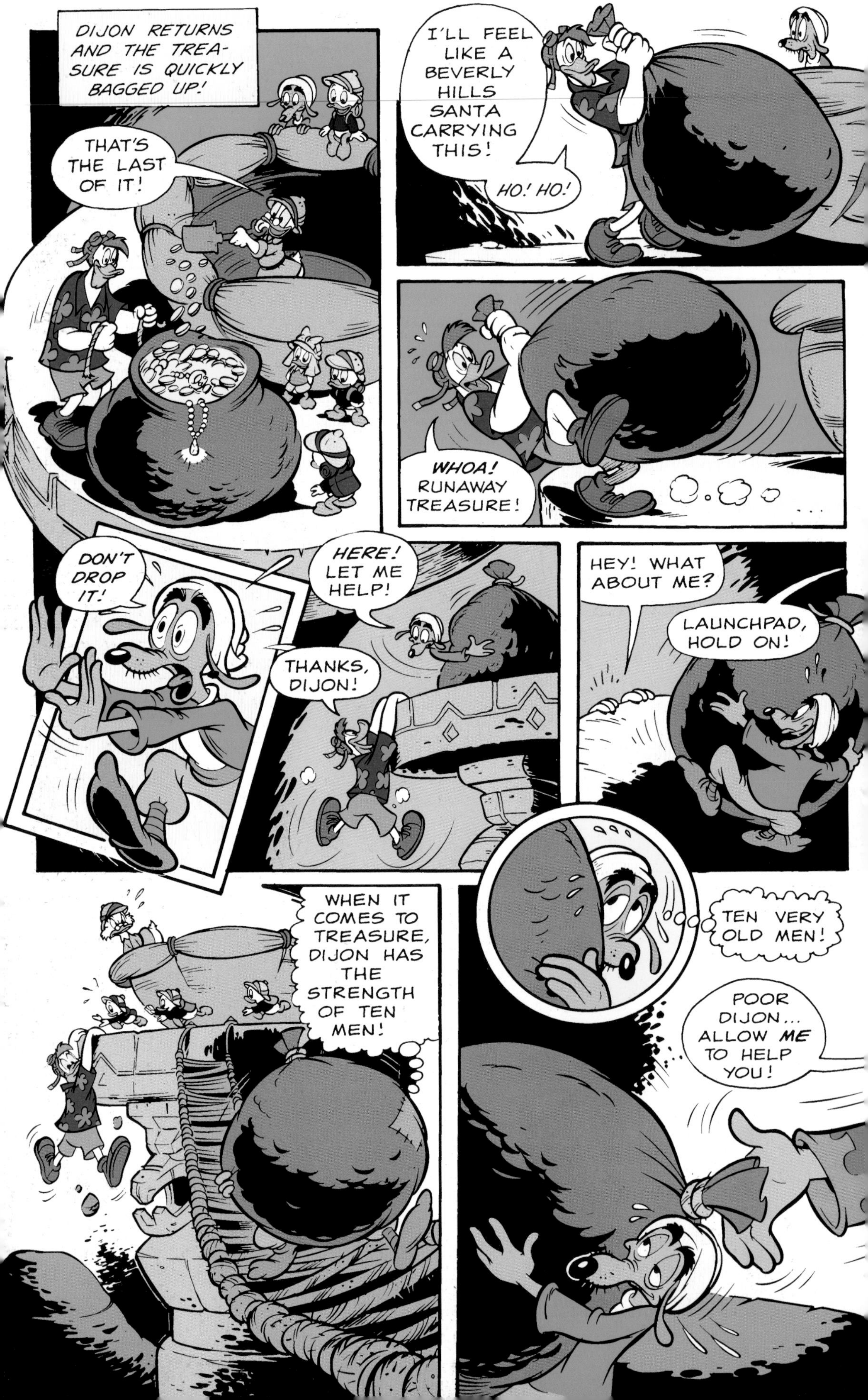
DIJON RETURNS AND THE TREASURE IS QUICKLY BAGGED UP!
THAT'S THE LAST OF IT!
I'LL FEEL LIKE A BEVERLY HILLS SANTA CARRYING THIS!
HO! HO!
WHOA! RUNAWAY TREASURE!
DON'T DROP IT!
HERE! LET ME HELP!
THANKS, DIJON!
HEY! WHAT ABOUT ME?
LAUNCHPAD, HOLD ON!
WHEN IT COMES TO TREASURE, DIJON HAS THE STRENGTH OF TEN MEN!
TEN VERY OLD MEN!
POOR DIJON... ALLOW ME TO HELP YOU!

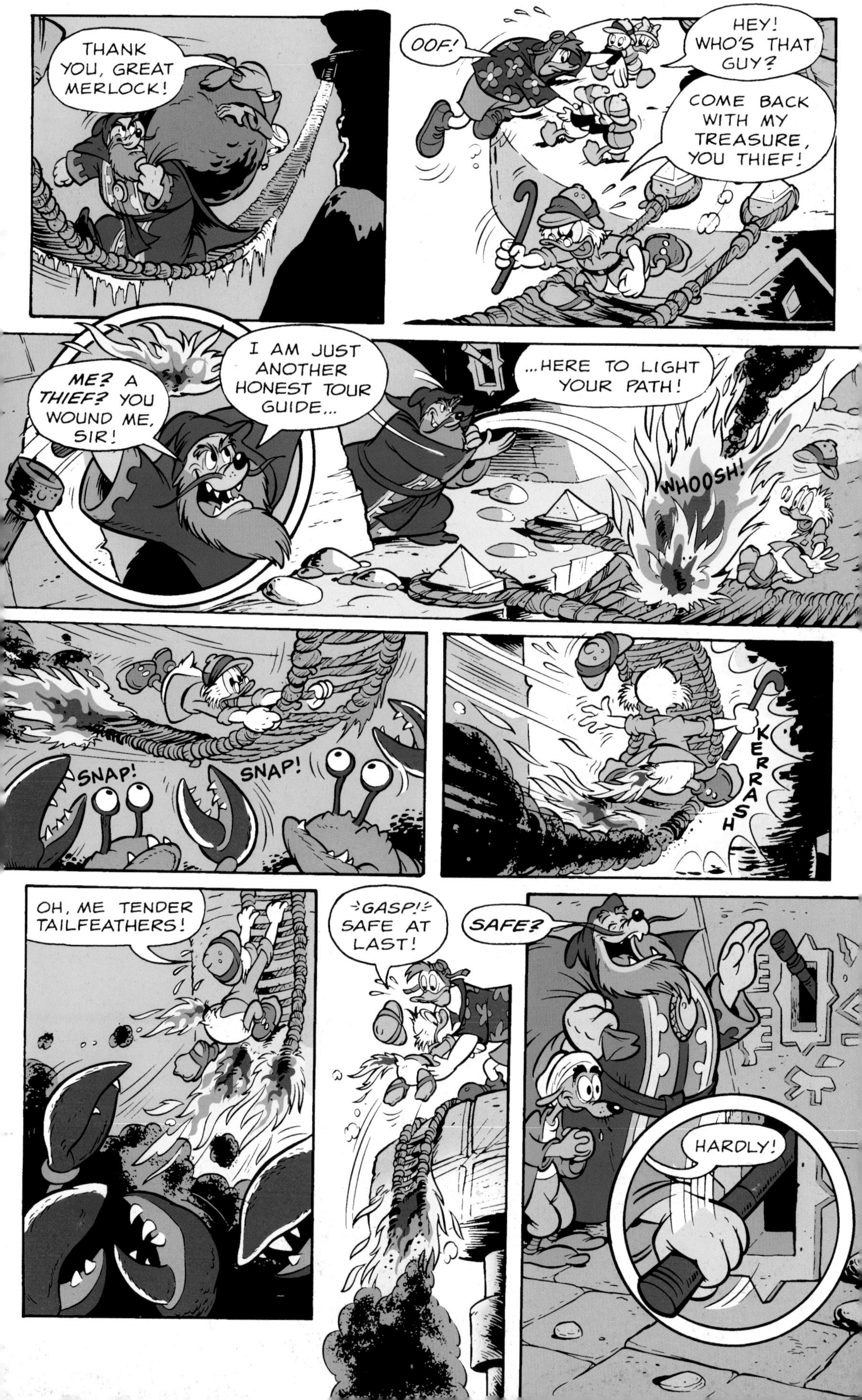
THANK YOU, GREAT MERLOCK!
OOF!
HEY! WHO'S THAT GUY?
COME BACK WITH MY TREASURE, YOU THIEF!
ME? A THIEF? YOU WOUND ME, SIR!
I AM JUST ANOTHER HONEST TOUR GUIDE...
...HERE TO LIGHT YOUR PATH!
WHOOSH!
SNAP!
SNAP!
KERRASH
OH, ME TENDER TAILFEATHERS!
GASP! SAFE AT LAST!
SAFE?
HARDLY!

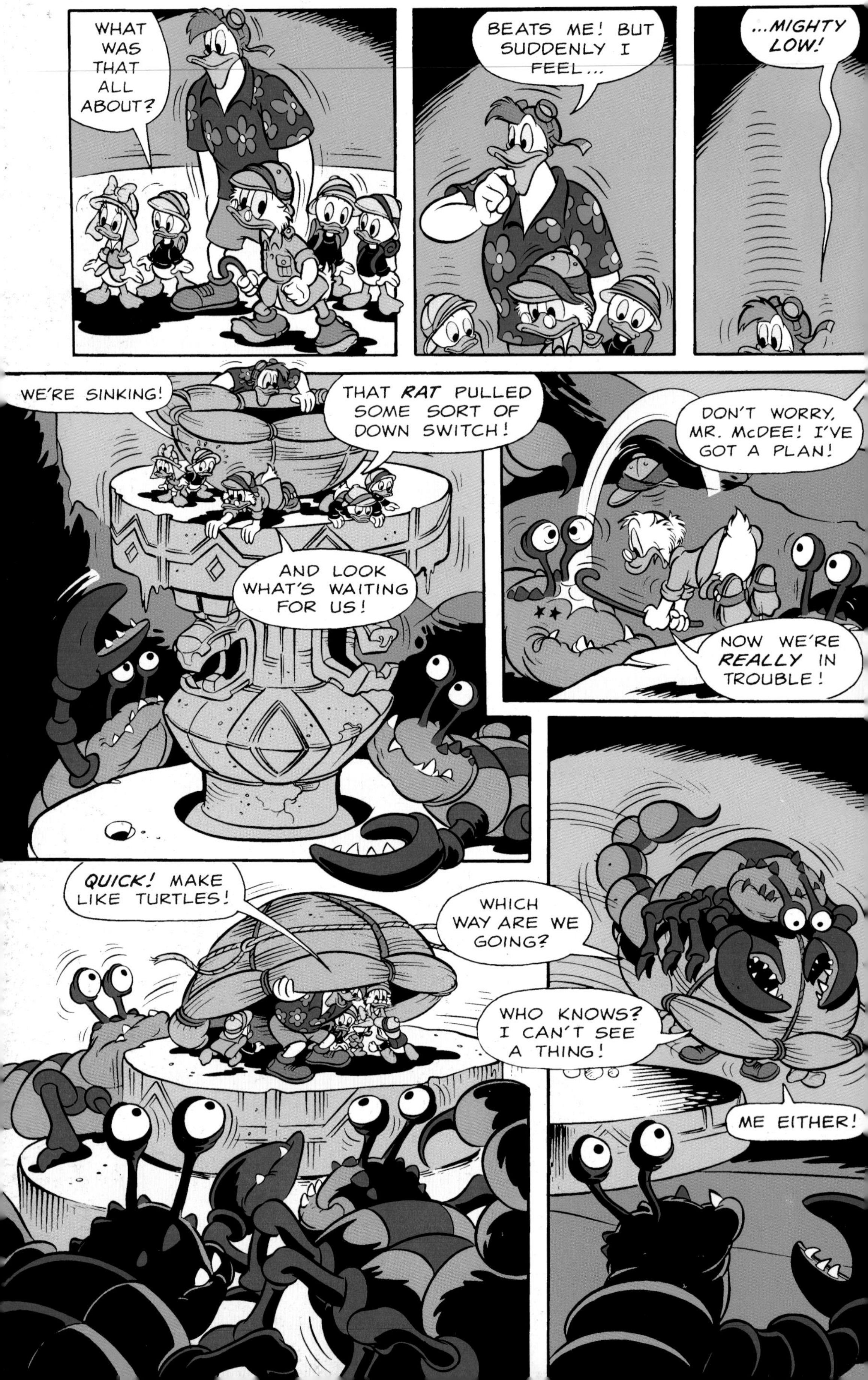
WHAT WAS THAT ALL ABOUT?
BEATS ME! BUT SUDDENLY I FEEL...
...MIGHTY LOW!
WE'RE SINKING!
THAT RAT PULLED SOME SORT OF DOWN SWITCH!
AND LOOK WHAT'S WAITING FOR US!
DON'T WORRY, MR. McDEE! I'VE GOT A PLAN!
NOW WE'RE REALLY IN TROUBLE!
QUICK! MAKE LIKE TURTLES!
WHICH WAY ARE WE GOING?
WHO KNOWS? I CAN'T SEE A THING!
ME EITHER!

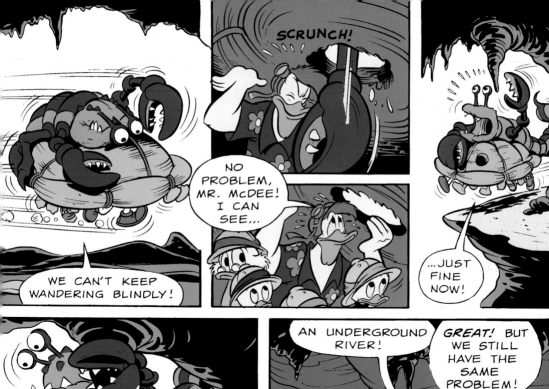

SCRUNCH!

NO PROBLEM, MR. McDEE! I CAN SEE...

WE CAN'T KEEP WANDERING BLINDLY!

...JUST FINE NOW!

YEOOOWW!

SPLASH!!!

AN UNDERGROUND RIVER!

GREAT! BUT WE STILL HAVE THE SAME PROBLEM!

WE DON'T KNOW WHERE WE'RE GOING!

ROAR!

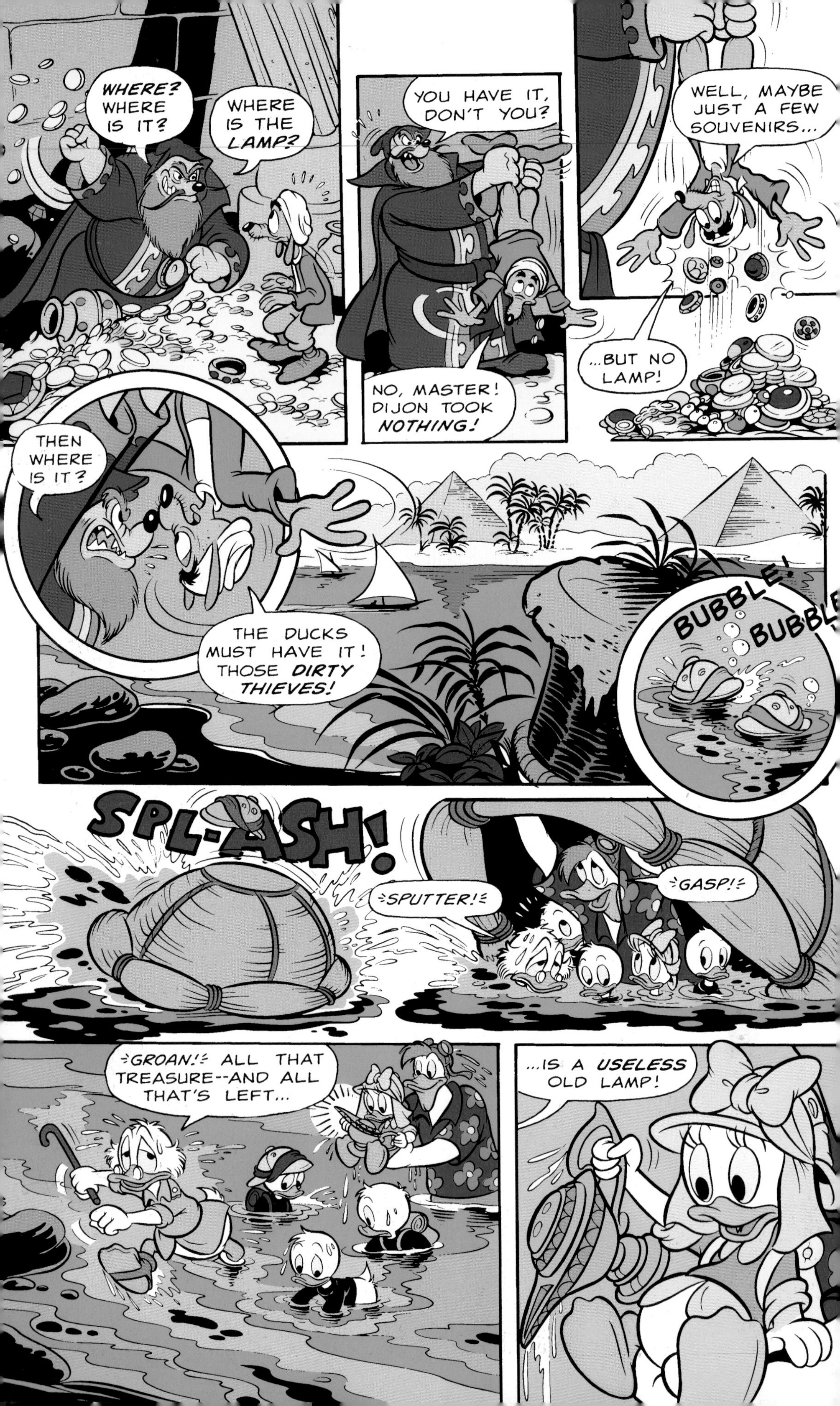
WHERE? WHERE IS IT?
WHERE IS THE LAMP?
YOU HAVE IT, DON'T YOU?
NO, MASTER! DIJON TOOK NOTHING!
WELL, MAYBE JUST A FEW SOUVENIRS...
...BUT NO LAMP!
THEN WHERE IS IT?
THE DUCKS MUST HAVE IT! THOSE DIRTY THIEVES!
BUBBLE!
SPL-ASH!
SPUTTER!
GASP!
GROAN! ALL THAT TREASURE--AND ALL THAT'S LEFT...
...IS A USELESS OLD LAMP!

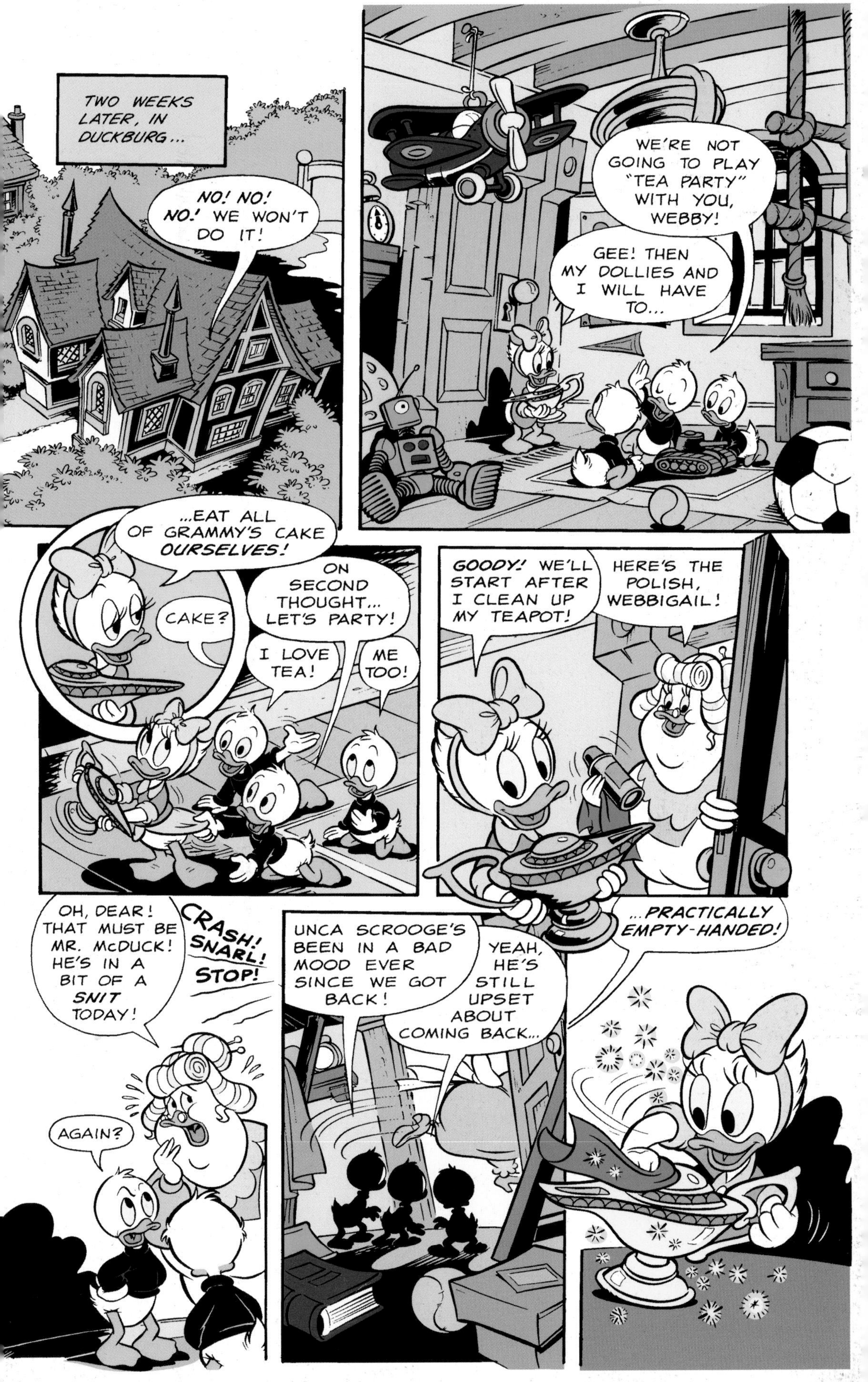
TWO WEEKS LATER, IN DUCKBURG...
NO! NO! NO! WE WON'T DO IT!
WE'RE NOT GOING TO PLAY "TEA PARTY" WITH YOU, WEBBY!
GEE! THEN MY DOLLIES AND I WILL HAVE TO...
...EAT ALL OF GRAMMY'S CAKE OURSELVES!
CAKE?
ON SECOND THOUGHT... LET'S PARTY!
I LOVE TEA!
ME TOO!
GOODY! WE'LL START AFTER I CLEAN UP MY TEAPOT!
HERE'S THE POLISH, WEBBIGAIL!
OH, DEAR! THAT MUST BE MR. McDUCK! HE'S IN A BIT OF A SNIT TODAY!
CRASH! SNARL! STOP!
AGAIN?
UNCA SCROOGE'S BEEN IN A BAD MOOD EVER SINCE WE GOT BACK!
YEAH, HE'S STILL UPSET ABOUT COMING BACK...
...PRACTICALLY EMPTY-HANDED!

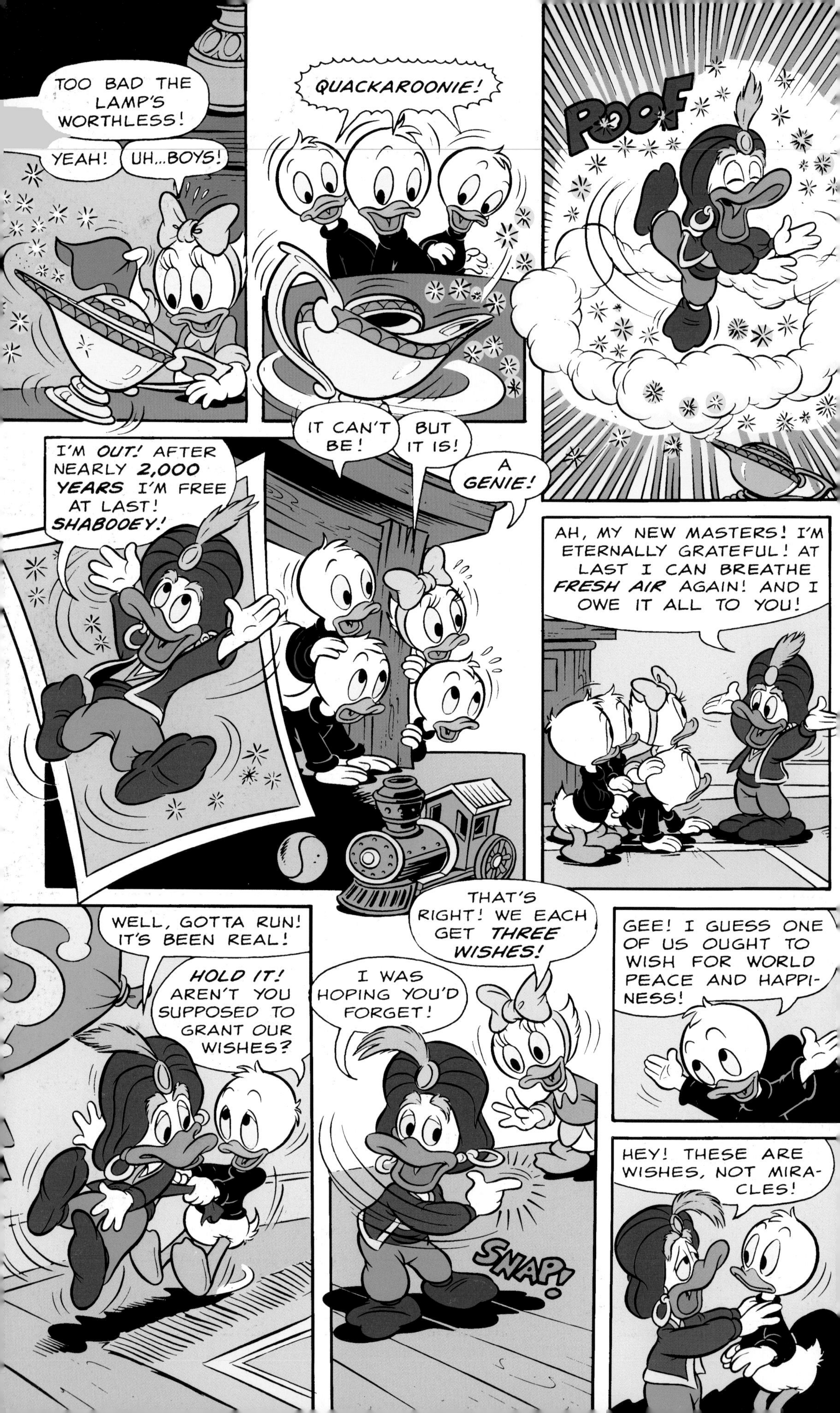

TOO BAD THE LAMP'S WORTHLESS!
YEAH!
UH...BOYS!
QUACKAROONIE!
POOF
I'M OUT! AFTER NEARLY 2,000 YEARS I'M FREE AT LAST! SHABOOEY!
IT CAN'T BE!
BUT IT IS!
A GENIE!
AH, MY NEW MASTERS! I'M ETERNALLY GRATEFUL! AT LAST I CAN BREATHE FRESH AIR AGAIN! AND I OWE IT ALL TO YOU!
WELL, GOTTA RUN! IT'S BEEN REAL!
HOLD IT! AREN'T YOU SUPPOSED TO GRANT OUR WISHES?
I WAS HOPING YOU'D FORGET!
THAT'S RIGHT! WE EACH GET THREE WISHES!
SNAP!
GEE! I GUESS ONE OF US OUGHT TO WISH FOR WORLD PEACE AND HAPPI-NESS!
HEY! THESE ARE WISHES, NOT MIRA-CLES!

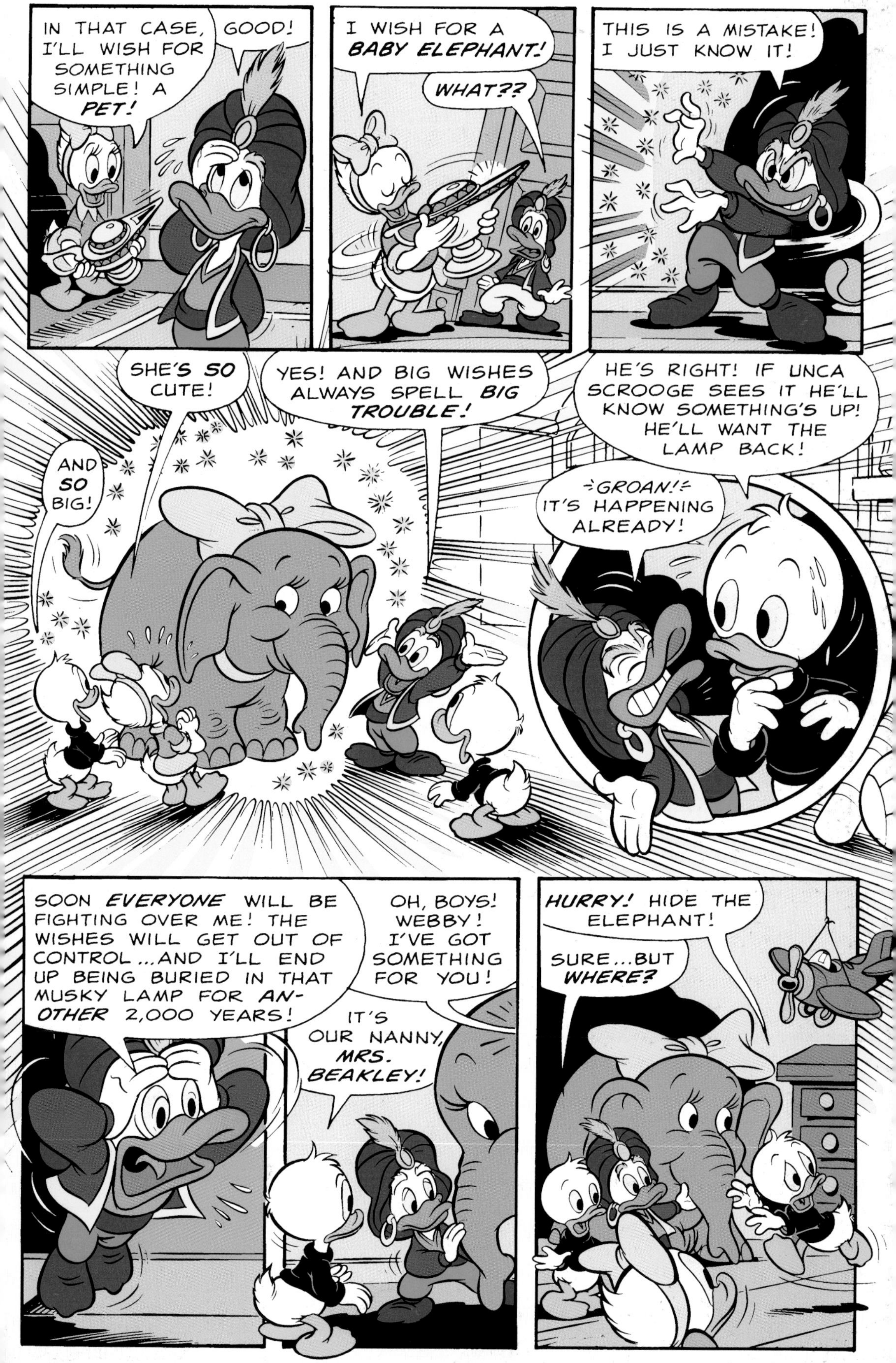
IN THAT CASE, I'LL WISH FOR SOMETHING SIMPLE! A PET!
GOOD!
I WISH FOR A BABY ELEPHANT!
WHAT??
THIS IS A MISTAKE! I JUST KNOW IT!
SHE'S SO CUTE!
AND SO BIG!
YES! AND BIG WISHES ALWAYS SPELL BIG TROUBLE!
HE'S RIGHT! IF UNCA SCROOGE SEES IT HE'LL KNOW SOMETHING'S UP! HE'LL WANT THE LAMP BACK!
GROAN! IT'S HAPPENING ALREADY!
SOON EVERYONE WILL BE FIGHTING OVER ME! THE WISHES WILL GET OUT OF CONTROL... AND I'LL END UP BEING BURIED IN THAT MUSKY LAMP FOR AN-OTHER 2,000 YEARS!
OH, BOYS! WEBBY! I'VE GOT SOMETHING FOR YOU!
IT'S OUR NANNY, MRS. BEAKLEY!
HURRY! HIDE THE ELEPHANT!
SURE... BUT WHERE?

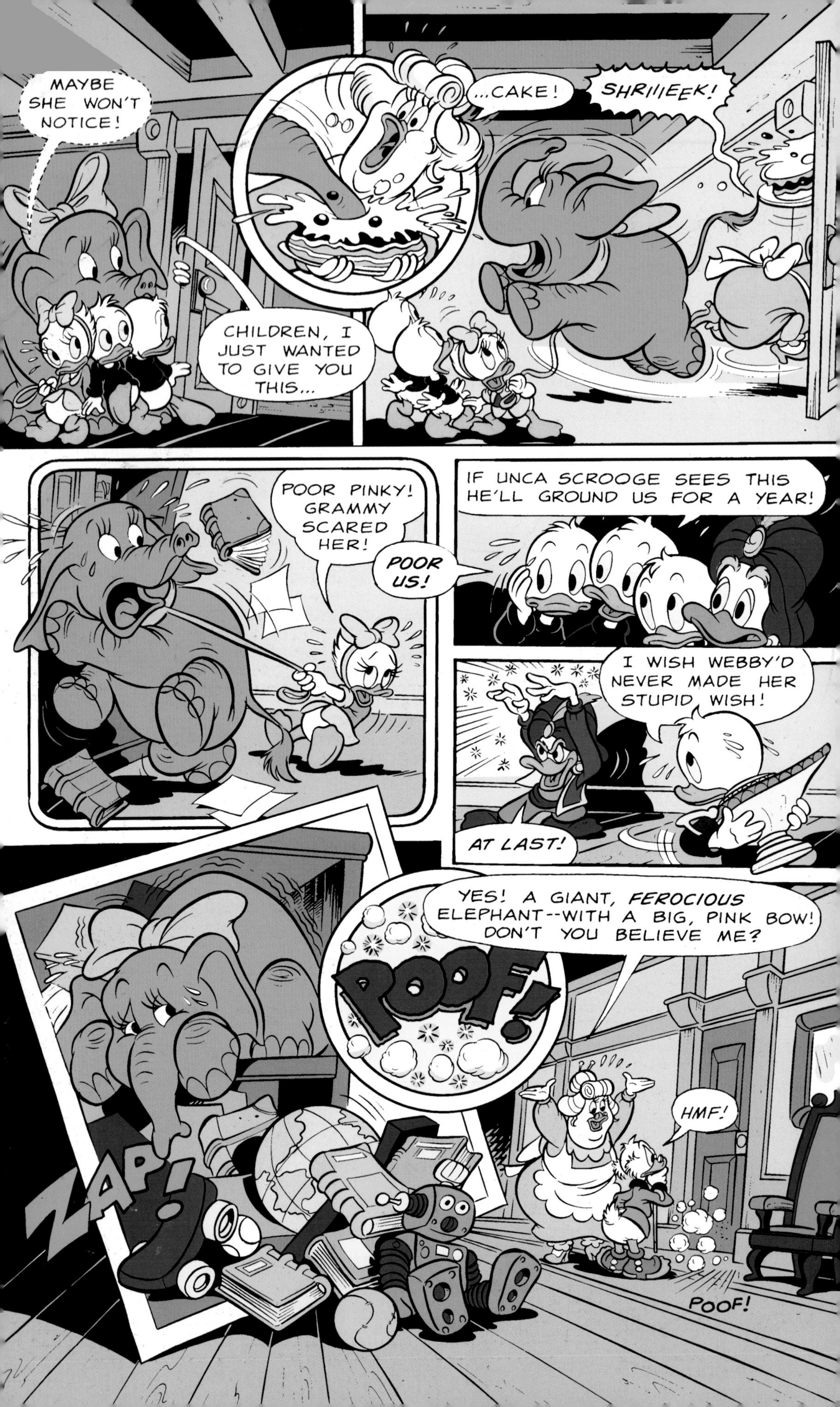
MAYBE SHE WON'T NOTICE!
CHILDREN, I JUST WANTED TO GIVE YOU THIS...
...CAKE!
SHRIIIEEK!
POOR PINKY! GRAMMY SCARED HER!
POOR US!
IF UNCA SCROOGE SEES THIS HE'LL GROUND US FOR A YEAR!
I WISH WEBBY'D NEVER MADE HER STUPID WISH!
AT LAST!
ZAP!
POOF!
YES! A GIANT, FEROCIOUS ELEPHANT--WITH A BIG, PINK BOW! DON'T YOU BELIEVE ME?
HMF!
POOF!

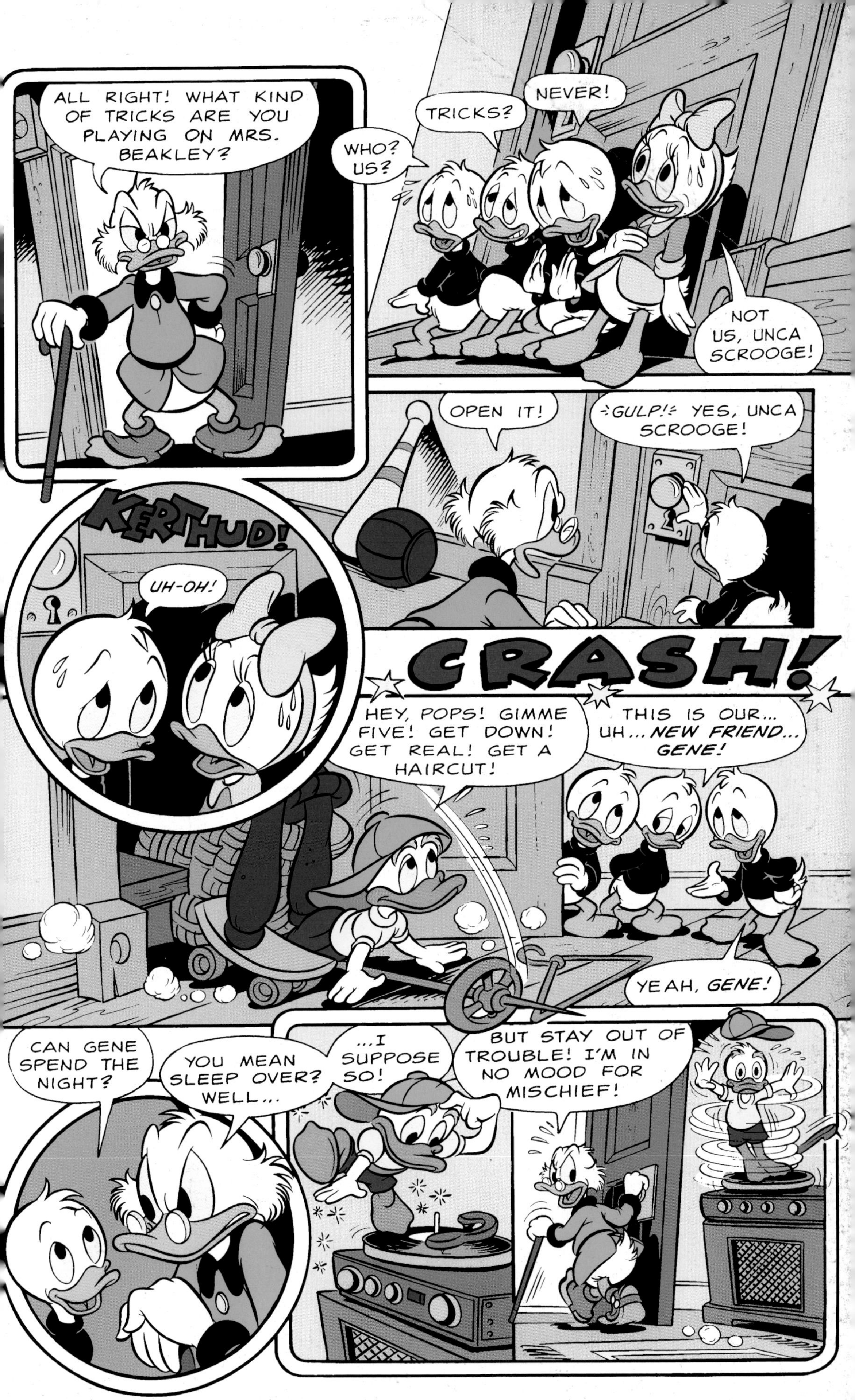
ALL RIGHT! WHAT KIND OF TRICKS ARE YOU PLAYING ON MRS. BEAKLEY?
WHO? US?
TRICKS?
NEVER!
NOT US, UNCA SCROOGE!
OPEN IT!
-GULP!- YES, UNCA SCROOGE!
KERTHUD!
UH-OH!
CRASH!
HEY, POPS! GIMME FIVE! GET DOWN! GET REAL! GET A HAIRCUT!
THIS IS OUR... UH... NEW FRIEND... GENE!
YEAH, GENE!
CAN GENE SPEND THE NIGHT?
YOU MEAN SLEEP OVER? WELL...
...I SUPPOSE SO!
BUT STAY OUT OF TROUBLE! I'M IN NO MOOD FOR MISCHIEF!

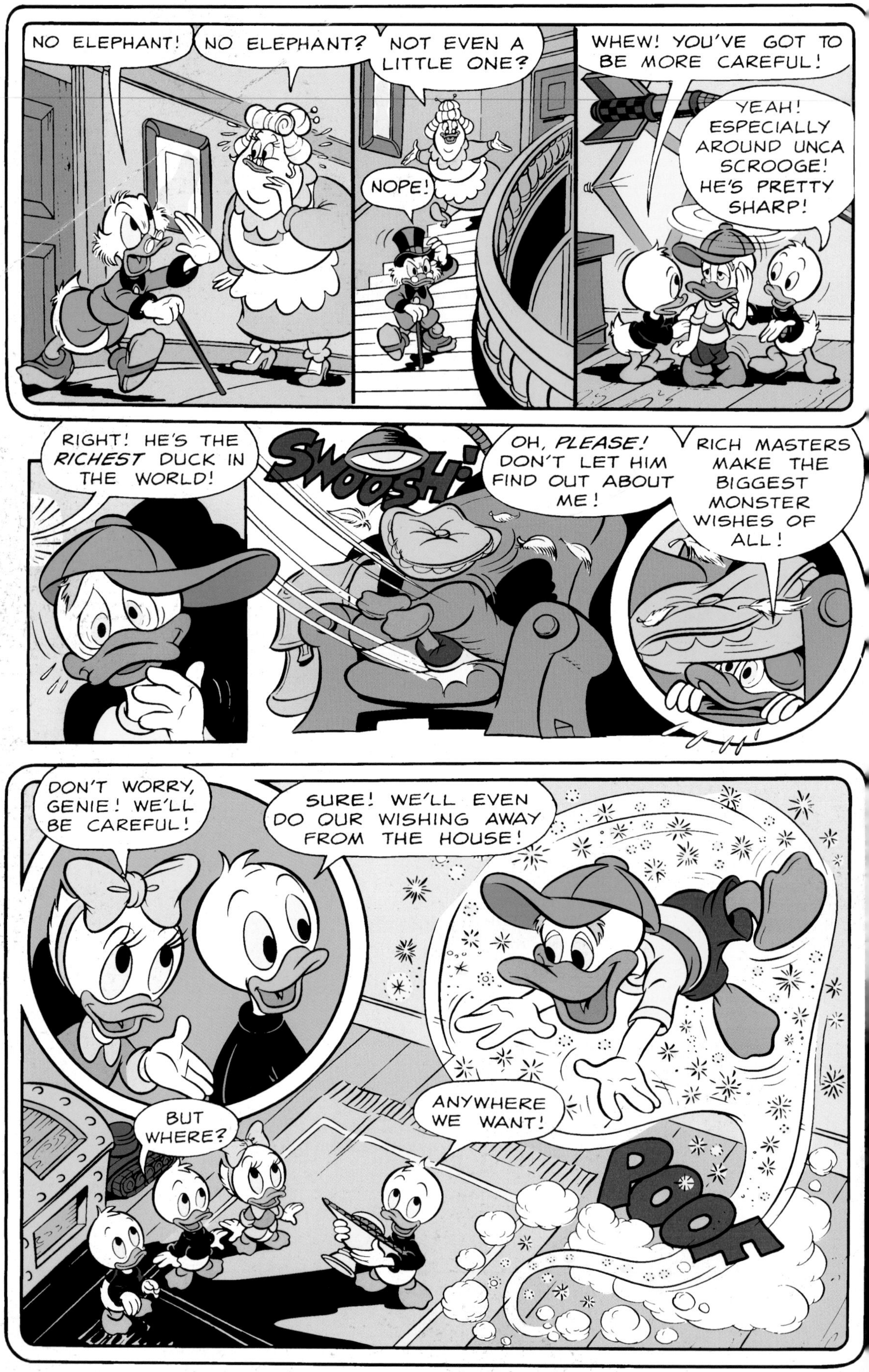
NO ELEPHANT!
NO ELEPHANT?
NOT EVEN A LITTLE ONE?
NOPE!
WHEW! YOU'VE GOT TO BE MORE CAREFUL!
YEAH! ESPECIALLY AROUND UNCA SCROOGE! HE'S PRETTY SHARP!
RIGHT! HE'S THE *RICHEST* DUCK IN THE WORLD!
SWOOSH!
OH, *PLEASE!* DON'T LET HIM FIND OUT ABOUT ME!
RICH MASTERS MAKE THE BIGGEST MONSTER WISHES OF ALL!
DON'T WORRY, GENIE! WE'LL BE CAREFUL!
SURE! WE'LL EVEN DO OUR WISHING AWAY FROM THE HOUSE!
BUT WHERE?
ANYWHERE WE WANT!
POOF

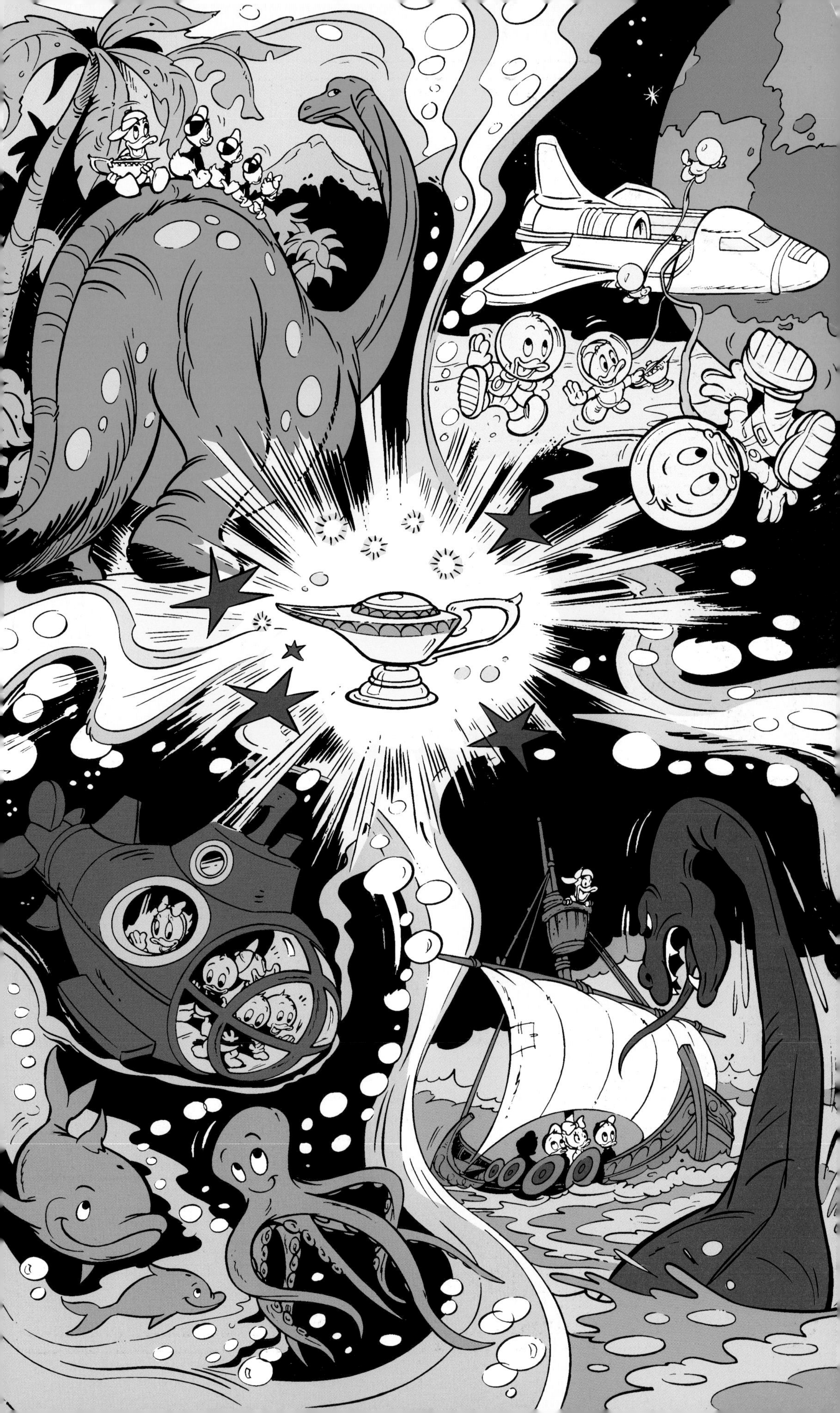

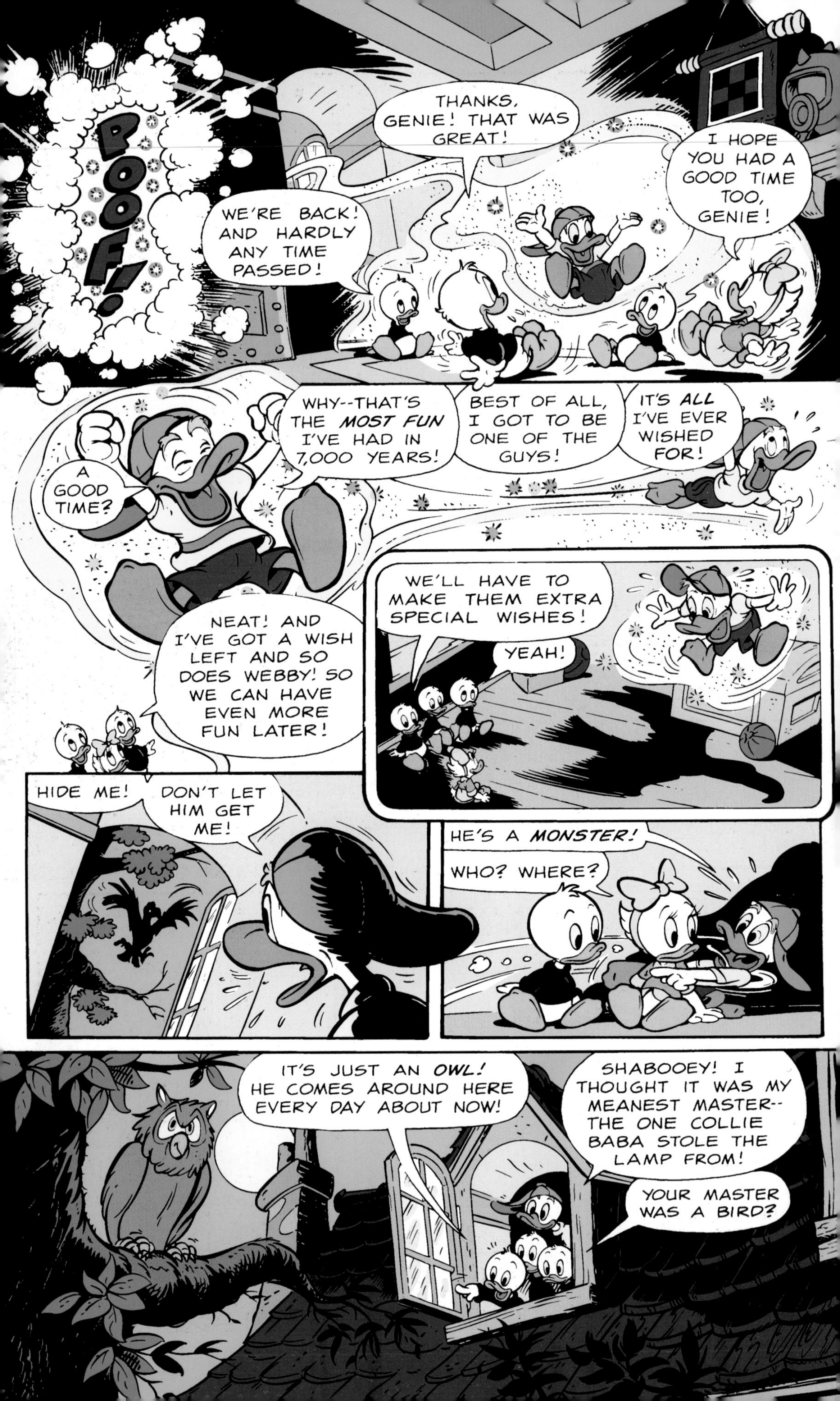
POOF!
THANKS, GENIE! THAT WAS GREAT!
I HOPE YOU HAD A GOOD TIME TOO, GENIE!
WE'RE BACK! AND HARDLY ANY TIME PASSED!
A GOOD TIME?
WHY--THAT'S THE MOST FUN I'VE HAD IN 7,000 YEARS!
BEST OF ALL, I GOT TO BE ONE OF THE GUYS!
IT'S ALL I'VE EVER WISHED FOR!
NEAT! AND I'VE GOT A WISH LEFT AND SO DOES WEBBY! SO WE CAN HAVE EVEN MORE FUN LATER!
WE'LL HAVE TO MAKE THEM EXTRA SPECIAL WISHES!
YEAH!
HIDE ME!
DON'T LET HIM GET ME!
HE'S A MONSTER!
WHO? WHERE?
IT'S JUST AN OWL! HE COMES AROUND HERE EVERY DAY ABOUT NOW!
SHABOOEY! I THOUGHT IT WAS MY MEANEST MASTER-- THE ONE COLLIE BABA STOLE THE LAMP FROM!
YOUR MASTER WAS A BIRD?

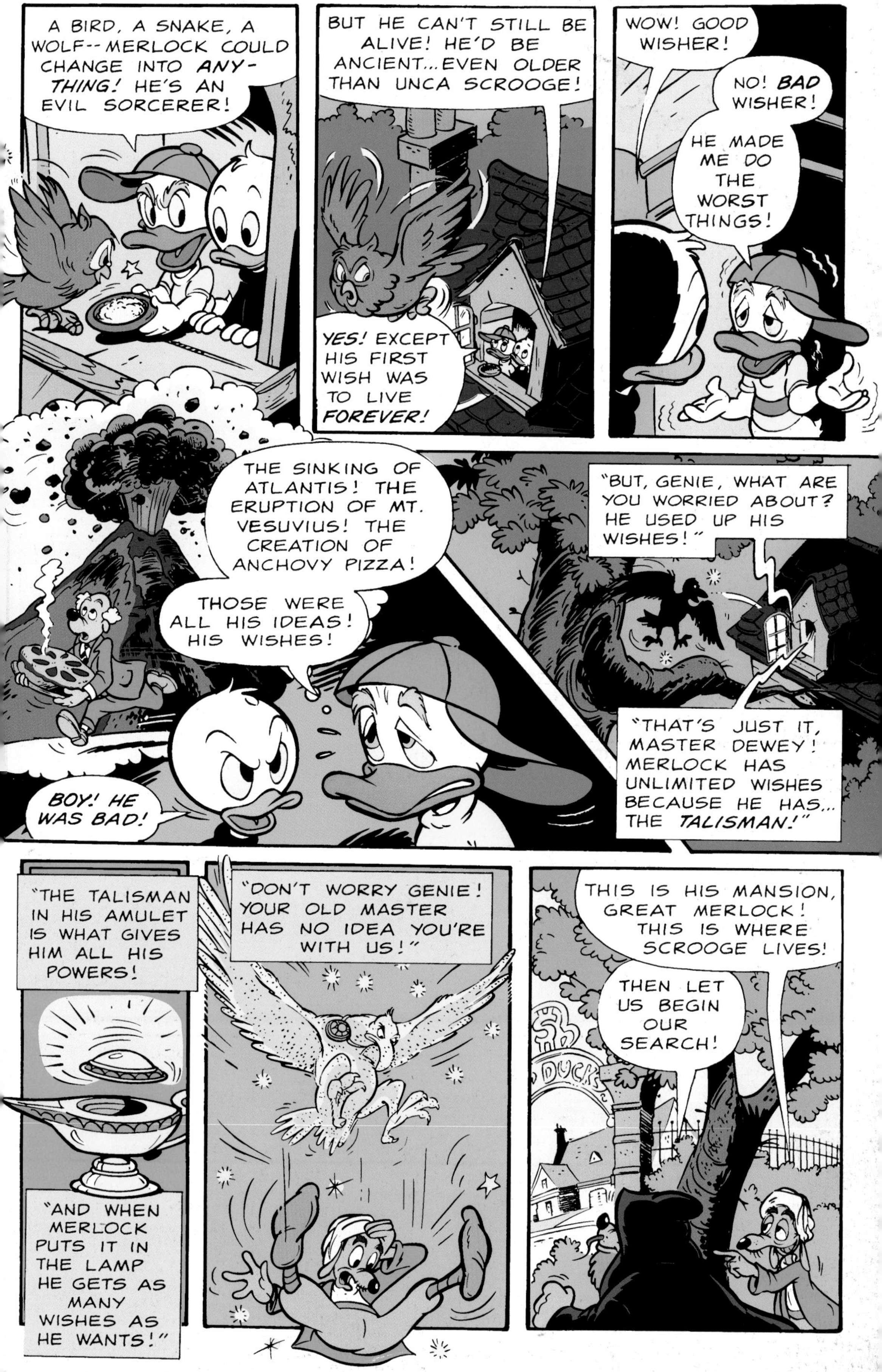
A BIRD, A SNAKE, A WOLF--MERLOCK COULD CHANGE INTO ANY-THING! HE'S AN EVIL SORCERER!
BUT HE CAN'T STILL BE ALIVE! HE'D BE ANCIENT...EVEN OLDER THAN UNCA SCROOGE!
YES! EXCEPT HIS FIRST WISH WAS TO LIVE FOREVER!
WOW! GOOD WISHER!
NO! BAD WISHER!
HE MADE ME DO THE WORST THINGS!
THE SINKING OF ATLANTIS! THE ERUPTION OF MT. VESUVIUS! THE CREATION OF ANCHOVY PIZZA!
THOSE WERE ALL HIS IDEAS! HIS WISHES!
BOY! HE WAS BAD!
"BUT, GENIE, WHAT ARE YOU WORRIED ABOUT? HE USED UP HIS WISHES!"
"THAT'S JUST IT, MASTER DEWEY! MERLOCK HAS UNLIMITED WISHES BECAUSE HE HAS... THE TALISMAN!"
"THE TALISMAN IN HIS AMULET IS WHAT GIVES HIM ALL HIS POWERS!
"AND WHEN MERLOCK PUTS IT IN THE LAMP HE GETS AS MANY WISHES AS HE WANTS!"
"DON'T WORRY GENIE! YOUR OLD MASTER HAS NO IDEA YOU'RE WITH US!"
THIS IS HIS MANSION, GREAT MERLOCK! THIS IS WHERE SCROOGE LIVES!
THEN LET US BEGIN OUR SEARCH!
DUCKS

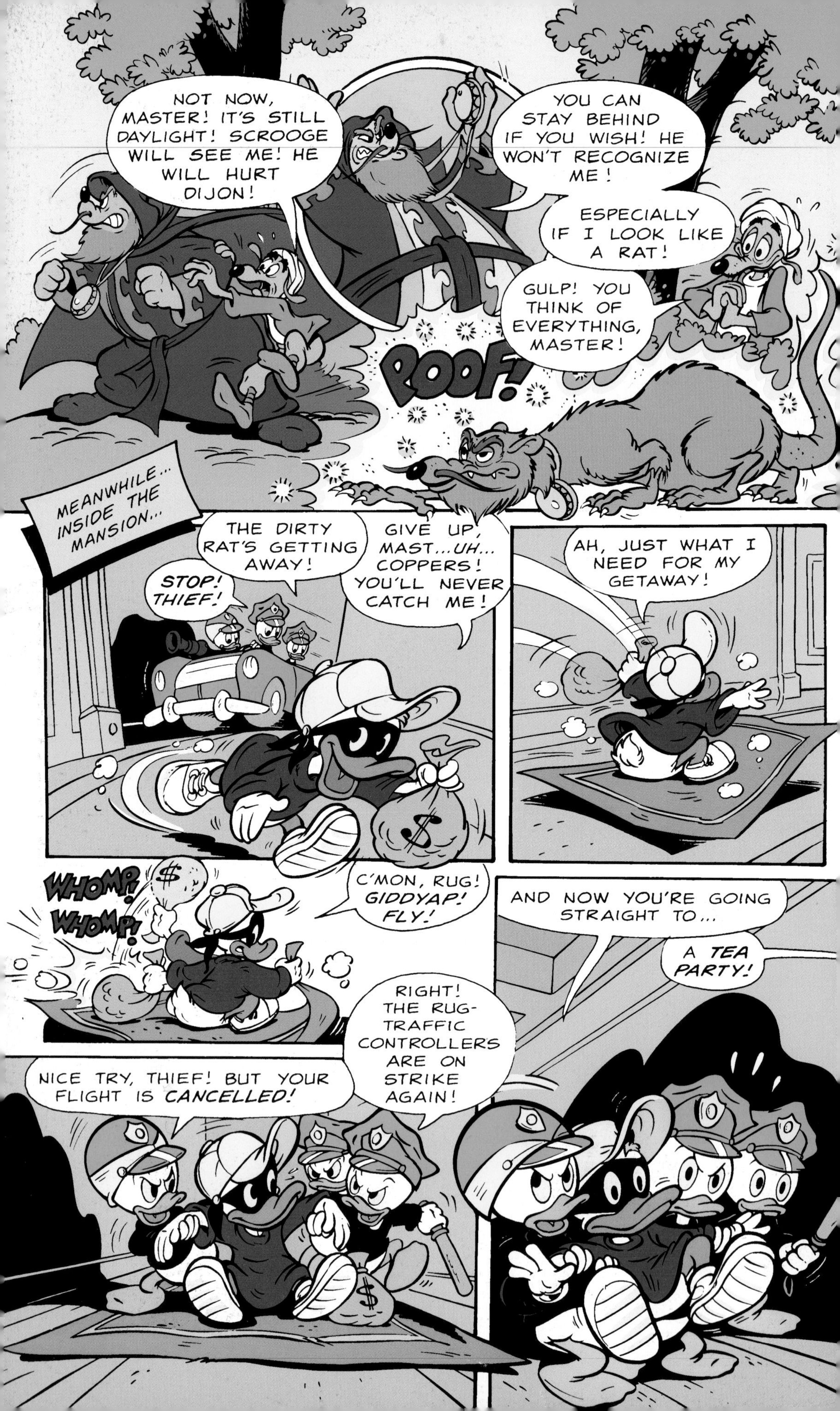
NOT NOW, MASTER! IT'S STILL DAYLIGHT! SCROOGE WILL SEE ME! HE WILL HURT DIJON!
YOU CAN STAY BEHIND IF YOU WISH! HE WON'T RECOGNIZE ME!
ESPECIALLY IF I LOOK LIKE A RAT!
GULP! YOU THINK OF EVERYTHING, MASTER!
POOF!
MEANWHILE... INSIDE THE MANSION...
STOP! THIEF!
THE DIRTY RAT'S GETTING AWAY!
GIVE UP, MAST... UH... COPPERS! YOU'LL NEVER CATCH ME!
AH, JUST WHAT I NEED FOR MY GETAWAY!
WHOMP! WHOMP!
C'MON, RUG! GIDDYAP! FLY!
NICE TRY, THIEF! BUT YOUR FLIGHT IS CANCELLED!
RIGHT! THE RUG-TRAFFIC CONTROLLERS ARE ON STRIKE AGAIN!
AND NOW YOU'RE GOING STRAIGHT TO...
A TEA PARTY!

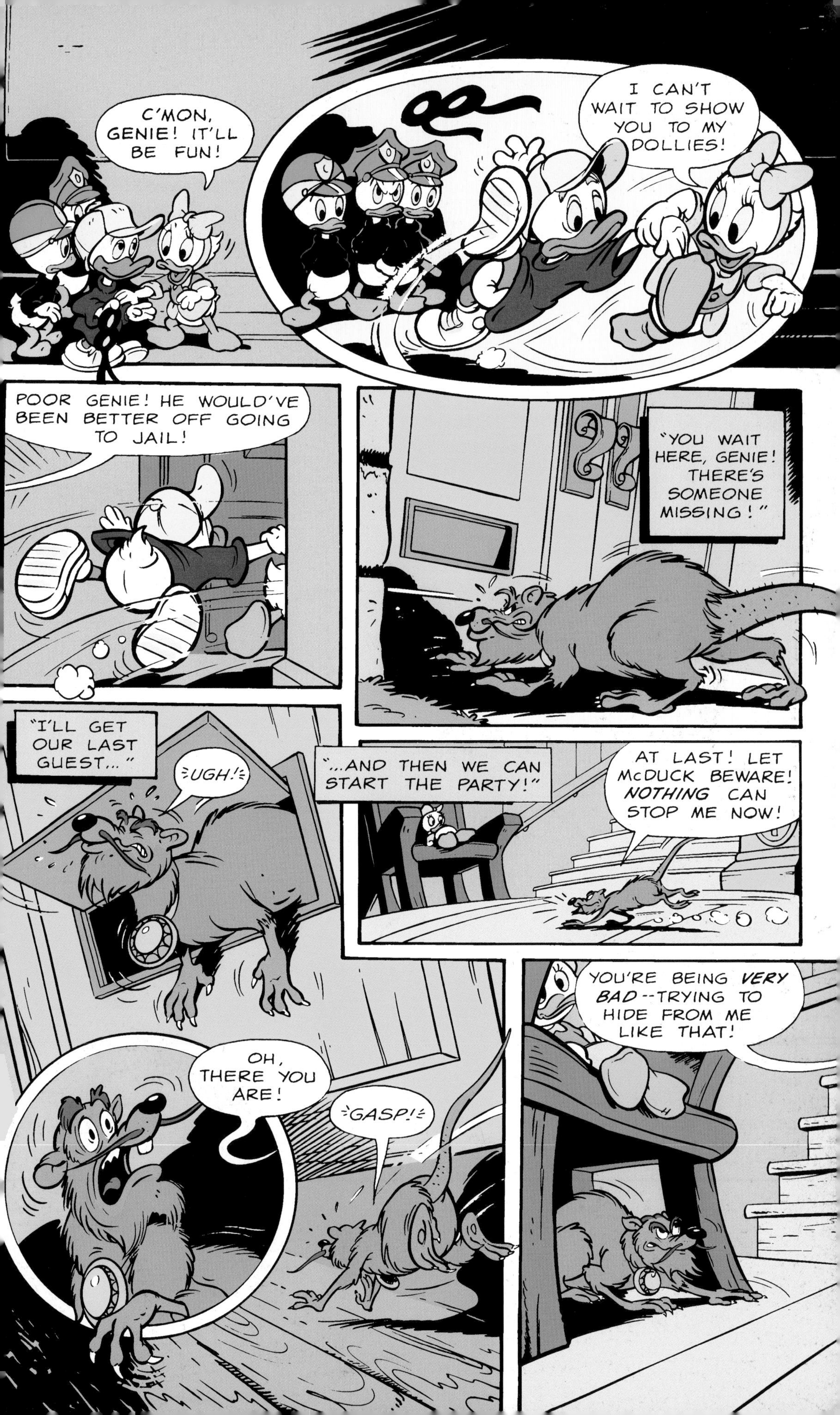
C'MON, GENIE! IT'LL BE FUN!
I CAN'T WAIT TO SHOW YOU TO MY DOLLIES!
POOR GENIE! HE WOULD'VE BEEN BETTER OFF GOING TO JAIL!
"YOU WAIT HERE, GENIE! THERE'S SOMEONE MISSING!"
"I'LL GET OUR LAST GUEST..."
UGH!
"...AND THEN WE CAN START THE PARTY!"
AT LAST! LET McDUCK BEWARE! *NOTHING* CAN STOP ME NOW!
OH, THERE YOU ARE!
GASP!
YOU'RE BEING *VERY BAD*--TRYING TO HIDE FROM ME LIKE THAT!

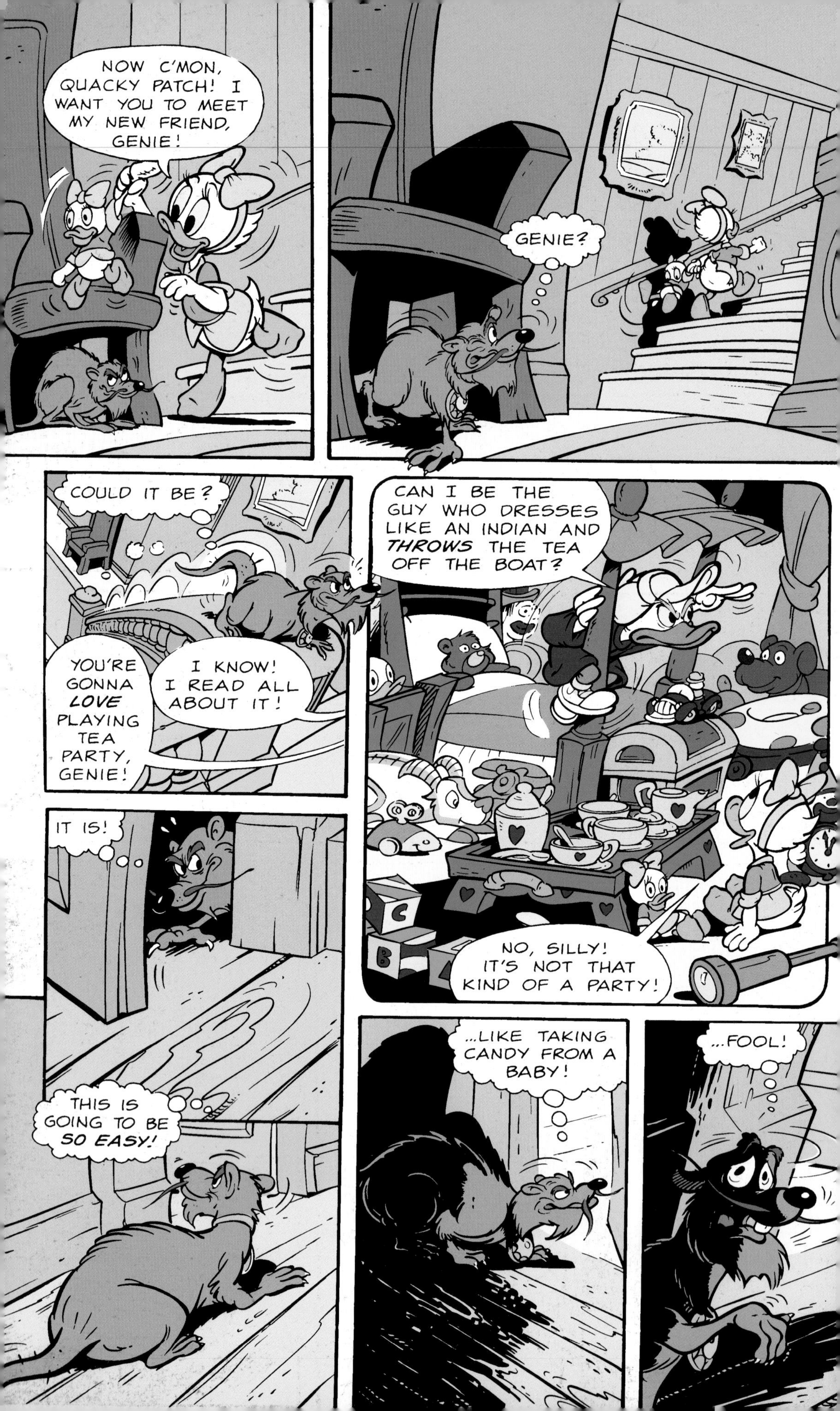
NOW C'MON, QUACKY PATCH! I WANT YOU TO MEET MY NEW FRIEND, GENIE!
GENIE?
COULD IT BE?
YOU'RE GONNA LOVE PLAYING TEA PARTY, GENIE!
I KNOW! I READ ALL ABOUT IT!
CAN I BE THE GUY WHO DRESSES LIKE AN INDIAN AND THROWS THE TEA OFF THE BOAT?
IT IS!
NO, SILLY! IT'S NOT THAT KIND OF A PARTY!
THIS IS GOING TO BE SO EASY!
...LIKE TAKING CANDY FROM A BABY!
...FOOL!

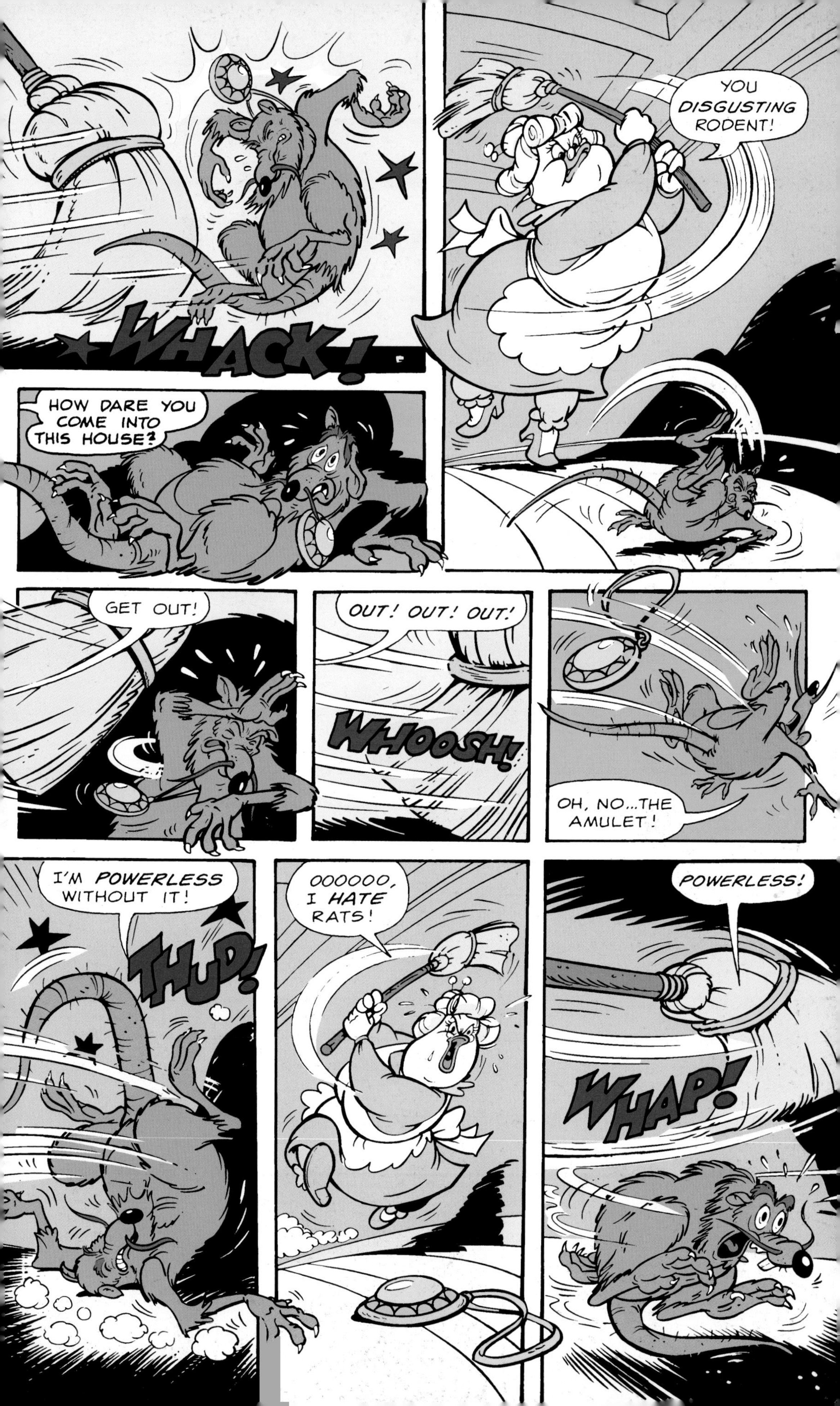
WHACK!
YOU DISGUSTING RODENT!
HOW DARE YOU COME INTO THIS HOUSE?
GET OUT!
OUT! OUT! OUT!
WHOOSH!
OH, NO...THE AMULET!
I'M POWERLESS WITHOUT IT!
THUD!
OOOOOO, I HATE RATS!
POWERLESS!
WHAP!

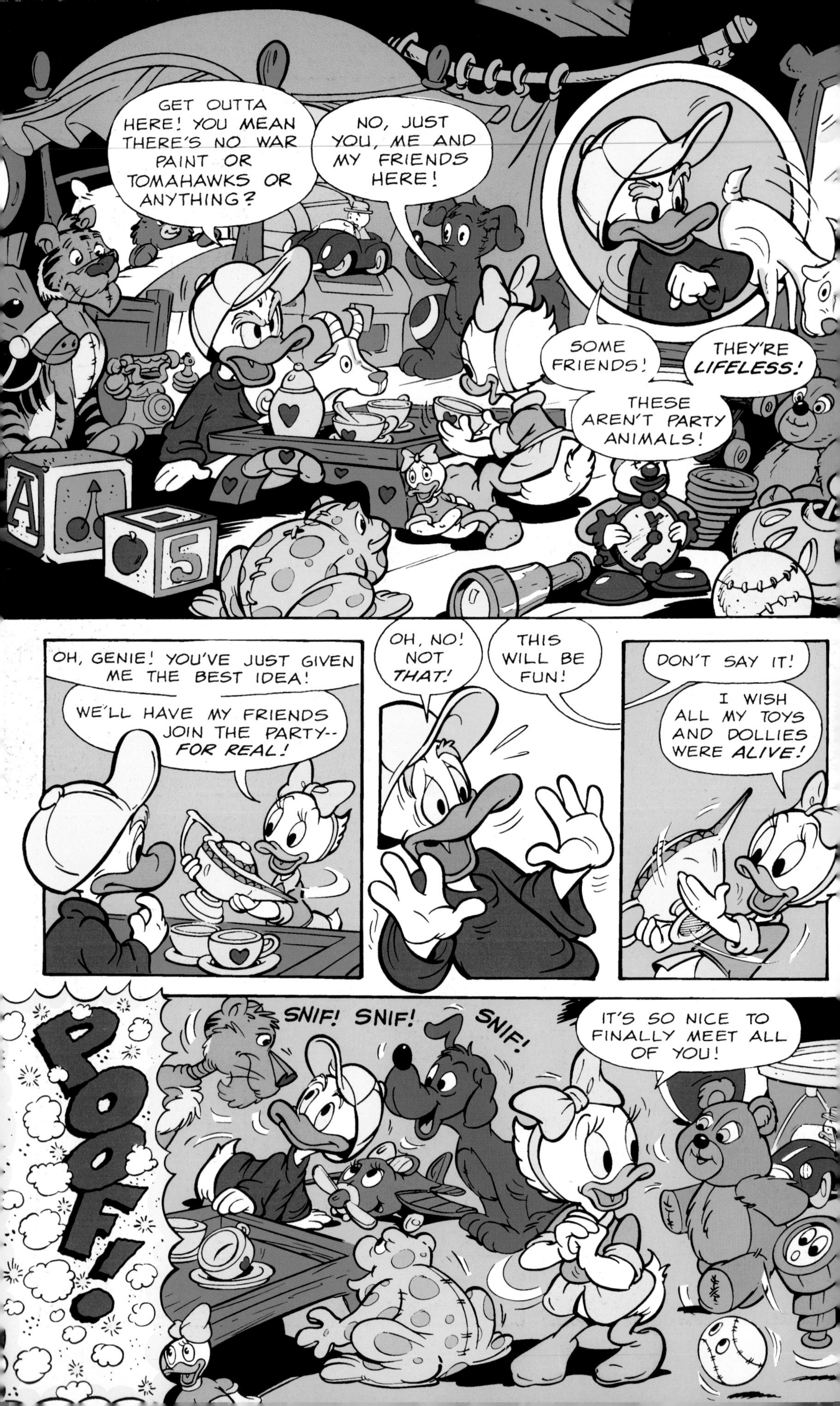
GET OUTTA HERE! YOU MEAN THERE'S NO WAR PAINT OR TOMAHAWKS OR ANYTHING?
NO, JUST YOU, ME AND MY FRIENDS HERE!
SOME FRIENDS!
THEY'RE *LIFELESS!*
THESE AREN'T PARTY ANIMALS!
OH, GENIE! YOU'VE JUST GIVEN ME THE BEST IDEA!
WE'LL HAVE MY FRIENDS JOIN THE PARTY-- *FOR REAL!*
OH, NO! NOT *THAT!*
THIS WILL BE FUN!
DON'T SAY IT!
I WISH ALL MY TOYS AND DOLLIES WERE *ALIVE!*
POOF!
SNIF! SNIF! SNIF!
IT'S SO NICE TO FINALLY MEET ALL OF YOU!

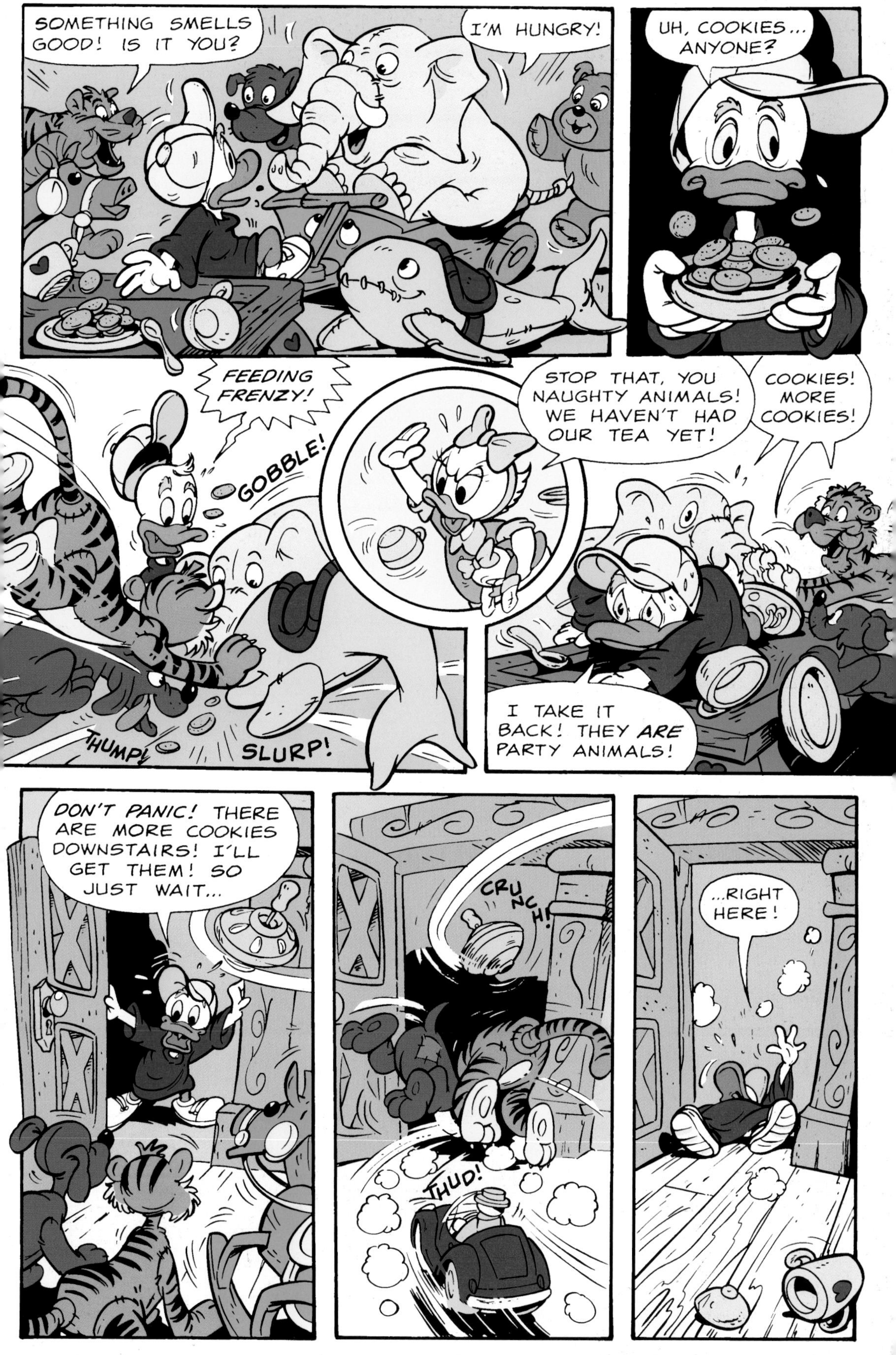
SOMETHING SMELLS GOOD! IS IT YOU?
I'M HUNGRY!
UH, COOKIES... ANYONE?
FEEDING FRENZY!
GOBBLE!
THUMP!
SLURP!
STOP THAT, YOU NAUGHTY ANIMALS! WE HAVEN'T HAD OUR TEA YET!
COOKIES! MORE COOKIES!
I TAKE IT BACK! THEY ARE PARTY ANIMALS!
DON'T PANIC! THERE ARE MORE COOKIES DOWNSTAIRS! I'LL GET THEM! SO JUST WAIT...
CRUNCH!
THUD!
...RIGHT HERE!

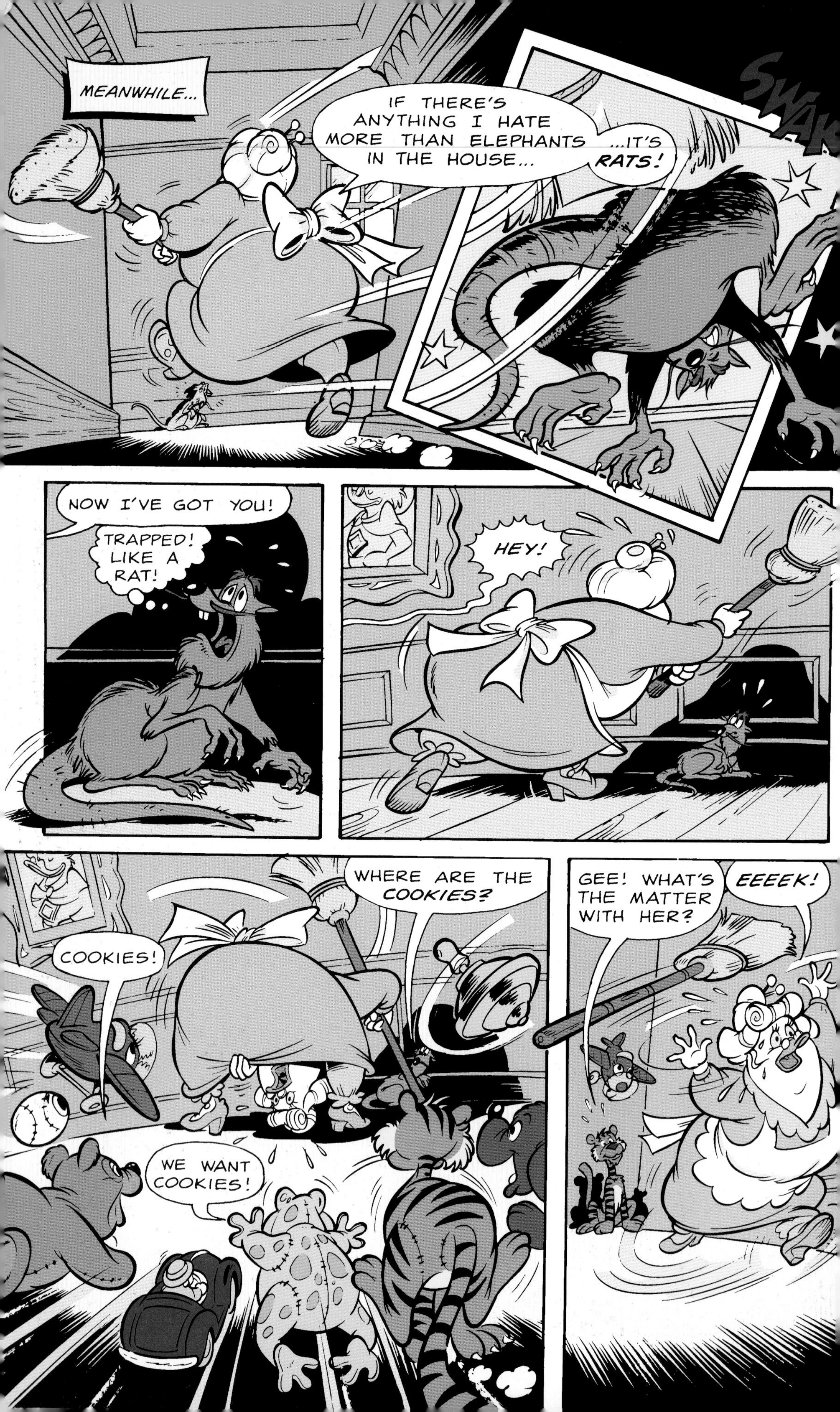
MEANWHILE...
IF THERE'S ANYTHING I HATE MORE THAN ELEPHANTS IN THE HOUSE...
...IT'S RATS!
NOW I'VE GOT YOU!
TRAPPED! LIKE A RAT!
HEY!
COOKIES!
WHERE ARE THE COOKIES?
WE WANT COOKIES!
GEE! WHAT'S THE MATTER WITH HER?
EEEEK!

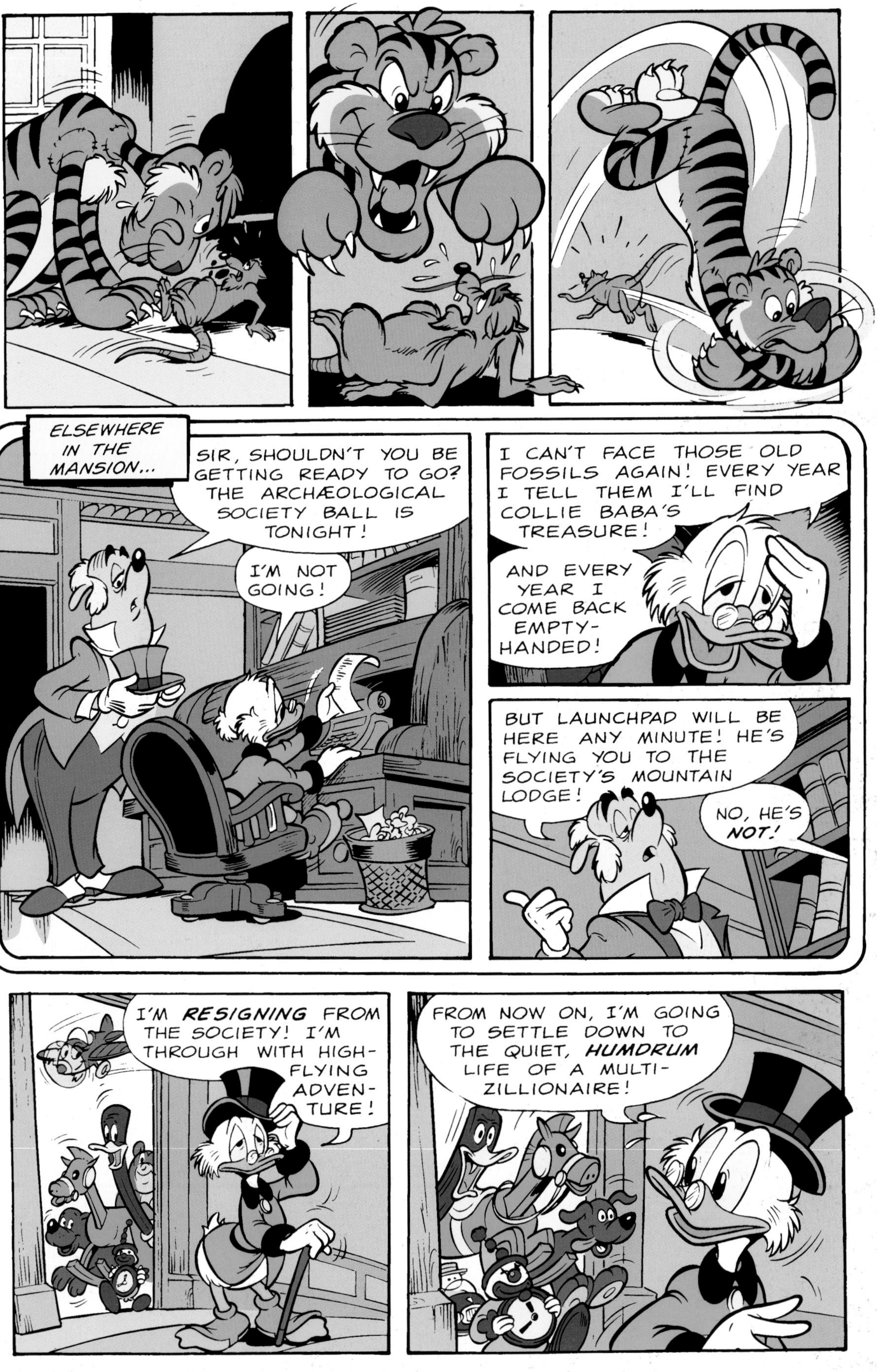
ELSEWHERE IN THE MANSION...
SIR, SHOULDN'T YOU BE GETTING READY TO GO? THE ARCHÆOLOGICAL SOCIETY BALL IS TONIGHT!
I'M NOT GOING!
I CAN'T FACE THOSE OLD FOSSILS AGAIN! EVERY YEAR I TELL THEM I'LL FIND COLLIE BABA'S TREASURE!
AND EVERY YEAR I COME BACK EMPTY-HANDED!
BUT LAUNCHPAD WILL BE HERE ANY MINUTE! HE'S FLYING YOU TO THE SOCIETY'S MOUNTAIN LODGE!
NO, HE'S NOT!
I'M RESIGNING FROM THE SOCIETY! I'M THROUGH WITH HIGH-FLYING ADVENTURE!
FROM NOW ON, I'M GOING TO SETTLE DOWN TO THE QUIET, HUMDRUM LIFE OF A MULTI-ZILLIONAIRE!

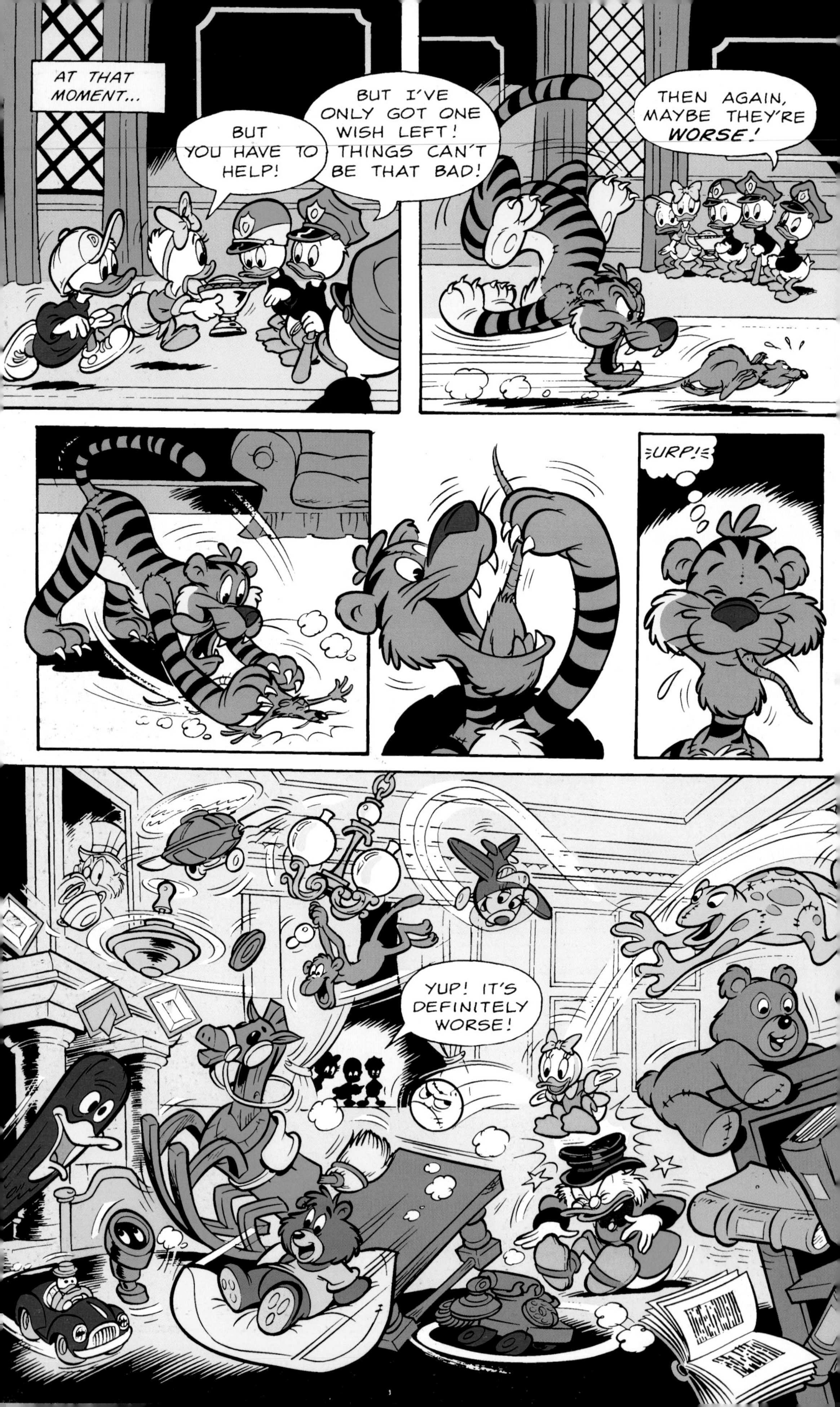
AT THAT MOMENT...
BUT YOU HAVE TO HELP!
BUT I'VE ONLY GOT ONE WISH LEFT! THINGS CAN'T BE THAT BAD!
THEN AGAIN, MAYBE THEY'RE WORSE!
URP!
YUP! IT'S DEFINITELY WORSE!

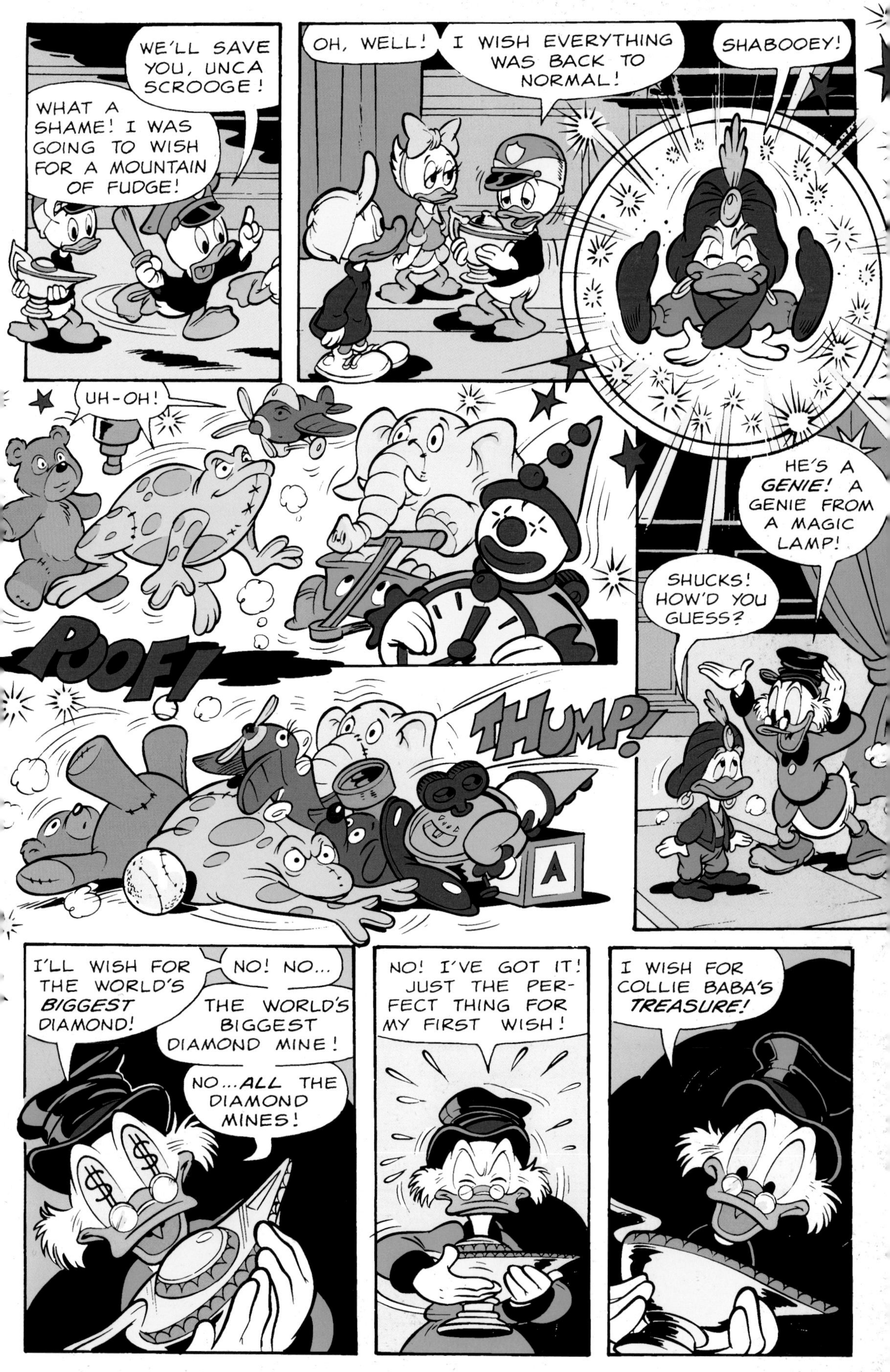

WHAT A SHAME! I WAS GOING TO WISH FOR A MOUNTAIN OF FUDGE!
WE'LL SAVE YOU, UNCA SCROOGE!
OH, WELL!
I WISH EVERYTHING WAS BACK TO NORMAL!
SHABOOEY!
UH-OH!
POOF!
THUMP!
HE'S A *GENIE!* A GENIE FROM A MAGIC LAMP!
SHUCKS! HOW'D YOU GUESS?
I'LL WISH FOR THE WORLD'S *BIGGEST* DIAMOND!
NO! NO...
THE WORLD'S BIGGEST DIAMOND MINE!
NO... *ALL* THE DIAMOND MINES!
NO! I'VE GOT IT! JUST THE PERFECT THING FOR MY FIRST WISH!
I WISH FOR COLLIE BABA'S *TREASURE!*
A

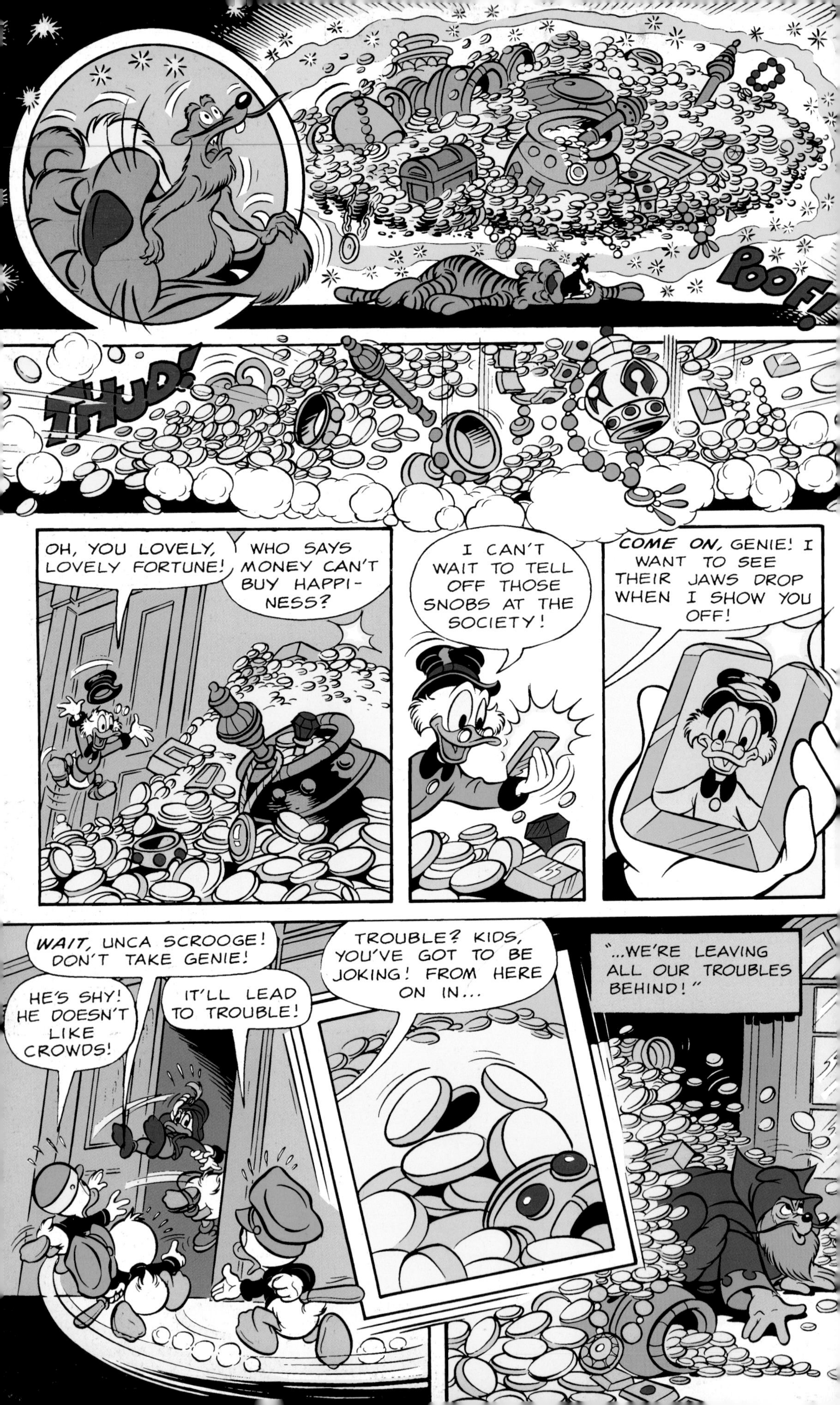
POOF!
THUD!
OH, YOU LOVELY, LOVELY FORTUNE!
WHO SAYS MONEY CAN'T BUY HAPPI-NESS?
I CAN'T WAIT TO TELL OFF THOSE SNOBS AT THE SOCIETY!
COME ON, GENIE! I WANT TO SEE THEIR JAWS DROP WHEN I SHOW YOU OFF!
WAIT, UNCA SCROOGE! DON'T TAKE GENIE!
HE'S SHY! HE DOESN'T LIKE CROWDS!
IT'LL LEAD TO TROUBLE!
TROUBLE? KIDS, YOU'VE GOT TO BE JOKING! FROM HERE ON IN...
"...WE'RE LEAVING ALL OUR TROUBLES BEHIND!"

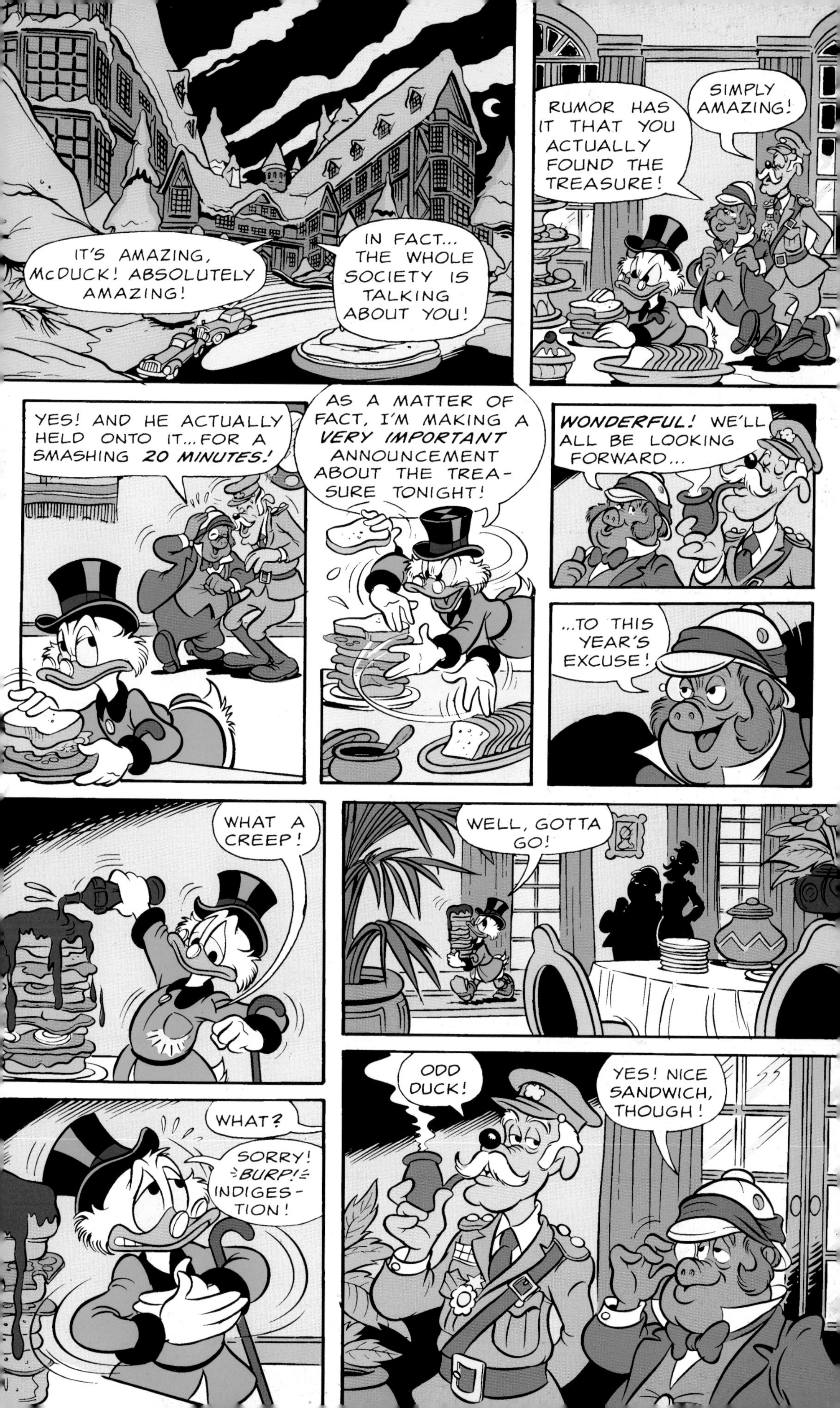
IT'S AMAZING, McDUCK! ABSOLUTELY AMAZING!
IN FACT... THE WHOLE SOCIETY IS TALKING ABOUT YOU!
RUMOR HAS IT THAT YOU ACTUALLY FOUND THE TREASURE!
SIMPLY AMAZING!
YES! AND HE ACTUALLY HELD ONTO IT...FOR A SMASHING 20 MINUTES!
AS A MATTER OF FACT, I'M MAKING A VERY IMPORTANT ANNOUNCEMENT ABOUT THE TREASURE TONIGHT!
WONDERFUL! WE'LL ALL BE LOOKING FORWARD...
...TO THIS YEAR'S EXCUSE!
WHAT A CREEP!
WELL, GOTTA GO!
WHAT?
SORRY! BURP! INDIGESTION!
ODD DUCK!
YES! NICE SANDWICH, THOUGH!

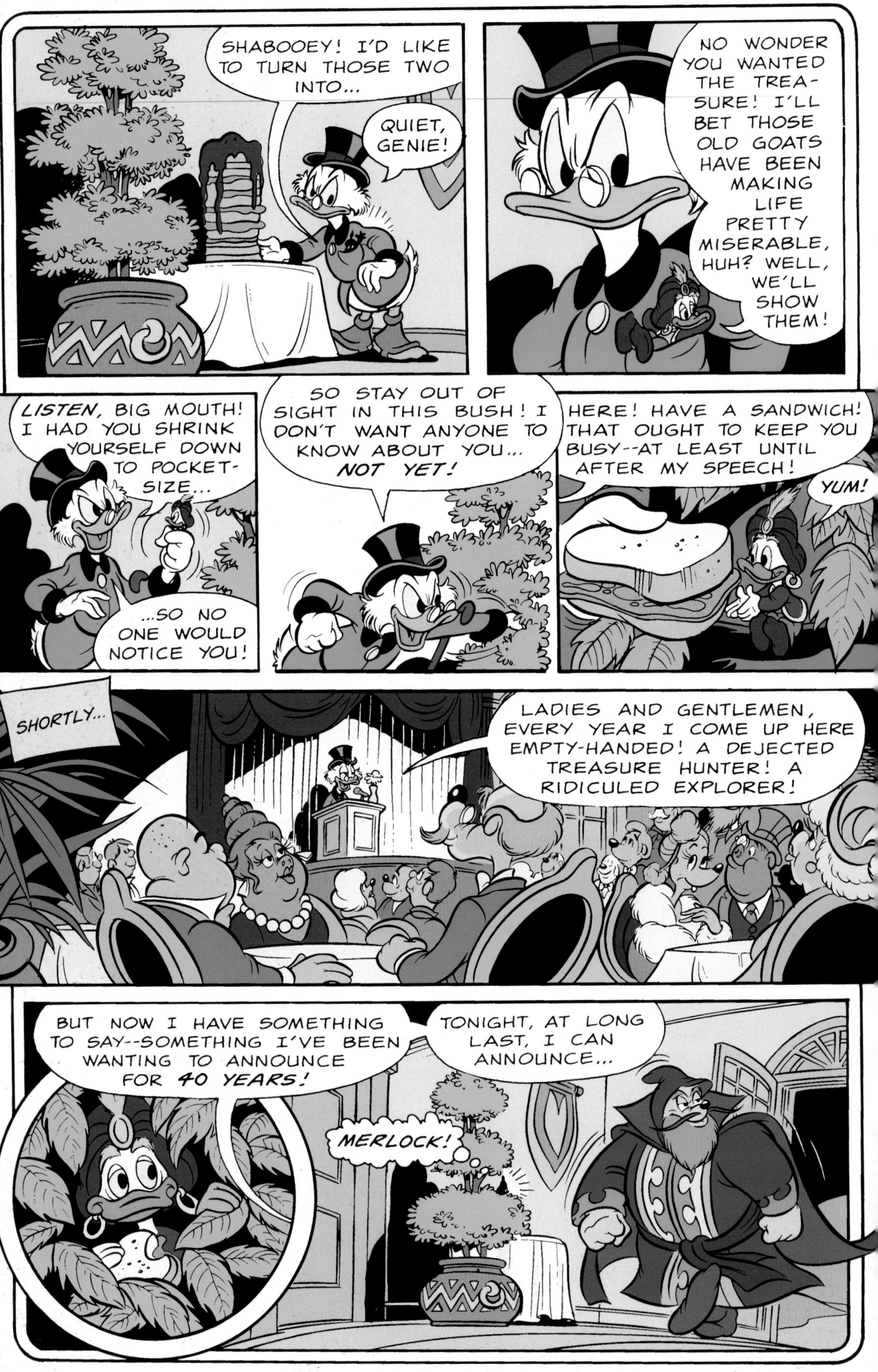
SHABOOEY! I'D LIKE TO TURN THOSE TWO INTO...
QUIET, GENIE!
NO WONDER YOU WANTED THE TREA-SURE! I'LL BET THOSE OLD GOATS HAVE BEEN MAKING LIFE PRETTY MISERABLE, HUH? WELL, WE'LL SHOW THEM!
LISTEN, BIG MOUTH! I HAD YOU SHRINK YOURSELF DOWN TO POCKET-SIZE...
...SO NO ONE WOULD NOTICE YOU!
SO STAY OUT OF SIGHT IN THIS BUSH! I DON'T WANT ANYONE TO KNOW ABOUT YOU... NOT YET!
HERE! HAVE A SANDWICH! THAT OUGHT TO KEEP YOU BUSY--AT LEAST UNTIL AFTER MY SPEECH!
YUM!
SHORTLY...
LADIES AND GENTLEMEN, EVERY YEAR I COME UP HERE EMPTY-HANDED! A DEJECTED TREASURE HUNTER! A RIDICULED EXPLORER!
BUT NOW I HAVE SOMETHING TO SAY--SOMETHING I'VE BEEN WANTING TO ANNOUNCE FOR 40 YEARS!
TONIGHT, AT LONG LAST, I CAN ANNOUNCE...
MERLOCK!

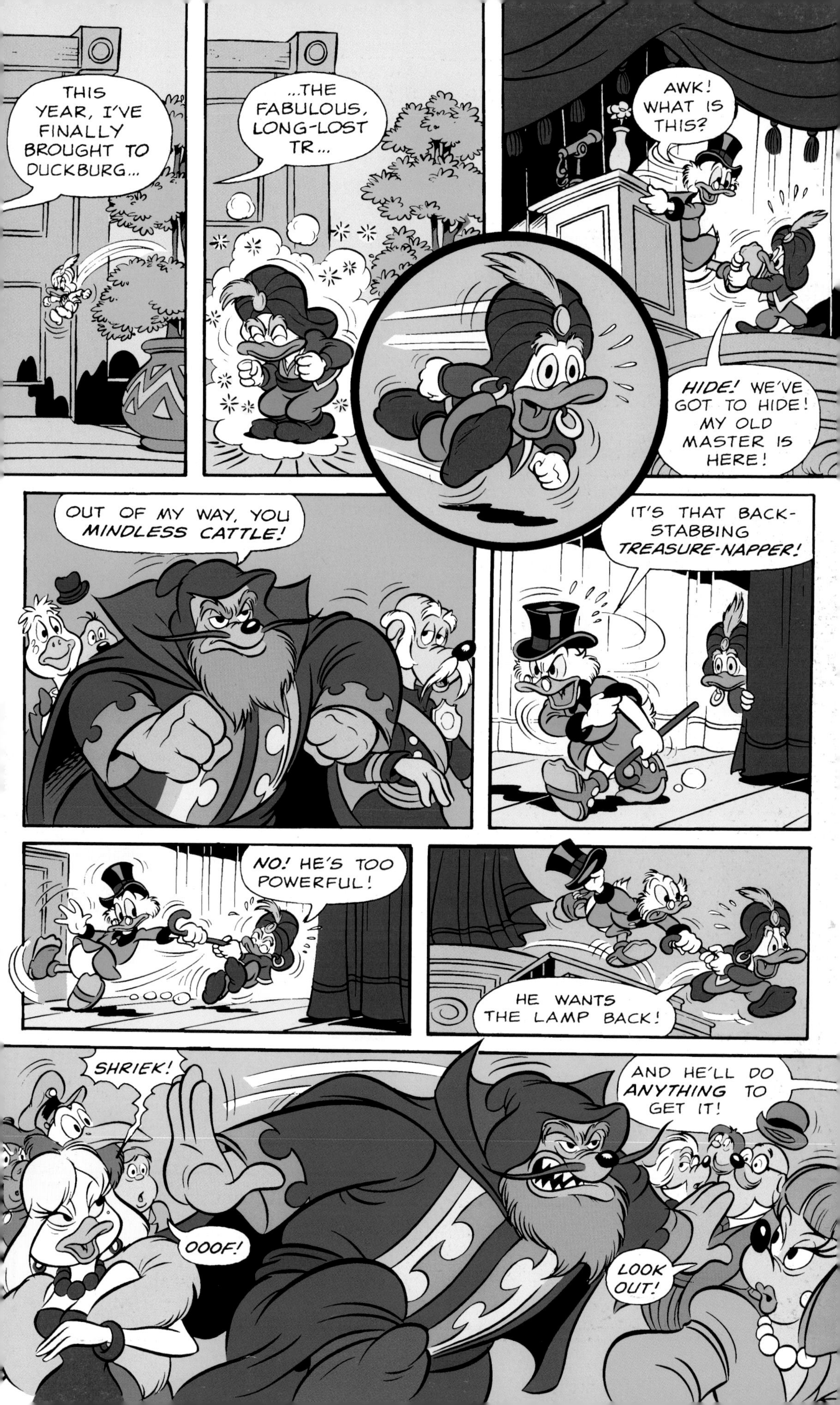

THIS YEAR, I'VE FINALLY BROUGHT TO DUCKBURG...
...THE FABULOUS, LONG-LOST TR...
AWK! WHAT IS THIS?
HIDE! WE'VE GOT TO HIDE! MY OLD MASTER IS HERE!
OUT OF MY WAY, YOU MINDLESS CATTLE!
IT'S THAT BACK-STABBING TREASURE-NAPPER!
NO! HE'S TOO POWERFUL!
HE WANTS THE LAMP BACK!
SHRIEK!
AND HE'LL DO ANYTHING TO GET IT!
OOOF!
LOOK OUT!

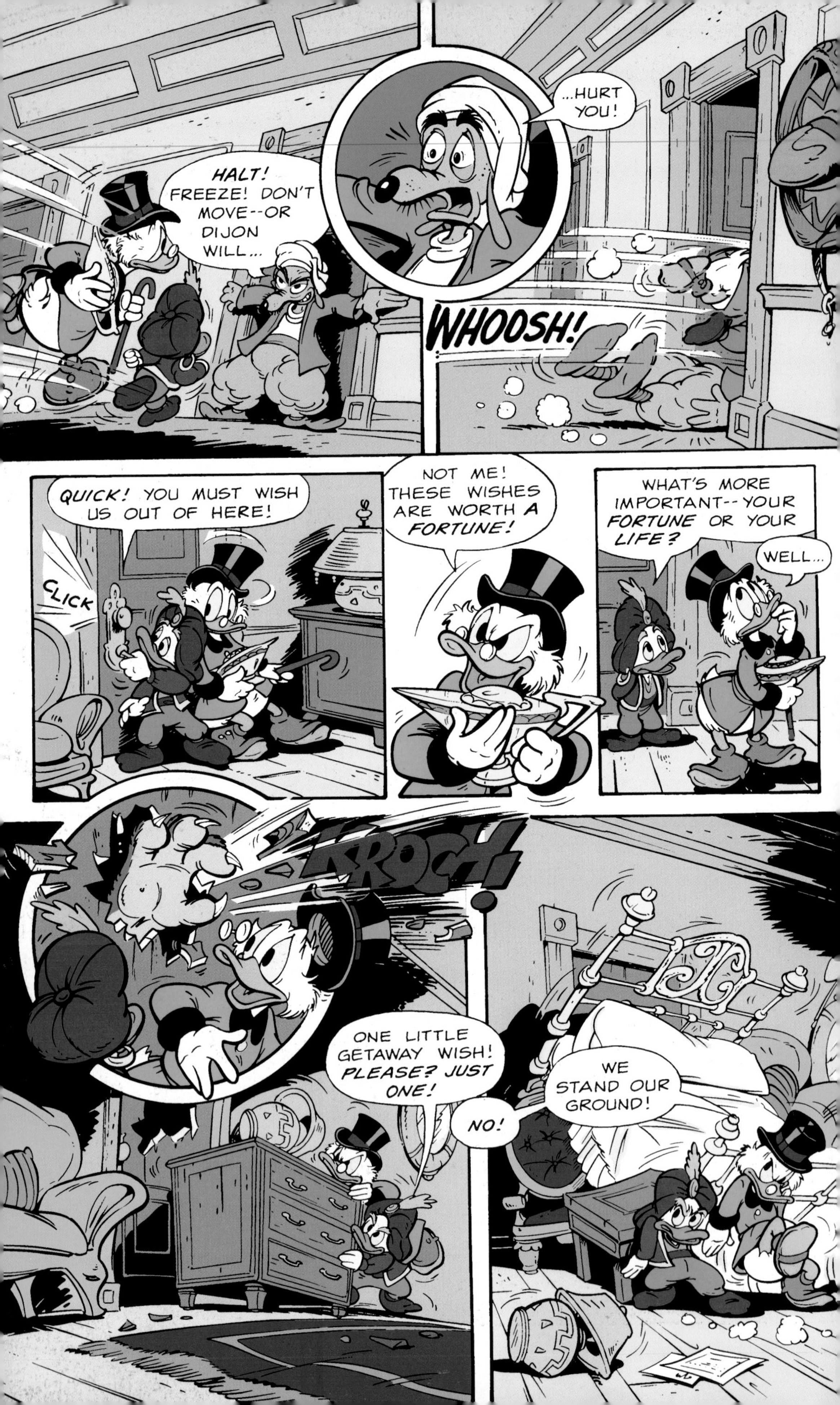
HALT! FREEZE! DON'T MOVE--OR DIJON WILL...
...HURT YOU!
WHOOSH!
CLICK
QUICK! YOU MUST WISH US OUT OF HERE!
NOT ME! THESE WISHES ARE WORTH A FORTUNE!
WHAT'S MORE IMPORTANT--YOUR FORTUNE OR YOUR LIFE?
WELL...
KROCH!
ONE LITTLE GETAWAY WISH! PLEASE? JUST ONE!
NO!
WE STAND OUR GROUND!

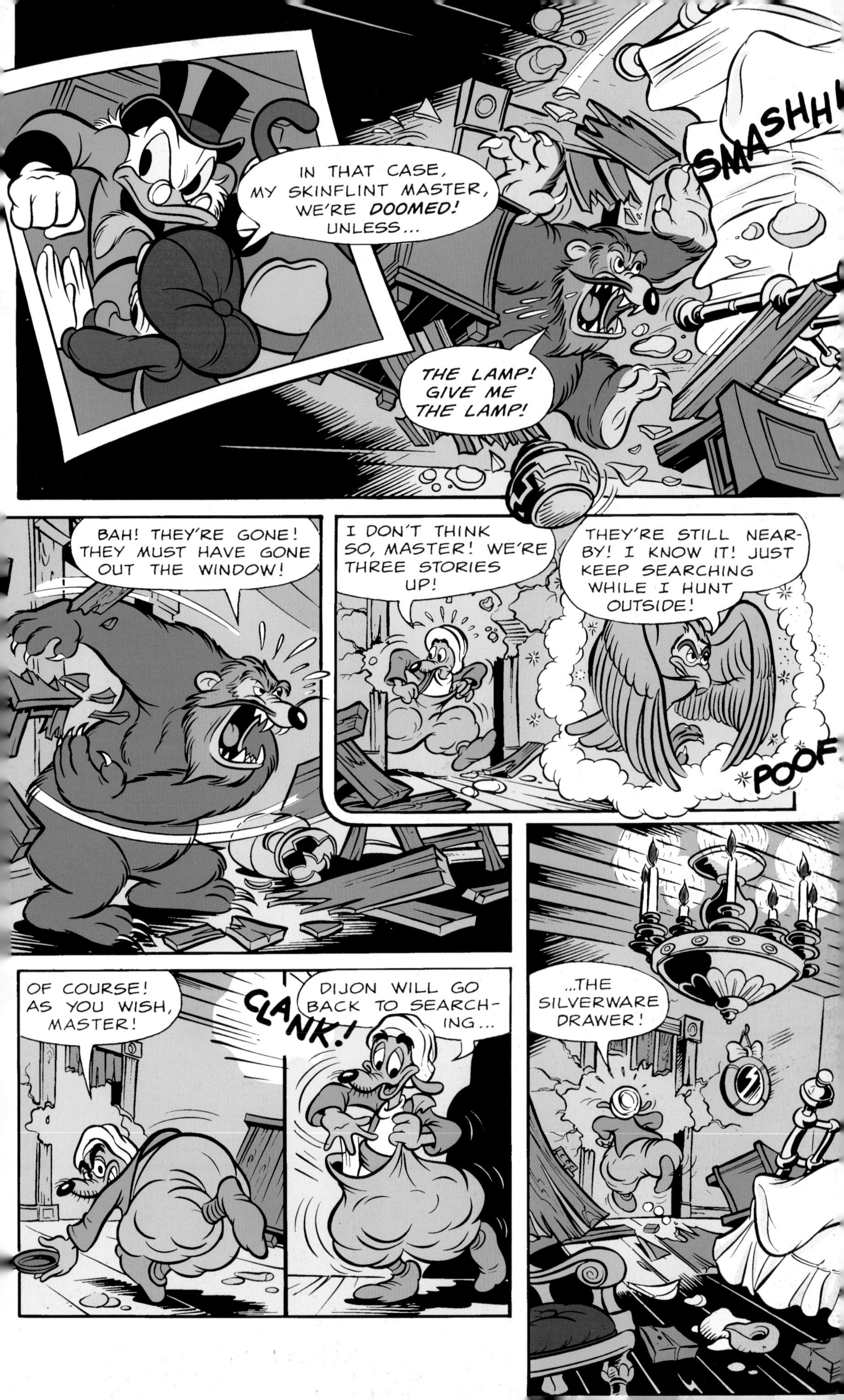
IN THAT CASE, MY SKINFLINT MASTER, WE'RE DOOMED! UNLESS...
SMASHH!
THE LAMP! GIVE ME THE LAMP!
BAH! THEY'RE GONE! THEY MUST HAVE GONE OUT THE WINDOW!
I DON'T THINK SO, MASTER! WE'RE THREE STORIES UP!
THEY'RE STILL NEARBY! I KNOW IT! JUST KEEP SEARCHING WHILE I HUNT OUTSIDE!
POOF
OF COURSE! AS YOU WISH, MASTER!
CLANK!
DIJON WILL GO BACK TO SEARCHING...
...THE SILVERWARE DRAWER!

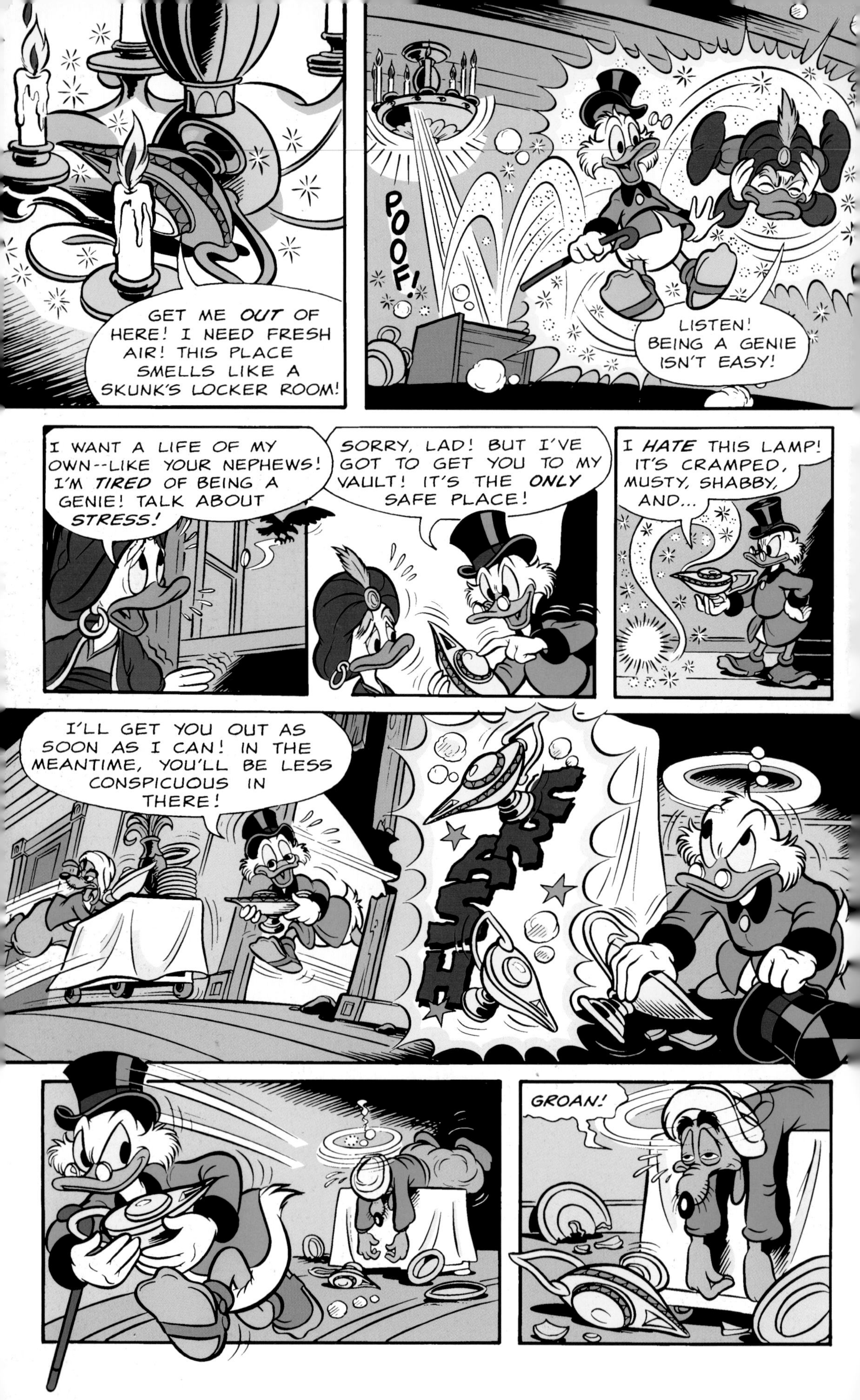
GET ME OUT OF HERE! I NEED FRESH AIR! THIS PLACE SMELLS LIKE A SKUNK'S LOCKER ROOM!
POOF!
LISTEN! BEING A GENIE ISN'T EASY!
I WANT A LIFE OF MY OWN--LIKE YOUR NEPHEWS! I'M TIRED OF BEING A GENIE! TALK ABOUT STRESS!
SORRY, LAD! BUT I'VE GOT TO GET YOU TO MY VAULT! IT'S THE ONLY SAFE PLACE!
I HATE THIS LAMP! IT'S CRAMPED, MUSTY, SHABBY, AND...
I'LL GET YOU OUT AS SOON AS I CAN! IN THE MEANTIME, YOU'LL BE LESS CONSPICUOUS IN THERE!
GROAN!

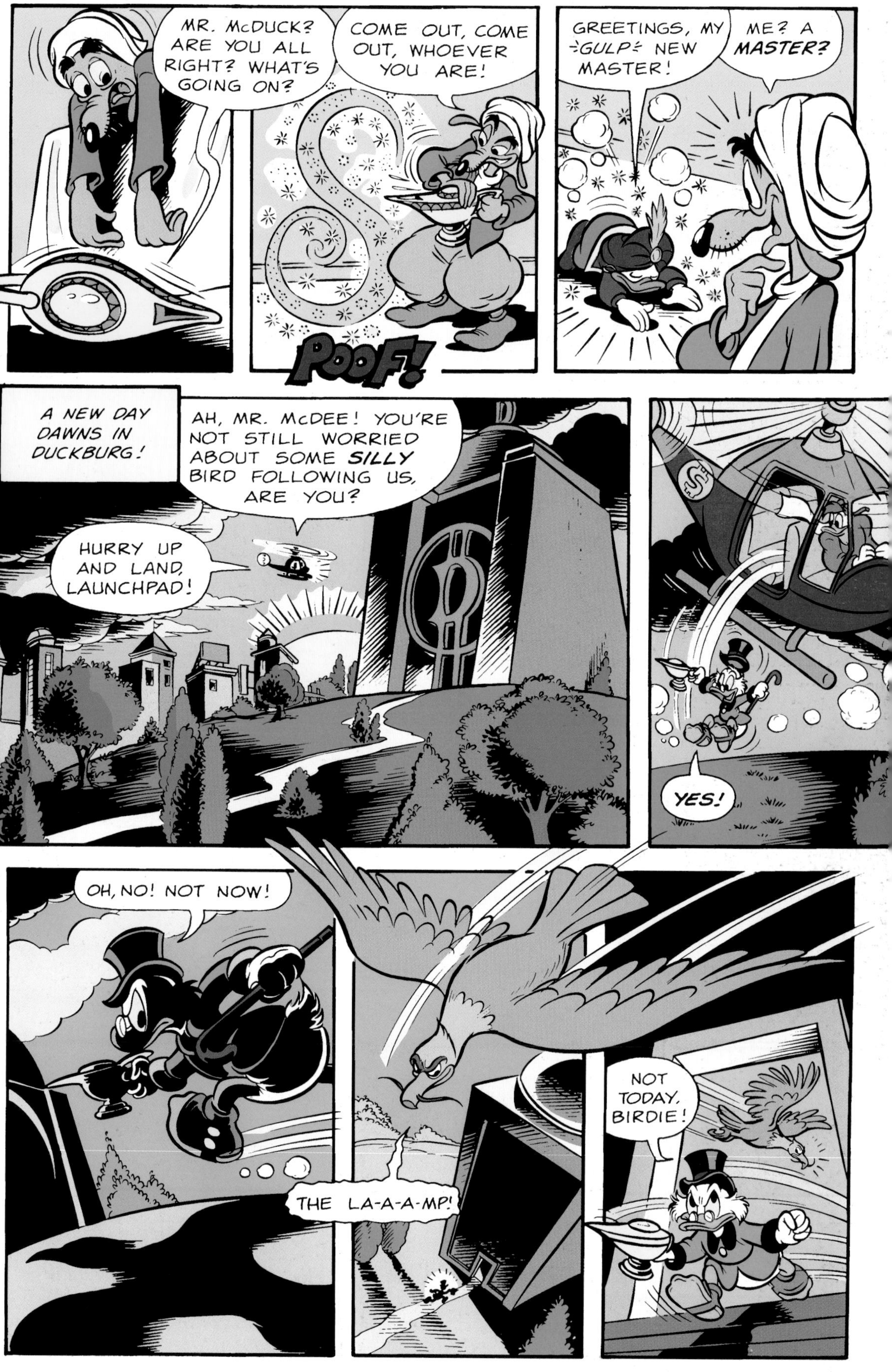

MR. McDUCK? ARE YOU ALL RIGHT? WHAT'S GOING ON?
COME OUT, COME OUT, WHOEVER YOU ARE!
POOF!
GREETINGS, MY *GULP* NEW MASTER!
ME? A MASTER?
A NEW DAY DAWNS IN DUCKBURG!
AH, MR. McDEE! YOU'RE NOT STILL WORRIED ABOUT SOME SILLY BIRD FOLLOWING US, ARE YOU?
HURRY UP AND LAND, LAUNCHPAD!
YES!
OH, NO! NOT NOW!
THE LA-A-A-MP!
NOT TODAY, BIRDIE!

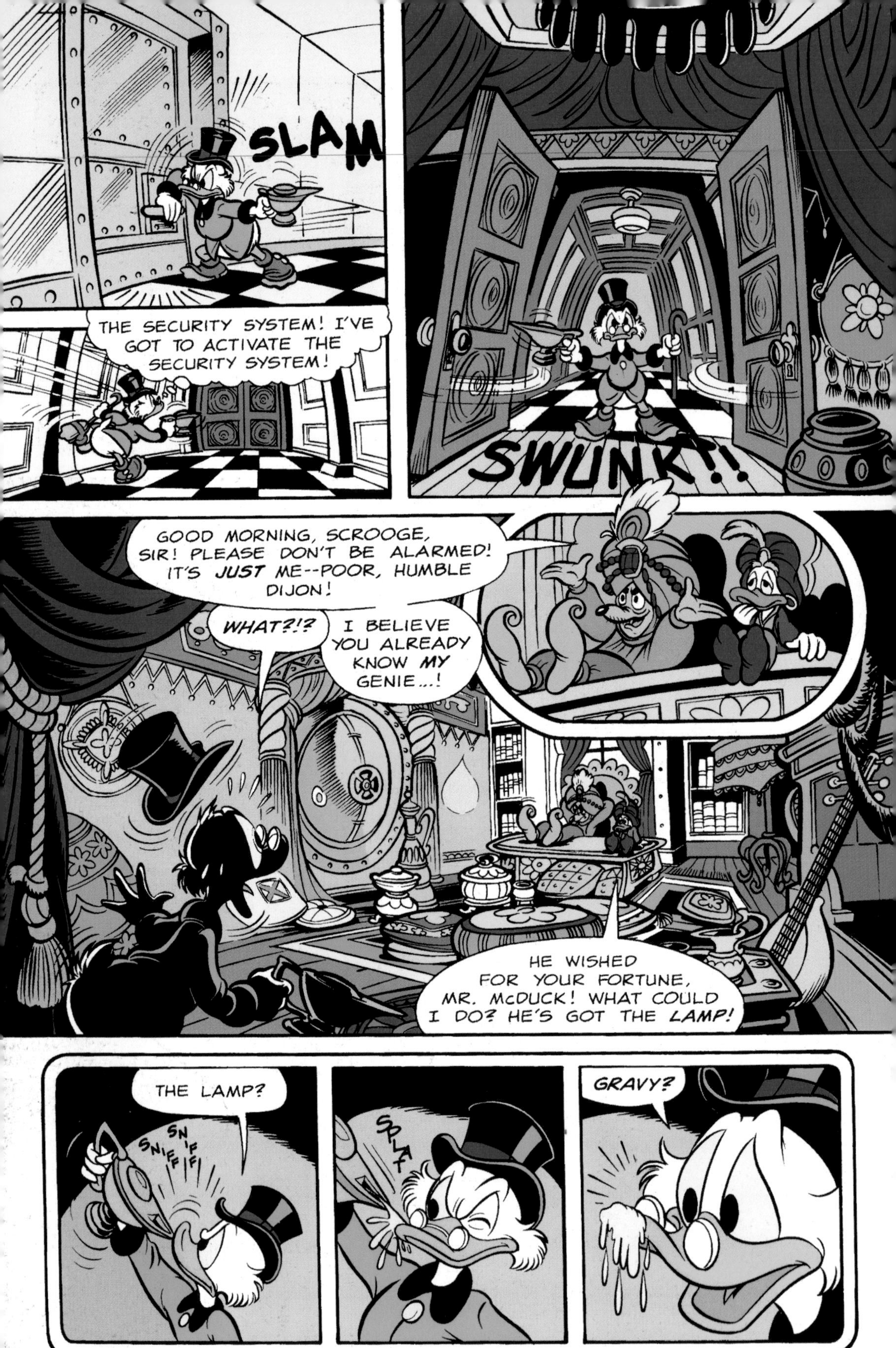
SLAM
THE SECURITY SYSTEM! I'VE GOT TO ACTIVATE THE SECURITY SYSTEM!
SWUNK!!
GOOD MORNING, SCROOGE, SIR! PLEASE DON'T BE ALARMED! IT'S JUST ME--POOR, HUMBLE DIJON!
WHAT?!?
I BELIEVE YOU ALREADY KNOW MY GENIE...!
HE WISHED FOR YOUR FORTUNE, MR. McDUCK! WHAT COULD I DO? HE'S GOT THE LAMP!
THE LAMP?
SNIFF SNIFF
SPLAT
GRAVY?

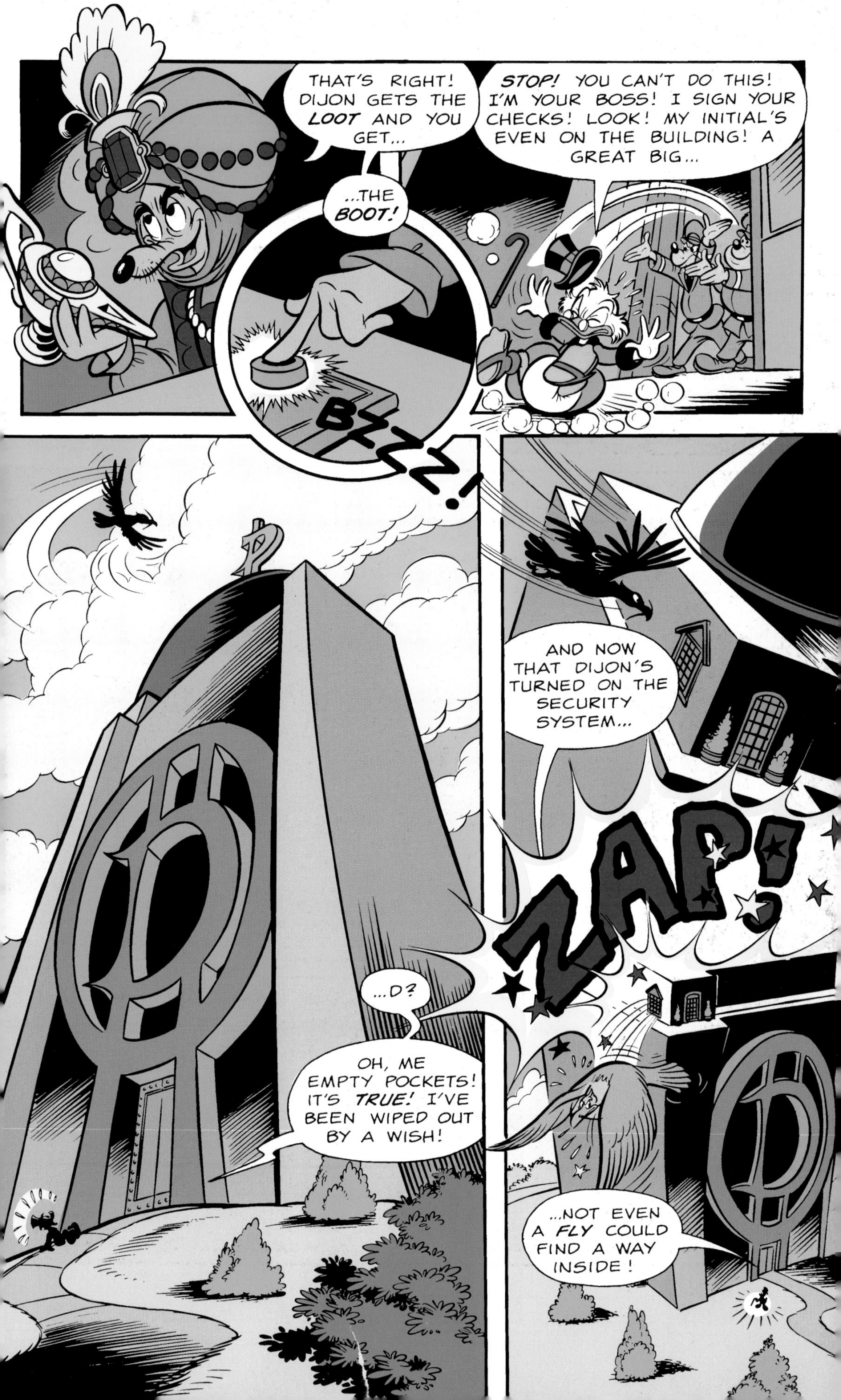
THAT'S RIGHT! DIJON GETS THE LOOT AND YOU GET...
...THE BOOT!
BZZZ!
STOP! YOU CAN'T DO THIS! I'M YOUR BOSS! I SIGN YOUR CHECKS! LOOK! MY INITIAL'S EVEN ON THE BUILDING! A GREAT BIG...
...D?
OH, ME EMPTY POCKETS! IT'S TRUE! I'VE BEEN WIPED OUT BY A WISH!
AND NOW THAT DIJON'S TURNED ON THE SECURITY SYSTEM...
ZAP!
...NOT EVEN A FLY COULD FIND A WAY INSIDE!

≈GROAN≈ THERE ARE 14,657 ALARMS AND TRAPS!

IT'S HOPELESS! *NOBODY* CAN BREAK IN THERE!

YES! IT'S HOPELESS...

...UNLESS--*LIKE ME*--YOU KNOW 14,657 WAYS TO SHUT THEM OFF!

OF COURSE, IT'LL STILL BE DANGEROUS! I'LL NEED HELP! THE BEST I CAN GET!

AND SO...

ARE WE ALMOST THERE?

YUP! I'VE GOT THE BIN AT TWELVE O'CLOCK HIGH!...

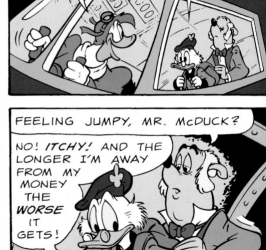

...GIVE OR TAKE 10 MINUTES!

FINALLY!

FEELING JUMPY, MR. McDUCK?

NO! *ITCHY!* AND THE LONGER I'M AWAY FROM MY MONEY THE *WORSE* IT GETS!

MAD DUCK TO WOODCHUCK WARRIORS! BEGIN OPERATION "LIFT THE LAMP!"

ROGER! COMMANDER BEAKLEY IS SCANNING THE PERIMETER NOW!

THE COAST IS *CLEAR*, GENERAL HUEY!

OK, MAD DUCK! WE'RE GOING IN!

DELICIOUS! ≷SNIFF! SNIFF!≷ DELICIOUS! EVERYTHING SMELLS MORE DELICIOUS WHEN YOU'RE RICH!

HEE! HEE! ≷SNIFF! SNIFF!≷ EVEN DIJON!

A THOUSAND PARDONS, MY FRAGRANT MASTER... BUT SHOULDN'T WE BE BIRD WATCHING?

DON'T WORRY! MERLOCK WOULDN'T DARE CONFRONT THE *GREAT* AND *POWERFUL DIJON!*

PERHAPS, YOU'RE RIGHT, MASTER! BUT COLLIE BABA SAID THE SAME THING...

...JUST BEFORE MERLOCK TURNED HIM INTO A *TOAD!*

...WITH A $1.99 ARMY SURPLUS PARACHUTE!

WITH LUCK, I COULD'VE FOUND A *NAVY* PARACHUTE FOR $1.49!

≷GROAN!≷ I MUST BE *CRAZY* RISKING MY LIFE LIKE THIS...

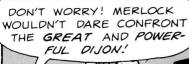

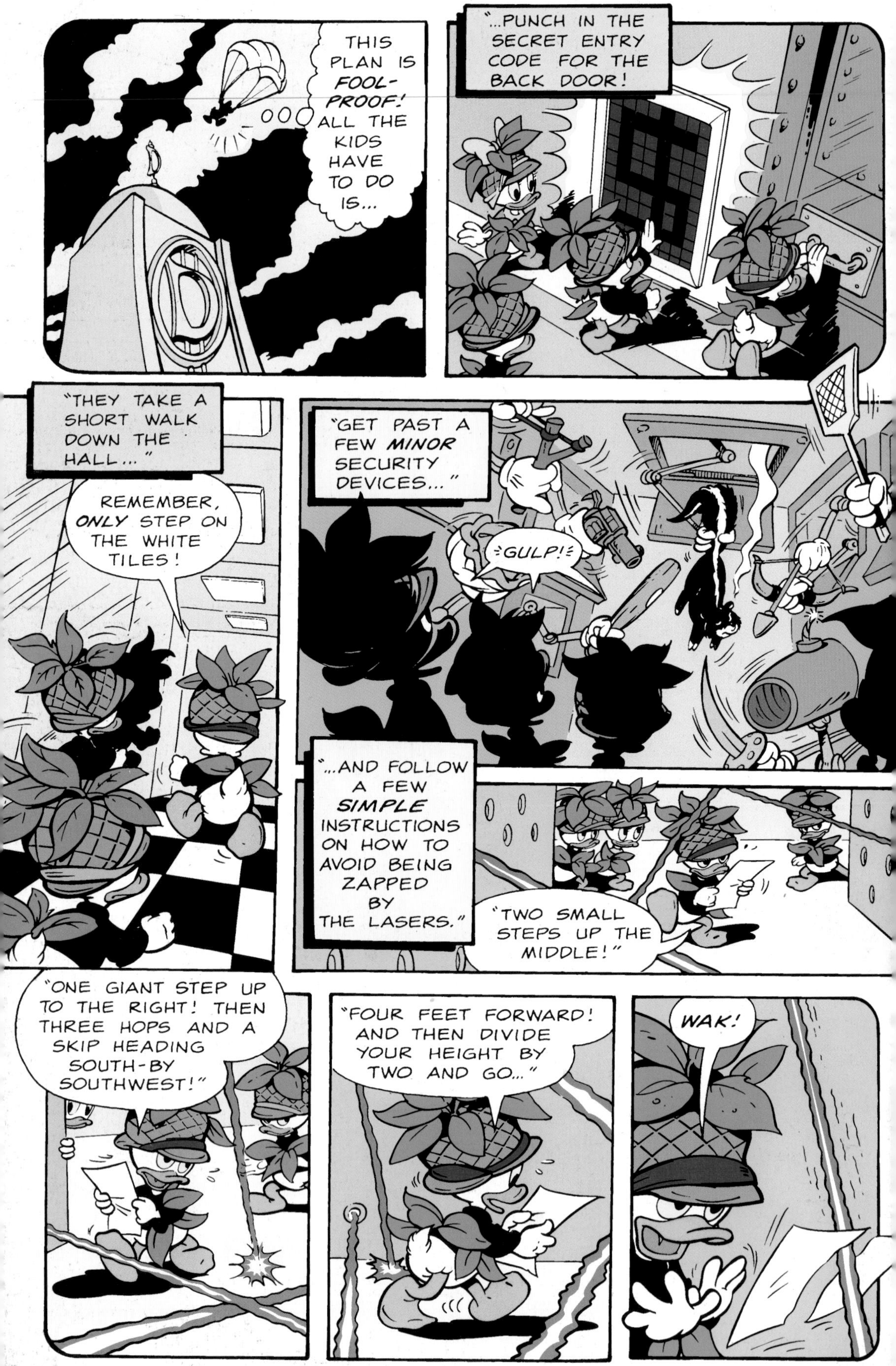
THIS PLAN IS FOOL-PROOF! ALL THE KIDS HAVE TO DO IS...
"...PUNCH IN THE SECRET ENTRY CODE FOR THE BACK DOOR!
"THEY TAKE A SHORT WALK DOWN THE HALL..."
REMEMBER, ONLY STEP ON THE WHITE TILES!
"GET PAST A FEW MINOR SECURITY DEVICES..."
GULP!
"...AND FOLLOW A FEW SIMPLE INSTRUCTIONS ON HOW TO AVOID BEING ZAPPED BY THE LASERS."
"TWO SMALL STEPS UP THE MIDDLE!"
"ONE GIANT STEP UP TO THE RIGHT! THEN THREE HOPS AND A SKIP HEADING SOUTH-BY SOUTHWEST!"
"FOUR FEET FORWARD! AND THEN DIVIDE YOUR HEIGHT BY TWO AND GO..."
WAK!

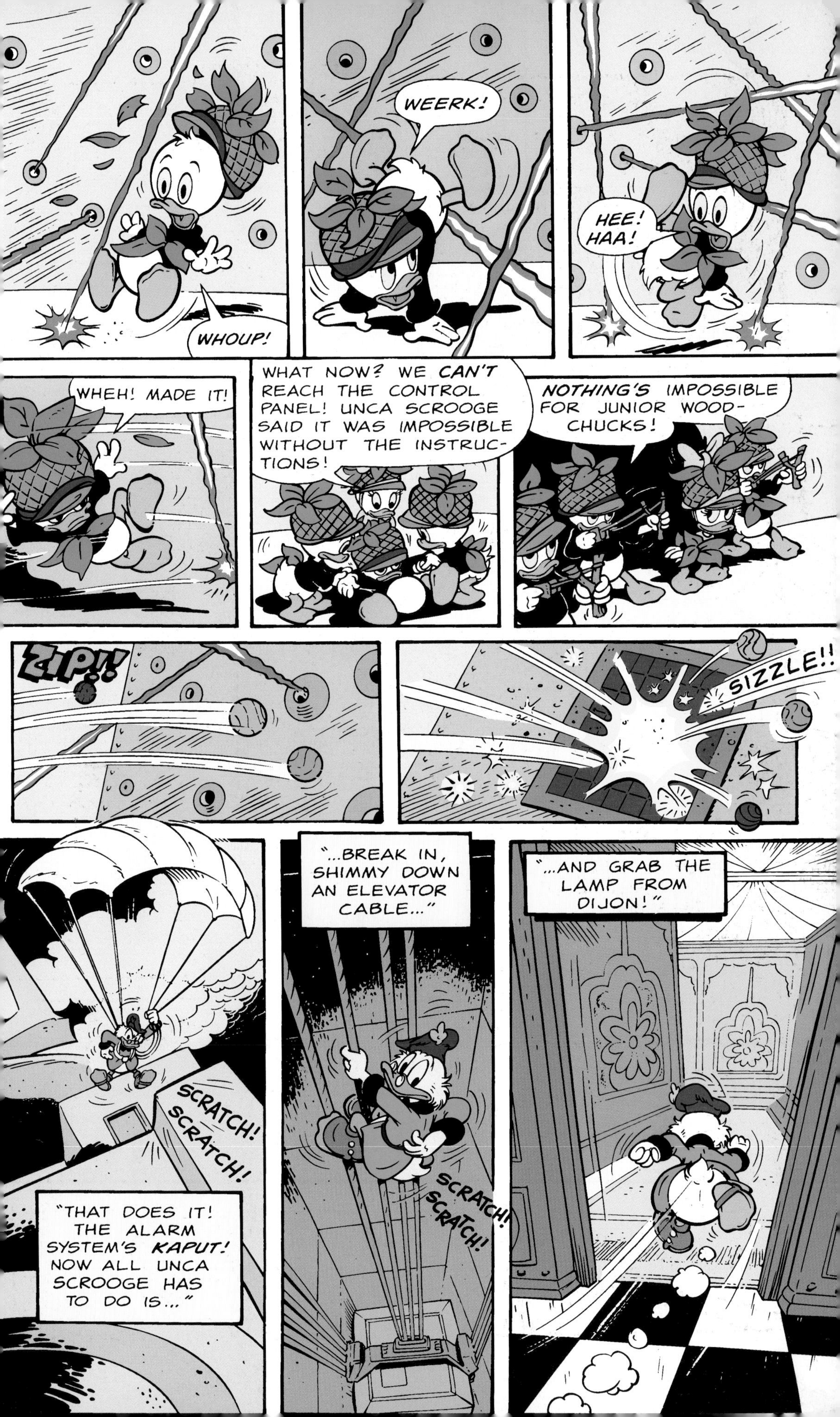
WHOUP!
WEERK!
HEE! HAA!
WHEH! MADE IT!
WHAT NOW? WE CAN'T REACH THE CONTROL PANEL! UNCA SCROOGE SAID IT WAS IMPOSSIBLE WITHOUT THE INSTRUCTIONS!
NOTHING'S IMPOSSIBLE FOR JUNIOR WOODCHUCKS!
ZIP!!
SIZZLE!!
"THAT DOES IT! THE ALARM SYSTEM'S KAPUT! NOW ALL UNCA SCROOGE HAS TO DO IS..."
SCRATCH! SCRATCH!
"...BREAK IN, SHIMMY DOWN AN ELEVATOR CABLE..."
SCRATCH! SCRATCH!
"...AND GRAB THE LAMP FROM DIJON!"

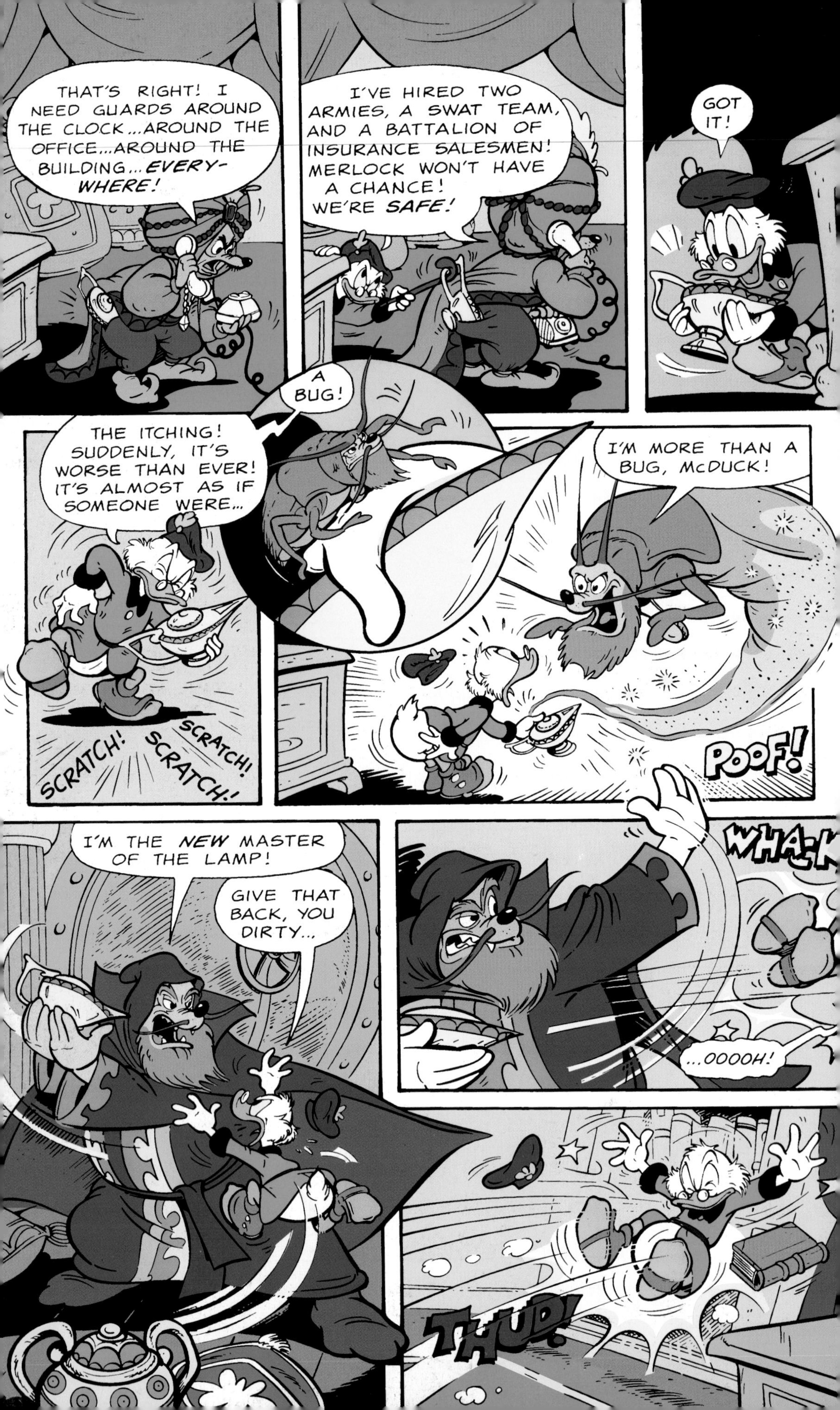
THAT'S RIGHT! I NEED GUARDS AROUND THE CLOCK...AROUND THE OFFICE...AROUND THE BUILDING...EVERY-WHERE!
I'VE HIRED TWO ARMIES, A SWAT TEAM, AND A BATTALION OF INSURANCE SALESMEN! MERLOCK WON'T HAVE A CHANCE! WE'RE SAFE!
GOT IT!
A BUG!
THE ITCHING! SUDDENLY, IT'S WORSE THAN EVER! IT'S ALMOST AS IF SOMEONE WERE...
SCRATCH! SCRATCH! SCRATCH!
I'M MORE THAN A BUG, McDUCK!
POOF!
I'M THE NEW MASTER OF THE LAMP!
GIVE THAT BACK, YOU DIRTY...
WHA-K
...OOOOH!
THUD!

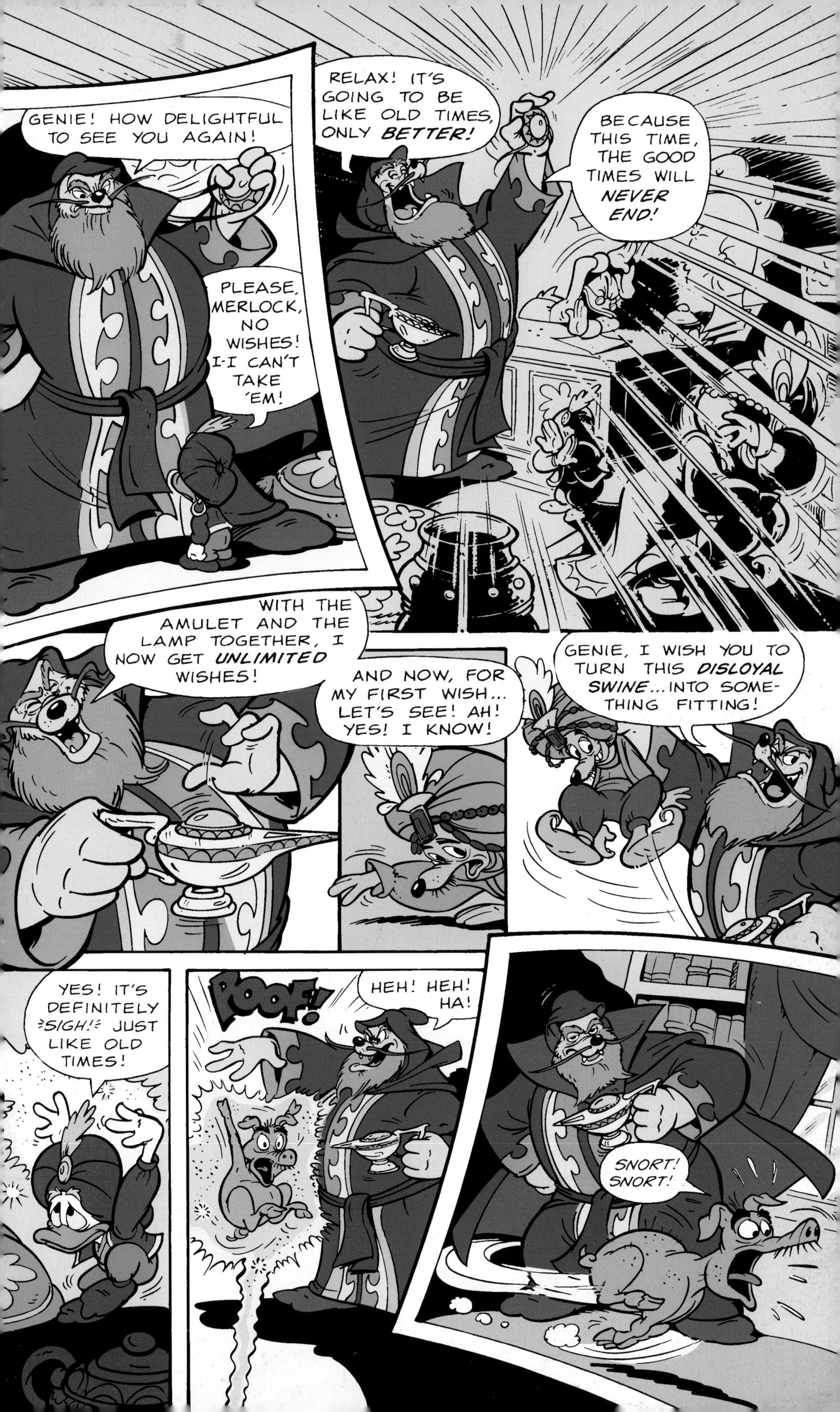
GENIE! HOW DELIGHTFUL TO SEE YOU AGAIN!
PLEASE, MERLOCK, NO WISHES! I-I CAN'T TAKE 'EM!
RELAX! IT'S GOING TO BE LIKE OLD TIMES, ONLY BETTER!
BECAUSE THIS TIME, THE GOOD TIMES WILL NEVER END!
WITH THE AMULET AND THE LAMP TOGETHER, I NOW GET UNLIMITED WISHES!
AND NOW, FOR MY FIRST WISH... LET'S SEE! AH! YES! I KNOW!
GENIE, I WISH YOU TO TURN THIS DISLOYAL SWINE... INTO SOME-THING FITTING!
YES! IT'S DEFINITELY *SIGH!* JUST LIKE OLD TIMES!
POOF!
HEH! HEH! HA!
SNORT! SNORT!

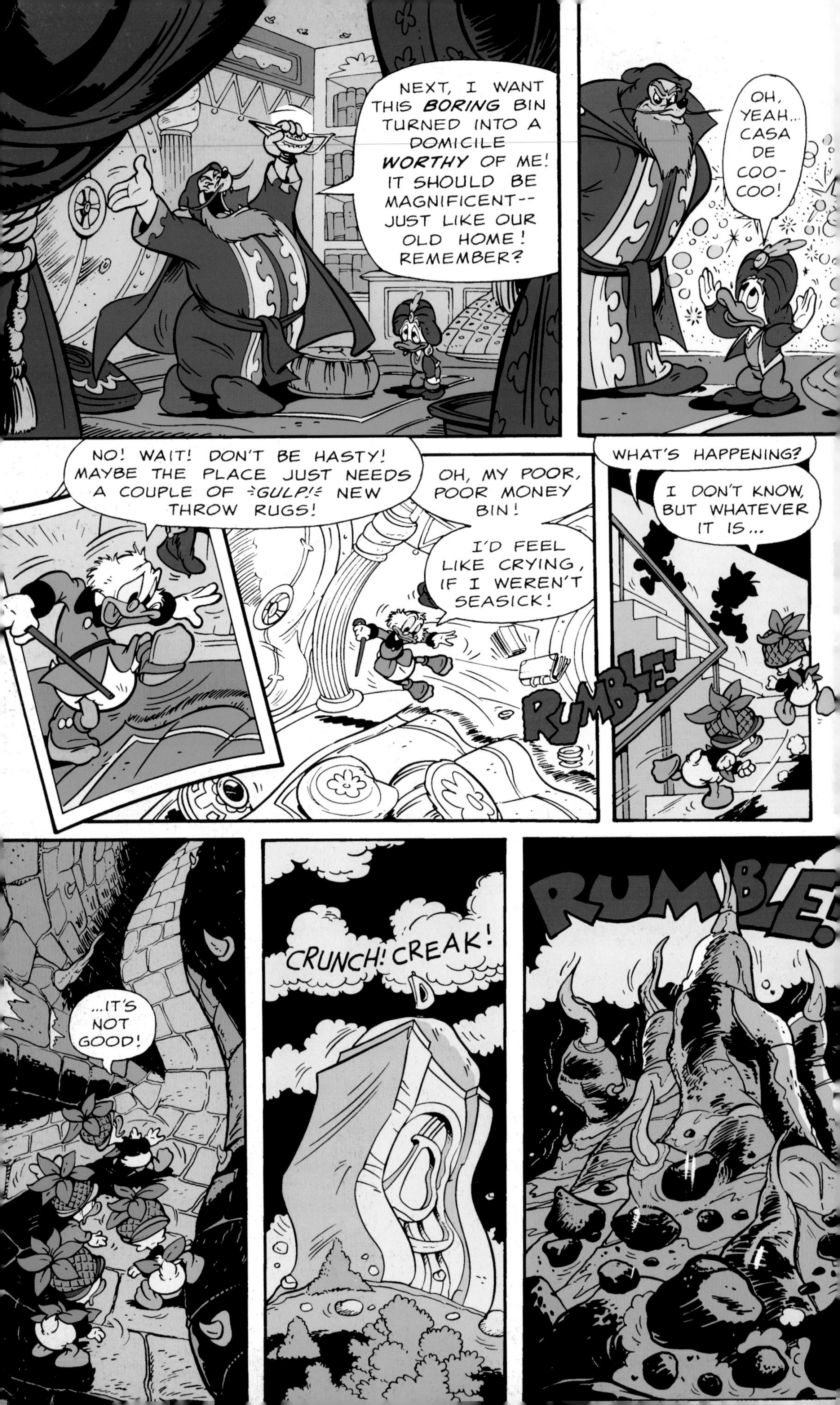
NEXT, I WANT THIS BORING BIN TURNED INTO A DOMICILE WORTHY OF ME! IT SHOULD BE MAGNIFICENT-- JUST LIKE OUR OLD HOME! REMEMBER?
OH, YEAH... CASA DE COO-COO!
NO! WAIT! DON'T BE HASTY! MAYBE THE PLACE JUST NEEDS A COUPLE OF GULP! NEW THROW RUGS!
OH, MY POOR, POOR MONEY BIN!
I'D FEEL LIKE CRYING, IF I WEREN'T SEASICK!
RUMBLE!
WHAT'S HAPPENING?
I DON'T KNOW, BUT WHATEVER IT IS...
...IT'S NOT GOOD!
CRUNCH! CREAK!
RUMBLE!

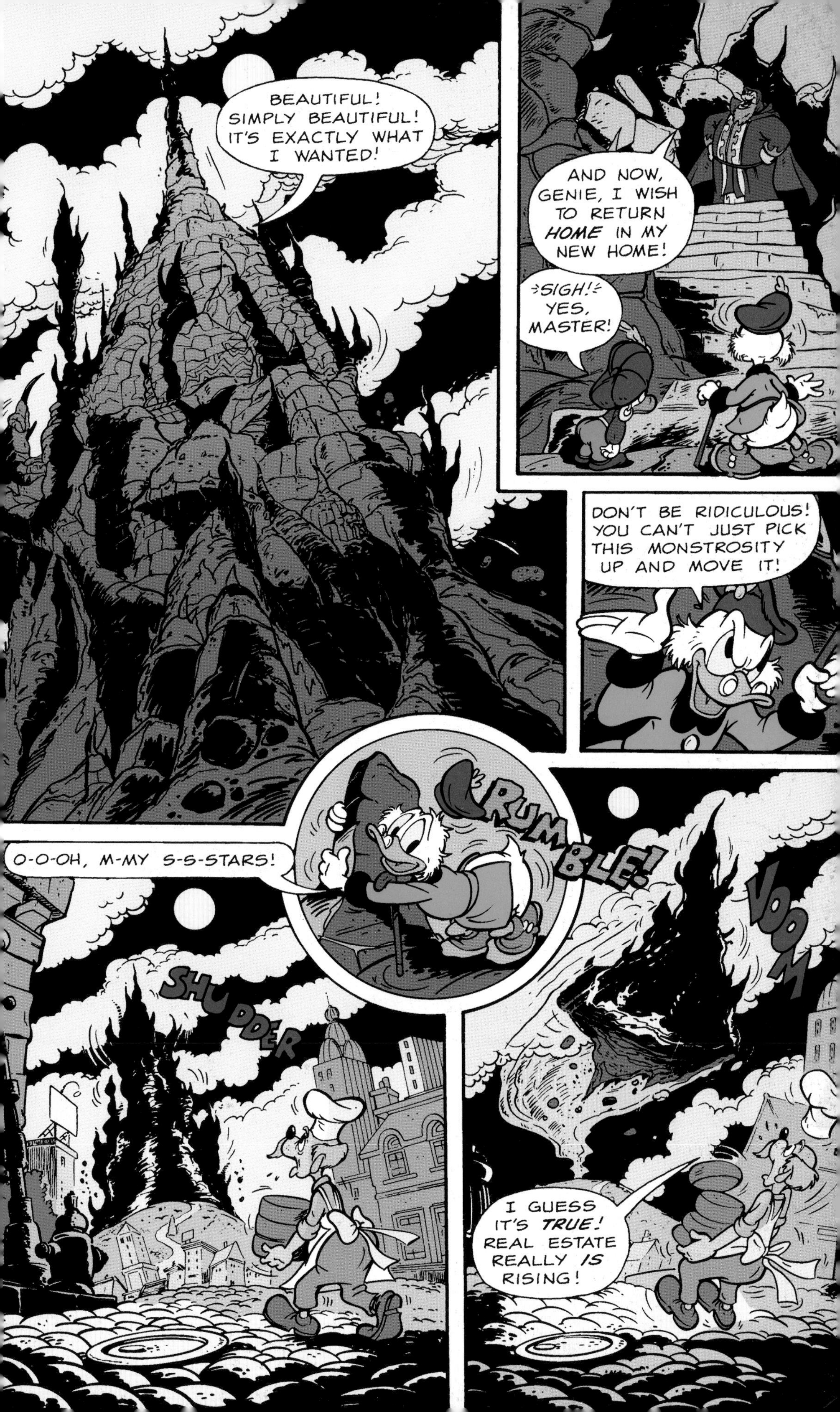
BEAUTIFUL! SIMPLY BEAUTIFUL! IT'S EXACTLY WHAT I WANTED!
AND NOW, GENIE, I WISH TO RETURN *HOME* IN MY NEW HOME!
SIGH! YES, MASTER!
DON'T BE RIDICULOUS! YOU CAN'T JUST PICK THIS MONSTROSITY UP AND MOVE IT!
O-O-OH, M-MY S-S-STARS!
RUMBLE!
SHUDDER
VOOM
I GUESS IT'S *TRUE!* REAL ESTATE REALLY *IS* RISING!

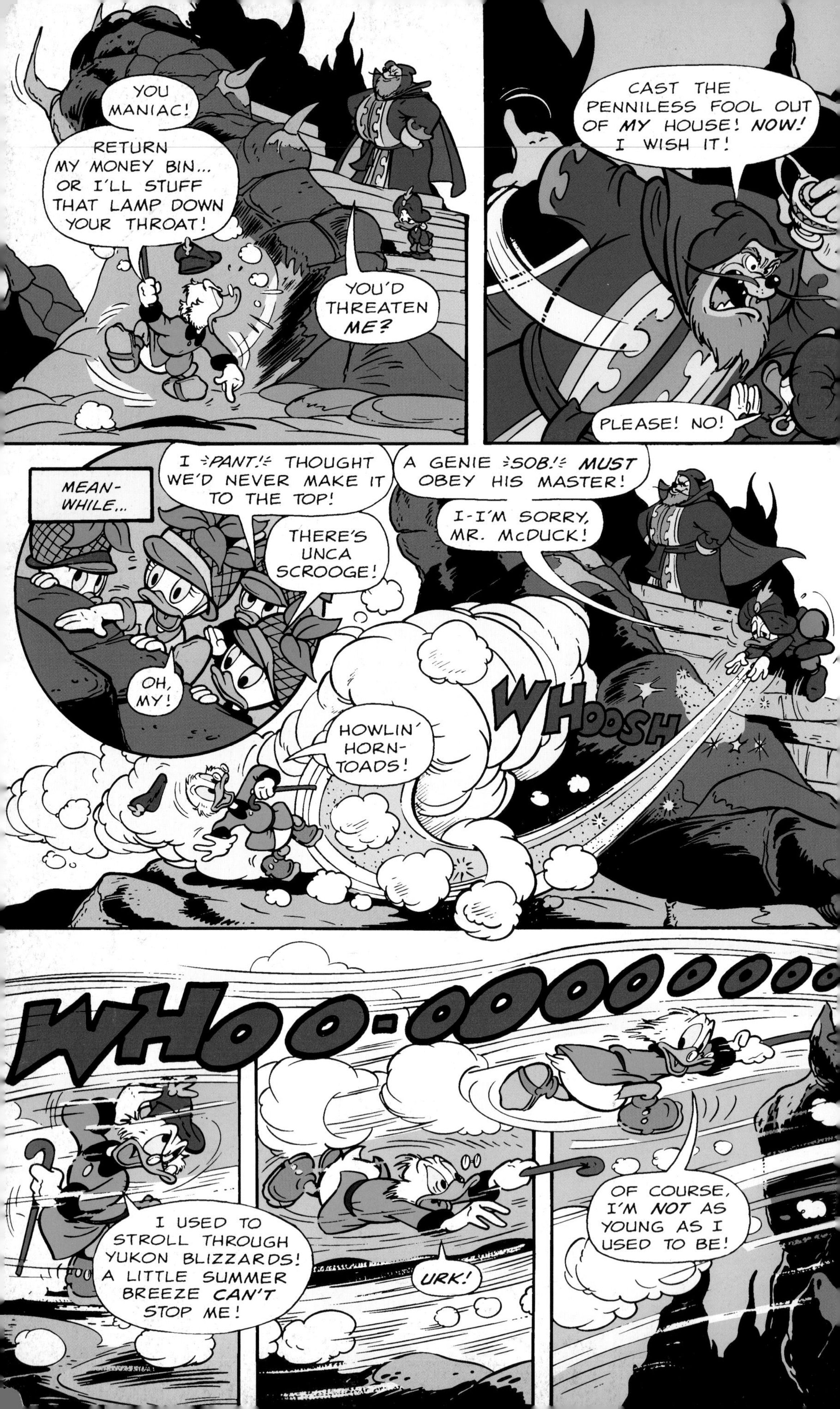

YOU MANIAC!
RETURN MY MONEY BIN... OR I'LL STUFF THAT LAMP DOWN YOUR THROAT!
YOU'D THREATEN ME?
CAST THE PENNILESS FOOL OUT OF MY HOUSE! NOW! I WISH IT!
PLEASE! NO!
MEAN-WHILE...
I *PANT!* THOUGHT WE'D NEVER MAKE IT TO THE TOP!
A GENIE *SOB!* MUST OBEY HIS MASTER!
I-I'M SORRY, MR. McDUCK!
THERE'S UNCA SCROOGE!
OH, MY!
WHOOSH
HOWLIN' HORN-TOADS!
WHOO-OOOOOOOOO
I USED TO STROLL THROUGH YUKON BLIZZARDS! A LITTLE SUMMER BREEZE CAN'T STOP ME!
URK!
OF COURSE, I'M NOT AS YOUNG AS I USED TO BE!

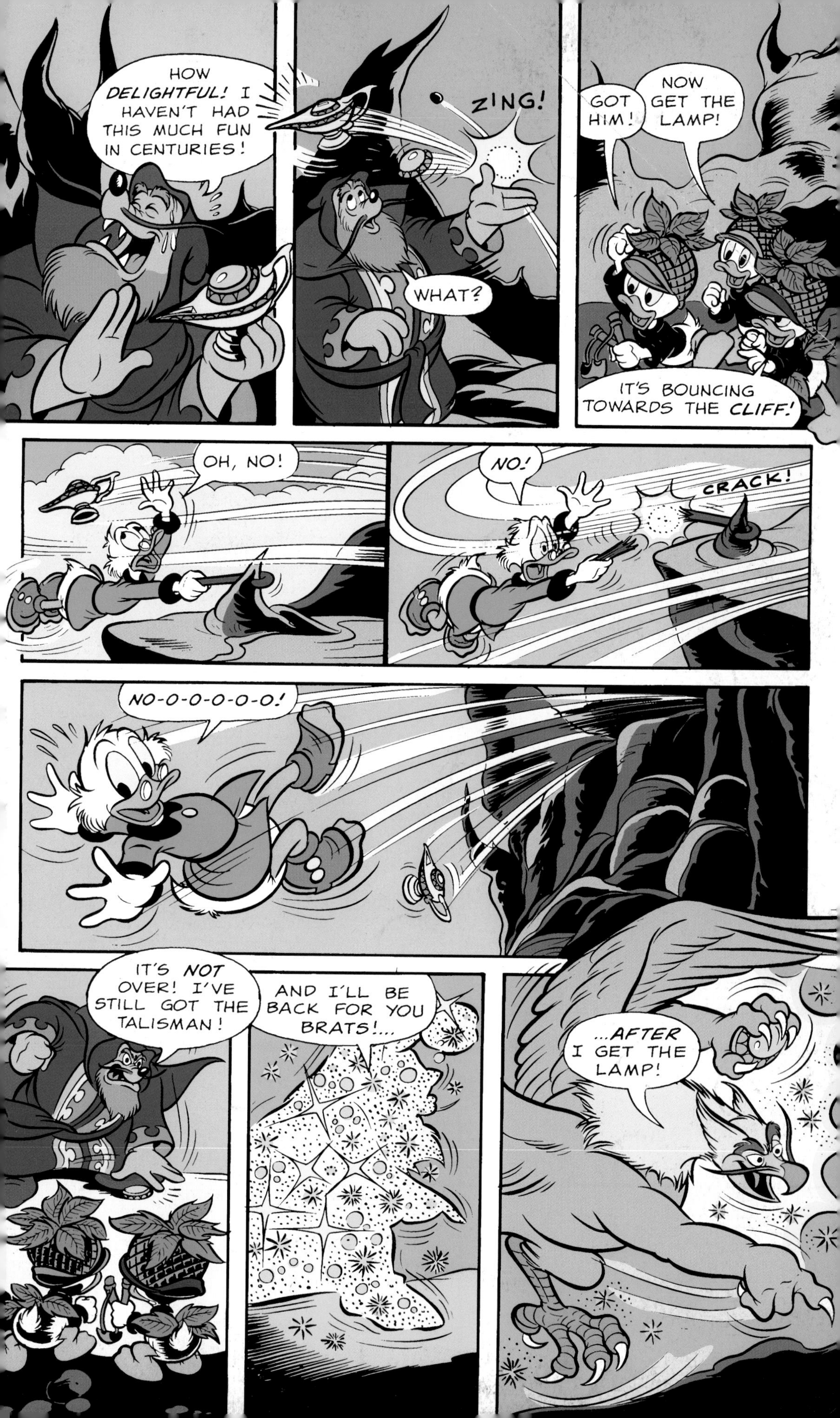
HOW DELIGHTFUL! I HAVEN'T HAD THIS MUCH FUN IN CENTURIES!
ZING!
WHAT?
GOT HIM!
NOW GET THE LAMP!
IT'S BOUNCING TOWARDS THE CLIFF!
OH, NO!
NO!
CRACK!
NO-O-O-O-O-O-O!
IT'S NOT OVER! I'VE STILL GOT THE TALISMAN!
AND I'LL BE BACK FOR YOU BRATS!...
...AFTER I GET THE LAMP!

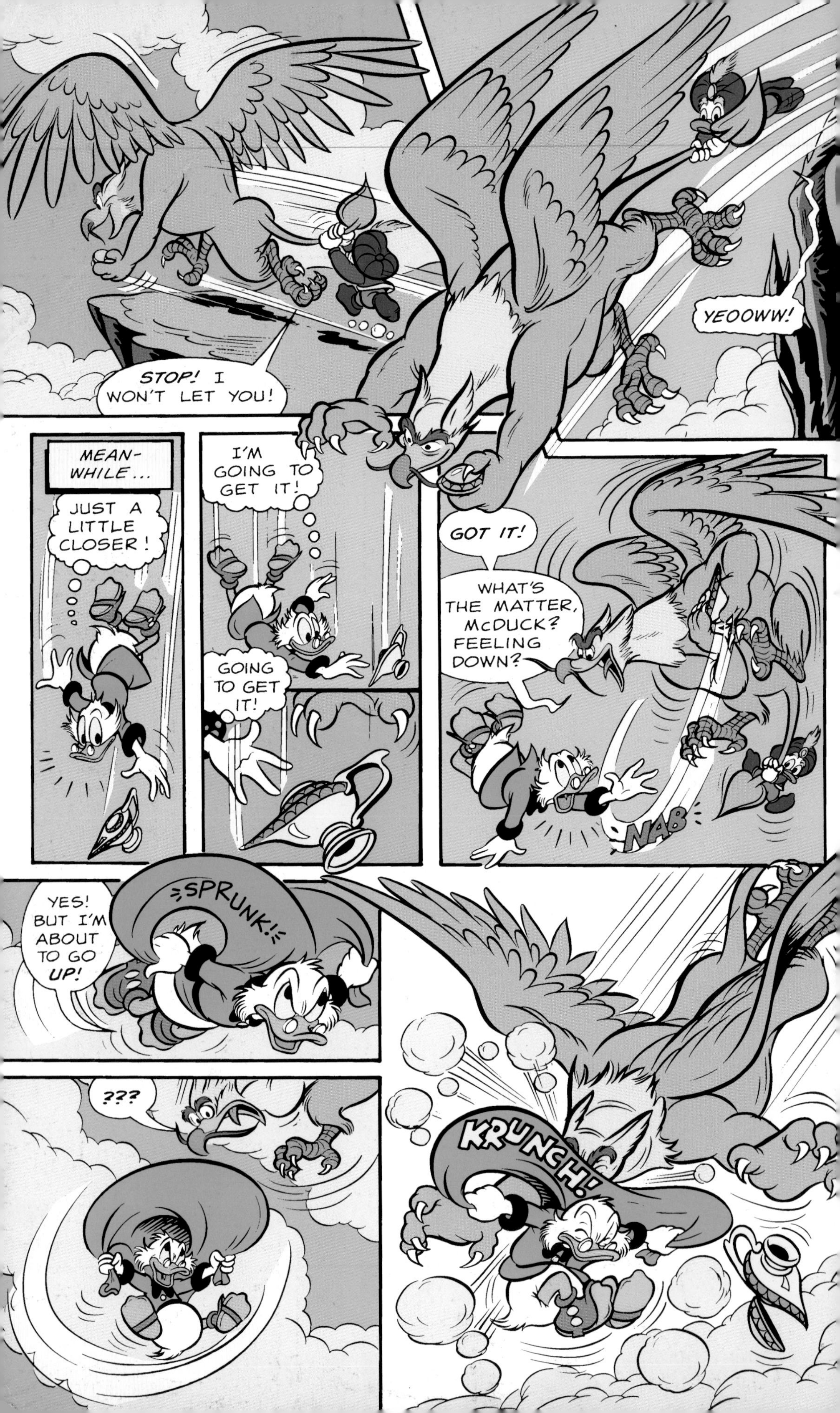

YEOOWW!
STOP! I WON'T LET YOU!
MEAN-WHILE...
JUST A LITTLE CLOSER!
I'M GOING TO GET IT!
GOING TO GET IT!
GOT IT!
WHAT'S THE MATTER, McDUCK? FEELING DOWN?
NAB
YES! BUT I'M ABOUT TO GO UP!
SPRUNK!
???
KRUNCH!

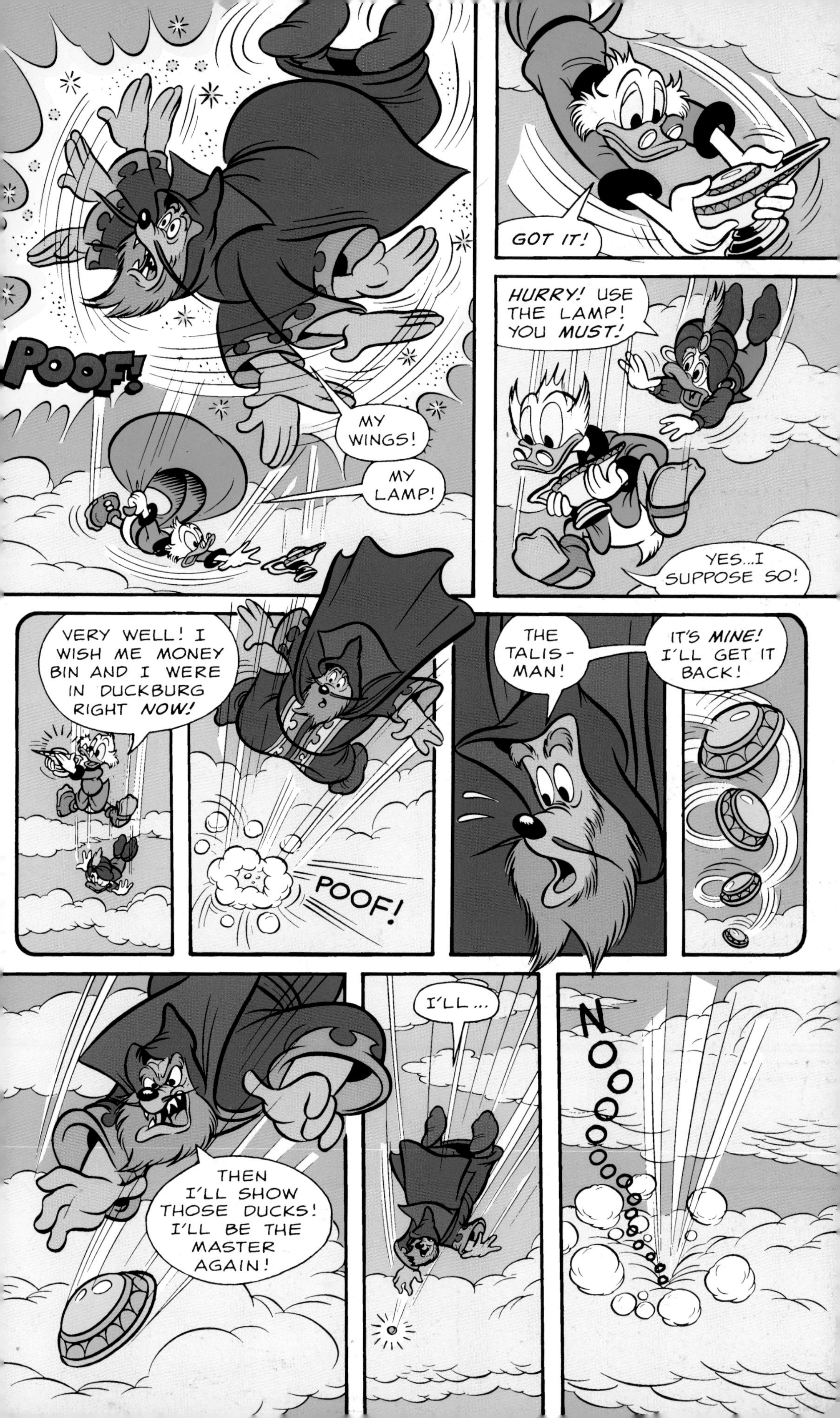
POOF!
MY WINGS!
MY LAMP!
GOT IT!
HURRY! USE THE LAMP! YOU MUST!
YES...I SUPPOSE SO!
VERY WELL! I WISH ME MONEY BIN AND I WERE IN DUCKBURG RIGHT NOW!
POOF!
THE TALISMAN!
IT'S MINE! I'LL GET IT BACK!
THEN I'LL SHOW THOSE DUCKS! I'LL BE THE MASTER AGAIN!
I'LL ...
NOOOOOOOOOOOOO

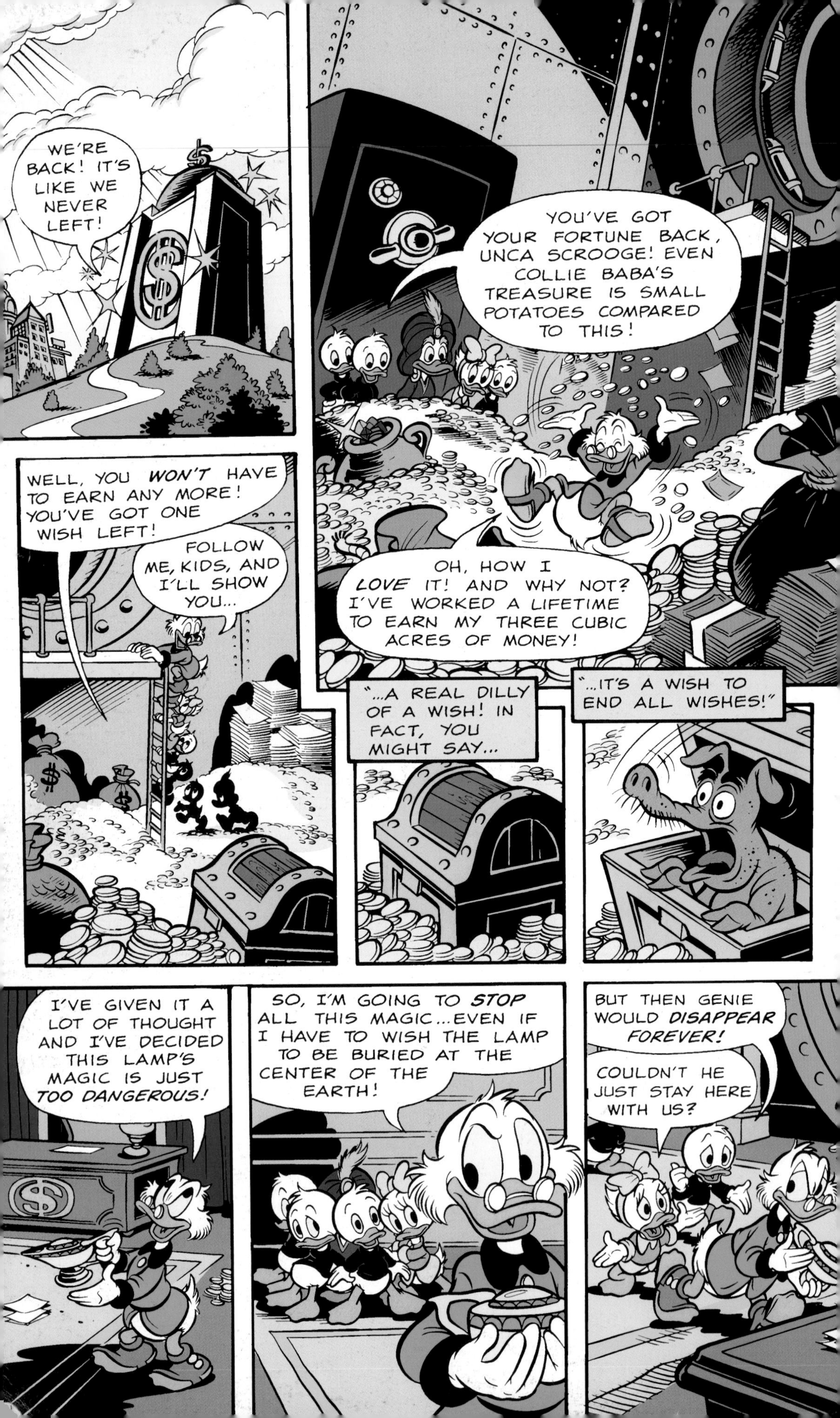

WE'RE BACK! IT'S LIKE WE NEVER LEFT!
YOU'VE GOT YOUR FORTUNE BACK, UNCA SCROOGE! EVEN COLLIE BABA'S TREASURE IS SMALL POTATOES COMPARED TO THIS!
OH, HOW I LOVE IT! AND WHY NOT? I'VE WORKED A LIFETIME TO EARN MY THREE CUBIC ACRES OF MONEY!
WELL, YOU WON'T HAVE TO EARN ANY MORE! YOU'VE GOT ONE WISH LEFT!
FOLLOW ME, KIDS, AND I'LL SHOW YOU...
"...A REAL DILLY OF A WISH! IN FACT, YOU MIGHT SAY...
"...IT'S A WISH TO END ALL WISHES!"
I'VE GIVEN IT A LOT OF THOUGHT AND I'VE DECIDED THIS LAMP'S MAGIC IS JUST TOO DANGEROUS!
SO, I'M GOING TO STOP ALL THIS MAGIC...EVEN IF I HAVE TO WISH THE LAMP TO BE BURIED AT THE CENTER OF THE EARTH!
BUT THEN GENIE WOULD DISAPPEAR FOREVER!
COULDN'T HE JUST STAY HERE WITH US?

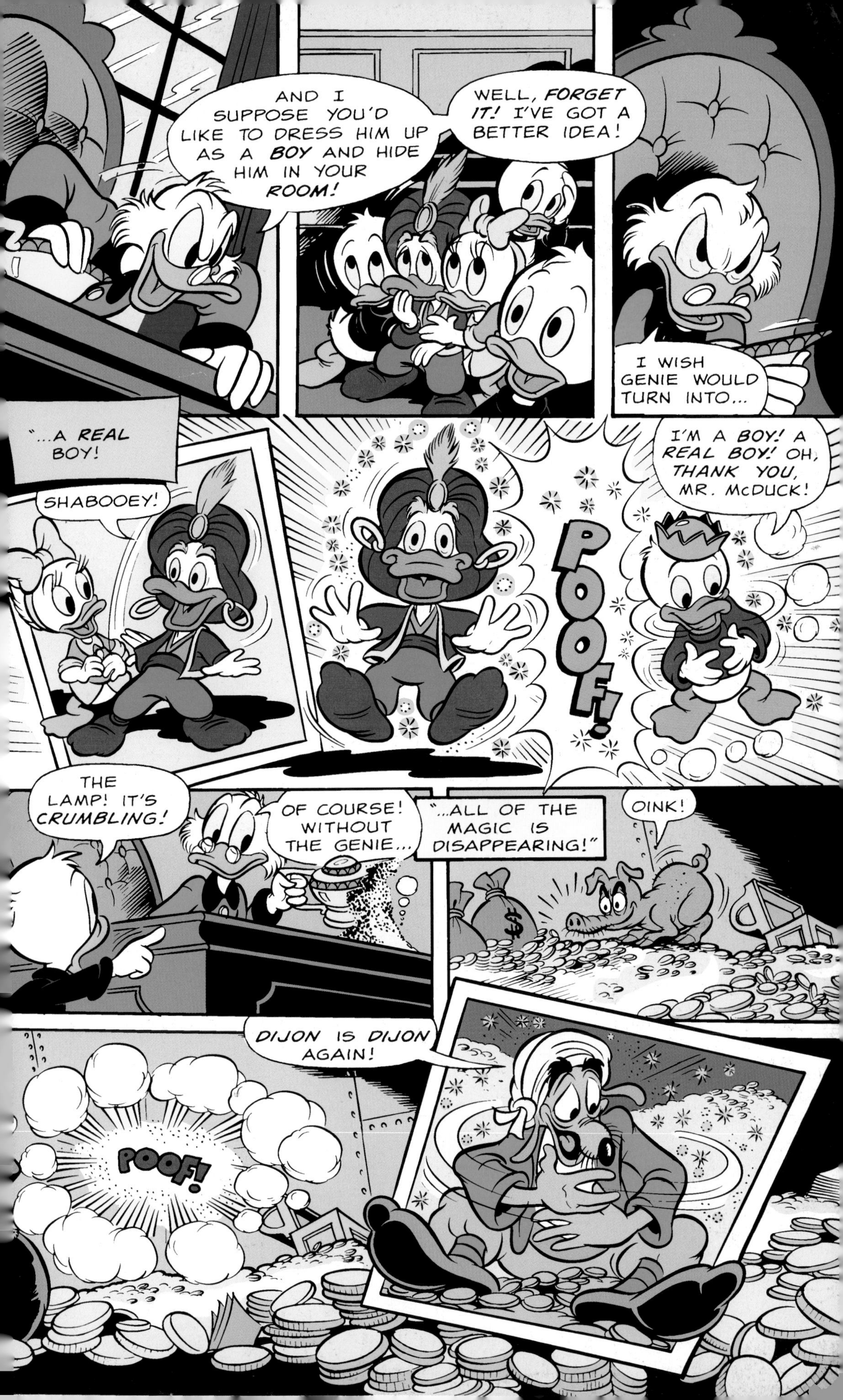
AND I SUPPOSE YOU'D LIKE TO DRESS HIM UP AS A *BOY* AND HIDE HIM IN YOUR *ROOM!*
WELL, *FORGET IT!* I'VE GOT A BETTER IDEA!
I WISH GENIE WOULD TURN INTO...
"...A *REAL* BOY!
SHABOOEY!
POOF!
I'M A *BOY!* A *REAL BOY!* OH, *THANK YOU,* MR. McDUCK!
THE LAMP! IT'S *CRUMBLING!*
OF COURSE! WITHOUT THE GENIE...
"...ALL OF THE MAGIC IS DISAPPEARING!"
OINK!
POOF!
DIJON IS *DIJON* AGAIN!

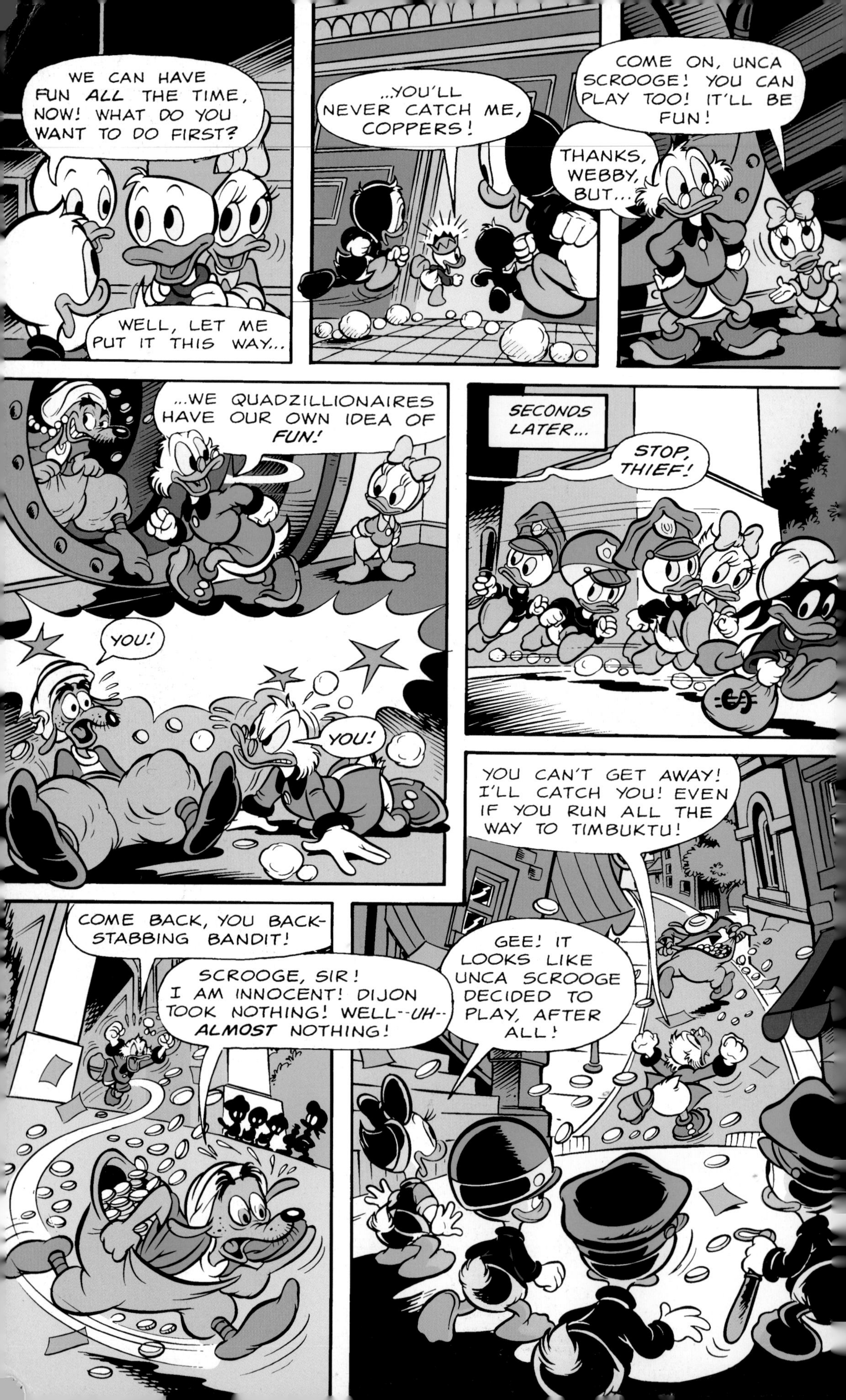
WE CAN HAVE FUN ALL THE TIME, NOW! WHAT DO YOU WANT TO DO FIRST?
WELL, LET ME PUT IT THIS WAY...
...YOU'LL NEVER CATCH ME, COPPERS!
COME ON, UNCA SCROOGE! YOU CAN PLAY TOO! IT'LL BE FUN!
THANKS, WEBBY, BUT...
...WE QUADZILLIONAIRES HAVE OUR OWN IDEA OF FUN!
YOU!
YOU!
SECONDS LATER...
STOP, THIEF!
YOU CAN'T GET AWAY! I'LL CATCH YOU! EVEN IF YOU RUN ALL THE WAY TO TIMBUKTU!
COME BACK, YOU BACK-STABBING BANDIT!
SCROOGE, SIR! I AM INNOCENT! DIJON TOOK NOTHING! WELL--UH--ALMOST NOTHING!
GEE! IT LOOKS LIKE UNCA SCROOGE DECIDED TO PLAY, AFTER ALL!

From *DuckTales* [series I] #10, 1989

Artist: **William Van Horn**

Colorists: **William Van Horn and Digikore Studios**

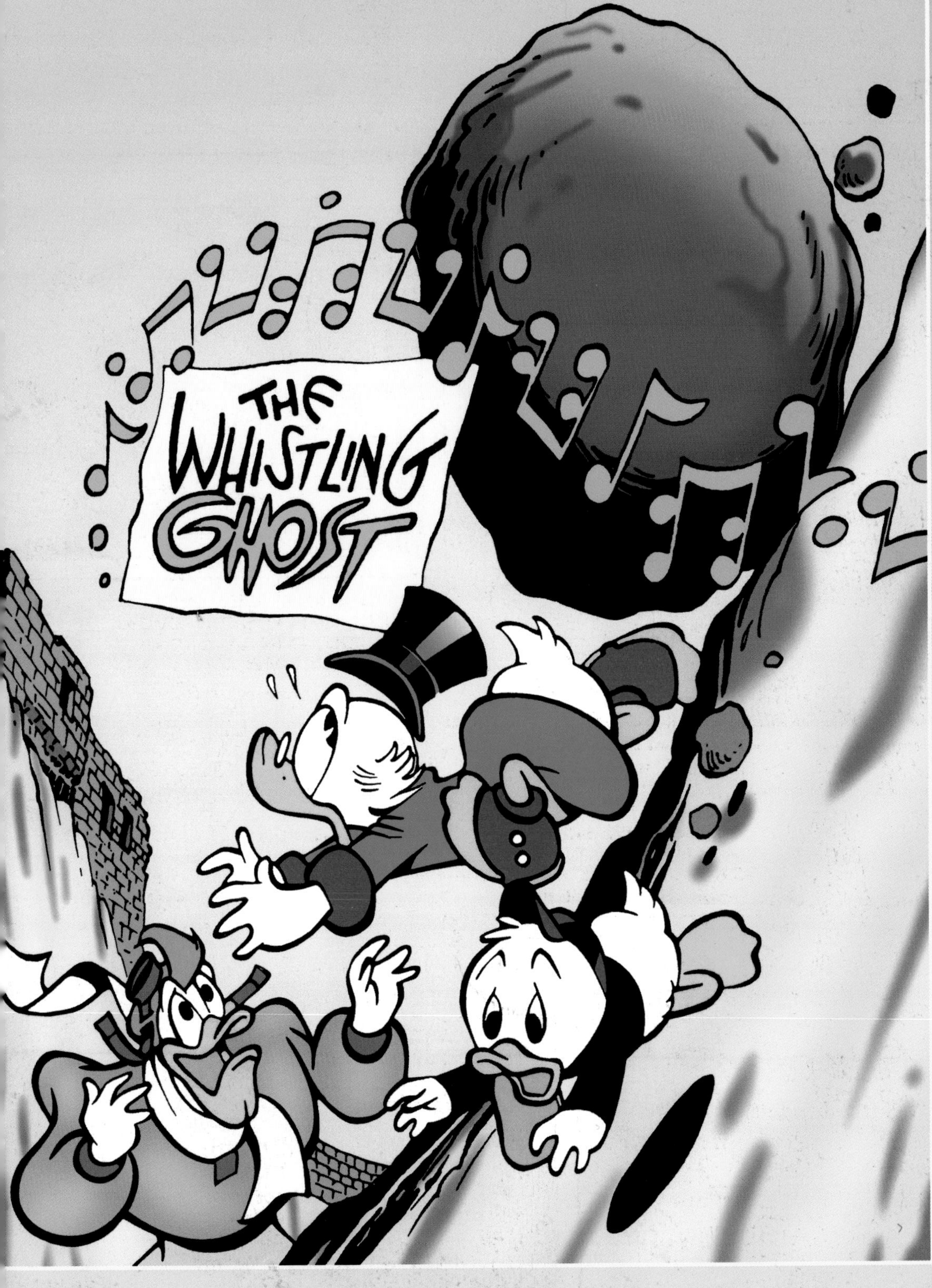
THE WHISTLING GHOST

From *DuckTales* (series I) #13, 1990
Artist: William Van Horn
Colorists: William Van Horn and Digikore Studios

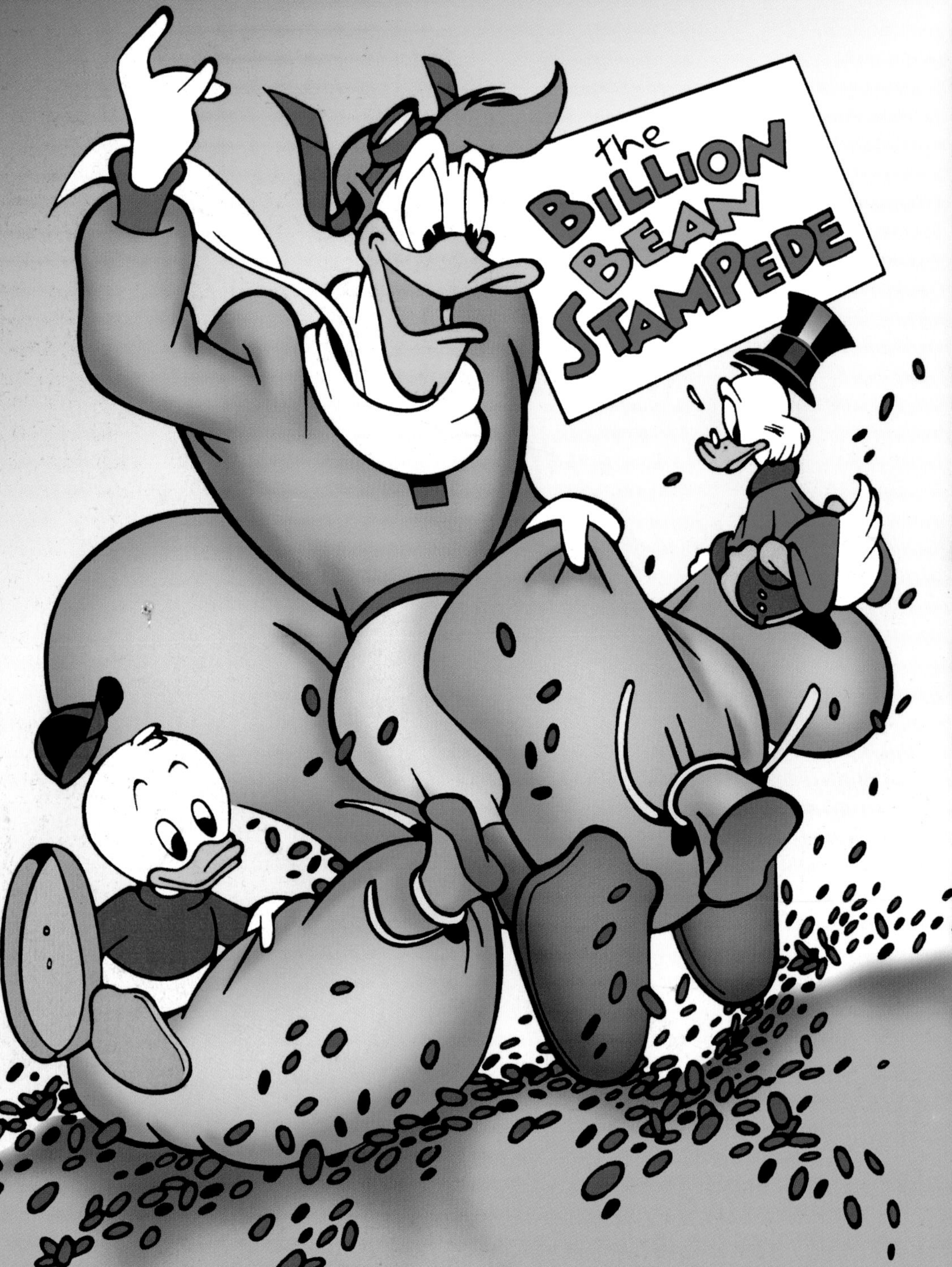
the BILLION BEAN STAMPEDE

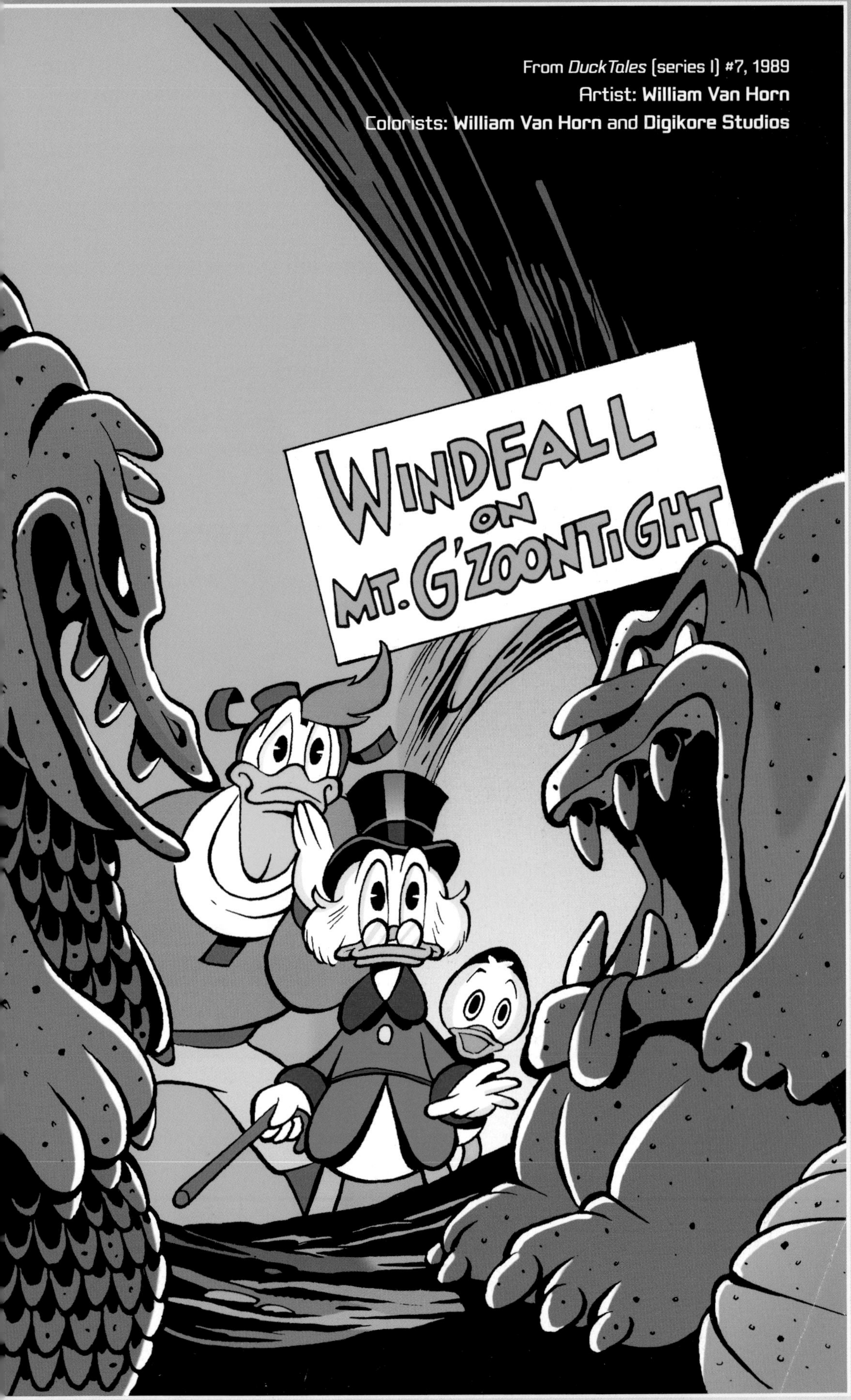
WINDFALL ON MT. G'ZOONTIGHT

From *DuckTales* (series I) #7, 1989
Artist: **William Van Horn**
Colorists: **William Van Horn and Digikore Studios**

From *DuckTales* (series I) #11, 1990

Artist: **William Van Horn**

Colorists: **William Van Horn and Digikore Studios**

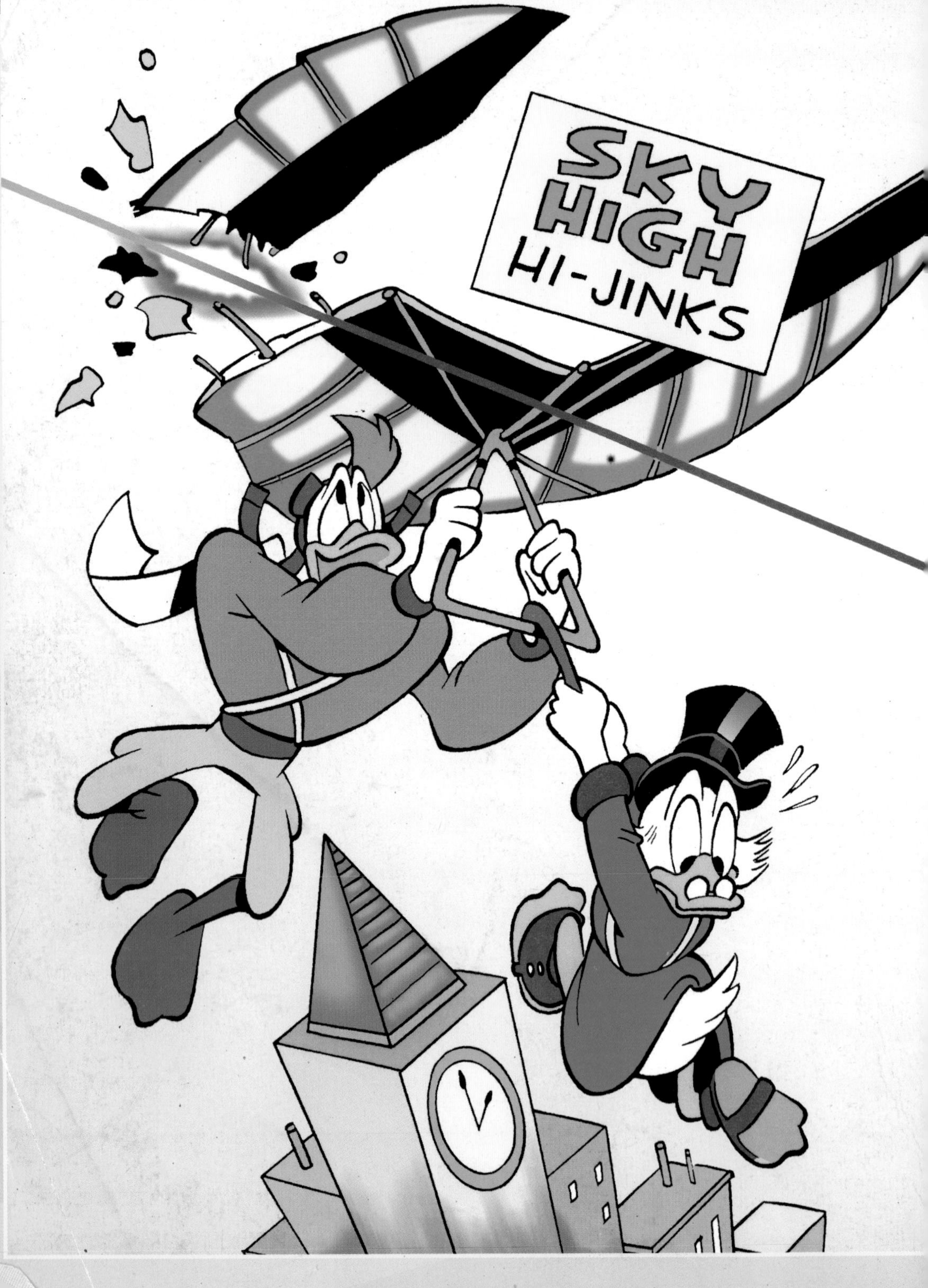
SKY HIGH HI-JINKS